Web of Lies

The Mowbray Chronicles – Book 3

Mette Holm

2nd edition: 2024

ISBN-13: 978-87-94404-11-2

Cover Art and Design by Tairelei
https://www.instagram.com/tairelei/

DEDICATION

To my readers and all those who faithfully devote their time and energy to creating their own worlds full of wonders.

Fiction is a mirror.

GALLERY OF CHARACTERS

HOUSE MOWBRAY

John Mowbray
Baron of Mowbray
✝1368

— married —

Elizabeth Mowbray
b. de Seagrave
✝1368

Children:

- Margaret
  b. 1361
  m. Reginald de Lucy
  m. 1380
- Joan
  b. 1363
  m. Sir Thomas Grey
  1382
- Eleanor
  b. 1364
  m. Baron John de Welles
  1385
- John Mowbray
  Baron of Mowbray
  b. 1365
  ✝1383
- Thomas Mowbray
  b. 1367
  m. Elizabeth le Strange
  ✝1383
  2nd m. Elizabeth FitzAlan
- **Argyle Mowbray**
  b. 1368
  m. Isobel Thorne

HOUSE PLANTAGENET

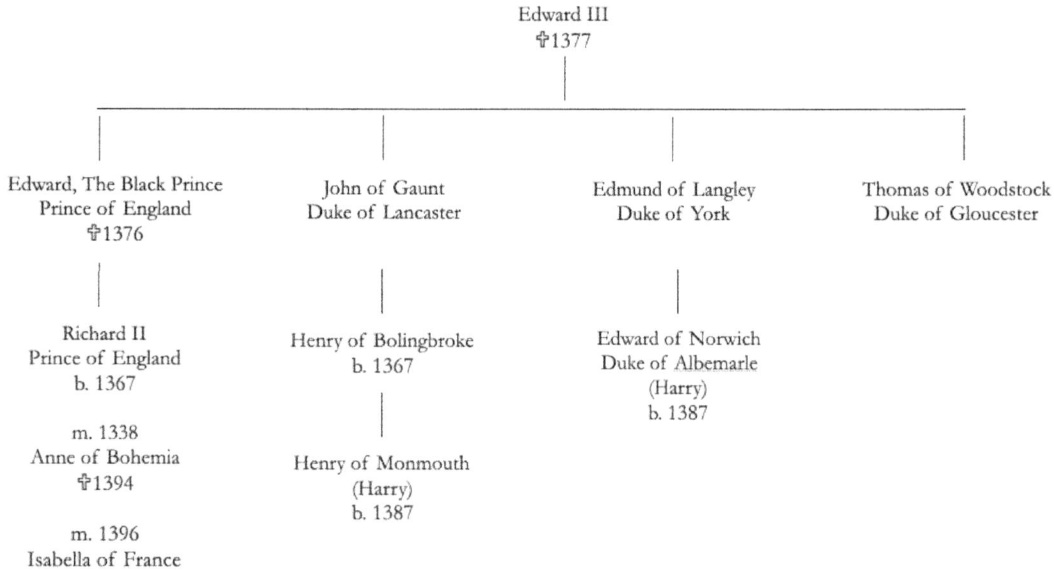

OTHER KEY CHARACTERS

Thomas Holland, Earl of Kent [half-brother to King Richard]
John Holland, Earl of Huntingdon, Duke of Exeter [half-brother of King Richard]
Thomas Holland, Duke of Surrey [nephew to King Richard – by Thomas Holland]
Edmund Holland, Earl of Kent [nephew to King Richard – by Thomas Holland]

John Beaufort, Earl of Somerset [half-brother to Henry of Bolingbroke]
Thomas Beaufort [half-brother of Henry to Bolingbroke]

John Montagu, Earl of Salisbury [English nobleman]
William de Courcy [English nobleman]
Thomas le Despenser, Earl of Gloucester [English nobleman]
Thomas Percy, Earl of Worcester [English nobleman]
Henry Percy, Earl of Northumberland [English nobleman]
Sir Harry Hotspur [nephew to Worcester and son of Northumberland]
Sir William Bagot [King Richard's long-time advisor]
Thomas Arundel [Archbishop of York and later Canterbury – exiled for 2 years]
Richard le Scrope [Archbishop of York, 1398-1405]
Richard of Conisburgh, [King Richard II's godson – second son of Edmund of Langley, Duke of York]

Jean-Pierre de Reines [French nobleman]
Marie de Reines [daughter of French nobleman]
Grand-Maman de Reines [mother of Jean-Pierre and grandmother of Marie]
Joan II, Countess of Boulogne [aunt to the French King Charles]
King Charles VI [King of France]
Queen Isabeau [Queen of France]

Lucia Visconti [Milanese aristocrat, daughter of Bernabò Visconti]
Agnese Venier [Dogaressa of Venice]
Orsola Venier [daughter of the Doge and Dogaressa of Venice]
Nicolò Venier [son of the Doge and Dogaressa of Venice]

Maud la Furniér [Madame, married to a maternal cousin of the Count of Valois]
Eloise la Furniér [mistress to King Charles]
Jacques la Furniér [bastard son of la Fourniér]

Philip Windham [prison warden of Calais]
Stephen Smith [Master of Arms at Beauworth]
Jasper [minstrel]
Adam [stable boy in London]
Felix [messenger for the Duke of York]
Coxcombe [the fallen knight]

ADRIFT

A head splitting scream ripped Argyle from the sweet embrace of sleep. He gasped as something cold washed over him, salt filling his mouth making him choke. Spitting and coughing, he rolled onto his side. Hard, coarse sand poked his body and when he wiped his eyes they burned from the salt. He tried to sit up, but the earth shifted under him and he fell back, closing his eyes to the whirling sparks.

Slowly, he got to his knees, eyes closed, and began crawling to escape the freezing sea. His mouth burned with sour, warm water. Once he felt dry sand under his hands, he lay down gingerly and slipped into a welcoming darkness.

When he woke again, he tried to open his eyes. Sand had seeped into his clothes and was stuck to his eyelashes. His throat was dry and sore and something crunched between his teeth. Once more, he got up on his hands and knees and steadied himself before trying to look around.

The surroundings were foreign, a few rolling hills on the horizon, the stretch of grey and unwelcoming beach. Argyle had to work hard to keep his world steady, his stomach churned and his head ached when he turned it. Gently, he leaned on his left hand and reached up to touch his right temple. His hand came away sticky, a shooting red flame of pain following his touch. Blood.

He fell clumsily to the side and, despite his better judgement, struggled to get up. If he closed one eye and focused with all his might he was able to keep the ground steady and the world level. Water lapped at his already soaked boots.

The tide must be changing. It would not be long before he was back in the sea.

He groaned and staggered, squinting against the pain and the strange shifting under his feet. For a while, he crouched, swaying with the world before he straightened and the world exploded in a burst of stars.

'All hells!'

He fell over, stretching his arms to ease his fall. His hand hit stone. Fumbling around, Argyle managed to drag himself up onto the rounded rock. He hung his head to stop his nausea but too late. Warm vomit hit his legs and splashed onto his newfound safety. When he coughed, the shaking stirred a pain in his temple. Carefully, he lay down on his back and closed his eyes against the light.

As he drifted out of consciousness again, he hoped he was at least safe from the sea.

ꙮ ꙮ

Part I Dream-scapes

CHAPTER 1

8 June 1399 – Kells, Ireland

Argyle lifted his gaze from his shield. It was a battered old thing, the top right corner had cracked long ago, and the rugged edge was worn smooth by years of use. It sported a prancing unicorn made out in silver, its horn now dull and almost white. He sometimes wondered if the blue field had once been covered in stars. Today, he kissed the iron rim and sent La Fontaine a flicker of gratitude before he turned to face the enemy.

Behind him, his men rallied, their energy almost pushing him into the saddle. In the face of battle, the destrier's calm seeped through Argyle's armour and quelled his concerns. Across the field a black pennant picked up the increasing wind and snapped.

He turned the horse and rode alongside the rows of men, spears, lances and bows ready, maces and axes by their sides. Shields carrying the King's white hart stood side by side, protecting the fragile bodies behind them. Argyle grabbed the hilt of his sword and loosened it in the scabbard. The moment he drew it, the soldiers' roar rushed past him pressing against his breastplate.

The enemy returned the call. Argyle turned his destrier and looked upon the foe. Yesterday, he had prayed they might make swift work of it; today, he was far from certain that God had seen fit to answer his prayer. Then again, God heard from him so rarely that he could not expect an answer. He hoped that more pious men might prevail and catch God's attention in time. At the low summit behind the English army a solitary figure stood, framed by the rising sun. The priest knelt.

Argyle turned back to the field, raising his sword; he let it sing the song of battle and released his men. The Irish rushed across the wet field, horses and men pushing to meet their enemy first. Along with the other mounted men, Argyle spurred his horse into a controlled canter. Behind him, the bowmen strung their bows and notched their arrows.

A thousand arrows blackened the skies. He slammed down his visor only when he could see the white of his enemy's eyes, the two narrow slits forcing him to focus on what lay immediately ahead. Steel rang as Argyle's horse smashed into the Irish horseman's side. Argyle swung his sword, blocked the attack and plunged a blade into the opening just above the armpit. The horseman's soul quit his body even before he fell from his seat. Argyle's horse never missed a step.

He looked right, seeing an almost unbroken line of knights charging into the midst of the enemy's lines; horses breaking spears and splintering shields. The left side fell back, providing a minute opening. Argyle turned his horse and charged, bringing with him a dozen knights who pushed through the opening and forced apart the unshielded men.

Next to him, two knights engaged; steel glittering they fell to the ground entangled and the horses made short process of both knights trampling them to death. Argyle gritted his teeth and pressed his heels into his horse's flanks. It took down five men as he thundered to the centre of the battle, blood spattering its plate.

'Sire.'

Argyle turned towards the shout and took a lance to his shoulder. Grunting, he swung his sword at what little he could see and sunk it deep into the enemy's horse. Its legs folded and Argyle followed the motion only dragging out his sword when he hit the ground.

He ducked, a mace hissing past his helmet. He thrust his sword with both hands and dragged it up, splitting his adversary in half. With his sight impaired, the spray of blood stung his eyes and honed his instincts. Stumbling forward he fell to his knees, the smash of a mace against steel turned his two little slices of the world sideways. He rolled and felt the vibration of a lance missing its mark by inches. Argyle looked up just in time to see an English soldier block a blow from an axe, his own weapon spinning out of his hand as his face exploded.

Cursing, Argyle got up and pulled at his helmet, the dent scraped against his temple. His sweat made swift work of releasing the steel from his head. He threw the ruined helmet at an enemy, caked in blood and dirt, but missed and had to grab his sword with both hands to block a blow. The axe slid down the blade and struck his armoured shoulder. His hand still on the blade, Argyle forced it down the attacker's face, the sound of steel rippling through skin and tissue following him as he turned to face the next challenger.

All around him, arrows pierced armour, horses, men and the ground, the whistle and twang sometimes audible above the cries of war, the screams of dying men and the thunder of battle.

Further away, Argyle glimpsed the pennant of Worcester and saw the English left flank round on the Irish, mounted knights and soldiers on foot charging, the enemy scattering before them. In the brief breathing space, Argyle sensed that perhaps this battle might soon be over.

Then the tide changed, and a fresh host of soldiers surged across the field. With the thrum of battle in his veins, it seemed the Irish were charging in slow motion, the movement running up through their chainmail, their boiled leather and armour clearly visible. For a fleeting moment, Argyle missed only seeing the world through narrow slits; when the enemy came upon him this time, he would see them all.

'Sire.' A hoarse, trembling voice cried behind him. 'Sire, I have your horse.'

Reaching out to grab the reins, Argyle never took his eyes of the advancing soldiers. 'Well done, boy. When this is over, I shall reward you.'

He took firm hold of the pommel and felt hands cup beneath his steel-clad foot. With an effort, Argyle hauled himself into the saddle, pulled the reins and looked about. Some twenty mounted knights had followed his squire's progress on the field, gathering under his dark blue pennant dusted with silver stars. One of them yanked off his helmet and offered it to Argyle, who shook his head.

Let the enemy see my face, let him know who took his life on this God-forsaken day. Let him gaze upon me and know what has descended upon him and his cursed land.

The knight put his helmet back on. 'A second wave,' he shouted through the still-open visor.

'We will be the bulwark that breaks all the Irish waves!' Argyle roared and the knights around him pointed their swords to the sky and joined in the infamous English battle cry.

'For Saint George!'

Time blurred as more enemies flooded the field, dragging behind them a trail of blood and destruction.

Argyle's breath rattled, his eyes burned from sweat mixed with Irish blood. At some point, he had fallen off his horse. His arms ached and every step he took felt as if he was walking through a bog. He could not be seen to be weak, though his shoulder blazed and his shield-arm hung limp at his side. Was it his own blood caking across his brow?

All around him, the King's soldiers were making short process of the few stragglers running in vain for the forest. There would be precious few survivors and only those who could be ransomed would live beyond sunset. The battle today was more than a lesson; it was retaliation.

'You…'

Argyle turned at the croak, his grasp iron on the sword once more. His eyes raked the field strewn with corpses and dying men, bleeding, crawling and bawling. The ground blood-soaked, the stink of death tore at his nose. How had he not noticed the carnage before?

His own men were walking about the field, giving foes and friends merciful deaths. Argyle saw two soldiers from another company pull the boots off a man not yet dead and heard him scream when one of the soldiers yanked at the boot and then held it triumphantly in the air. Red tendrils dangled from the leg of the boot. Next to them, an Irish soldier was reaching his hands to the sky, half his face gone from an axe-blow.

'You!'

The roar came from behind, and as he turned, he swung the sword and slashed the air.

'A ghost…'

Argyle looked down. 'No. I am very much alive.'

'You chase a ghost…'

There on the ground, defenceless at Argyle's feet lay his old enemy, whom he had once believed burned to death, and since hunted through the streets of London to no avail. Coxcombe. One of his hands had been hacked off and a dagger was buried in his side.

'Is that so?' Even at the miserable sight, Argyle felt only cold hatred. 'Well, it seems the ghost found me.'

'I'm not speaking of me…' Coxcombe's rattling cough shook fresh blood from his wounds. 'I'm speaking of your master. That's why you're here, isn't it?'

'In part.' Argyle planted his sword in the dirt and leaned on it. No need to tell Coxcombe the pathetic truth. That Argyle was here to avoid the Tower. He stared at the fabled fallen knight.

'Are you prepared to meet your maker, old man? For I think, this time, you cannot escape. I hope you have made peace with God.'

Coxcombe flashed a set of cracked, bloodstained teeth. 'You're offering to be my confessor?'

'No.'

'Good.' Another rattling cough. 'I'm not in need of salvation. I've made my peace with what's to come. I've got a parting gift for you though, a rare secret.'

'What is that?' Argyle asked.

'You think La Fontaine went to heaven? Don't disappoint a dying man, I'd hate to die thinking I've been fleeing a fool.' Coxcombe appeared delirious, his eyes shone with malice. 'Do you think he never offended God?'

'I harbour no such illusions,' Argyle said tiring of conversing with a living corpse. He wanted to plunge his sword through Coxcombe's black heart and be done with it. Still, he had to know. 'He had seen too much battle, but he always fought on the side God favoured. That says something do you not think? If you will not tell me your secret I shall leave you to die a slow death, birds pecking your eyes from their sockets while you still breathe.'

Coxcombe attempted to wipe his face with his bloodied stump, no trace of pain. 'I swore before a priest – on the eve before battle – that if you were here, today, if you were to be the master of my destiny, I'd tell you all.'

'You care nothing for God or priests, and you can have nothing to tell me that I do not already know.'

Here lies a madman. He hates God even more than I do, Argyle thought and turned away. I cannot give in to his lies, he calls me master of his fate and I must be watchful not to let him master mine.

'You break house arrest, kill a royal servant, you come all this way and now, now you care not?' Coxcombe said. 'You will not hear what I have to say?'

'How can I know you will tell me the truth?'

Coxcombe waved his raw stump. 'I'll not live for long. You want to discuss truth? I can tell from your expression that you're curious, no, craving knowledge. You need to know. You want me to tell you. You won't forgive yourself if you let me perish here without pausing to hear. You've come too far, sacrificed too much…' A cough rattled Coxcombe's bones, blood bubbling from his mouth.

'Then tell me, since it seems to weigh heavily on your conscience.' Argyle kicked his heel in the churned-up mud. 'You know you have my attention. You have had it since you returned from whatever rock you cowered under, while you watched as we carried a charred body from the docks in Calais. I have all the time in the world, yours will run out soon. So, tell me and I shall deliver you to purgatory.'

Coxcombe's eyes were clouded, the bubbling blood seeping down his chin. When he tried to sit up, the dagger did short work, and he fell back with a faint curse on his breath. Argyle waited. Once before, Coxcombe had returned from the dead. Not again. This time, Argyle meant to watch him die.

Not until Coxcombe grabbed for the dagger, did Argyle interfere. He pushed the hand away with his foot. If the wretched man succeeded, he would bleed out in an instant and Argyle's curiosity would never be satisfied. 'Tell me.'

'Stubborn to a fault. Just like him.' Coxcombe blinked, sweat beading on his pale brow. 'Dogged. Never able to let a cause go. Should've, you know, should've – in Limoges. He made himself too many enemies. Though the greatest enemy he never knew until it was too late.'

'Who?' In the distance, soldiers wearing the King's crest were looting the dead and they drew ever closer. He dropped his voice. 'Who was his enemy? Who killed him, for I know Lockley was merely an instrument.'

'I told your brother, you know.' Grim satisfaction flashed against Coxcombe's streaked red cheeks as he eyed Argyle. 'You didn't know.'

'Why?' Leaning on his sword, Argyle knelt. Gore and mud seeped through the slits of his armour. 'What were you to Thomas?'

'Informant,' Coxcombe whispered. Close up, Argyle could smell death on his breath. 'Everyone's got a price. Even you. May not be money, titles, lands, whores… We've all got a price. So did La Fontaine.'

'You waste your breath keeping me here with your muddled words,' Argyle snarled, though the truth was slowly sinking in. Everyone did have a price – Argyle's was truth, had always been truth. He wanted closure so bad that he could not even will himself to move.

Coxcombe grabbed his arm with surprising strength. 'Heritage.'

'Go on.'

'When I told your brother, he didn't believe me. It wasn't until I warned him of the enemy brooding in Paris, thirsty for revenge, that he believed me.' Coxcombe leaned back, dragging Argyle with him. 'La Fontaine's dirty little secret could topple a kingdom.'

'You make no sense.' Argyle willed his hands to stay where they were rather than close around Coxcombe's traitor neck. The din of battle ebbed in his ears and the hushed silence of a field of death encroached.

'Your master, the King's friend…' Another cough jolted Coxcombe and little ruby droplets washed Argyle's face. Still, he could not tear himself away.

'I told Thomas to write to the courts abroad, to seek for himself the truth. About why Woodstock loathed the valiant Sir Edmund. Why Gaunt ran hot and cold at the mere mention of the fabled knight. The King signed La Fontaine's death warrant in the hand of his uncle Woodstock on a document hailing from the days when he ruled in the King's name. The perfect plan.' Coxcombe's words came out ever further apart, the pain of waiting nourished terror in Argyle's frozen blood.

'He wanted Sir Edmund destroyed. The seed planted long ago …' The steady flow of blood from Coxcombe's mouth had subsided, it was a weak trickle now, his words stuttered and low. Life faded away.

'Who planted the seed?' Argyle locked a hand around Coxcombe's wounded arm and crushed it. 'Who!'

'There it is… I told him. I told him what I saw plain as day.' Coxcombe's eyes came into focus through the fresh pain. With a red smile, he welcomed Death to his side. 'He knew… but it's of no matter…'

'It matters to me. If you hope salvation will come while you spin me a tattered tale, you hope in vain. All that is left now, Sire,' Argyle spat, 'is to hope that I will end your misery – and that will only come to pass if you stop veiling your words.' He released Coxcombe's arm. 'I ask one final time and if you fail to satisfy, Hell will be nothing to what you shall face here.'

Argyle leaned in and raw fear flickered in Coxcombe's eyes for the very first time. 'Who planted the seed?'

'Woodstock.' The admission rode on crimson bubbles as Coxcombe continued, 'By word of his brother Gaunt. I know not if it was by design. On their father's deathbed, he'd let slip some secret that'd set fear into the heart of his sons. There was a bastard in the court. Half-bred.'

While Coxcombe's life poured out of him, emptying his body, laying bare his soul for Death to take, Argyle stared into the eyes of La Fontaine's so-called friend. What was the connection?

'Who? Tell me who.' Desperation clutched at his throat.

'Secret never revealed…' Coxcombe coughed, a pitiable sound, and Argyle drove his gauntleted hand into the stump to force out Coxcombe's confession. It came in blows. 'He knew. I told your brother. Woodstock died for it. Ask your brother. Find him. There's a change coming… Enemy at your door…' His chin dropped to his chest and Argyle cursed.

A slain body looks nothing as a man. It is a pile of bones, its features contorted and unfamiliar.

Rising was struggle, his body ached as if suddenly awake and suffering the beatings he had taken on the field. All around him, soldiers milled, killing the last of their enemies and comrades, offering what mercy they could, picking the corpses clean of valuables. The gory aftermath of battle was rarely discussed. The soldiers needed to be paid and would take what they could from the dead. After all, corpses had no use of coin or clothes.

Turning his back on the clump of useless meat that would begin to rot before the day was out, Argyle tried to sort through the last rush of disorganised warnings and demands.

He took a few paces, unseeing eyes trained on the ground. Then he paused, rooting around in the trampled grass with his foot. He kicked a severed hand towards Coxcombe.

Let us see if Death lets you bring your limbs to Purgatory or not, though I do not doubt that you are hell-bound, and I am glad of it for then La Fontaine need never set eyes on you again.

Though he tried not to, Coxcombe's words about La Fontaine's own merits haunted his steps as he made is way across the field, raising a hand on reflex when one of his men called out. Had the King truly wanted his friend destroyed? It made no sense, there had to be something more to it.

When he got to the outskirts of camp, he sheathed his sword. Could a dying liar be trusted? He knew not, but then he could not reason why Coxcombe would lie when he knew he was dying.

A sickening notion surfaced, bobbing on waves of fear, how long had Thomas known? And what had he kept from Argyle?

CHAPTER 2

8 June 1399 – Cork

The missive made out in the King's hand lay before Argyle. What was to be a quick trip to subdue the Irish princes and prove that England was not to be toyed with had already stretched and demanded sacrifice.

When word had reached the King that his Lieutenant had been killed, the news had been received with mixed emotions. Argyle knew that Roger Mortimer, the Earl of March, had been stripped of his office because the King wanted to gift the title his maternal nephew, Thomas Holland, the notorious Duke of Surrey.

Harry of Monmouth, son of the King's exiled cousin Henry of Bolingbroke, cleared his throat. He had been the one to convey the King's decision and had received orders to ride with Argyle and his three thousand men to ensure that all was managed with as little cost as possible. While they faced battle, the main host would make its way from Waterford to Kilkenny where it would await reinforcements from Edward of Norwich, the Duke of Albemarle.

Since their departure from the main host, they had no news. Argyle did not know whether to think it a solace or an ominous sign that something was wrong. Either way, he knew better than to voice his concerns and instead, he turned to Monmouth.

'First battle, I believe Master Harry.'

The youth started. 'It was glorious.'

'It was mayhem. Such is battle whatever the cause of it.' Argyle covered the royal order with a blank piece of paper. 'The King will want word?'

'He is certain you will do your duty by him, Sire. That is why he gave you command.'

'And why he ordered you to go with me.'

'It was time for me to have my first experience.' Trouble clouded Harry's words. 'I… We won. My uncle will be pleased.'

'I am glad to hear it. Still, I warn you. This will not subdue the Irish. If anything it will push them further in their rebellious ways.' Argyle clicked his fingers for a squire. As with all who were allowed close to him, the boy was a stranger. Such was the penalty for crossing the King. At least, he had let Argyle bring his own soldiers trained at Beauworth and loyal to his command.

The boy bounced on the balls of his feet as Argyle said, 'Bring refreshments. We have earned it. And tell the men I will be with them shortly.'

'You take such measures to care for the soldiers.' Harry kept rubbing his hands together as if he might remove the invisible stain of bloodshed.

'It was impressed upon me by my master, Sir Edmund La Fontaine. He proved to me that to keep such numbers as these in check you need to be among them. It is half the measure of instilling loyalty.' Argyle was reminded of his promise to reward the squire who had caught his horse and brought it to him in the midst of battle. Jeremy. That was his name.

'When?' Harry sat down. He might have seen his first battle today, but at his age any tale of bygone times was enough to push aside fresh fear.

'I began my training at Beauworth, which was La Fontaine's estate back then. He drove home the point when we joined the King for his march against the Scots.' The horrible memory still made Argyle reel. He had been roughly Harry's age and so eager to prove he was a man grown that La Fontaine had been forced to put him in his place. 'I learned the hard way that much depends on the man who leads the attack – or seeks to prevent it.'

Harry rubbed his chin. 'My uncle never speaks of Scotland.'

'Not his finest hour, I fear.' Argyle turned when the flaps of his tent opened and let the returned squire interrupt.

'Sire, there are spits of pork and sides of ox. Only they're not ready yet. All I could scrounge up was this.' He held out a tray of dried meats and oatcakes and a pitcher of watered wine. 'Want me to keep looking?'

'No, this will do, Peter. Find me Jeremy, he did well on the field today and I owe him a debt.' Argyle smiled when Peter bowed before leaving.

'My uncle will be pleased that you made such short work here.' Harry picked an oatcake and bit off a large chunk. 'He was concerned it would be a long siege and that, when they finally gave battle, the Irish would prove hard to defeat.'

Is that so, Argyle thought, or did the King merely say so because he did not want you to know that he would take great pleasure in seeing me fail? After all, the King still had more than twenty thousand men at his disposal and a plan to take on MacMurrough at Dublin. A siege with just three thousand men would be hard graft at the best of times. With so few to spare, open battle was the best Argyle could hope for and he had gotten it. He would have to get a count of how many they had lost but it could wait until the morrow.

'I still wonder why the Irish opened their gates to us.'

Harry scratched his smooth cheek. At twelve, he was on the cusp of manhood and yet looked like a boy. 'The element of surprise, Sire?'

'I doubt it, Master Harry,' Argyle said and pushed away his plate, contemplating the King's true motives had driven away hunger. 'Will you join me in the camp?'

Any other man would have been ordered to attend, however as the King's nephew Harry was used to being treated with deference. No doubt any slip would be reported and added to Argyle's already long tally of missteps.

'Gladly. For all that I love the King, he has not the ease of manner with common men that you possess.' He got up, oatcake quite forgotten. 'When I come of age, I shall have a position of great import in the army. My uncle has promised me so.'

'He is fond of you.' Better not commit to an opinion. Argyle rested his hand on Harry's shoulder for a moment. The boy's head reached Argyle's shoulder and he looked so like his father that Argyle sometimes thought Bolingbroke was trailing in his wake.

'And I of him.' Harry pushed through the outer tent-flaps and gave a tentative smile to a company of soldiers passing by. 'Do you think he will be pleased with me?'

'Of course. You have proven yourself to him on the field, I will attest to that. His Majesty will have no reason to be disappointed.'

That has never stopped him. Argyle paused at the roasting spits to replace a spit-boy for a couple of turns. The wide grin on the boy's sweaty face was a strange comfort.

'Sire. We'll do that.' The cook looked troubled at the prospect of having not only a knight but also the King's nephew working the spits. 'It's hot work.'

'Which needs doing,' Argyle said and let the spit-boy have his place back, the heat from the large smouldering fire had him sweating already. 'And I have always enjoyed the smell of roasting meat.'

'It'll be ready soon,' the cook assured him and swung his ladle. 'If only 'em lazy boys'd do their bit.'

'We're going fast as we can. We can't be dropping 'em spits.' The boy flashed another smile, broken tooth and all. 'I've seen the men fight, da', I'll not risk me neck over a couple o' pieces o' meat.'

'Snotnosed lad!' The cook's voice was full of pride. 'The bottom two're ready, get 'em off.'

'Best we get out of your way then.' Argyle signalled for Harry to follow him. He lowered his voice, 'the King's dispatch only gave orders about our march here…'

The insinuation lingered in the air and Argyle let Harry writhe. Reluctant to divulge what he knew, the youth looked afield unable to hide the red blotches on his cheeks.

'It matters not. The men will have a well-earned rest.' Argyle decided to push harder next time. 'The spoils will be enough to entertain them for now.'

Harry's face soured. 'Looting the dead.'

'The payment our soldiers receive is meagre. Many of the men come for the chance to make a small fortune. They risk their lives in hopes that they may prosper if victory falls in their favour.' Argyle cared little for the trinkets of dead men. 'I have forbidden them to raid the city. The women and children…'

'Are enemies too.' Harry looked straight ahead.

'Are innocent. Men make war.'

'Do you think my uncle agrees with you?'

Argyle smiled. 'As most of the men here would say they are not paid to think. They will take pay to fight.'

'Then they are fools.'

'They are poor.' Harry sniffed and Argyle awarded him a harsh look. 'Do not pretend to know their lives, Master Harry. We are blessed never to wake hungry not knowing when we shall eat again.'

'I stand corrected, Sire.'

'In order for the King to afford his journey here, he knows full well that the men who do his fighting will steal what they can. It is their reward. There were few enough prisoners taken and I doubt the Irish will pay much in the way of ransom.' A cart came rumbling by, the harnessed oxen making slow progress. Argyle watched them go by. 'You may not like it, Master Harry, but there it is. They fight for what they can carry from the field.'

'You say that my uncle cannot afford his war?' Harry chewed his lip.

'I am saying that most Kings cannot afford their wars, not if they are to pay the men in gold from their own coffers. The spoils of war go to the men who are brave enough to pick up a bow, mace or axe and wield it against an enemy they have never before set eyes on.' Argyle raised his hand to groups of men eating outside their tents. 'If they do not fight for riches, why should they fight at all?'

'Is that true for the knights too?'

Here was a boy unaware of the worries of the real world for which Argyle was pleased. 'Some of them. We are all here at the mercy of God and the King. His gifts are what enable us to arm our men, keep horses and houses, and in return we are at the King's disposal. Few knights are as lucky as I – and none are as lucky as you, Master Harry. Trust me when I tell you that our soldiers enjoy no favours at all.'

Harry saw the point. 'It is a brave action.'

'Desperate more like,' Argyle remarked and called out to a company of Beauworth men. 'Ho! How is the food?'

'Roasted by a knight, I've heard.'

To the roar of laughter, Harry and Argyle continued their progress, stomachs growling in unison. He decided to dole out a short lesson. 'Any man can rule by fear, Master Harry. For men to keep true to you, even when they go hungry, even when fear gnaws at their hearts, you need their loyalty and devotion.'

'Turn a spit and earn their love?' Incredulous, Harry looked up at Argyle. 'Is that all it takes?'

'Would that it was, but no. I train in the field with my men whenever I can. A visible leader wields more power than a distant one.' Argyle knew he was walking a fine line. Harry was devoted to the King; he would refer any conversation that went against the King in a heartbeat if he felt his uncle's honour soiled. Argyle smiled. 'His Majesty has been fortunate that he has had little cause to engage enemies.'

'He keeps France at bay with his wife,' Harry mused and clapped a hand to his mouth. 'I only mean he was wise to marry for peace.'

'Indeed.'

They reached the far edge of the camp and began circling around it. The stench from the cesspits reached them and Harry cringed. 'We should dig new latrines.'

'We are to stay here then?' Argyle asked.

Harry coloured again, his hand shown. 'My uncle expects us to return before June is out, he told me as much before we left. However, we are to await his command.'

'Then we must look further afield for provisions,' Argyle said and made for the horse-pens. 'The King has enough mouths to feed, and grain, greens and meat here is plentiful for now. We cannot live off it forever.'

'I am certain that once word of our victory reaches the King.' Harry paused and looked at the horses, grazing in the twilight. 'I only mean…'

'No need to explain, Master Harry.' Argyle clicked his tongue and his destrier pricked up its ears. He was still not used to the sight of brown hide rather than Noble's grey flanks. Since the King would not let him send for his own horse he made do with this one. 'I am out of favour. Anyone with eyes and ears knows as much.'

'Perhaps not for long.' Harry reached out and patted a golden gelding. 'Is he not wonderful? He was a gift.'

'From your uncle?'

Harry's face knotted. 'My grandfather. To my father.'

'Now, it obeys you which makes it yours. No matter from where it hails.' The brown destrier shied away from Argyle's hand. 'Unlike this one.'

'It was my uncle's. Perhaps you are not so out of favour as you believe, Sire.'

You know not what happened, Argyle guessed and nodded to appease Harry's concern. 'I live in hope.'

'I shall speak for you.' His earnest promise should have warmed Argyle's heart. 'He shall have no other choice than to forgive you now that you have secured Kells for him. Whatever your past transgressions surely they are dwarfed by your victory in his name.'

'Is it true that the Duke of Surrey is to take the office of Lieutenant?' Argyle tried to make his voice light. Talk of the King drew worry into his bones and he would rather speak something other than his own situation.

'My uncle plans to make his nephew grander still,' Harry said with a grudge. 'They whisper that he is to be King of Ireland.'

Argyle's hand floated in the air in front of the horse's muzzle. Harry stroked his golden steed with a grim smile. 'He is to swear eternal fealty to England of course, and reign in my uncle's name. At last, he is to be given a royal title.'

'Truly?'

'A crown was commissioned before we left.' Harry turned his back to the horses. 'If not for Thomas Holland then whom?'

If the King had his wits about him, he would crown you King of Ireland, as you must have contemplated yourself, Harry. Then, the King would appease those who believe he has wronged you and your family by reverting your inheritance to himself. But he would also acknowledge that you have a place in the succession and that will not do. Argyle's thoughts brought with them fresh concern.

For all that the King paraded about Bolingbroke's estranged son as if Harry was his own, he would never bestow any real power on the young man.

They returned to the centre of camp in silence, Harry with his head hung, Argyle deep in thought. Occasionally, he roused long enough to return greetings from the fires that had sprung to life outside the tents. The Duke of Surrey to be raised to King of Ireland, the first of his kind, and no more than a maternal connection to the Crown to forward his claim. Was the King unravelling?

'I shall find men to dig the latrines, Sire.' Harry's voice was muffled by Argyle's musings. 'Sire?'

'Yes, thank you, Master Harry, that would be a great help.'

'We will soon be called upon to join my uncle.' Harry's brisk walk indicated a clear desire to be away. 'He cannot be long without me.'

Argyle watched the shadows swallow up King's nephew. I should wager he would be best pleased to be without me forever.

CHAPTER 3

13 June 1399 – Cork

The smell of rotting flesh clung to the air and had Argyle, Harry, Sir William Bagot and Thomas Percy, the Earl of Worcester, huddled around a small fire in the early morning. The herbs they had thrown on the flickering flames did little to mask the stench.

Argyle had been worried about feeding his men, but for the past five days no one had wanted for food, the stench of the slain sickened every soul in camp with the meat spits hanging empty over old coals.

'We need to bury the dead.'

'Let the crows have them.' Sir William sniffed his sleeve.

'Hiding behind thyme, Sir William?' Harry spoke with revulsion. 'The crows are overfed. They cannot take flight anymore and the field is still littered with corpses.'

'Then let the women come to fetch their rebel men.' The knight snapped before he realised his mistake. 'My Lord.'

Before Harry could speak again, Argyle cut in. 'We will bury them. You cannot imagine anyone daring to leave the city with an enemy army at their gates. They have witnessed what our men did to their husbands and sons, they will not come even if we make promises of safe passage. Who could blame them for their caution?'

'You think them that clever?' Worcester looked surprised.

You worthless fool. Argyle swallowed his comment and said, 'Clever or not, the women will not come and the bodies are festering. Call your men to dig, my Lord.'

'Will yours?'

'I set them the task yesterday, they begin after breakfast.'

Sir William's laugh was muffled by his sleeve. 'They will get started before then.'

'Every able soldier – every able man and boy – will dig.' Argyle was losing his temper fast.

'We do not take orders from you, Sire,' Sir William remarked and Worcester nodded along, a ridiculous smile on his face. Not for the first time, Argyle wondered why the King put such stock in Thomas Percy. He would be better off trusting a fox to guard the hens, at least the fox had a brain.

'Everyone will dig,' Harry said with a look so like his father's that Argyle felt a pinprick of pride. 'Before the sun sets, the corpses shall be buried. Are we agreed?'

'Yes, my Lord.' Worcester gave a cowered yelp and Sir William glared, but Harry returned the glare without blinking.

'The King has granted me authority to make decisions on his behalf, Sir William.' Harry spat disdain. 'If you mistrust me, I urge you to write the King to voice your concerns.'

'While we await the King's pleasure on the subject,' Argyle said, 'the men may fall sick from the stench and there will be fewer to dig more graves.'

Worcester looked up his face bright. 'We might move camp.'

'No.' Although the sun was little more than a thought on the horizon, Harry's brow already beaded sweat. 'We dig the graves today. If you are disinclined, my Lord Worcester, I shall convey your lack of cooperation to my uncle when we re-join his forces. I am certain he will listen with great interest.'

Worcester made a queasy noise. 'Very well, my Lord.'

'Right away, my Lord.' Sir William stomped off with Worchester in tow.

Stirring the flames, Argyle dreamed that the smell of burning wood could burn away the underlying decay that played in his nose and on his tongue. 'Well played, Master Harry.'

'You are the only one to call me that, Sir Argyle.' Harry's gaze was miles away, his shoulders hunched. 'You think the men will fall sick from the stench?'

'Perhaps not, but the decay will foul the water soon enough, and then they *will* fall sick.'

Harry yanked at his collar. 'My grandfather once told me a tale of how the King's father fell sick after a battle. He never truly recovered. In fact, grandfather said it killed him slowly stealing away his famous strength and power.'

'I heard a similar tale as a child,' Argyle said. 'The sickness was for want of clean water. Half of Prince Edmund's camp fell sick and died within a week. It was said to be a great miracle that the Prince survived.'

'To think that our enemies can kill us even from their graves.'

'Lack of graves more like, Master Harry.' Rising, Argyle worked his hands which were still stiff from the battle. 'Nothing for it but to get it done.'

'You mean to dig?'

You have much to learn still. Argyle offered a tired smile. 'Sickness has no regard for rank or family, it falls prey on any man, as the tales from our childhood prove. If I want my men to work hard until sunset, I shall sweat with them. To lead is not merely to ride ahead of the forces into battle, though I would take glory over decay any day.'

Harry spread his hands. 'Then I dig too.'

'Not today, Master Harry.' Argyle ignored the pleading noise Harry made and clamped a hand on his shoulder. 'The King will never forgive me if I put you into the path of sickness, even if your willingness does you credit. I shall be sure to tell his Majesty for your intent once we are back with his main host.'

'But the men…'

Argyle acknowledged the boy's good intentions. 'You can stay for a short while and make a start of one of the graves. I will not have you stay for longer than that the men to see you there and acknowledge your resolve.' Harry tried to argue, but Argyle spoke over him. 'I have another task for you – to procure fresh water.'

'I will haul water if you wish me to,' Harry said with an earnest nod. 'You see, Sire, I am willing to learn; I am willing to lead. I understand, though you think I do not.'

Despite the stomach-churning air around them, Argyle laughed. 'You have put me in my place, Master Harry. You will need help with the water. Round up the spit-boys, horse hands and squires and equip them with buckets. Take a cart or two. There is a stream a few leagues from here. Go there, taste the water and assess if it is worth drinking. You may have to go further up stream. Trust your nose and your mouth, not your eyes.'

'And now, you put me in my place, Sir Argyle.' Harry grinned. 'If my words were empty, you have filled them with purpose.'

'Fortunate for us all that you speak no empty words, Master Harry.' Argyle turned for the field, tugging his collar up over his mouth and nose and tying it in place with a leather string. 'You will be better for it to be away from this.'

Despite Harry's true reason for being at Kells, his ease of manner made for pleasant company and Argyle would have let him stay if not for the threat of an angry sovereign looming overhead.

He joined the waiting men, most of them wore stern expressions that were, no doubt, designed to make them look as if the reeking battlefield did not make their stomachs churn. What had been an enemy only a week ago was well past human, the bodies now bloated and crusted with dirt. The crows had had their feast; some bones picked clean, all dead opened, grey-green sludge oozing from ragged holes.

'We must make do with shallow graves,' Argyle said to the captains. 'Spread the word. Dig holes as big as you can as close to the corpses as is possible. We cannot move them far or they will break apart.'

'Dissolve more like, M'lord,' someone shouted further afield.

'Aye,' one of Worcester's captains said with a savage grimace. 'We'll make short process of it.'

'Anything to get them into the ground.' Argyle grabbed a shovel. 'Best get on with it.'

'You're staying?' The captain's question was laced with disbelief.

'More hands make for faster work. If we dig all through the day, we may be done by nightfall.'

'Where's the princeling going?' asked a soldier sporting Sir William's black raven crest on his chest.

Do not let the King hear you speak thus of Bolingbroke's son.

Argyle pointed to a couple of carts trundling out of camp to the west. 'My Lord Monmouth is assigned to find fresh water for us.'

'Three cheers for Prince Harry!'

Argyle let the men roar, making a mental note to caution his captains that once they returned to the King's forces in Dublin. There was to be no more talk of princelings. Though the King might show Harry special favour it was better to stifle the subject before he came to view his nephew as a threat.

At the end of the day, Argyle's arms and back ached, and he envied Harry his mission to secure clean water. They would not be done before nightfall, but at least today, everyone was too tired to care that no food was prepared when they returned to camp.

'The Prince's returned with water.'

'Three cheers…'

'No.' Argyle felt hundreds of eyes on him. 'You may cheer Lord Monmouth for his efforts as you please, as long as you remember that he is no prince. Be warned that if I hear you mention him thus again, discipline will be administered.'

What little laughter rose was soon smothered by the sombre looks of Argyle's men. He straightened and rammed the shovel into the hard ground. 'We break for the night.'

As they made their way back to camp, stinking of death, he heard muttering in the encroaching darkness. He checked his pace when a soldier scoffed. 'He's not my commander.'

'He's the only one digging with us, ain't he? And he's the right of it. If you've got a brain, you'll listen to him.' Argyle recognised the cook by his coarse retort.

'I hear the King dug him out of the Tower, how'd he get in there?'

Curiosity travelled alongside him and would most likely be a constant companion as long as they were on campaign. Argyle had tried to make his peace with it.

'Not our business,' the cook said and spat. 'All's we need know is he's here. Where's your fancy Lord, eh? Hiding his horn in a bunch of thyme, he nicked from me stores.'

The darkness hid the laughing men and Argyle's smile.

'He's a right prick,' the gruff voice agreed. 'Don't know what he's doing most of the time. Mayhap I'll ask to enter into Sir Argyle's service.'

'He'll not want you.' The cook hawked another glob.

'And why not? I'm good with an axe, and I'll dig as many graves as need be to get home.'

'Aye,' someone said behind him. 'We'll all want to work for the golden knight. He'll just not know where to stick us.'

'King's man he is,' someone else said, the dark swallowed up everyone now, only footsteps revealed where men were walking.

'You think?' A curse followed and then a short laugh. 'God's blood, where's the torches?'

'You know what I think? I think he's a clever man, and he'll know what to do.' The voice was vaguely familiar, though Argyle could not place it. 'If he says don't call Lord Monmouth a princeling, I'll go on his advice. We're all the King's men, aren't we?'

'Three cheers for the King!'

A ragged choir reached for the skies above. Argyle could not help but notice that not all of the men joined in. He blessed the clouds that hid the moon, in the darkness he could not be accused of his silence for the men did not know he walked among them.

As soon as he could make out the camp fires, he hung back until he was fairly certain all of the soldiers were in front of him. Then he veered left and took the long way back to his tent. All he wanted was a wash, perhaps some of the cook's oat cakes and then sleep. Tonight, surely, he would be too tired to dream. Argyle pushed through the tent flaps.

'Sire.' Harry's voice betrayed his fatigue.

'Master Harry, you did well.'

'The men are watered,' Harry gave a tired laugh and tumbled to the cot. 'As are the horses.'

'A long day for us all.'

'I fool myself into thinking I cannot smell the corpses anymore.' Harry put his arm over his forehead. 'But I can.'

'The ground is proving a greater enemy than the Irish,' Argyle said and splashed his face with water. 'What you smell is an incomplete job. We shall finish tomorrow.'

Harry dragged himself to his feet. 'I should have taken your advice and harnessed an ox. One of the dray horses kicked a spit-boy.'

'Bad?'

'We think his hand broke, though the physician says it did not.'

Argyle rubbed his face with a clean shirt, it felt as if his skin took a breath of relief. 'Good, the cook needs the boy at the spits. Once we are freed of the rank stench and hunger gnaws at our innards again he will be hard at work.'

'We brought enough water to last us three days.' Harry plunged his hands into the bowl of water and drove them through his tangled hair, grit trickling down his cheeks. 'It will suffice.'

'You have had word from the King?'

Rummaging the folds of his shirt, Harry produced a scrap of paper, a whisper of red wax on the edge. 'The summons came at night fall.'

'Tullow.' Argyle ran his eyes over the brief message.

'My uncle grows weary of waiting for the Duke of Albemarle to arrive.' Harry lay down, his white chest shining in the weak light of the candle. 'I wish he would be more patient, for what can we do before he does? And he is to bring one hundred barges.'

'So I gather.'

Harry laughed, half asleep. 'I forgot I gave you the paper to read.'

'We are both tired.'

'To the bone.' There was a rustling from the cot. 'I thought I knew what that meant. It turns out, I did not.'

'Now you do.'

Argyle assumed Harry had fallen asleep when he muttered, 'He will have to forgive you now, Sir Argyle. Your praises are sung at every fire in the camp.'

The golden knight. Argyle shivered despite the heat.

ADRIFT

Strange sounds and voices dragged Argyle from his disorganised dreamscape. He kept his eyes closed and tried to steady his breath. Until he knew where he was, there was no reason to let anyone know he was conscious. First, he needed to know if they would find him, then he could worry about the rest.

Soft hands brushed against his cheek and lifted his hair. Argyle steeled himself when fingers began examining his wounded temple. Someone said something and he could tell by the crunching on the sand that at least two people walked a little way away. He heard their muffled voices, one of them definitely female. She sounded angry and then exasperated. The other might be a boy or perhaps a young man who clearly wanted to leave Argyle where he lay. A few more words were exchanged before one set of footsteps returned. The hands stroked his neck, warm breath tickled his ear.

Footsteps indicated that more people had arrived. The other voice spoke again and Argyle could make out a few French words. The accent was strange, warping the speech. The woman agreed with a 'Oui'.

People grabbed his arms and legs and Argyle forced himself to relax. Pain shot up his leg when a gloved hand pressed into a wound on his calf and he groaned. The manhandling stopped briefly. In the distance, a horse whickered. He was lifted and then there were boards beneath his back. Strangely, it steadied the shifting sensation for a moment. As the cart began moving, nausea washed over him and he just managed to turn his head before he retched.

Then darkness folded him in a perilous embrace.

CHAPTER 4

18 June 1399 – Grennan, Ireland

Argyle sliced the darkness with his dagger, rolling out of his cot. A cloaked figure yelped and fell back, narrowly avoiding the blade. In his grip, the stranger's arm shivered and panic ebbed in his veins.

Whoever was foolish enough to enter Argyle's tent was forced to his knees, his face hidden beneath the dark hood. 'Please Sire, I bring a message.'

Argyle shook sleep from his mind. 'Message?'

The man made to stand, but froze when Argyle pressed the blade against his jaw. 'Stay down. I do not know why you are here…'

'I bring news from England,' the messenger said and gulped when Argyle twisted the blade.

'From whom?'

'The Duke of York.' The messenger pushed back his hood revealing a young, haggard face, streaked with dirt and sweat. 'I'm Felix. The Duke has tasked me with delivering this news to you.'

Argyle released Felix and peered into the dark. All seemed quiet in camp but he knew what happened in the shadows. He pushed the flaps shut and bound them from inside. What could the King's uncle, Edmund of Langley, want? They had scarcely exchanged five words with each other in all of Argyle's life.

He kept his dagger in hand. 'How did the Duke know where to find me?'

Felix held out a letter, seal down, his ghostly hand still shaking. 'I'm told all will be clear once you have read this, Sire.'

Argyle snatched the paper. The seal was not broken, nor was it the royal seal of Edmund of Langley's. The crest was one he had never expected to see. 'I ask you again, who sent you? And you had better speak the truth this time.'

'My Lord the Duke…' Felix's voice trailed away his eyes fixed on Argyle's blade, which was turning in his restless hand. With an effort, the young man met his gaze. 'The winds of England are changing, Sire.'

I dare say if York has hold of Bolingbroke's personal seal, Argyle thought. Was it such a stretch of the imagination that Gaunt had left the Lancastrian seal in the hands of his younger brother for safe keeping?

Argyle snapped the red wax. 'How is the Duke?'

'In good health, when I left, Sire.' Felix kept his distance. 'He was among friends.'

'I should hope so, for all our sakes.' He stoked the little brazier and held the letter close to the flames, fighting an urge to just let the fire devour the thin paper.

In all his life, he had never believed that an English lord would defy a royal sentence and break exile, let alone sail for England as soon as his King was gone. What madness was this? Had Bolingbroke lost his mind?

Gaunt's death and the King's choice to revert the Lancaster heritage to his own uses was the worst decision of his reign. Even Argyle could not blame Bolingbroke for wanting revenge, but if he thought anything good would come of this, he was wrong. Such an extreme measure could only end in disaster. Then again, why would York lie in a missive that could easily be intercepted?

Of late, Argyle had often wondered when the English nobles would turn against their King.

Ever since he had watched Bolingbroke being cheered by crowds thronging the streets of Dover as he made his way to the ship that would take him to exile, Argyle had known for certain that the English people put more stock into Bolingbroke than their own King.

He had suspected that the English nobles might even turn against the King if he did not mend his rift with them. Now, here was Bolingbroke returned, embraced by the noblemen of England. Would they support a man they believed wrongly exiled rather than the King they had once sworn to serve?

If this letter was indeed authentic it seemed the nobles of England were willing rally to the side of an exile. Bolingbroke had taken measures for any eventuality. According to the message he had arrived in England with three hundred men in tow. How many did he have now?

Argyle put down the missive and locked eyes with Felix. It was not until just now that Argyle noticed how young he was, perhaps only a year or two older than Harry.

'How long have you served the Duke?'

'Five years. I hope to join his service as a steward once I'm of age.' Felix chest swelled with pride.

'How much of your future rides on my reply?'

Felix wiped his brow. 'I'm instructed not to leave your side until you've decided.'

The youth seemed in much distress though fervent in his obedience to York, and Felix reminded Argyle of himself when he still had a master to serve.

'And if I return to the King, you shall join me? He will know you are not part of my retinue, nor that of any other knight or nobleman.' Pallid, Felix shirked back from Argyle's harsh tone. 'This is no game, boy. What you bring to me are words of treason. How would you have me react other than to seek an audience with the King as soon as we meet with him and tell him what you have brought? This is treason.'

'Only…' Felix' courage finally failed.

Argyle turned his attention to the letter. Bolingbroke was riding hard for London. He already had the support of the northern Lords and expected the rest of the country to follow suit in due course. Argyle suspected that the Archbishop of York, Thomas Arundel, had sent word to Bolingbroke the moment the King decided to make for Ireland and that the only element detaining his return would have been the weather.

If he was already in England the King's days were numbered that much was certain. The Lords were done being disgruntled. They were ready to act and Bolingbroke had given them a common cause behind which to rally.

York had turned his back on a nephew who had trusted him to govern England while he settled old scores in Ireland. Now, the Duke of York seemed almost too eager to let his exiled nephew step in and claim England for himself. For certainly that would be the end of this disaster, if indeed, Bolingbroke would emerge victorious.

At the mention of Beauworth, Argyle's pulse quickened. Bolingbroke had posted soldiers on Argyle's own lands, the threat was plain; Bolingbroke demanded that Argyle turn his coat to save his family. His eyes lingered on the last line.

– *Which will it be, Sir Argyle? Your family or your King?* –

'What are your orders?' Argyle tried to keep his voice steady.

'I'm to take back a letter sealed with your crest. I'm to put it into the hands of the Duke and no one else. If I'm intercepted, I'm to discard the letter and throw myself on the mercy of the King.'

Felix had the fierceness of youth and an unyielding loyalty that Argyle had long since lost. For a second, his heart ached to be back in the service of La Fontaine for this not to be his decision to make but rather to have it made for him.

'How many are backing Lord Bolingbroke?'

'All of the Lords, save the ones currently in the King's retinue,' Felix said. 'Although the Duke believes that they too will come to find that it's time for a change once they are made aware of the situation.'

'How many messengers were sent?'

Felix looked up. In the weak flickering light from the brazier his fatigue leaped from the circles around his eyes to his sunken cheeks. 'I was tasked with locating you. If there are others in Ireland, I know nothing of them.'

CHAPTER 5

24 June 1399 – Leighlinbridge Castle, Ireland

Harry was weary of his uncle's many messengers hurrying their return to the main host, and he complained that the King had too soon forgotten their triumph at Kells.

'He did not bury the dead.' Harry's voice trembled. 'He did not sleep in the stink nor tend to the wounded.'

'He has his own to contend with, Master Harry. We cannot begin to understand the pressure of his office.' It was all too easy to give in and agree, but that would not do and, so far, Argyle had mastered his own malcontent. Now that they were about to merge with the rest of the army he felt the pressure of the King's watchful gaze and knew that the tiniest misstep would secure him a long stay in the stocks.

'The more he speaks of battle, the more I fear it. Has he ever been in the fray? Does he know that the Irish are a real danger to us?' Harry shook his cloak, bristling. 'How can he be this ignorant?'

'We shall soon see Dublin, Master Harry.' Argyle shielded his eyes with a rain-swollen hand. 'We shall be out of this miserable weather and perhaps even blessed with a warm fire and food to fill our bellies.'

'We had better be awarded much more than that, Sire,' Harry sounded years older than he was. 'Or I shall have to have words with my uncle.'

As the camp went up around him, tagging onto the main site, Argyle walked a round to cheer up his men and hastening the cooks to raise makeshift shelter, build fires and get food under way. He had brought three thousand men with him to Kells and had returned just shy of two thousand four hundred. By all accounts a fine result, though it remained to be seen if the King agreed.

Harry turned for Leighlin castle the moment they reached the outskirts of camp. With him went Sir William and Worcester, and Argyle would not miss their company. Instead, he was left to wonder what tales they would spin around the King's head and if Harry was a match for them once surrounded by luxury.

As Jeremy removed the armour, several bruises and cuts awakened. The long, wet ride had offered no relief, sweating in the iron casing had only added to his discomfort and Argyle grunted as he shrugged off his inner kirtle, his left shoulder still stiff and distended. The rain had wreaked havoc with the metal, rust creeping into every joint.

'Find a barrel of sand and roll it.' Jeremy nodded and gathered the pieces lingering inside the tent flaps in hopes the rain might let up. Argyle shifted. 'It cannot be put off, who knows when MacMurrough decides to rebel again?'

The boy was so tired it was all he could do to shoulder his burden and wobble into the encroaching darkness.

'Sand, Jeremy, and then bed. Get Peter to help you, he should be done stabling my horse by now.'

'Sir Argyle, the King awaits your company.' A soldier sporting the King's white hart crest on his chest peered into Argyle's tent. He recognised the man as one of the retinue that had greeted them just outside of camp. The soldier kept glancing over his shoulder, fiddling with his lance which looked in need of honing and oiling.

A quick splash of cold water washed salvation and punishment over the cuts and bruises on Argyle's face and arms. Pulling a clean robe over his head, he tried not to jerk when the fabric tangled with his wounds. He slung his belt around his hips, winding the ends through the ornate belt ring and tying the saturated leather as best he could.

Wishing he had a change of boots, Argyle nodded. 'Lead the way.'

The winding walk through camp made it clear how long the main host had been stuck here. Argyle noted that new latrines needed digging to accommodate his own troops as well as Albemarle's men once they arrived. The fields were empty except for a few cows soon to drop calves and, in the coops, chickens worked hard to keep the army in fresh supplies.

As they emerged from the camp and made their way towards the castle, Argyle asked, 'How do you sustain the men?'

'There's good hunting and last year's harvest was generous,' the soldier replied and almost tripped over the uneven cobbles of the castle courtyard. 'There's clean water and the monastery has plenty of greens. We want for nothing.'

Clearly, Argyle thought when he saw a couple of women slipping out of the yard, giggling and sniggering. The men deserved what entertainment they might scrounge up while they waited to see what MacMurrough might have in store for them.

Perhaps it would come to nothing if the King had had word that Bolingbroke was coming back. Argyle had long considered whether to broach the topic with Harry, but then they would have had orders to return to England, not join the King for his march on Dublin.

What remained to be seen was if Albemarle carried any orders from his father, the Duke of York, or if he remained loyal to the King. One thing was certain, the longer they stayed in Ireland the more fealty would shift to Bolingbroke's cause.

Doors swung open and Argyle entered a vaulted space where the lords and captains were enjoying their meal. Worcester and Sir William were already washed and redressed, glittering at one of the lower tables. Harry was nowhere to be seen, though he might be in with the King who was likewise absent.

'Sir Argyle.' John Montagu, the Earl of Salisbury, made space for him at the trestle table near the dais. 'Join us.'

'My Lords.' Argyle sat down, conscious that he was inspected by all at the table, which had fallen silent. He pulled close a pitcher and poured, the rich scent awakening his appetite. 'What news?'

'The King!'

Everyone leapt to their feet as the King entered, Harry trailing behind. Even at this distance, Argyle could tell the boy was tired, his feet dragging and his head ducked. The King made a sweeping gesture and all resumed their seats.

'His Majesty seems in fine spirit.'

'Word is that Albemarle will be in Dublin by the time we arrive.' Salisbury leaned in. 'The King has been sending out small vessels for the past week to scout for the Duke. We all wonder what has taken him so long, but then a lack of wind can prolong any journey at sea.'

'Then it is a fine thing he has been sighted at last.' Argyle drank deep, relishing in the good wine. He would have to pace himself or risk falling down drunk if he did not eat something soon. 'This is a welcome change from the sour piss we had in Kells.'

'Anything would be better than that, I imagine,' someone said and the men around the table laughed.

'Where is Lord Surrey?'

Salisbury skewered a baked onion. 'In a state.'

'Master Harry has informed me that Surrey is to have a great position soon.' Argyle caught the King's eye and saw him send a dish in his direction, no doubt for Salisbury. 'If that is the case, I wonder why is he in a state, my Lord?'

'He felt slighted that you and Lord Monmouth were sent to Kells while he was to stay behind.' Salisbury watched the servant turn left before the table and pick his way towards Argyle. 'He believes you cheated him out of battlefield glory. The King, however, is pleased.'

Owning that this rare favour was probably the work of Harry, Argyle picked out the best pieces from the dish before raising his cup to the King. 'If only I had known, I would have exchanged charges with him.'

'Could not be done. The King has his heart set on keeping Surrey close, so that the Irish shall see him enter Dublin at the head of the army.' Ever a staunch supporter of the King, Salisbury lowered his voice. 'I believe he also wanted you to redeem yourself. I cannot lure the tale from the King and so, I would have you tell me what transpired? Why were you dragged off to the Tower by all accounts bleeding from so many cuts you should have died? Only weeks later to be remitted to the King's favour?'

'If the King has said nothing, it is not my place.' Argyle stuffed a big lump of bread in his mouth as if to contain the truth. Every night he was visited by past horrors, all he wanted was to lock them away forever.

'How did the peacocks do?' sneered Richard of Conisburgh, the King's godson, awarding Worcester a condescending glare.

'They put up with the battle and then ran when the dead needed burying.' Argyle wondered if the younger son of the Duke of York knew about his father's betrayal, but the two had never been close and Conisburgh favoured his godfather in both faith and looks.

'They would not bury their own?'

Argyle scratched his cheek with the tip of his knife, he needed a shave. 'They would not bury their enemies.'

Conisburgh folded his arms. 'And you would?'

'They were rotting on the field, fouling the air, carrying disease. If it had not been done, we would have fallen sick and died ourselves.'

Argyle noticed a few of the Lords push away their plates. War makes dirty business. If rotting corpses is enough to put you off your food what will happen when you are in the thick of battle?

'Good decision then.' Salisbury tipped his cup to Argyle before drinking. He wiped his chin on the beautiful, beaded sleeve of his opulent attire. 'I suppose we must await the full tale until you have been with the King.'

'We need not wait long.' Conisburgh nodded and Argyle turned.

'The King will see you now, Sire.'

The antechamber had the same vaulted ceiling as the hall, though it was sparsely lit and scantly decorated. Although the castle looked to be in some disrepair, at least, it was dry and the King had put up a few of his curtains and tapestries to lend it a regal air. No doubt new wall-hangings were commissioned to ensure that the King of Ireland could receive his subjects in splendour once he was set up in Dublin, and most likely those commodities waited for them once they arrived.

'Sir Argyle.' The King waved him forward. 'No need to stand on ceremony. Come, let me congratulate you on your victory. I am best pleased.'

'Thank you, Majesty.' Argyle endured the King's drunken, crushing embrace. He would have to bury Coxcombe's last words and his own feelings deep within to ensure the King did not take notice. 'The Irish made it easy for us.'

'I told you they were getting too big for their boots. It needed attending to, my council agreed.'

This is the story we are to spin? This is what we anchor our cause to and call it just. It is to hold no trace of your nephew about to assume a title far beyond his station?

'And you ensured that Mortimer was avenged as I desired. You dealt them the first blow, and now, we can begin our preparations for the main event.'

'Will MacMurrough give battle, Majesty?'

The King laughed and clicked his fingers. 'I should think not, now that he knows you are here at the head of my army. Most likely he also knows that Albemarle is speeding this way. I had word today that Edward's fleet was spotted two days ago, so I assume he will be in Dublin well before we arrive.'

Once more the King clicked his fingers, looking about with displeasure. 'Harry.'

'Here I am, uncle.' Harry carried a tray of fruit. 'I was preparing your refreshments. I am sorry to have kept you waiting.' Fatigue rode on his words and his leaden movements.

'My nephew has been praising you, Sire. Relating how you get on with the men, how much they all love you.' Something in the King's tone made Argyle's hair stand on end.

'Most men like to follow orders, Majesty. It is only natural.'

'Some do not.' Huffing, the King picked up an apple and sliced it open. 'You know, of course, of whom I speak. But enough of that. I am pleased with you tonight and you may ask any favour of me that you like.'

'I should like to send a message to my wife, she deserves to know that I am still alive. I left in haste and she has had no word from me since then. That is all I ask.' Better to be humble and meek even if it lodged in his craw and made his words taste bitter.

'She certainly does, for she cannot have been pleased by what you did to deserve being holed up here with me.' The King grabbed his cup and inclined it, the glitter from a ruby ring on the King's middle finger turned Argyle's stomach. 'To the good women of England.'

'Majesty.'

There was no way of telling if the King was appeased or if his immediate praise was only skin deep. Argyle wanted rest and to get back to Beauworth, power plays between cousins be damned. No amount of wishing could release him from his sworn duty and the only thing he could truly take pleasure in was the memory of Coxcombe bleeding out before his feet.

The King took a swig of wine. 'Can I count on you to be loyal to a fault from now on, Sir Argyle?'

'I honour my pledges, Majesty.' Argyle tasted the easy lie.

'Honour is fickle, Sire. Do not believe I have forgotten why you are here in fetters,' the King said and smirked. 'The past is what urges me to ask. Have you been sending messages to your brother under cover of darkness?'

Awarding the King a neutral glance, Argyle shook his head. 'No. To my dying day, I will advocate his return for I believe his punishment was too harsh, of which you are aware, Majesty. I have sent no messages since we arrived, as you demanded. Tonight, I will send one to my wife if it pleases your Majesty, and I hope to tell her that soon I shall return home.'

All the while, Harry had been lingering near the King's elbow, holding a tray that was wobbling in his shaking hands. The boy looked prone to collapse when the King poked him in the side.

'My dear Harry will return with you and watch as you compose a message for your glorious wife. Once Sir Argyle is done, Harry, you are to ensure that it contains only assurances of his affections and timely return, and you will fix the wax upon the letter yourself.' The ruby sparkled when the King raised his cup to Argyle. 'Then you are to return here and relate to me the content. Only then can you put it in the hands of the messenger we are dispatching at daybreak.'

The King turned the cup in his hands. 'You have my leave to assure your wife that you will return to her side soon, Sir Argyle. I only wonder what she might do to you when you are left alone. I hear she has a fierce temper.'

'Yes, Majesty.' Argyle bent his knee, Harry kneeling next to him, his face a lethargic mask.

'Be quick about it, Harry needs to rest.' The King gestured to the door.

The darkness swallowed up Argyle and Harry, the wind whipping noises from camp around and smashing them against the castle walls. In the scant light of a few torches, Argyle looked up to spy a light moving from window to window as if someone was following their progress through the courtyard. For once, he was glad to sleep in his tent and not in the castle with the rest of the lords and royal favourites.

'My uncle is fearful.' A gust of wind carried Harry's candid admission. 'He finds he can trust only a few men these days.'

'War nurses suspicion,' Argyle said with careful indifference. 'Once we make for Dublin he will be himself again.'

In the dark, a hand touched Argyle's sleeve. 'Fear can be supplanted by hatred.'

'Master Harry,' Argyle began and was cut short by a tug on his sleeve.

When, at last, they were inside his tent, he pulled out a scrap of paper and wet the dry ink. Swirling the liquid in the wooden inkwell, he looked at Harry. 'Your concern for your uncle does you credit. You have no doubt felt the brunt of his wrath, and yet, I believe you still love him.'

Harry peeked out of the flaps. 'Beware what you say, Sire.'

'The camp has ears.' Argyle echoed what Henry of Bolingbroke had once said to him in a land far to the east.

'I would add that it has eyes and far too many wagging tongues. If indeed the King is harbouring concerns, mark my words, most of the camp already knows.'

Harry tied the strings in the tent flaps with loose knots and turned around. 'Then you and I can easily agree that some words are best left unsaid. I confess nothing to you that I would not repeat to my uncle if he willed it of me.'

Be careful what you admit to. Argyle motioned for Harry to continue.

'There are rumblings.' Harry sat on Argyle's cot, an uneasy look upon his tired face. He had borne the rushed march to reach the King's camp with some good cheer which had slowly washed away as they approached the King's host.

Now, he looked ready to come undone. 'The men are uneasy. They do not believe that our victory is enough to subdue MacMurrough. In fact, they doubt it will make any difference at all.'

'MacMurrough will not come crawling like a cowed dog, it is simply not his way, nor the way of his people. La Fontaine once said that the Irish were Scotsmen stranded on an island, just as impossible to predict and make to give battle and as sly and cunning too.' Argyle wet the tip of the quill on his tongue, the ink tart and earthy.

Would that the King had never set his sights on subduing the Irish. He would happily exchange this act of war for a lifetime in the Tower short though it might be.

'Do you know why there is such unrest in camp? We came here to bring the Irish to their knees. It was never going to be easy.'

'I suspect only a very few know anything. Perhaps Surrey, though I cannot say for a certainty.' Harry got up and paced the tent, glancing every once in a while, to gauge

Argyle's progress. 'Why does the King not issue his appointment? Perhaps hold back on making Thomas King of Ireland, for the time being. He could still be Lord-Lieutenant. Though that is a title tainted by blood.'

'He was promised a better prize, he is hardly going to settle to anything less than what the King has granted in private,' Argyle said, forming a few sentences that he hoped would inspire faith in Isobel. If Bolingbroke's men were at Beauworth's gates the chances of her receiving anything from him were slim. Still, he had to try.

If it were up to him, he would crown Surrey King of Ireland this instant if it might stem the changing tides, but to what end? In England, another sought to usurp the King, and in that game, Surrey was nothing more than a pawn.

Argyle paused to dip his quill. 'No one can be crowned until the Irish are subdued. How is Surrey to achieve such a feat without the King's men? No, the Irish must be put in their proper place or they will discard of a would-be King as easily as they did Mortimer.'

'You never told me what landed you in the Tower?' Evidently, Harry was spoiling for a change of topic. 'Why does the King not trust you to compose a letter to your wife? Now that you have brought him glory in Kells and he has made a public display of his appreciation.'

'We had a difference of opinion.' In Argyle's mind, the King's unfortunate mistress, Celeste, died once more. Just as La Fontaine, her ghost must be put to rest. Argyle scratched a few more lines. Perhaps they danced together in Heaven now, they would make quite the couple. Both dead at the hand of an erratic man if Coxcombe was to be trusted.

'Must have been quite a difference to land you in the Tower.'

Argyle signed the letter and held it out to Harry. 'There, you can read it. As for the rest, if your uncle has not seen fit to explain the situation to you, neither shall I.'

Harry seemed to accept that some things he would not be privy to, and he read the letter carefully three times before he picked up the bar of wax and dripped it onto the paper. 'Do you wish to put your mark on it?'

One look at the gold ring with the unicorn was enough for Argyle to shake his head. 'She will know my hand.' He put her name on the outside of the folded paper and held it out to Harry.

'I shall relate your message to the King,' Harry said and the letter disappeared inside his shirt. 'I shall ensure that he knows you did not attempt to put in a coded message. He still worries you communicate with your brother.'

Biting his cheek not to laugh out loud, Argyle loosened the strings and let Harry out. 'My brother is in exile. What could he do even if I did try to reach him?'

If he were to send Thomas a coded message, he would never include it in a letter to Isobel. She would let it smoulder on the Beauworth fire warming her cold hands.

Who would tell the King that he was better served turning his suspicions on his own family?

CHAPTER 6

25 June 1399 – Tullow, Ireland

Mounted, it was easy for Argyle to see the King's sweeping gestures and the line of young men whose hearts no doubt throbbed in anticipation of their coming glory.

Last in line, Harry's dark hair moved with the same gusts of wind that made the King's standards snap and twirl high above the provisional dais erected late last night. The soldiers who had been set the task had come back groaning with fatigue just before dawn. If they expected praise or even a courteous nod from their King they would wait for an eternity. Argyle had let his men stay in the camp, huddled under their stinking hides to catch what rest they could.

The wind carried fragments of the King's speech towards him, but Argyle did not hear them. The words from the long since burned letter carrying the Lancaster seal kept surfacing, disrupting his quiet contemplations. He tried to push it back in its lair; it did no good to dwell on the actions of the past – even the recent past. He found himself once more wondering if Felix had got away. How foolish he had been to accept the young man's word that he was sent by York and Bolingbroke himself.

At first light, Argyle had awoken from a startling dream once more certain that the King had set a trap. That soon he would have his revenge over the last bothersome Mowbray brother still free to roam around England.

A drop of sweat escaped from the nape of Argyle's neck and made its slow, clammy descent down his spine. It was as if Ireland had decided to bless the King in his endeavour, the sun was high on a clear sky, the air thick with the scent of rosehips and chamomile. The heat beneath his plate made his blood boil, bubbling with concern that the King would call forth Harry only to cut off his head.

How could the King not be aware that Harry's father had returned to England almost the moment the royal fleet had set sail for the Irish shore? Nothing travelled faster than gossip and rumours.

Argyle was sure that many men had been dispatched to send word to the English nobles once loyal to Gaunt and the royal Lancaster line that the heir had reappeared and was mustering an army. Looking around, he paused at each noble face and tried to decide if there was an air of secrecy or a tremor of doubt as the King moved slowly down the line of young men, tapping each shoulder with his ceremonial sword. In all his regalia, he lit up on the dais as a peacock in a guinea fowl enclosure. King Richard was in his element.

Argyle's thoughts drifted. What would Bolingbroke do when he took London and discovered that the King had brought with him all the royal regalia? Would he simply shrug and set about making his own, or would he pursue the King to secure the treasure?

Certainly, Bolingbroke had not come back merely to secure his inheritance. If that were the case would have been no need to despatch messengers to the far corners of the English realm. In fact, all he had to do was to write to Harry and implore that he be made Duke of Lancaster.

The idea must have crossed Bolingbroke's mind, and yet, he had returned though he must know that the King had brought Harry to Ireland.

Locking eyes with Thomas Holland, Duke of Surrey, Argyle gave a small nod and noticed his lips curl. Here was a man secure in his position. Or so it would appear. Surrey would achieve a title that not even Mortimer, who gave his life to defend the King's supremacy, could ever have aspired to.

Argyle wondered if the King's nephew would be as adept in the art of negotiating with the proud Irishmen as Mortimer had been. And yet, it had not been enough. In the end, the Irish had taken Mortimer's life – and head if rumours were to be believed. Put it on a spike and paraded it far and wide around the restless island. Perhaps Surrey's mild temper might prove to be the counterbalance everyone before him had wanted for.

Stifling a sigh of relief when the cool wind picked at his hair, he watched the King's slow progress. At the end of the line, Argyle spied Harry cocking his head slightly to better see how far he was from earning his spurs. He was the only one kneeling before the King who had actually made war on the Irish.

It was well known that the King was in a state over MacMurrough's retreat into the fasthold of Wicklow. With a small force compared to the King's twenty-eight thousand men, Argyle could not blame MacMurrough that he chose to make war on his own terms. If he were to go into open battle and survive he would gain nothing except shackles around his ankles and a noose around his neck.

Those who had encountered the Irish during the march from Waterford to Leighlinbridge had great respect for the Irish determination and spirit, but to be outnumbered almost ten to one would make any commander worth his salt take a different route. Now, MacMurrough sat laughing in his stronghold, no doubt conjuring up plans of how to best deplete the English enemy.

Yesterday, Argyle had said as much to the King when in council. He had advocated that small bands of men be sent to scout for the Irish, arguing that, if nothing else, they would be able to send word where the enemy might strike next, for strike they must surely do. The King had laughed him off and asked if he had not already proven himself more than an equal to their adversaries? When Harry had voiced his own concerns the King's gaze had gone black and he had fumed that if Harry was unhappy with his spurs, he need not accept them. Nothing more had been said on the subject, and yet, Argyle already knew that he would speak up again against the superior neglect of the Irish will.

To his left, Salisbury's dapple-grey scraped the ground. The horse and its master decked out in yellow, green and red, the unique standard of red diamonds on white squared with the green eagle on yellow flying above their heads. Salisbury sat straight-backed his helmet nestled on the high pommel of his saddle. At almost fifty years old, John Montagu was still a match for men half his age or younger, and though he was slight of build he had a blow that could knock a man off his horse. His eyes were fixed on the King who had come to the end of the line. To Harry.

In Argyle's mind, Harry's slender body transformed to that of Thomas, his head bent as the King stood before him in the torch-lit hall of Westminster Palace, hesitating for a brief moment before creating him Warden of the East Marches. Since then, the Mowbray name had been soiled and tainted, left to waft in tatters over a once great house.

On the dais, the King paused before Harry, bending his head to impart some words of wisdom no doubt. How curious that man who had never seen actual battle should speak of it to someone who had killed his first enemies only weeks ago. Harry looked down, his hands folded on his left knee, the right knee placed firmly on the sanded grass. The King raised his sword, the gold hilt long and glittering in his slim hands. When the flat of the blade touched Harry's shoulder, Argyle exhaled relief.

The King held out his hand and Harry took it, rising from the dust an anointed knight of England. The crowd let out a collective roar of delight, many banging the hilts of their daggers against their shields or stomping their feet in celebration. To create knights was a centuries old tradition intended to bring about good fortune in the war to come. Argyle wondered if perhaps, this time, it would prove fortuitous to impart new titles upon young men when it had not in Scotland. Then again, the King had not promoted a favourite to a seat well beyond his station in life.

There was not to be another de Vere. At least not until they reached Dublin and Surrey got his crown.

The ceremony completed, the crowd dispersed and the King retreated to his immense pavilion, his Holland family in tow.

'What a sight.' Salisbury had edged close without Argyle noticing.

'They will be eager to prove their worth to the King.'

Salisbury began the slow trot back to camp. 'Indeed. You have already given Monmouth his first taste of battle. Tell me, Sire, how did he like it?'

'How do any of us like taking the lives of others?' Argyle shook his head. 'Forgive me, my Lord, I am in ill humour today.'

'Might it be because you will not be acknowledged for you efforts, Sire?'

Argyle gave Salisbury a bleak glance. 'I should hope you know me better, my Lord. When we left my wife was pregnant with our second child. I find my thoughts often travel to her and to our new little boy or girl.'

'I was unawares she was expecting. This shines a different light on the matter. I shall pray for her and the child.' Salisbury gathered his reins and patted his horse. 'I know what it is to leave a pregnant woman behind. We must allow that she is in God's hands when the day comes for her to birth and whether we are close or far afield we are helpless to change the course of events.'

'Though you will admit, my Lord, that Ireland is a little further afield than most men can boast.'

Salisbury laughed. 'That I do. Let us speak of other things, Sire, to take your mind off domestic life for a while. I am proud to say that we had Monmouth live in our household for some time.'

'I recall, my Lord.'

'He is a fine young man,' Salisbury said. 'And very devoted to his uncle. I doubt his Majesty could find another such a subject.'

Casting a shadow on me. Argyle inclined his head. 'He is very devoted and loyal. I found him useful in the field, in no small part a testament to his time in your household, my

Lord, and if he keeps on learning, he will make a fine commander one day.'

'He is fair young, but shows much potential.' Salisbury put a hand on his helmet, still perched on the pummel. The bright green feathers fluttered between his fingers. 'You and he share the stain of family, Sire. Perhaps that is why he is so at ease in your company. In you, he has found someone who understands his situation better than anyone – not that I envy you. In that, I am happy to let you be the one to provide some succour.'

As well you should be. Argyle bit back a sour response.

For all he knew, Thomas might well still be in England although he had no word from him since the visit in the Tower. He did not even know if Eleanor knew where Thomas was, though she must know that he was in England long after his exile for it was she who sent a physician to close Argyle's gaping wounds. Just as Thomas had promised. He survived on the mercy of a brother's ghost.

'I do what I can, my Lord.'

Salisbury turned towards the pens. 'I am pleased that we are moving on to Dublin. The King grows restless that MacMurrough will not give battle.'

'Would you, in his position?' Argyle acknowledged Salisbury's smile. 'Any news of the Duke of Albemarle?'

'Only that his fleet was sighted near a week ago. Though the King will never admit it, Albemarle's absence is causing great distress.' Salisbury stroked the plume of his helmet. 'What might we expect when we enter Dublin do you think, Sire? Shall they cheer for the King as they do in London?'

'The Irish thirst for freedom.' Argyle turned to the mounting block. 'We would be better off preparing for a hostile entry than one of glory and happiness.'

'A bleak prospect.' Salisbury threw his reins to a boy and swung from his saddle. The mounting block teetered a little under the weight of man and armour.

'I prefer to be pleasantly surprised than taken aback.' Argyle dismounted and took off his helmet, the dark blue plume fluttering. His battle helmet was lost in Kells and the smith had been hard at work forging not one but two, since the King had demanded that all knights and noblemen wear their finest armour at his ceremony. This one was all for show, the one he might don if the Irish decided to give battle was made from stronger steel and unadorned.

'If an enemy came to England, we would not cheer for them either.' Which was not entirely true. Bolingbroke would have returned to a roar of triumph, Argyle had no doubt.

'There are times when I am reminded of your affinity.' Salisbury looked up with a smile. 'Do not take offence, Sire, for in many ways I respected your brother for his abilities and his way of keeping the King happy. Though in the end…'

Argyle's breastplate bit into his shoulder. The black bruise he sustained had faded but the pain persisted. 'There are days, my Lord, when I dream that my brother had been allowed to ride against Lord Bolingbroke. Perhaps then his legacy would not be such a burden to bear. I believe he attempted to do what was best for the King, however misguided. It happens to us all if we stay too long at court.'

'If you feel thus why do you not wear your family's colours?' There was no sarcasm in Salisbury's question, only genuine interest.

'Let my nephews sport the Mowbray colours. My inheritance came from La Fontaine.'

'Sir Edmund, yes. A great man.' Salisbury stroked his plume again and let a few fluffs of green fly away. 'I understand.'

They watched their horses career across the wide field towards the hedge, dirt and grass flying from their hooves free from heavy saddles and restraining headgear. Salisbury handed his helmet to a squire and pulled off his gloves. 'I would ask you something, Sire.'

'Yes?' Argyle wanted to go back to his tent and get out of his plate. He needed to cool his wounds, especially those sustained in London; they burned and itched. They were mended not healed.

'What happened?' Salisbury made for the shade of a small bent tree stretching its longing branches to the west. 'In London. Before the King decided to come here.'

'If the King has not seen fit to explain his actions, neither can I, my Lord, as I told you not long ago.' Tasting the bitterness of having to repeating himself he shook his head.

'Such headstrong behaviour feeds the rumours. People are saying you tried to kill the King, others that you threatened the Queen – or worse that you sullied her.'

In the shade, the wind cooled his brow, stemming the tide of anger. Queen Isabella was not yet ten years old, the mere notion that theirs was an adult relationship irked. 'I have ever only attempted to be the Queen's friend. Why would I act against her?'

'On your brother's command?' Doubt frolicked in Salisbury's comfortable deep voice.

'My brother may be charged with many faults, as we have already discussed, my Lord,' Argyle said and earned a nod. 'But to lay before him any command that might have me act against the King or the Crown is folly. I was raised in the house of La Fontaine, the King's most ardent friend and adviser. I would be tainting his legacy, his afterlife, if I did anything such as that. Not even my own kin would dare ask that of me.'

'Bolingbroke then? You went on pilgrimage…' Salisbury shook his head. 'No. I have seen the two of you together and there is no love lost between you. Bolingbroke is a difficult man to accommodate. I cannot see you on his side.'

Laying down his helmet, Argyle drew a hand through his damp hair. 'You shall hear no words to the contrary from me. I sent him into exile. Although he knew I was only there at a royal command, he will not have found me better company in his last hours in England than he did when we travelled to the Holy Land.'

And yet he asked for my allegiance, Argyle thought.

Salisbury leaned against the tree, a speculative air about him. 'Then I cannot guess.'

'Best you do not attempt it, my Lord. As I said before, if the King has not seen fit to involve you it is not for me to speak.'

'Surely your victory at Kells has set it right?'

You are very eager that I improve myself in the King's favour. Argyle wondered why that might be. He chose his words carefully. 'Master Harry says it must and I put my fate in his young hands.'

Salisbury looked out over the wide expanse of tents, the first fires coming to life. 'I know what Monmouth is made of, after all, I raised him. You could do worse.'

Swallowing guilt, he refrained from adding, I did do worse. I put my fate in the hands of his father.

CHAPTER 7

14 July 1399 – Dublin

The small brazier was red-hot and offered a warm embrace as Argyle closed the flap, muffling the noises from camp. They had left the warmth of summer in Kells and though the sun had briefly kissed their necks in Tullow, relentless rain had since cooled the air, churned the road and left the men marching in silence.

When at last they had reached Dublin, they were met with war cries and shouts of defiance. Salisbury had waylaid Argyle and, with an irritated glare, acknowledged the premonition that the Irish were far from thrilled to be visited by the King.

It had been some time before the population had settled with housing their oppressors. Now, the soldiers had forgotten past hardships and enjoyed their time of leisure in Dublin. Often, Argyle met men coming back just before dawn from a night of drinking and whoring. Accepting that such activities helped sate the thirst for battle, he let it pass.

While the men in the camp sought female company, Argyle spent his nights discussing the immediate future with Thomas' ghost. It was easily summoned and offered an endless flow of words, none of which gave the consolation, he craved.

Even in his own mind, Thomas would weave his webs and turn Argyle's thoughts dark and sinister. He knew it was the secret of Bolingbroke's return that kept sleep from his door, and yet, if he decided that, tomorrow, he would tell the King, Thomas' ghost would laugh and change Argyle's mind as easily as he had done when they were children.

Keep your peace, brother, Thomas' voice would whisper, a smile lurking in the words. Keep your peace and wait to see what happens. If Bolingbroke does what he plans to do, you have already given him your word to back him when the time comes. If he does not succeed, if the English lords turn on him, as they may well do, you are no worse for wear. What will come of you admitting that you know the King's enemy has returned? He will twist your body and mind until you break and confess that you have known for weeks, and to what end?

You will be put back in the hole from which he dragged you. Do you desire to return to the Tower? For that is the best you can hope for, Thomas' ghost would continue. If he finds out, if you tell him that you have long known that Bolingbroke is returned and that England has thrown herself in his arms, the King may well decide to make an example of you and string you up. No. Wait and watch. Do not change your allegiance until you know the outcome for a certainty. Then and only then choose which master to serve.

I swore loyalty to the King, Argyle would argue, his inner voice weak and trembling. I told the King that I was his. That I would obey any order.

To save your family, Thomas would counter. Which is all anyone can do. And you did not swear loyalty to the King. Not this last time, brother. You swore to protect the Crown, and so you shall, regardless of who wears it.

Is this what it is to be you, Argyle would ask and before his mind's eye, Thomas would give a wolfish smile.

I have taught you well, he would say with pride. I who feared I had failed in my endeavours. I am so proud that, at last, you understand how to be a courtier. How to ensure you get what you deserve, even if everyone else does not. It warms my heart.

Argyle would rub his eyes and grit his teeth. In his mind, he tried to reach out and shake his brother, though it was all for naught. Thomas would avoid his hands and laugh.

I knew you were a Mowbray at heart. Let everyone else talk, what do they know? You are a true Mowbray, and you know that to keep secrets is the only true way to wield power, for what are we if we have no power? You almost lost your power when you let a woman's fate govern you. Do not be so foolish as to fall into such a trap again. I cannot keep rescuing you every time you make a bad decision.

Bad decision, Argyle would growl back, I vowed to keep her safe. What would you have me do?

Stop being a glorified knight, Thomas would whisper, his words curling like the smoke from Argyle's small brazier. Let others have glory, and much good may it do them. You are destined for greater feats. It will not do that you lose sight of what truly matters.

Family, Argyle would argue and sense Thomas balling his fists.

Our family, Thomas would shoot back. Never mind that brood mare you married, she is nothing, a nobody. Have your fun with her if you wish. It is only the Mowbray name that matters.

I have my heirs to consider. They too are Mowbrays. Argyle felt the crush of not knowing if Isobel had gifted him with another boy, if she had even survived the birth, if it was done already. I must choose wisely for them.

And you have. Satisfaction would ride on Thomas' whisper. You have by waiting. It will not be long before you know whom to back and when. Bide your time and wait.

This morning, as every other morning, Argyle emerged from his tent, dark circles around his eyes and an ache in his bones.

Sleeping a few hours every night when he had lost another battle to his brother's ghost was taking its toll.

In the King's chambers, the mood was high-strung and tense. The Duke of Albemarle's absence was a source of constant concern for the King and his council, creating a rift between those who sought to comfort the King and those who dared speak their mind.

One moment, the King was elated and calm, the next he would curse and scream out his frustration. On one point, he never wavered. He insisted that the English fortune would change once Albemarle arrived, because then the Irish would be forced to give battle and be subdued.

Whoever had told the King that Albemarle's fleet was sighted weeks ago when the King's army was still in Tullow must have been disciplined by now. Argyle had not been able to find out who had told the lie. Or if it was a lie.

He sat through another council meeting listening to the Lords' crowing. The King was in a dark mood and pounded his fist on the table every time anyone dared venture that, perhaps, making peace with MacMurrough was the best hope.

'We *must* fight them and win. Albemarle will come!' the King shouted and slammed the door behind him.

In the echoing silence, Argyle noticed that Salisbury was deep in conversation with Surrey, both men wearing concern as heavy cloaks.

CHAPTER 8

19 July 1399 – Dublin

'How long is it since you have had news of your father?' Argyle attempted a cavalier tone but failed and Harry looked up at him, shrewdness chasing fear in his eyes.

'I have heard little since the King sent my wayward father into exile.'

'How little?'

'Is it your place to ask, Sire?' The tone suggested that Argyle was taking liberties, and yet, he could not let the matter rest. If Harry knew what Bolingbroke was about at this very moment he was in more danger than all of the other turncoat lords and knights – including himself.

'Whispers reach me that your father is returned to England.'

Harry stopped dead in his stride, his eyes darting around and his breath suddenly shallow. 'What?'

Argyle cocked his head towards the edge of the camp, leading Harry by the elbow when the boy seemed unable to walk on his own. At the height of a wet summer, the grass was tall and the trees heavy with leaves providing plenty of cover for a private conversation.

'A messenger brought a disconcerting message to me when we were in the north.'

'What?' Harry pulled at the knot of his cloak-strings. 'You have known for this long and never told me?' He wrenched free from Argyle's light grasp and turned. 'He would not dare…'

'Would not dare disobey a royal order? I believe you will find that most men are capable of much more dangerous choices when all else is lost to them.'

Harry's darting eyes fixed on Argyle and he was well aware that the boy was trying to decide if he was trustworthy.

'It is said that he has returned to challenge the King over the Lancaster estate, which was to be expected.' Argyle nodded to a grove of wilted trees beyond the makeshift horse-pen where his own destrier was grazing lazily on the dew-riddled grass. Yesterday had been hot, but the night had offered another shower to freshen the air. 'The Lancaster inheritance is vital to him.'

'I should be all the inheritance he needs.' Harry sounded as a petulant child though Argyle suspected his tone was to disguise his fear. 'Am I to understand that he cares not that mere contemplation to return puts me in harm's way? He cares not that I am in the charge of the one man who can – who will – break him?'

Argyle had often wondered at Harry's reverent behaviour towards his gaoler uncle. Time and again, he had proved his devotion to be strong and steady. Could it be that Harry had not questioned the King's decision to render him a pauper with nothing to his name? Or had the King made other promises? Had ambition blinded Bolingbroke?

'I love my uncle.' Harry's outburst finally persuaded Argyle that he did indeed know nothing of his father's return. 'How can my father be so callus? How can he care naught for me? Is money everything in this world?'

'No, my Lord, power is.' It took no more to silence Harry and Argyle continued. 'Your father has come for his inheritance to be sure, just as he comes to ensure that whatever was his a mere couple of months ago will revert to you when he is gone.'

'And you support his cause?' Harry backed away from Argyle, shaking his head. 'You who are such a great friend to the King? You who speak of honour and refuse to talk about your time in the Tower.' Harry paused as if sorting through his thoughts. 'Will you earn your freedom if you back my father? Has he made such promises?'

'Your father has made no promises. And I have yet to make up my mind,' Argyle lied.

'And when you do?'

He pushed up his sleeves. Today, the heat burned his scars and wounds. 'What I say next must never be repeated.'

Harry nodded, but Argyle was far from convinced he could trust a boy who loved his uncle so fervently that tears brimmed in his eyes. 'I will have your word of honour, my Lord.'

Gritting his teeth, Harry placed a hand on his heart, covering the illustrious emblem of his own house entwined with the King's white hart. 'I give you my word, Sire, that nothing will transpire from what is spoken next.'

'Not even to the King.'

Harry's eyes blazed in anguish. 'Not even the King.'

'If your father decides to fight, the King will lose.' He reached out to steady Harry when he tottered. 'His best choice is to declare a readiness to meet your father when he learns of his return. It is your only chance to change what might otherwise happen. You must act swiftly to ensure all is not lost. You can change the outcome.'

'I…' Harry swallowed and balled his fists. If he was shocked before, he looked to be in Death's grip now. 'I…'

A couple of squires were making their way to the horse pen, carrying buckets of water. The moment would soon pass and he decided to push.

'All of England supports your father's claim.' Argyle turned his back to the squires and fixed Harry's eyes, little flecks of bright green floating in a sea of grey. 'They will stop at nothing when he has back his inheritance. They will have him on the throne. You must be careful not to be caught on the wrong side of what transpires.'

'I have declared my undying fealty to the King.'

'To the Crown,' Argyle corrected Harry in low tones. 'No one will ever chide you for standing by your father's side when it comes to it. Everyone knows what the King has stolen from your father – from you. If he had not, the Lords would never have suffered his return. He is come back to salvage much more than his own fortune. He is here to save England. This is what they believe.'

Harry turned and stumbled from the grove, hugging himself tight despite the dry, warm wind that wafted around the camp. Argyle watched him go and hoped that he had done enough to ensure Harry realised the danger he was in, and most importantly, whether a boy could change the fate of thousands.

ꙮ ꙮ ꙮ ꙮ

The very next day, Salisbury led the way across the inner courtyard and through a panelled door to the east. Holding out a hand, he stopped Argyle. 'While the King is grateful for your victory, I must impress upon you that he intends to publicly honour someone else.'

'Dear God, let it not be Worcester.' Argyle barked a laugh. 'He would not know his horse's head from its arse and he is worthless with a sword.'

Salisbury flashed a smile. 'As well I know, for I tried and failed to train him. He is good for nothing but prancing about and drinking with the King. So unlike his brother. At least Henry Percy understands what it is to be an Earl.'

They resumed their progress the wooden building at the heart of the walled enclosure. Argyle ran his fingers along one of the circular towers. 'I hear rumours that Albemarle is finally arrived?'

Salisbury's face darkened. 'Yes.'

'And?'

'The King is livid.'

'Did the Duke forget his barges?' Salisbury's hunched shoulders shattered Argyle's banter. 'What has happened, my Lord?'

A door opened and golden light pooled around their feet. Even at the height of summer, hundreds of candles burned bright in the great hall of Dublin Castle, washing the ominous décor in butter.

'Sir Argyle. My victor. Come and entertain me with your tales of battle…' The screech of the King's voice tore at Argyle's ears.

Bad news came in spades, and what little pleasure the Kells victory had created it had only lasted for a few fleeting moments. Just inside the door, Harry was arranging food on a couple of silver platters.

'It is bad,' he whispered when Argyle passed him.

Together with Salisbury, he bent his knee. 'What does your Majesty wish me to relate?'

'Your triumph. Though we may have to defer such pleasantry until later.' The silence that ensued spoke volumes. 'Get up. We have pressing matters to attend to. Food? Drink?'

'Thank you, Majesty.' Argyle took the offered cup and pretended that the reek of fear did not settle on him as a second skin.

'Tomorrow I shall grant you the lands and castle of Kells and you will refuse.' The King tore a bite from a chicken leg. 'You will then offer your reward to my nephew in lieu of an oath I can no longer keep. I intended to make him Lord Lieutenant of Ireland.'

'Intended, Majesty?' Argyle asked, and in his mind he added, not kingship?

The King ignored the question. 'You will surrender the lands to Surrey, is that understood?'

'Yes, Majesty, I shall happily renounce my prize and gift it to my Lord Surrey.' Argyle tested the wine and found it weak. 'I hear the Duke has arrived?'

'Oh, Edward has arrived has he not, Harry?' The words came out in blows. 'He has arrived and brought with him a great surprise. Indeed, such was my astonishment that it stirs me to return to England without delay.'

Harry took the trembling silver cup from the King's hand and replenished his drink. 'All true, uncle.'

When he turned, the brightness of the massive candles revealed a fresh bruise under his eye. The King ogled him and prompted that Harry taste the wine before handing over the cup. He knew.

'What news, Majesty?' Argyle played his part. 'What can possibly make you give up subduing the Irish, now that you have fresh men and more ships?'

Documents, maps, platters and food flew from the table. The King pounded his fist into the oak top, ablaze with rage. 'The filthy, rotten lie that my cousin Henry has returned!'

Argyle's eyes sought Harry, and the King soared into a rant. '*He* says he did not know. How can he not? His father returns with an army at his back, and *he* does not know? Has he recruited you? Are you to be my jailor as once you were Henry's? The moment I turn my back, my despicable uncle calls for Henry to return: Come Henry,' the King squealed as a woman would. 'Come to me and I shall install you on the throne of England now that nasty Richard has left it in my charge. I will kill York with my bare hands!'

Harry stood impassive, letting the King's malice rain over his head. When it rained – it poured. 'I will have your father in a dungeon before he can reach London. I will make such a spectacle of him that no man will ever dare oppose me again. I shall summon all my archers, call all my lords to me and we shall see who dare defy a royal command. As for *you*…' A curled fist shook inches from Harry. 'I shall lock you up and throw away the key!'

'Majesty,' Argyle intervened. 'For all the time we have been in Ireland, Master Harry has not left my side except to serve you. He is loyal to you. He names you his beloved uncle and I have no reason to doubt that he means it.'

Gratitude ran across Harry's anxious face, but the King was deaf to Argyle's words. 'I shall trample all traitors, root out the evil of my own kin, move the earth and skies if needs be. You watch me, Sire, for you know of what I am capable.'

In a flash, Harry was on the floor, pitcher clattering away. Blood from where the King's ruby ring had struck his face mingled with wine. 'Uncle…'

'Do not uncle me.' The King lifted his foot, poised to kick his nephew. 'I am your Majesty!'

'Majesty, please…' Harry scrambled for safety, his nose dripping on the bare stone. 'I knew nothing. All this time, I have heard nothing from my father. I have been your faithful servant.'

'Traitor father.' The King's foot struck air when he kicked for Harry and missed. He tottered. 'Begone you vile creature. Begone and prepare for a better defence!'

Lurching from the room, Harry put a hand to his nose, shock plain on his face. Argyle spared him a single glance before focusing on the King. His infamous temper had brought back memories of honeyed hair drenched in blood. Argyle pushed the images away.

Salisbury slid through the door, closing it with a soft snap. 'Majesty, may I be of service?'

'Can you deliver my cousin to the Devil? For that would be a great service.' The King's wrath began to ebb, sanity crept into his features. 'Send someone to see to Harry, he fell and hit his head.'

Alone again, the King took his cup and twirled it slowly, silver glittering gold. 'This was to be my crowning moment, Sir Argyle. Here in Ireland, I would put to rest the question of supremacy, I would install a King true to England, I would bring the Irish princes to heel – or to their deaths, whichever was quicker. Now… I have to turn tail and run back from whence I came.'

'You are not turning tail, Majesty,' Argyle said. 'You are protecting your realm. Only a fool would question your decision, however hard it is to make. No one will ever say that you ran from a war, but that you chose wisely when you returned to England to stamp out rebellion. Ireland can wait.'

Though if you were wise you would suspect every man in your service of plotting against you, including me. Now that I know what you did, now that I know it was by your hand La Fontaine died what little care I had for you has shrivelled and turned to dust. If not for my family, for my children, I would challenge you with La Fontaine's murder this moment. Argyle schooled his expression. I too can wait.

'I know… I know.' The King drank with greed. 'Harry truly never left your side?'

'Only when your messenger found him hauling water to our camp.' Argyle checked his disgust, folding his hands. 'He was gone for a day surrounded by my men, all loyal. They saw nothing untoward. Since Tullow he has been in your presence.'

'Loyal to whom?' His breath hitched with fear.

'You, Majesty – and me.' There was no need to coat his words. 'The day we received your order to return, the camp cheered for you.'

Though not all of them – far from all of them, Argyle remembered.

The King's smile flooded his face with pleasure, rendering him handsome once more. 'Good. I knew I could count on you. Though we have had our differences I know full well that La Fontaine instilled in you a deep sense of loyalty. Which you have demonstrated time and again. Close by and far afield.'

Any loyalty granted to you comes at a price I no longer wish to pay. Argyle nodded dutifully. 'What now, Majesty?'

'I would ask the same of you, Sire.' The King thrust forward his cup and Argyle took it. 'We both know that I cannot linger here and let Henry gather men to his side.'

'Of course not, Majesty. To do nothing would be to surrender England to the hands of a traitor. You must return and send Lord Bolingbroke back into exile.'

'I can do that. I am the King.' The murmur was barely audible. 'Now then, tell me of Kells for we have had little enough time to ourselves and I am in need of diversion.'

As changeable as the Irish weather, Argyle thought and decided to play his card. 'I encountered Coxcombe. You remember him, do you not, the knight we all thought dead in Calais and later discovered to be alive and well in London.'

The King's eyes widened for a breath before they shied away. 'Is that so?'

'He is dead, at long last, he is truly dead.' Argyle tried to read the King.

'By your hand?'

'Would that I could claim such triumph. An axe took his arm. He bled out before me.' What to say next, Argyle wondered, how much to reveal? Pouring wine gave him respite from the King's probing eyes.

Accepting the cup, the King gave a sombre nod. 'No doubt seeing this old enemy on the field must have stirred memories. I demand that we put the matter of La Fontaine to rest. His untimely death and the circumstances surrounding it have poisoned your life – and mine – long enough. We must rest assured that, on the day of judgement, God will know what is befitting those who took his life.'

'Yes, Majesty. We must.' Argyle wondered if the King counted himself among the men who took La Fontaine's life.

'When La Fontaine chose you as his heir I remember wondering if he was doing the right thing.' A sigh. 'When you sent your brother into exile, I knew whose man you were. Family can be fickle. As my uncle York has just confirmed.'

'When do we return to England, Majesty?'

The King leaned back. His anger had evaporated and he was all business. 'Messages are slipping from camp. Missives that might find their way into the wrong hands. We cannot wait for long or we will lose what little element of surprise we can hope to have.'

Argyle waited for the King to continue, but he just twirled his cup. The silence ate up the air in the room.

'I want to trust Harry, Sir Argyle. I truly do.'

'You are more a father to him than his own father ever was,' Argyle said. 'If you let him, he will love you. Not as his King, but as his flesh and blood, as the father he wanted.'

'Spoken as a true courtier. I was rash…' Lost in thought, the King put the silver cup aside. 'Have you heard from your brother?'

Thomas, always Thomas, I will never outlive him. It matters not what royal faction I support, the Mowbray stain will never wear off. And at night, for all my sins I continue to summon him for counsel I do not care for.

'No, Majesty. Since he was exiled I have had no news.'

'Not a word?' Was that a veiled threat or mild disinterest? Argyle could not tell.

'I believe he wrote to his wife Elizabeth once or twice, but I have been…'

'Yes.' The King waved about the silver cup. 'Your wife must be worried. It is well you sent word to her when you did. When we have caught Henry and put this madness to rest, you can go home. Beauworth is yours, I will not break my promise to La Fontaine. Let that be the prize you get for Kells, though we will have to keep it between us.'

You have been promising me that I can return home for so long that I dare not believe in your reassurances any more. No more than I believe, you will ever release me from your command. I only wonder if another King would do the same as you, keep me close simply for my family name, or if I may at least be allowed to return home. Only time will tell.

'Will you go to Harry, Sir Argyle?' The King pushed back his chair, wood scraping against wood. 'See that he is well and patch what needs patching?'

'He has rooms here in the castle, Majesty?' Argyle tried to gauge the King's fickle mood. 'Perhaps he will be more comfortable in camp?'

The King's gown snapped as he turned. 'So that he might send word to his father? So that he might sneak away? He stays here. Now leave me, I have matters of state to attend to. A return journey to plan. Fetch me Salisbury.'

Argyle ducked through the low door that Harry had left the room by and found Salisbury lingering in the dark. 'My Lord, the King wishes your council. Do you know where I might find Master Harry?'

Salisbury pushed the door closed. 'Do you think he might have known? About his father's return?'

'No, he is innocent. To this day, Harry's loyalty to the King has never wavered,' Argyle said. 'His rooms?'

'In the western tower.' Salisbury hesitated and admitted, 'He turned me away. Perhaps you will have better luck interceding.'

It was a short distance from the free-standing main hall to the tower. Scaling the steps two at a time, Argyle tried not to wince when his leg smarted.

He knocked twice on the massive wooden door, the frame unadorned, the walls to either side bare. 'Master Harry?'

The door opened to reveal Harry's bruised face. 'I knew it was you before you spoke, Sire. I know your stride, as if you are always on a mission, going somewhere important.' He gestured. 'Come in, I was just bathing my face.'

'You seem to get more bruises here than in battle, Master Harry,' Argyle said and earned a painful smile. 'Your uncle sends his apologies. He is much distressed by the news of your father's return. It has turned his mood. Once he calmed down, he regretted what he had done.'

Harry wiped his hands, his bloodied shirt abandoned on the floor. He stared at it for a long time. 'I understand why he is angry and I do not blame him, how could I? He has taken me in, and now, he cannot be certain that I am loyal. If he trusted me completely I could not respect him as I do. I swear to you, I am loyal, Sire.'

'I know.' The anguish in Harry's voice made Argyle's heart jitter. 'You would do nothing to betray the King as I have already attempted to reassure him and shall continue to do so until he sees sense. It does you credit that you do not blame him for his actions.' He inspected Harry's face. 'If the swelling has not come down by tomorrow you must let the physician take a look at it.'

'That butcher?' A groan followed Harry's smile. 'I saw him hack off limbs by the dozen at Kells.'

'He can mend a broken nose without hacking it off,' Argyle said drily. 'I think.'

Laughter spilled fresh blood from Harry's nose, the sound a welcome reprieve from the malice and foreboding that crested the walls of the castle. He was a kind boy who was about to tip the scales. Argyle did not know where he would put his stake, though hard pressed, he believed that, for the moment, Harry would back the King. They might yet turn out to be enemies.

'Had the King any orders for me?'

'Only to stay within the castle.'

Pressing the linen into his nostrils Harry coughed. 'I am hardly going to slip away in the night.'

Argyle's words fell heavily. 'There will be a guard posted by your door, Master Harry. The King is concerned for your safety.'

'He does not trust me.' Perhaps his declaration that he did not blame his uncle was only skin-deep.

Argyle opened the door. 'He is the King.'

CHAPTER 10

23 July 1399 – Waterford, Ireland

'A word, my Lord Salisbury.' Argyle had long attempted to find an excuse to get John Montagu on his own. He needed to know if Salisbury was still the King's man. It was becoming ever more important to know whom to trust, and Salisbury was about to leave for Chester, tearing a chunk of the King's forces away to rally his personal army of archers.

Falling in with John Montagu, Argyle matched his stride as they exited yet another fruitless council meeting in the King's pavilion. The mood had been as sombre as the weather, the prospects bleak.

'I wonder, what do you think of the King's decision?'

Veering left, Salisbury lowered his voice. 'What can he do but return at once? He has a kingdom to rule and the moment he is gone, it is tearing itself apart. What strain he must be under. I am surprised he can act at all, especially since half his council are imbeciles.'

'I try to give as good advice as can be, I hope you know that, though in this case, I do not know what to say. Perhaps the King's men will be able to hold London for him, I am certain they will if you lead them… If the rumours are true then Bolingbroke is backed not only by the northern lords, but many more.' Argyle threw on his cloak. 'Sometimes, I think La Fontaine was wrong to choose me as his heir; it seems he saw something in me that I do not recognise myself.'

'We are all forced to make hard choices,' Salisbury said in a non-committal tone. 'The King…'

'You are lucky. You get to return to England.'

'And deliver the message that the King sends armed men marching on London.' In the fading light, Salisbury looked displeased. 'Hardly a task anyone envies me.'

'Would you join me in a drink, my Lord?' Argyle glanced at the greying skies. 'I fear the weather will turn soon. If that is so, the King will be most discontented.'

Salisbury smiled briefly. 'Even he cannot dream to control the weather. And yes, I should like a quiet word, Sire, especially if you can rustle up a decent drink to wash it down with.'

Argyle led the way to his tent, dismissed his squire and poured refreshments. 'Have you had any news from England?'

'I might.' Salisbury accepted the cup. His bright green cloak had a coating of dust and muck on it. 'My wife wrote a while back, but I could not believe the rumours. I dismissed them as idle talk meant to divert the women as they went about their chores.'

'Rumours?'

Salisbury sampled the wine. 'Rumours we now know to be true. I should put greater stock in my wife, she has never before let me down.'

'Bolingbroke.' Argyle caught Salisbury's penetrating stare and sized up his companion. 'I had similar news.'

'From whom?'

'"The Duke of York sent a messenger.'

Silence filled the tent. Argyle had played his hand, now, he waited to see if Salisbury was friend or foe. His decision to change sides had no doubt long since reached York and through him Bolingbroke. Whatever came next, he hoped at least to save his family from ruin, even if it meant he had to pay with his own life.

'I received a letter in Bolingbroke's hand, bearing the Lancaster seal.' Argyle scratched his cheek, the stubble was long and coarse with grime. 'He must have reached London already. You will forgive me, I hope, that I spoke differently while we were making our way here. Camp is never a safe place.' He sat by the brazier. 'It is only a matter of time before he turns his attention to his real goal.'

'The King.'

Argyle nodded. 'Securing the King.'

Salisbury drove a hand through his thinning hair. 'He has his eye on the ultimate prize.'

'Some might argue it is his by rights.' That would be the way it would be coined with the population. Lancashire was vast and many Londoners viewed Bolingbroke as their own. The King had never managed to transfer the love they bore him as a child into adulthood.

'What does he have on you?'

'My family. He has guards stationed at Beauworth, and since the King called all my able men to his side I left Isobel and the children with a skeleton crew…' Argyle pretended distress. The stark truth was that the King had lost a servant long before then. He decided to push his luck. 'Mine was not an easy choice.'

'Even after the King had you in the Tower?'

'He is the King I swore my fealty to. He released me on orders that I follow him wherever he commands and ask no questions. If not for him, I would be in London myself, awaiting my sentence behind bars. Do you think Bolingbroke would let me out of my cell?' Argyle drank and wiped his chin. 'What of you?'

'My niece is in the Queen's household.' Salisbury toyed with the plain clay cup, tracing the faint indentations of whoever made it. 'If you were going in my place what would you do?'

'Offer the men a choice. The King is little loved in England, though he commands Chester as his own. Unlike the rest of the country, they may stay loyal. You cannot hope to persuade them to change their fealty if that is what you plan, but you might remind them what may come to pass.' Argyle had lowered his voice to a whisper. 'The entire north has turned out for Bolingbroke and most of the south loves him, I saw that for myself when I sent him into exile. They lined the streets and threw flowers before his horse as if he was a hero, not a man sent away in disgrace. The south holds no love for the King. If the Cheshire archers know how many ride with Bolingbroke perhaps they will have the common sense to understand their situation.'

'And what if they do not? What would you do then?'

Argyle took Salisbury's cup and poured another measure of wine. 'The King commands that you raise Cheshire for him, and raise it you must. His command also entails that you take London and hold it for him. Something you can scarce hope to achieve. In that you are right, it is not a task I envy you. No one would.'

'And yet I must do it.'

'Unless you make him see reason,' Argyle said. 'Behind closed doors you might be able to achieve what we cannot hope to do in public.'

Salisbury's expression darkened. 'Change his mind?'

'What other choice do you have? When all of England stands between you and a few hundred archers.'

CHAPTER 11

26 July 1399 – Milford Haven, Wales

Boards creaked beneath the weight of horses and men. The barges were being tied up, rope coiling along the docks. In the distance, the royal flagship rolled on the waves primed to enter the harbour and Argyle knew that the King would waste little time before visiting Thomas Becket's chapel. He needed all the strength and divine intervention he could conjure up. Since the initial message brought over by the Duke of Albemarle, the King's court had been flooded with reports of Bolingbroke's progress. Many had already absconded to the other side, leaving the remaining Lords on edge.

Nearby, Argyle's brown destrier tugged at its rope, causing soldiers to curse. The crossing had been smooth, although none of the horses took kindly to being forced onto a ship and penned into precious little space. A nimble boy ran up the planks, the Beauworth crest on his shoulder.

He reached up and put a gentle hand on the massive flank. The horse calmed and the boy took the rope, guiding it onto firm ground.

'Sir Argyle.'

'My Lord Surrey,' Argyle tore his gaze from the horse to look at the King's nephew, who was robbed of his Irish crown. Behind Thomas Holland stood the King's half-brother, John Holland, keeping a wary eye on his nephew. He inclined his head when Argyle said, 'My Lord Huntingdon.'

'The King does not wish to linger here it is too exposed.' Huntingdon's detached tone did not match his fiddling hands. 'We must make our way to Pembroke castle at once. It is in the King's keep and they will hold faith with him.'

Most likely it was in disarray since the King had precious little coin with which to ensure proper upkeep of his many estates. Part of his decision to revert Bolingbroke's inheritance to the Crown was no doubt that he wanted to remedy his poverty. Instead, his act had brought home an enemy he could not possibly hope to defeat.

Argyle knew better than to voice his concerns. 'We will make camp around the city, but I do not advise that we stay for long.'

'And why is that?' Surrey still had the look of a seasick man about him, as well as the odour.

'It too is exposed.' The salt in the air stung his face and he wanted more than anything to be far away from the sea. He kicked a piece of driftwood. 'We must find a place where the fortifications are strong and that can take most of the men.'

Huntingdon shook his head. 'The men are here to defend the King and they will camp where we order them to, Sire. If we are to make accommodations for thousands of men there is nowhere to go.'

'There are some of the old castles.' Doubt rode on Surrey's suggestion. 'In the south we could make for Cardiff.'

'It is a long march.' Argyle sidestepped a regiment of soldiers hammering for shore. 'Now that we are in the north why not consider Beaumaris or Conwy?'

'Beaumaris.' Huntingdon snorted. 'You would have us holed up in a nowhere place without enough farmland and woods around to support the men? You jest at an odd time, Sire.'

'Ideally, I would split up the army,' Argyle said and suffered the aghast stares. 'You are in the right, my Lords, there is no place here that can hold thirty thousand men for any duration. If we were to split up the forces and leave the main host with the King for his protection, a small contingent might be able to slip south and march on London. No one would expect it. When Salisbury comes down from Chester and a contingent emerges from the south it may just be enough to take back the capital.'

'It is a futile plan.' Huntingdon scratched his cheek. The Irish summer had not been kind to him. 'Futile and absurd. The King will never concede.'

'He may, my Lord, if you propose it.'

'Or if you do, Thomas.' Huntingdon looked for an escape. 'You are owed.'

'I cannot. I cannot put such a proposition to him. How could I at such a time?' As his uncle, Surrey was trying to avoid the inevitable. No one wanted to suffer the King's wrath and surely, he would be livid. Surrey's expression turned wily. 'No. It must be you, Sire. You alone can convince him.'

If only I had such powers. Argyle shook his head. 'The King has little love for me these days, as you well know. He trusts me even less…'

'You won Kells.' Huntingdon interrupted as the flagship perched its oars and the faraway roll of drums reached the shores. 'You are a hero, the only one to take on the Irish on the open field. Your triumph is all he speaks off early and late. He recognises that, without you, he would never have taken the north of Ireland so easily.'

'That was then.' Argyle watched the royal ship approach, no King in sight on the deck. 'This is now.'

'Does he have cause to distrust your loyalty?'

A little part of him wanted to divulge the tale of how he ended up in the Tower, to drive the gossip into the ground and make the two Hollands realise that he was powerless to change the course of events. 'It matters not what I say – or even what I do – for he will never listen to me as he might once have done. He will look to his family for council, and so he should, for you will give it free of complaint.'

'Yes, of course.' Surrey tugged at a loose thread on his thick travel cloak; it came away reluctantly. 'Yes, he will look to us. We must make sure he is not disappointed… Beaumaris you say?'

'Or Conwy.'

'Conwy, yes, it might well be a good place. The city walls have been maintained as I understand it; it will welcome its King; do you not think?' The trace of doubt on Surrey's face convinced Argyle that Conwy was a last resort.

Huntingdon gestured. 'We must await the King to disembark. Perhaps he has already made plans for his return to England. It may well be, we shall not linger in these parts but for a day or two. Until we know what he has in mind, Sire, best you give the men orders to make for Pembroke.

The camp must be up before the King arrives it must look as if we are in control.'

'As you command, my Lord.'

The wind picked up as the King's vessel made its entry, smaller barges and ships scuttling out of the way, some retreating back into the deep waters. At the top of the road, Argyle turned to watch the ship being secured, vast ropes securing the vessel to the docks. At the bow Harry stood, alone and no doubt frightened.

Having despatched the orders to set up camp at Pembroke, Argyle returned to the harbour. The flagship was being unloaded, supervised by a frantic Surrey who called contradicting orders at a pace that had everyone running around as headless chickens.

'My Lord, the troops are marching for Pembroke.'

Surrey tugged at the large emerald and pearl brooch that held his cloak in place. 'The King has gone to the shrine. He will have words with God on how to proceed.'

'What might you advise him?' Argyle was curious if Surrey had it in him to make his own decisions. Often enough, he turned to his uncle Huntingdon for advice, perhaps this might be an awakening for the King's maternal nephew, a way for him to prove that, given time, he would make a good feudal king of Ireland. Should the King triumph.

'What are my words to those of God?' Surrey's voice revealed agitated dejection. 'Those were my uncle's words upon his setting foot on land. "What are your words to those of God, nephew?" His Majesty paused only long enough to ensure that Monmouth was at his heel.' He spat, a little spittle dripping down his chin. 'Whipped dog.'

'His father threatens the King's supremacy. I should not envy his position.'

'It is not his position I envy, Sire. He is as wily as his father. He will know how to appease the King. You wait and see. I should be sorely surprised if it is not Monmouth who offers up the royal regalia to his father before long.'

'You care not for Master Harry?'

Surrey's laugh carried shards of glass. 'Only you are fool enough to call him that. The rest of us see him for what he is, a cuckoo in the nest. A Lord without land is the most dangerous kind of opponent, Sire. He will push all of us out, and in the end, he will hand over the King on a silver platter should the opportunity arise.'

'You seem certain he will not come out victorious, my Lord.' Argyle knew full well that he might be the cuckoo, the wretch who sacrificed the King to save himself. 'Your words disturb me. I should not speak so in front of his Majesty if I were you.'

'And what do you know, Sire?' Surrey's snarl twisting his handsome Holland features. 'The King dragged you from the Tower. And I know why he threw you in there in the first place. Despicable. What stays his hand from returning you to your pathetic cell once we have London? You need his favour more than I do.'

'He is the King.' Argyle spoke without emotion, careful to conceal his deep-felt resentment. 'If he wishes me back behind bars, he will put me there. What I will not do is prophesy the future when none of us know what may transpire. If you were wise, my Lord, neither would you.'

Surrey stayed his shaking hand, clutching his ornate sword hilt. 'If you speak thus to my uncle, I shall deny everything.'

'He needs loyal men, not frightened bullies. Let us make truce, my Lord, and speak no more on the subject.' Argyle held out his hand and felt Surrey's reluctance from his grip.

'Soon enough, we will learn what has passed between the King and God.'

'Let us hope it tips the scale.' John Holland startled them both. He beat his gloves against his palm, an inscrutable look on his face. Of all the Hollands, he was the shrewdest. 'Word has reached us that, every day, more men bolt for Bolingbroke's cause. We have no time to delay.'

And yet, we are stuck here until the King has spoken to God. Argyle joined a contingent of Beauworth men marching for Pembroke. What happens if he does not like what God demands?

CHAPTER 12

28 July 1399 – Pembroke Castle

'I must advise against this, your Majesty.' When the King turned his feverish gaze on him, Surrey staggered but he held his ground.

The King had spent much of the previous day conversing with God and had come away without telling anyone what had transpired. When Argyle had met Harry walking aimlessly through the makeshift camp, he could not nudge a single word from the boy.

Today, standing next to the King, Harry wore an empty expression, his hands locked behind his back. Although he wore no new bruises something was amiss.

'Harry, my dear boy, you heard me plead with God did you not?' The King put a hand on Harry's shoulder when he nodded. 'Did you hear the answer?'

'No, Majesty.' Harry's nose had been pushed back to its natural place, a little nick at the base the only evidence of the King's wrath.

The great hall, which was small and dark, oozed of abandonment and mould, the walls weeping although the sun hammered down outside and pushed against the dirty, high-set windows.

'No, because God speaks only to me. We conferred and his divine advice was that I rally troops to my cause in the south. I shall leave with a suitable host for Carmarthen, which has great love for its King.' The King beamed. 'My Lord Salisbury.'

John Montagu knelt, no doubt feeling the weight of the King's command even before it was spoken. 'Majesty?'

'You shall go to Chester and rally my archers. They are to join our forces as reinforcement. Once you have succeeded, you are to muster an army in the north of Wales. Gather the forces at Conwy and make provision for war. If my wayward cousin is not quickly subdued, any pretender might rise against his rightful King and make mischief.' Malicious satisfaction laced the King's words leaving no doubt that he meant to staunch any unrest, starting with the return of his own cousin. 'We must stamp out this madness.'

'Yes, Majesty.' Salisbury got to his feet, brushing dirt from the knee. Today, he had foregone his usual, bright green attire and wore dark, drab clothes made for travelling. 'I shall make my way there at once.'

'Do. And take young Harry here with you.' Sweeping the room with his eyes, the King sought strife and found none. 'I wish him safe and out of harm's way.'

Out of the corner of his eye, Argyle noticed Harry's shoulders sag. The King's idea of keeping him safe was to put him in the arms of the most loyal of men in England. Although Salisbury had once provided a home for Harry, he was loyal to the King before all others. Harry knew this, as did everyone in this room. Sweat travelled down Argyle's spine despite the clammy coolness.

'I cannot rouse suspicion that I am on the move south. Therefore, I cannot take many men.' The King sat on a chair draped in the royal coat of arms, his hands stroking the thick silk. He had brought it from London and used it countless times during their expedition, by now, its colours were faded in places and it showed signs of fraying at the edges. 'What say you, my Lords? How many men can go undetected?'

'A thousand,' Huntingdon ventured and won a royal smile.

'No more than two hundred, Majesty, if that,' Argyle said. The rumble of the room was oddly comforting. He spoke what the others had secretly speculated.

Albemarle glanced in his direction when the King laughed. 'Two hundred? Sir Argyle, you jest.'

'No, Majesty. If you mean to create an army in the south there is no need to bring more than two hundred. It is enough to keep you safe, yet no more than a nobleman of some standing might bring on a prolonged journey.' Scattered nods confirmed Argyle's words. 'The more you bring, the more mouths to feed and you need all the food you can procure for your new recruits. Leave the main host to Lord Salisbury and let him recruit in the north. Bring him fresh troops from the south, well-fed and battle ready and you shall not regret it.'

The King stroked his smooth cheek. 'What say you, Thomas?'

Surrey puffed out his chest. 'Let me come with you, Majesty, and I shall pick out the best of my men.'

'Outfit me with Surrey men?' The King held out a hand for his nephew to take. 'Most promising.'

'Let me come too, Majesty,' Huntingdon offered. Half again the age of his nephew, John Holland looked much older. Argyle knew he had not slept well since returning to Wales and probably would not until his half-brother's seat on the throne was once more safe. 'Between us, Thomas and I can provide the best troops.'

More lords chimed in, and Argyle let them. He wanted his Beauworth host in the north. Going south might prompt many to scurry off into the night if they came too close to the border. Until he had no other course to follow, Argyle would keep his men in line and under his command.

'Majesty,' Albemarle cut across the noise that climbed to the worn, tar blackened rafters. 'What of the rumours?'

Argyle watched him shrink under the King's angry glare. 'Hearsay. We cannot build an army if we are not willing to take chances. You are to come with me, Edward. Or is that too disagreeable to you?'

'No, Majesty.' Albemarle wiped his brow. His delay in bringing the fleet to Ireland had caused much suspicion, and every day, he had to brush off rumours that he was not to be trusted. That his delay was instigated by his father, the Duke of York who now harboured an exiled Lord bent on bringing the King to heel. 'I am here to serve.'

'Too true.' The King fiddled with the silken shroud. 'Surrey, Huntingdon, you are my natural choices. Outfit me with fifty men each, and Albemarle will bring with him another fifty, chiefly made up of my own reserves.' He tapped his fingers on his thigh. As ever, he was opulently dressed, even if dust clung to the edges of his garb and his boots were dirty. 'Sir Argyle. You will provide the remaining fifty from the Beauworth contingent.'

'I am honoured, your Majesty,' Argyle said swallowing an argument. Albemarle had just proved that all objections would be smothered in disdain and threats.

The King would ride for the south to gather troops to his banners and he hedged his bets on bringing the men he trusted most and least. Keeping friends and enemies close.

At the King's pleasure, the men filed out the door two abreast and Argyle matched his pace to Harry's. 'The north for you, Master Harry.'

The boy looked despondent. 'With my gaoler, Salisbury.'

'He is a friend too, as you well know. You grew up in his house.'

'He was a friend.' Harry brushed a finger over his nose, wincing. It might have healed to look at, but it would be sore for months. 'Behind closed doors, you know not what goes on, Sir Argyle. If I did not before understand what true leadership is, I do now, for I have seen you perform it and I have seen others fail at it. I would wish you came north with me for I fear what might happen once we arrive at Conwy.'

'Salisbury is a fierce leader. He instils much loyalty in his own men and will in others.' Argyle had hoped Harry would be relieved that he was not to come south but rather retain troops in the north. In Salisbury's care, Harry would be kept out of trouble and free from conspiracy rumours. 'He is still fond of you, which means you have little to fear.'

'He is not the failed leader of whom I speak.' Looking up, Harry met Albemarle's eyes in the crowd. 'I would keep my eye on that one. He may well be in the King's favour for bringing men and barges, but all is not what it seems. I have enquired and the weather has not been as abysmal as he claims, most of the dockworkers laughed when I asked if there had been storms to thwart the fleet setting sails. I cannot shirk the feeling that he is not to be trusted.'

'The King adopted him as his own brother.'

'And we both know that blood and promises cannot hold back those who wish for a different future. I have learned my lesson from you, Sir Argyle, take heart and believe in me.'

Argyle watched Harry get swallowed up in the throng of men stomping into the fading sunshine. Autumn would soon be upon them, settling as an uneasy kernel in the pit of his stomach.

He would have to keep his own council once they rode south and not trust any of the men surrounding the King. Argyle snorted: was he trying to convince himself that he was the King's most ardent defender amongst the four hand-picked to accompany him? Of them all, he was the worst for he had turned his cloak many weeks ago and did not regret it.

'Something you find amusing, Sire?' Albemarle gripped Argyle's elbow. 'A quick word.'

'If you wish, my Lord.'

Never alone, never unseen, such had Thomas said to him in bygone years whenever they had met at court. As a Mowbray you were never alone and never unseen. Thomas had meant to sound grand, his words a veiled warning never to let your guard down. Now, Argyle acknowledged the truth of his brother's portent.

'We are to be brothers in arms.' Albemarle led Argyle into a nook cast half in shadow. 'Quelle surprise.'

'The King means to keep me close. He has cause to be uncertain of me, a cause I gave him many months ago.'

'And yet he will not speak of it to anyone, though God knows I have asked far and wide.' Albemarle settled on a high stone plinth running along the narrow window. 'It makes a man wonder.'

'I am sworn by the King to secrecy and so I cannot alleviate your concerns, my Lord. But yes, you and I are to protect the King in his endeavour – along with his brother and nephew.'

At least, two of them would stay loyal no matter the course events might take. As for the remaining two, time would tell.

'Do you find it brave or perhaps foolish?' Still the Duke made no eye contact.

'The King's plan is daring. I shall not deny that I fear it may not be the glorious journey he hopes it to be, nor that we will succeed. I believe that, in the face of danger, bravery and sometimes even a foolhardy approach are required, my Lord.'

'If you say so.' Albemarle kept his gaze on the windows, the view blurred by years of grime and dirt. 'I hear that you are a great warlord, Sire, and that I am to be honoured to ride with you.'

'As I am honoured to ride alongside the King's brother.'

'Adoptive.'

'Yet still beloved and entrusted, I have no doubt. Together we will be a suitable guard to his Majesty, and no doubt, he will look to you to give him honest counsel.' The more Argyle spoke with Albemarle, the more Harry's words rang true. 'We may yet face a great adversary. You may have been spared the Irish blades but the Welsh are no different. Make no mistake, we are far from safe as long as we linger here. Welsh oaths of fealty are as brittle as a dry leaf.'

A few servants began lighting torches, casting warped shadows around the narrow hall. Albemarle produced a small knife and picked his teeth. 'I was shocked to learn of the return of Lord Bolingbroke. Were you not?'

'It chilled my bones. I wonder what might have possessed him to act as he has. He must be desperate, my Lord.' This was one dance, he would rather sit out, if for no other reason that Albemarle still had the King's ear and it was impossible to tell what he might divulge – and what he might keep to himself.

To shirk the oppressive silence, he turned his mind to the task of picking men to bring south. He would have to select the young and brave, for in Wales there was ever unrest. His most seasoned captains he would send north with secret orders to keep Harry safe.

'Then we are agreed that the King must be kept safe at all costs.' Albemarle rose and slipped his knife back into its sheath looped into his long, leather belt. 'That is good to know. I have often wondered what the King saw in you – outside your obvious traits and appearance – and now I know. He recognised a true friend, Sire, and he is ever in need of true friends.'

'He has many.'

Albemarle caught Argyle's eye for the first time. The stare was cold and dead. 'He requires many more. God willing, we shall find them for him.'

ADRIFT

'Who is he?' A deep voice cut through the fuzzy, grey spectres in Argyle's head, yanking him from his harrowing dreams. 'Marie?'

'I do not know, Father.' The female voice from the beach replied. 'He lay on the rocks. If we had not taken him, the tide would.'

There was a warm darkness around Argyle and a strange but comfortable smell wafted in the air. He had been taken indoors while he was still out for the count, the wooden boards under his back replaced with a soft mattress. The two discussing him were clearly at odds about the woman's decision to rescue Argyle. He found it easier to understand their French now, and he wondered once more where he was. When he tried to move, he felt hands on his face, holding his head steady.

'You must not move.' The soft accent was odd but the

words understandable as if she was taking great pains to enunciate.

Argyle waved his hand to signal that he understood. His throat was raw and he dared not speak, so instead, he tried to open his eyes. Only half a room came into sight. His shock must have shown because the person attending him quickly stepped into view.

An elderly woman with bushy white hair and keen, bright eyes smiled reassuringly. 'Bandage.' She pointed past his left eye at the blackness. 'You understand French?'

Trying to nod made his vision blur and he gritted his teeth.

The white-haired woman issued an order in a low voice and turned back to him. 'Your neck is bruised as is your forehead. For now, you have to stay completely still.'

From the dark part of the room, someone offered him a cup and he drank deep, coughing when cold water hit his bruised throat.

'Careful.' Stern warning rode on the white-haired woman's clipped word. 'Do not drown on us now that we have saved you from the sea.'

In the background, someone's soft laugh ebbed when the woman glared. 'His wounds amuse you? Get out.'

'Grand-Maman,' the voice of Marie pleaded.

She had been on the beach.

He shifted towards the sound and the world swivelled, making him spit up the water he had just drunk, heaving and coughing.

A rain of curses sent Marie fleeing the room while two sets of rough hands turned Argyle on his side. His body shook as his stomach tried to rid itself of whatever illness caused the room to tilt.

'Merde!' One of the men came into view, shaking a hand

covered in Argyle's bile.

'Language, Pierre.' Grand-Maman's lecturing tone made the grown man shirk. 'Take his arm and hold him steady. I need to examine his back.'

Argyle twitched and moaned as her hooked, hard fingers prodded his spine and neck. Probing completed, she gave a satisfied nod. 'You will be able to walk again.'

'When?' Argyle croaked swallowing to keep from retching again.

'Patience.' She turned away and her assistants rolled him onto his back once more. 'You have suffered greatly and need rest. I cannot say if you will have the use of both eyes. The right one was closed up from blood and grime. Time will tell.'

Her calm statement made Argyle sigh, and she turned back to him, a serene smile on her face. 'Drink this. Tomorrow we will know more.' She held out a steaming cup, the smell a bitter and the taste worse still. When Argyle cringed, her smile deepened. 'You will live. Take heart.'

Argyle tried to nod and his world fell apart in great swoops. As two sets of hands grabbed his body the ghosts of his distorted past grew flesh on their bones and reached out for him.

CHAPTER 13

4 August 1399 – Wales

'Quickly, in here.'

Three shrouded figures dodged past Argyle into the dark room. One, a Franciscan friar, stopped, shook his drab garb and pushed back the hood, muttering curses under his breath.

'Majesty. We cannot take chances, you must remain in disguise.' Argyle's candle flickered when he closed the door.

'How the Hell did the wretch make it to Bristol without us knowing?' Huntingdon's voice trembled even more than his hands. 'The whole of the south rally to his side, and we are kept in the dark.'

Thomas Holland's eyes danced around the ascetic chamber no doubt taking in how sparse and coarse it was. 'Is this safe?'

'As safe as any place can be, my Lord,' Argyle said and hooked the door against intruders. He took comfort in knowing that, should anyone have followed them, he would hear them coming and deal with them accordingly. 'There is only one way in, the narrow window looks to have been boarded up long ago and we are on the second storey. It will have to do and we shall not stay for long.'

'What of food?' The King took the only chair in the room and tapped his fingers on the rickety armrest. 'Nephew, perhaps you could procure some sustenance for us?'

Something in the King's manner made Surrey flee the room, his hand gripping the hilt of his sword as he pushed past Argyle and shut the door behind him the latch clattering. Creaking accompanied his progress down the hall towards the rickety stairs which they had so recently ascended.

Huntingdon settled on the lumpy straw mattress, running his hands over the stained bedding, pushing down straws.

'Why did my brother abandon me?' The King looked up at Argyle as he dripped wax on the table and set the candle in it. Prodding the setting wax, he continued, 'I placed such trust in him. I considered him a true and honest friend – a brother of my choosing to replace the one I lost as a child…'

'He was no true brother to you, Majesty, not as I am.' None in the Holland family ever took kindly to being reminded that the King had gone over their heads to settle acknowledged brotherhood upon a cousin of the royal line. Now, Huntingdon would have his say. 'He was ever interested in furthering his own position and never had a care for anyone but himself, as we now know,' he growled and scratched his leg.

Fleas in the bedding no doubt. Argyle wondered when he too would steal away in the night as the Duke of Albemarle had done. When would Bolingbroke's command arrive? So far, Argyle had heard nothing from the Duke of York or anyone else who openly supported Bolingbroke in his endeavour. The loss of southern Wales was a stark reminder that the King was on his heels. His star was waning, Bolingbroke's rising.

'I would have given him anything.' Anguish in the King's words, pleading in his eyes. 'Anything he could wish for, he needed only to ask. All he has known from me is kindness.'

'Perhaps he heard what you had planned for our nephew, your Majesty. Edward always envied Thomas, it is the worst kept secret at court.' Huntingdon cringed under the King's harsh look, but Argyle thought he had the right of it. 'He may well have assumed himself in line for the title of King of Ireland. He may well have coveted the crown you made for Thomas.'

'Then Edward is a fool. After all, he is adopted. How would it look if I favoured him before my own kin?' The King flicked old dirt off the table, his misery replaced with disdain for the time being. 'You of all men should know, brother, how little it takes to come to terms with me.'

'Yes, Majesty.' Huntingdon looked at his hands as if willing them to stay still. Ever since they were forced to bolt, he shivered and jerked, his determination in tatters.

'What is being done to ensure my return? Sir Argyle?'

'We fled in the night, Majesty.' Argyle leaned against the door, the rough boards scraping against his armour and sticking to his cloak. 'On your command we abandoned the troops gathered. Some of them may come north, although…'

'You are saying that I – *I* – lost our troops?' A storm was gathering in the tight confine, the air thick with thunder.

'Your safety was all that mattered, Majesty. If we had not gone there and then who is to say what might have happened next? You made the right decision and those men loyal to your cause know they must seek north to find your main host.' Argyle hoped the King would stay his rage for it was impossible from one moment to the next to know what might happen.

The King resumed his work of flicking dirt from the table as if he might remove his despair along with the filth. 'How did Henry know where I was?'

'Since Albemarle has turned his coat, it is most likely Bolingbroke knew from the moment we set out.' Argyle's words made Huntingdon hang his head. Clearly, he had entertained the same notion though was too cowardly to voice it.

'Even before he came to me in Ireland?' Wrath smouldered in the King's question. 'You mean to have me believe that he came into my open arms a traitor? I shall have his head for this.'

'Majesty.' Argyle deliberately lowered his voice, they were on the run, drawing attention to themselves was the very last thing he wanted. 'I must caution you. If we are to get back to the north we must not be conspicuous.'

'Duck and cower? Is that your advice, Sir Argyle? Are you lecturing your King now?' Some of the fire had gone out of his rage, and yet, his fingernails scraped the layer of grime on the table with renewed energy. 'I who believed that you – of all men – would know what to do. I am given to think perhaps you lost me my new recruits.'

'We left before first light, Majesty. If we had lingered or told the men where we were going, anyone of them might be caught and made to reveal our plans. It was safer to go alone.' Argyle mastered his own temper with an effort. 'Tonight, I shall arrange for fresh horses. I shall send word to my men to make their way back to Conwy and take as many of the new recruits as possible.'

'Not good enough.' Huntingdon scratched his leg with more vigour, refusing to look up. 'Are we truly to make do with this disgusting place?'

'You are welcome to return for the soldiers, my Lord, or indeed to find better accommodation if it does not become you.' Argyle turned from Huntingdon. The fleas might bite, but at least they would not be deadly. 'Majesty, the decision to leave with as few men as possible was the right one. If Albemarle was in Bolingbroke's pay, your life was at stake.'

The King paused and looked at the boarded-up window. 'Your men will come to Conwy? You are certain? They will not turn tail and run for Beauworth or worse yet, to Bristol? To my traitor cousin?'

'My men are loyal to you, Majesty,' Argyle said. Or at least, they are loyal to me. How easy it was to lie.

For the first time, he hoped that Bolingbroke would send his command soon. The prospect to be much longer in the company of the King and his terrified family was almost unbearable.

Picking at the hem of his disguise, the King rubbed his forehead. 'Leave me.'

Huntingdon followed Argyle into the dark and narrow hall, casting a final glance over his shoulder before he closed the door and took a few steps further into the gloom. 'Was it necessary to point out that my brother lost himself an army?'

'Sometimes, I wonder at how we bend the truth and warp reality to have it fit the minds of the few,' Argyle said.

'Or the one. In this instance, I would school anyone who thought their lives were not on the line. We mean to survive, my Lord, and to do so we must sometimes say that which is disagreeable. I would rather offend in the present and live, than pander and die. I never was much of a courtier, my tongue is not made of silver. Truth is coarse and scrapes, but it is necessary.'

'You must have had some training in the art of being at court,' Huntingdon said grasping a different line of conversation. He disliked discord with a passion and was always attempting to smooth over that which offended his royal half-brother. 'In the household of the great Blanche of Wake, as a son of a Baron of Mowbray and the brother of two more. John most of us liked, but Thomas, he was a different creature. I often wondered what it was like to have your brother, just a year older than you, rise in the King's favour while you toiled under the watchful eye of an upstart knight?'

'Surprisingly pleasant, my Lord, and the King was ever a great friend of La Fontaine. I never cared for courtly affairs.'

Before Huntingdon could poke further, Surrey came scurrying up the stairs and stopped at the sight of them in the shadows. A bowl of brown slop wobbled on his tray. 'What is this? Why are you out here? Is something amiss?'

'His Majesty required some peace. I should imagine he is conferring with the only councillor he has left.' Huntingdon pointed skyward. 'For I am almost certain, he will no longer place his faith in either of us lurking here in the dark and why should he? If only Albemarle had been caught. If only someone had seen the traitor within and had convinced him not to defect to the losing side.'

'Bolingbroke a loser?' Surrey snorted and tipped the small wooden tray in his hands, the thick brown fluid revealing chunks flecked with white. 'It is as if you know him not at all, uncle. You and I cannot doubt that the King's cousin would only return if he was certain of the outcome.'

Huntingdon ignored him. 'Sir Argyle. What might we expect if…' He checked himself. 'When we arrive in Conwy?'

'If Lord Salisbury has been successful he may have raised enough forces to ensure we can march on London. To take back the capital will award us time to regroup and take stock of the situation.' Argyle doubted it, especially if Salisbury had taken his advice and offered the archers a choice.

'What is to prevent this happening?' Surrey asked in a feeble tone, wiping brown droplets off the tray with his sleeve.

'Men grow restless if they are kept too long in one place. Should news reach them that the King has been forced to abandon his plan and that Albemarle turned his cloak there is little to keep them loyal.'

The King might have lost more than his new recruits with his flight, and yet, what else was there to do?

'He is their King.' Huntingdon's repulsion echoed down the dark corridor and Surrey spilled more of the stew, fretting over the tray, his sleeve now soaked in brown mush.

'Men go where there is food and fighting to be had. Many have already chosen Bolingbroke over the King. The people are not as dependent on the King as you might believe, my Lord,' Argyle said to Huntingdon's shadow. 'Harvest is upon us, many of the men called to the King's service have obligations to their Lords and families. They may favour going home and tending their fields. Especially if Bolingbroke offers them safe passage. Most of the forces that answered the King's call in the south will be home before we reach Conwy, you mark my words. We are more easily replaced than the men farming the land.'

Surrey wiped sweat from his brow; his pale face came away streaked with slop. 'If Bolingbroke succeeds…'

Argyle shook his head. 'Changes will have to be made.'

A nod from Huntingdon silenced any further discussion. 'We Hollands cannot expect to be left with any offices of consequence. We can only hope to keep our heads.'

CHAPTER 14

6 August 1399 – Conwy, Wales

'What are they doing?'

Hundreds of men could be seen to be moving away from Conwy as the castle came into sight. The men were reluctant to step off the road and into the muddy ditches, squeezing against the high dikes, thorn bushes pricking their skin and tangling in their hair. Most were carrying big bags on sticks or slung over their shoulders, and Argyle caught more than a few eyeing him with malcontent.

'If I did not know better, I should think they are returning home.' Surrey reined in his horse when a few men were pushed back onto the road and into his path. 'Ho there. Step aside!'

Argyle moved closer to the King who was slumped in his saddle. The entire journey to Conwy he had been deep in thought or prayer, no doubt pleading with God. Since the uncomfortable night in the inn, they had slept in the open and he had retreated into himself, speaking to no one and only eating when Surrey urged him to.

Before they reached Conwy, rumours reached them that the southern forces amassed in the King's name now rode beneath Bolingbroke's banner, something that had brought on a royal silence much more menacing than his usual explosive rage.

'What are they carrying?'

Huntingdon was first to turn into the cobbled road leading up to the castle walls. 'What in the Devil's name?'

Following his gaze, Argyle's fears that the deserting men were not going home empty-handed solidified. The carriages that used to hold the King's furniture and personal treasures were upturned, the ground churned from hundreds of feet prowling the chests and crates.

Looking over his shoulder, he glimpsed a flicker of silver poking out of one of the men's sacks. The horse-pen was almost empty, no doubt the most daring had stolen a steed or two and would peddle them once they were clear of the King's encampment. It was a camp in upheaval, and yet, by Argyle's side, the King was silent. When he stole a look, the King still had his head down, the hood drawn against prying eyes.

He is frightened, and justly so, for I fear his end is imminent, Argyle thought. If Salisbury could not inspire loyalty among the troops gathered here what hope is there that he was able to inspire the Chester archers to join their Lord and King?

Surrey rode up next to Argyle, his horse skittish at the crush of the men. 'They are deserting,' he whispered in disbelief. 'They are abandoning their King. What has possessed them?'

'No doubt the rumours that reached us of Bolingbroke's massive army have also reached Conwy. Perhaps the rumours even started here,' Argyle whispered back, careful to let the King proceed ahead of him, trailing Huntingdon's horse. 'They smell defeat and will have none of it.'

'Traitors.' Surrey's grey face reflected Argyle's despair. 'They are all traitors.'

'Rich traitors.' Argyle pointed and Surrey's eyes bulged.

'The King's treasure?'

'Be quiet, man.' Argyle hissed. 'There are just four of us and thousands of them.'

Surrey's hands shook, the reins fluttered between his fingers. 'We are their Lords. He is their King. Have they lost their minds?'

'I would remind you, my Lord,' Argyle said with forced deference. 'I warned you that this might happen.'

'You said they might not stay, not that they would rob the King.' Shock made Surrey forget to be cautious, and Argyle noticed hostile stares from the men skirting the horses. His destrier snorted when a couple of grubby soldiers stomped by in supple leather boots, too fine to be theirs by right.

Turning on Surrey, Argyle hissed, 'I said, be quiet!'

In front of them, Huntingdon fell back to flank the King and Argyle left Surrey to secure the other side. A monk accompanied by two Lords and a knight would soon raise suspicion. He watched for the Beauworth crest on any of the men abandoning their King. In secret, he hoped not to be recognised as much as he hoped his men were still in the camp.

'We must get inside the walls.' Huntingdon too was on edge. 'How could Salisbury have failed his King so completely?'

'I am certain that Lord Salisbury has amassed troops, as he was instructed,' Argyle defended the King's most ardent supporter. 'Although he has failed to keep them here.'

'Then we are agreed,' Huntingdon snapped and took the King's rein, drawing the horse through the open portcullis. 'He has failed.'

Clattering through the grey shadows, Argyle realised that only a few of the King's White Harts stood guard and they made no effort to check who came and went. He turned right as soon as they emerged into the light and let Surrey and Huntingdon proceed to the inner courtyard.

'You there. Get word to Lord Salisbury to come to the royal chambers at once,' Argyle barked at one of the soldiers and turned his horse without waiting for an affirmative response. 'And you. Muster the royal guard and let down the portcullis.'

'Yes, Sire.' Exchanging a single, baffled look the soldiers' training kicked in. They were to obey and carry out orders, not ask questions.

Approaching the centre of the courtyard, he noticed that the King was still mounted and Huntingdon was screaming orders at servants and soldiers alike. Argyle searched in vain for some of his own men and acknowledged that he would have to go to the camp to ensure that none had deserted. Some of the certainty he had leaned upon while making his way back with the King now slipped through his fingers.

'The castle is secure, my Lord.' Argyle swung from the saddle and landed with a heavy thud as the portcullis chains clattered behind him. 'We must get the King inside.'

Surrey scuttled down the mounting block as Argyle drew the King's horse to it, steadying his leg when he dismounted. 'Majesty, you are safe. I have issued orders for Lord Salisbury to join us in your chambers.'

A grunt from underneath the hood was all he got in return. The hem of the King's plain robe dragged behind him, soiled in mud and dirt from the waste that covered the cobbles. A nervous stable boy reached for the reins in Argyle's hand.

'Why has the yard not been kept?' he snarled. 'Fetch some boys and get about cleaning it up. Your King is returned and he is not pleased.' That would put word about the camp that the King was back and perhaps put the fear in some of the deserting men or give them heart to stay. Argyle cared not either way.

The boy struggled with the horse, calling out to the other boys as he pulled and tugged it all the way to the stable. Surrey had a lost look about him when Argyle passed him on the stairs.

'Is it all gone do you think, Sire? All of it? The gold, the silver?'

'I cannot say, my Lord. I have sent word that Salisbury is to come directly that we may have a full report.' He had little hope that any of the treasure was still here. The soldiers had been cheated out of battle in Ireland which meant they had not been able to loot enemies for riches. Looting the King's stores would seem fair compensation, and a risk worth taking since so many had been in the coffers.

Waiting for Surrey to get inside Argyle pushed the big door closed. The smooth wood gave of a faint scent of forest and rain. In different circumstances they would be homely smells. 'Let us hope that the men were not bold enough to break into the King's quarters.'

The discarded monk's garb lay on the floor inside the castle and muddy boot prints suggested that the King had run the halls to get to his own chambers. A roar reached the outer rooms and, purely on instinct, Argyle loosened his steel from the scabbard.

'Thieves and whoremongers!'

With six soldiers in tow, Argyle threw open the doors to the royal bedchamber and found there a miserable sight. The King rooting through his chests, tears of rage running down his gaunt face. He was as white as a ghost except for a couple of red roses blooming on his cheeks.

'Majesty?' Argyle pushed his sword back in its sheath.

'I am robbed.' The King sunk onto a chest that gave off a hollow thud. 'My silks and robes gone. Gone! Fetch that traitorous cur Salisbury this instant.'

His gaze locked onto the throne, all gemstones plucked from the high back and armrests. Even the cloth of gold usually draping it was gone. Snarling, he stalked to the throne his fingers seeking the holes where jewels used to be.

The moment Salisbury stepped over the threshold, the King seized the Earl by his neck and forced him to his knees. 'You scoundrel. You villain!'

On their ride to Conwy he had been subdued and lethargic, now that he knew his own army had robbed him, his volatile nature sparked a red madness. 'How dare you fail me so utterly? So completely? I put my faith in you! I am robbed while I ride for my life. And you…'

When the King released his grip, Salisbury gasped for air, his face ashen. Nothing he might say would change the stark truth. The royal army was a thing of the past. Once news reached Bolingbroke's southern camp that the King was deserted, there would be no need for him to travel north. The King could merely hope he was offered favourable terms.

'Majesty…' Salisbury rasped and cowered when the King spun on his heels. Argyle noticed the tiny holes in his garb. It seemed the looters had left behind what was old and worn, and now, he had to wear rags if he did not want to redress in the monk's robe.

'How many?' the King hissed.

'Majesty?'

'How many men did you raise?' Outside, clouds gathered, thunder rumbling in the distance. The room darkened with the weather and lend heft to the King's fury.

Salisbury stayed on his knees. 'At its height, there were forty thousand men here, Majesty.'

Despite the dire situation, Argyle had to acknowledge that Salisbury had carried out his mission to perfection. Keeping even a few thousand men in check was quite a task for any Lord, and Salisbury had been almost alone in his endeavours. To gather such forces and keep them in one place was a monumental achievement.

A tinge of surprise laced the King's next question. 'And now?'

'Less than fifteen thousand.' Salisbury risked getting up, head still bowed. 'More are disappearing every day, Majesty. I have tried with all my might to keep them at bay…'

'You disappoint your King.' The words clattered to the floor as chips of ice.

'Is there nothing you can do, my Lord?' Argyle knew better than to offer advice, the King listened only to his divine councillor and what was a knight's words to God's divine edict?

Salisbury shook his head. 'I cannot think what it might be. My own men remain loyal, but since word reached us that Chester has surrendered to Bolingbroke, welcomed him with open arms…'

Shock tore across the King's face and he hid it in his hands. One more thing he had never imagined would come to pass. In the background, Huntingdon growled and Surrey looked ready to faint. For the first time since they had arrived, Argyle wondered where Harry might be. Why had Salisbury not thought to use him as a means of convincing the men to stay? If nothing else, Harry's face was well-known to all the men and his being Bolingbroke's heir might, in the short term, have made at least some men stay at Conwy.

'Leave me.'

The whisper crept around the room, and Huntingdon grabbed Surrey's sleeve to drag him out. Argyle was last to leave, closing the door on the King's misery. Salisbury hung back, some of the initial shock had worn off and his fear seemed to be evaporating.

'What happened, my Lord?'

'They rallied readily enough, cries going up in favour of the King,' Salisbury began as they made their way towards the gloom of late afternoon. 'I own, I was surprised at their eagerness to serve. They marched out in good spirits, settling easily into the camp. In the beginning, I stationed some of my own men in and around the new recruits to ensure they stayed loyal and ready, in case we were attacked.'

Argyle nodded along and ignored the first splatters of rain when they crossed the courtyard. 'What changed the tide?'

'The camp grew beyond control. Lord Monmouth attempted to keep the peace by visiting the men, instilling what courage and calm he might muster. It was a valiant attempt and one I owe to your good influence.'

'And the love of his uncle.' Argyle was pleased that Harry had offered his services on his own accord. The men would remember such conduct. 'Where is Master Harry now?'

The pause before Salisbury answered was enough to make Argyle's blood curdle.

'Once news reached us about Chester…' Salisbury spread his hands. 'And then the messenger arriving to inform us that the King had made a narrow escape, leaving behind the forces he had mustered in the south, well…'

'You feared Master Harry might inspire rebellion?'

'By then, the first men had deserted…' Salisbury's nerve failed. Argyle would swear he heard it snap clean off. All at once, the Earl looked his age and that was a terrifying sight.

For a while they walked about the overgrown inner courtyards and gardens, aimless in their silence, the rain increasing with every step. Argyle swallowed his questions about Harry, they would get there in the end. Salisbury seemed lost in contemplation, no doubt reliving his failure all over again.

The King might have sent them from his chambers, but this was far from over and they both knew it. They would have to prepare a plan, have proposals ready for the King to consider. It would not do to let the failure fester.

'My Lord.' A crack of thunder made him look skyward. 'Have you truly lost more than twenty-five thousand men?'

Salisbury nodded, unable to speak. Argyle put a comforting hand on his shoulder for just a moment before releasing it. At this rate, they would both be soaked to the bone before long.

'I am sorry. Keeping that many men in check without the King present is a task no man could hope to achieve. Not in the long run.'

'Your captains lent me what help they could.'

'Beauworth remains loyal.' Argyle heard the query in his own words. 'The men I brought south are making their way here.'

'What happened at Carmarthen?'

'Albemarle.'

Salisbury made a face and Argyle smiled for what felt like the first time in weeks. Overhead, slate clouds swirled the rain momentarily ceased. It was sure to come back with a vengeance.

'He must have been the one to warn Bolingbroke that we were mustering. Though he left with us when the King was first betrayed, he did not stay long. Stole away in the night and next we heard, he was riding alongside Bolingbroke to take over the forces we had rallied to the King's cause. I cannot shirk the notion that he planned it all along and that was the real reason his arrival in Ireland was delayed. Was he first receiving instructions from his new master?'

Stepping under a trellis overgrown with vines, Salisbury shook out his cloak. 'The King must have been appalled.'

'At the deceit of an adoptive brother? He is infuriated as are we all. I believe the deepest wound sustained was coming here to discover that all his treasure, gold, clothes even horses are gone.'

The rain returned, the leaves staunching the onset a little. When lightning struck not far afield, Salisbury hunched his shoulders. 'I tried to ward off the looting. In the face of such numbers, some of them our own kin, my men were reluctant…'

'I do not blame you, my Lord, it would serve no purpose. Though you must expect the King to feel differently, for he knows not what it takes to keep a camp of men satisfied even at the best of times.' Argyle drew a hand through his hair; it was greasy from sweat and dirt. 'I still remember when we went on campaign in Scotland, no doubt you do too.'

'This will be far worse.' Salisbury's face hardened. 'In Scotland…'

'Our enemy was mutual and our defeat one in a long line of fruitless attempts to seize an unwilling land. Not the first and not the last. You fear that, this time, all may be lost before we begin?'

'Is this to be another talk about which side to back, Sire?' Salisbury's voice boomed with the thunder. 'For I will never again do anything so utterly deceitful as I did that one time. I will never be sweet talked into treason to such a degree. I wanted the men to back the King for love.'

'He has given them very little love to live on,' Argyle said. 'Men cannot live on such scant provisions and, if all the rumours are to be believed, the whole of England and most of Wales are rallying in favour of Bolingbroke. Who would dare go against the army he is gathering?'

'Only a fool.' Salisbury stepped into the torrent. 'And the fool who loves him.'

CHAPTER 15

7 August 1399 – Conwy, Wales

'Cowards! Traitors! Bloody bastards!' The King's words whipped around the bleak room. Behind him, Harry looked out over the crowd, his face an immovable mask.

An unfortunate messenger cowered on the floor, covering his head and pressing his face into the grime and old rushes. Argyle fought a sudden urge to protect the young man.

'How dare they? It is *my army*. Before this is over, I will have their heads on spikes.' The King kicked the messenger, who fell sideways clutching his stomach. In fury, the King reclaimed some of his former glory, terrifying though it was. Even his patched clothes looked ablaze, the colours renewed by his flaming wrath.

'I shall never make terms with them. Never. They will rot in Hell!' His hand sought his sword, which still lay in the pile next to the cold forge, the blacksmiths had gone in the night.

That his soldiers had abandoned his cause was one thing. That his archers, his most beloved men, had changed sides had torn the fabric from the King's eyes to reveal the stark reality. At this very moment, he turned his rage upon an unsuspecting youth whose head snapped back when the King kicked him in the mouth.

Argyle decided to intervene. 'Your Majesty.'

'Sir Argyle. Why is there always a Mowbray on hand when something foul happens?' The high-pitched words came out in punches.

Argyle was still kneeling, weighing what to say next, trying to ignore the abuse he was forced to witness. The few who were present all stared at the stained floor.

'Well? What brilliant advice do you hold for me this time? Surely, you must know what to do.' Next to Argyle the messenger's breath rattled. 'Come now, Sire, enlighten me.'

He cleared his throat. 'Has Bolingbroke made demands?'

'What right has he to do so?' Again, the King clawed at his empty scabbard. 'And why should I listen to him? He is a traitor, he has broken his exile and if fools and turncoats did not surround me he would be rotting in the Tower until I returned with news of a new King of Ireland. He foiled my plans, spoiled my endeavour and stole my men. *My* men. He is playing with me, Sire, and I will not have it. What makes you think he will send demands? What moves you think I would respond?' He took a step towards the messenger who shivered.

'Majesty,' Surrey began and was silenced by the King's sweeping gesture.

'No, nephew. We must now adhere the great trove of Mowbray wisdom. As you well know, I used to rely on his brother. A brother who bled my Calais coffers dry while he smirked and smiled. A brother who once stood arm in arm with Bolingbroke and declared he would never turn against me, none of them would if only I would send from my court my most trusted friends and lean on their – *their* – advice. They promised, in one voice, that if I took their counsel England would love me and we would have everlasting peace.'

Surrey's head bobbed along, eager as ever to agree with his royal uncle. Every word twisted the dagger in Argyle's heart. The King would never forgive him Thomas' misdeeds. If only he knew that, until the royal sword took two innocent lives, Argyle had not for a moment contemplated turning against his King.

'Come now, Sire, pour that sweet Mowbray charm upon us all and make us smile as we embrace our doom. Is that not what you were trained to do? What you have secretly been doing all this time?'

If only you knew how close you are to the truth. Argyle raised his head. 'Since your treacherous cousin has returned to England surely he must want something?'

'My head on a spike, no doubt.' The cold laugh that followed the King's words bounced off the old, clammy castle walls. Behind the throne, Harry turned away his head. 'All I hear is that more and more men fall at his feet, grovelling and making pledges to stand by his side in the war to come. They will make war on their anointed King, on the Crown of England itself? What is that if not madness? If my cousin wants a war, I shall give it to him. If he makes demands, I shall show him what comes from reaching above his station. I shall have his head on a spike for betraying his sacred oath to the Crown!'

Argyle rose and turned to the messenger, stepping in front of his shivering form as much to shield him from the King as to question him. 'Was there other news than the Chester archers opening their gates to the traitor?'

The trembling figure before him was no more than a boy just beginning to sprout the first fuzz on his cheeks. When he shook his head, blood spattered Argyle's boot.

'Nothing? No note? No spoken words?'

Again, the boy shook his head. Argyle felt the King glaring behind him and dismissed the messenger with a stiff nod. It took two guards to lift him and carry him away, his wheezing filling the silence.

'You dare dismiss men from my presence, Sire?' The King hissed the last word.

'The boy had no more…'

'The *boy* has seen my enemy.' He stepped close but something stayed his hand when he looked Argyle in the eye. 'You would have me grovel before my cousin and plead for him to let me keep my crown? Is that how little you think of me, Sire? For if it is, I would remind you that you are only here because of the love I had for your former master and I can strip you of all your lands and leave you to beg on the very roads you once commanded. I can throw your wife and children in the Tower and force you to watch them waste away while you rot, chained to a pole, outside their cell.'

The love you had for my master sent him to his death, Argyle thought, so I shall be thankful if you do not show the same love for me. As for the rest, I can very easily imagine how you would relish in my demise.

'Majesty,' Surrey said, Huntingdon's elbow buried in his side. 'To squabble among ourselves is what the traitor Bolingbroke wants. We must not lose focus.' It was Huntingdon's words slipping from Surrey's mouth.

When the King moved it drew all air from the room. 'Is that so?'

Rather than dare to speak again, Surrey nodded with vigour. Next to him, Huntingdon only inclined his head.

'What do you think, brother?' The King's fury lurked just below the surface, dancing in the quiet of his tone.

'Sir Argyle saved us all from Albemarle's betrayal, Majesty. I agree that Henry must make demands – and soon.' Huntingdon fixed the King's gaze. For once, the Holland brother appeared disinclined to pander. Perhaps he was the one to make the King see reason.

He sat down, drilling his fingers into the empty holes on the armrests where gemstones used to sparkle. 'Very well.' His attention swung as a pendulum. 'Sir Argyle, you have the support of a man I trust beyond all others. I shall hear what you have to say.'

'Is there anywhere, here in Wales, where you might be safe? It will take Bolingbroke weeks to get here and as he is mustering along the way, it may be even longer. Your safety is paramount.' Next to Argyle, Huntingdon slapped his gloves into his palm. Argyle continued, 'Finding a good place for a siege might be your best choice.'

'I should run and hide?'

Huntingdon scoffed and earned a hard glare, and yet, he stood his ground. 'You must be able to defend yourself. You must take the men still loyal to you and find somewhere that they can defend. It is not a cowardly act if it is done to secure the Crown and your men.'

'A siege could tire our enemy,' Surrey agreed, happy to show support if someone else would carve the way. 'A siege would be the better option, your Majesty.'

'What else might be done?' The idea of a siege did not sit well with the King.

Argyle wondered if he knew what was at stake. He had been blind to the mood of England. Gone was the glamour and fame of the boy-king saving London from scores of desperate peasants. Gone was the grandeur of the King's young court with its chivalrous ideas. Left was a country ready to back a new pretender to the throne. Since receiving word from Bolingbroke, the only thing holding Argyle up was the possibility that his decision would, in time, reunite him with his family, something he desired more than anything, and that seemed to slip further from his grasp by the day.

'Well? Now is not the time to cower and hide, my Lords. I will have your ideas if I have to shake them from your bones.'

'Majesty, you must send a messenger to Lord Bolingbroke,' Argyle said.

'What?' If the King kept up this uncompromising attitude, Argyle was certain that many more would abscond, and soon, they would be too few to keep a siege anywhere.

'Offer terms first. The country may yet rally to your cause, Majesty.' Argyle knew his suggestion would make no difference, and yet, he had to play the game. Had to wait, glean which side might win before he showed his hand. Inside, derision rode on a sensation that it would not be long before the King's suspicion would be proven right. He would act as a Mowbray – turn his coat and back the enemy.

'Do you believe that, Sir Argyle?' The King ground out his question, his frayed fingernails scraping against the wooden armrests. 'Do you believe that an act of weakness will stay my cousin's hand and bring men to my side?'

'There is still time to change the tide. It will not be seen to be an act of weakness, your Majesty. This is an opportunity to prove that you are the King our country needs. The ruler we know you to be.' Argyle ignored the stolen glances from the few men in the chamber. 'Forgive me, but what other choice do you have?'

The King laughed. Although the sound was harsh and raw, it defused some of the tension. Behind the King's chair, Harry stood still as a statue.

'What choice indeed?' Contemplating his decision, the King rose to pace the floor. 'Although I am not ready to hear his terms he may well be ready to hear mine. Yes… very shrewd, Sir Argyle. I see how this might work to my advantage.'

Huntingdon nodded agreement. 'To be first to offer terms is a good solution, Majesty. Perhaps we should do so from a place of safety? Beaumaris is easy to defend.'

A smile spread on the King's face. 'Sir Argyle, gather what men we have left, we leave for Beaumaris immediately – send a couple of your men ahead to tell the castle master to make provisions. We shall march before daylight tomorrow.'

'Majesty.' Argyle turned to carry out the order.

'Why not consider Carnarvon, Majesty,' Surrey chirped, keen to make his own mark now that it was safe to speak. 'It is closer to Conwy and in good repair.'

'Sir Argyle, what do you suggest? Carnarvon or Beaumaris?' The King's question had Argyle turn, his brain churning, coming up short.

'Well? You have been lousy with advice of late.'

'Carnarvon provides the best shelter for our forces, Majesty.' Argyle noticed Surrey's surprised expression. Here was a man incapable of betrayal, Argyle had no such qualms. 'There we can make a stand. The walls are thick, there is room for the men and we can survive a lengthy siege if need be. Let it slip that we march on Beaumaris and you may yet confuse the enemy. Meanwhile, you should dispatch men to trait with Bolingbroke.'

'Send me to negotiate with Lord Bolingbroke,' Huntingdon offered. 'With the right kind of attention there will be no need to discuss where to lay down for a siege or indeed even to discuss terms. Let me go to ascertain what Bolingbroke might want from the Crown. Perhaps it is not what we think.'

Determination gave way to wariness. 'What if he decides to take you prisoner?'

'You have something that he wants more in the world than gold and lands, Majesty,' Surrey piped up and sent a shrewd look Harry's way. 'You have leverage.'

'Leverage?' The King looked over his shoulder at the boy, his scrupulous glare returned by blank eyes.

'If you are concerned, Majesty, decide for yourself whom you wish to send with Huntingdon for there are bound to be no end to the offers to protect your brother,' Surrey continued with confidence.

'Yes, Majesty.' Huntingdon grasped Surrey's idea and engorged it. 'If it pleases you, I shall go with a large retinue and bring with me whomever you deem fit to relay your terms. For terms there must be and it is only befitting that they come from you, the King, and not this traitor upstart.'

Tapping his foot on the floor, the King looked lost in thought and the whole room held its collective breath. Argyle made a small wager with himself about what the

King might say next, more to pass time than because he had any real idea what might spill from the King's lips.

He will decide to send Huntingdon that much is clear, Argyle thought stole a glance around the men assembled in the royal reception room. Perhaps Worcester too, for the King grows weary of young peacocks.

'And what do you suggest I do in your absence, dear brother?' The King's light tone made Huntingdon start.

'Perhaps it is wise to take the council of my nephew?' Huntingdon glanced at Surrey who bobbed his head with vigour. Clasping his hands behind his back, Huntingdon continued. 'Carnarvon is better situated than here, it will take longer for anyone to get to you and the fact that you are moving about may well spark ideas that you are mustering more loyal men to your cause.'

'Carnarvon is a grand fortress, Majesty,' Surrey said and earned a benevolent nod. 'It will fit your needs for the time being, and as Lord Huntingdon says, it may well give rise to speculations that you are in your strength. Perhaps, the enemy shall think again on his endeavour and decide that to bend the knee is the only path to choose.'

Argyle studied the King. There was no telling what he might decide, but to pull such wool over his eyes as to instil in him a false sense of supremacy was far worse than revealing the harsh truth and suffer the consequences. Though Argyle had chosen a side in this skirmish already, there was no need to spill any blood if such could be avoided.

'Majesty, though I wish as much as any man that I could agree with my Lord Huntingdon and my Lord Surrey, I cannot.' He suffered the sting of angry glares. The King folded his hands and rested his chin on the pyramid of his thumbs, nodding for Argyle to continue. As ever, when advice went against the grain it was impossible to decipher what he was contemplating.

'A few weeks ago, you were indeed in your strength and all of Ireland trembled before you. Since then, a series of most disadvantageous events have led us to this place and here we must acknowledge that your power has dwindled. By all means, my Lords, spread the rumour that the King is amassing troops, but know that Bolingbroke has taken so many men from the King that even if we were to raise ten or twenty thousand new recruits we will be well and truly outnumbered. A siege is all we can hope for.'

He turned his attention to the King. 'Majesty, do not make the mistake that the Irish did in Kells. Do not open your gates to the enemy for I promise you that Bolingbroke will show no more mercy to us than we did the Irish. Send your most trusted men to bargain with your cousin, it may well prove the best strategy. Still, I beg you, do not ignore that it is he who is in a seat of power, not you. Carnarvon will offer the kind of shelter you need, it is big enough to hold most of your troops and enough food to sustain a siege. It is by no means a perfect situation, but it will have to do.'

How well I lie, Argyle thought, careful to keep his expression bland. If I had not made plans of my own I would advise we go to Beaumaris, for only there can we hope to avoid an open confrontation with Bolingbroke's forces. Carnarvon might be bigger and certainly it can hold more men, but it is easy to access and its walls are crumbling.

Harry stepped forward his hands clasped behind his back. 'I know little about warfare and even less about the world in general, Majesty. What I do know is that men follow Sir Argyle. If he suggests Carnarvon, you may trust that he is giving you sound advice.'

Argyle hoped Harry knew what he was doing since he had never disclosed where his true loyalty lay. Even Harry, at the tender age of thirteen, must know that Carnarvon was the least suited place for a siege. Was this a sign that he too had accepted the only possible outcome of this situation? That he was ready to turn on his beloved uncle?

Surrey and Huntingdon locked arms and knelt before the King.

'We offer our services as your emissaries to Lord Bolingbroke, Majesty. Make your terms known to us and we will carry them to him without delay,' Huntingdon said.

'You are confident you will succeed, brother?' Rising from his seat, the King looked upon his depleted council with hard eyes. 'That you can bring about the surrender of my traitor cousin?'

'I am, Majesty. I will lay down my life for your cause if needs be, and I will secure you peace. I shall do all in my power to bring the traitor to you in chains.' Huntingdon gave a sombre smile when the King rested a hand on his shoulder.

'I shall think upon your words,' the King said and caught Argyle's eyes. 'I know that you wish to keep me safe, but let us not forget that I changed the tide of rebellion once before. What is to say I cannot do so again if only the people see me? Remind them that I am indeed their captain and their beloved King such as they themselves proclaimed when I was but a child?'

A weak cry went up and a few even applauded.

There are some here who are genuine in their support. I only wonder how many are playing false, as I am, waiting for the right moment to switch sides? How many families sit in house arrest or have strangers roaming their lands deciding how far they can go? How many look out of their windows and see soldiers in arms guarding their gates? How many here know that the only way to keep their families safe is to bend the knee to a new contender? Argyle resisted the urge to glance at each face to determine if they, as he, had chosen blood over oath.

The King dismissed them all, his slim, brooding frame the last thing Argyle saw before the doors closed. In these past days, he had grown lean and haggard. Gone was the illustrious, golden King whom all gazed upon in wonder and awe, left was a man who teetered on the brink of sanity.

'You have an avid admirer, Sire.' Surrey sidled up beside him. As ever, he was dressed in the colours of the King and his own house, his crest picked out in rich thread on his chest. 'How ever did you manage?'

'Perhaps I simply did not try, my Lord.'

'Then you are a fool.'

'A fool with an admirer.' Argyle joined in when Surrey laughed. 'What do you make of this, my Lord?'

The King's nephew tugged at his sleeve, a tell-tale sign that he was as uneasy as ever. Thomas had once called Surrey frail; Argyle had witnessed that often enough on their flight from the south. On one subject he never wavered, he was entirely loyal.

'My uncle is the King.' Surrey failed to look calm. 'I still cannot fathom that any lord of the realm would dare oppose him. Perhaps my blood prevents me from understanding the ways of fickle men.'

'You have not been approached then, as I have heard many others have been?' While it was not wise to show his hand, Argyle had to know.

'No.' Surrey snorted derision. 'Most certainly not. Bolingbroke knows better than to ask for loyalty within the King's own family. Would he dare it, do you think? He is a foul creature and cares not a jot for family himself or he would know that every league he closes in, he puts his own son in ever more danger.'

Argyle ran a hand through his sweaty hair. The August heat was proving unbearable. 'The King would harm Master Harry?'

'Such liberties you take and are granted, Sire, it baffles me. To the rest of us he is a royal nephew and a Lord. To think that a man who was, not long ago, a prisoner, can speak of the King's close relation with such intimacy.' The shrill undertone in Surrey's voice spoke volumes. 'I do not believe my uncle would harm Monmouth, but he may well be forced to dispense hard justice to prove his point. For now, he is a ward. Should his father fail to see reason, he will become a prisoner.'

'No one would blame the King for taking measures.'

'Just so.' Surrey led the way along walls that wept in the oppressive heat. The castle was an abysmal place to be holed up and whenever possible everyone chose to be out of doors. 'I can only hope that my uncle accepts Huntingdon's offer and that I might be allowed to barter with Bolingbroke. Between us, surely, we can make him see reason, make him understand that what he is doing will earn him the short journey to the executioner's block. Does he not remember what happened to his old allies?'

Before Argyle's eyes flickered the image of Arundel casting out his arms, the executioner swinging his sword. It was gone as quick as it came while nausea lingered. 'No one present at those trials could ever forget, my Lord.'

'I know you have little regard for me, Sire,' Surrey said. In the corridor his voice echoed along the large stones. 'Be not remiss. I love my uncle and my greatest desire is to be the one who offers up to him Bolingbroke's surrender. I shall not rest until I have secured the result we all must strive for.'

In some ways, it was refreshing to be in the company of someone who would never waver. Argyle's cloak snapped around his calves. 'You are wrong about one thing. Being close to the King is a difficult privilege, as many of us know. His command is ever the precipice upon which we wander, we must carry out whatever order he deems necessary and without delay.'

Surrey snorted and indicated at a green cloak that was consumed by the stark light of high noon. 'I for one do not envy Salisbury. Has he no sense?'

'Sense enough to know that the King doubts his loyalty.' Acknowledging the shock that marred the Duke's features, Argyle said, 'Salisbury may have failed to keep together the army. However, he did not fail to amass the self-same army nor did he fail in Cheshire. Add to all these merits that he loves the King and he would be wise to keep Salisbury close. Keeping this large a camp of soldiers at bay cannot be achieved by one man alone. You know this as well as I.'

Surrey adjusted his garb and pretended away his initial dismay. 'And what of you?'

'We all have a care for the King.' How unfortunate that the love had dried up – if it had ever existed. It was hard to tell with all the lies and deceit that bobbed in his wake and Argyle could no longer remember any cause he might have had to love a fickle King.

'He is now to be holed up in Carnarvon.'

'By your suggestion, my Lord.'

'And by your sanction, Sire.' Surrey gave a nervous chuckle. His left hand kept straying to the massive chain that hung around his neck, pinned by the shoulders to take some of the weight and prevent him stooping. 'Be prepared for the King's command. It may well be that you will have to depart at dawn if not before. Since you sanctioned the notion of Carnarvon, I should be surprised if you are passed over when the charge of the army is allotted.'

With a nod, Argyle left the damp and stuffy hallway. If he was quick about it, four of his best riders could be out of camp within the hour streaking for Carnarvon to make ready for the arrival of the depleted army. Many men had slipped away since they had returned to Wales, surely it was only a matter of time before the Beauworth men decided to abscond too.

Why do I linger here, he wondered, why not leave? I have already decided to place my fate in the hands of Bolingbroke, and the more news we get, the more I congratulate myself on the decision, though I would not have changed it, even if Bolingbroke was losing momentum. He holds my family's fate in his hands.

'Sire.'

Argyle started at the voice. 'Master Harry. Do no sneak up on a man lost in thought.'

Harry gave a weak smile, his face pale. 'Beg pardon, Sire, but I had to see you. I am worried. My father sends no word to me… Has he forgotten me?'

'I cannot imagine that he has.' Argyle looked about to ensure they were alone. These were dangerous words, especially when most of the lords still by the King's side believed Harry loved his uncle and hated his own father. He would have to play his part well to stay alive.

'He has other heirs.' Harry's voice pleaded for comfort.

'You are his eldest.' Argyle put a hand on Harry's shoulder. 'The firstborn son is special to all men. If you do not hear from your father it is because he seeks to protect you. He knows that the King is… he knows the King. They grew up together. He seeks to keep you out of harm's way as much as he can.'

Harry's shoulder shook. 'I can only hope it is a sentiment the King shares.'

CHAPTER 16

10 August 1399 – Carnarvon Castle, Wales

'The King wants your council, Sire.'

Argyle nodded at the soldier, a filthy and threadbare White Hart clinging to his chest with tattered stitches. 'See that you mend that, soldier.'

'Yes, Sire.' He turned and scampered through camp, Argyle striding along behind him, enjoying for once that he got to stretch his legs. 'It's true then? We're for Conwy once more?'

'Yes.'

'It's not my place, Sire, but all this running about, it's tiring out the men…' The soldier did not finish his sentence.

'No, it is not your place.' Although Argyle agreed wholeheartedly with the poor man whose beard was as bedraggled as his appearance, he had to let nothing show through. 'I shall find the King on my own accord. Take this order to every tent on your way: we ride for Conwy without delay. Make ready the King's horse and take down the tents. Pack the carriages and get under way.'

'Yes, Sire.'

The soldier vanished into the measly camp and Argyle sighed at the sight of canvas riddled with mould, holes letting in water. They needed to make permanent camp soon or there would be nothing to under which to huddle and find shelter. In a few weeks, they had flitted about and tired out what men were left going from Carnarvon to Beaumaris and back again – and now to Conwy once more. All to cater to the whims of someone who had lost his way.

Argyle scraped his boots on the raised slab in front of the doors before he entered. The castle was dry for the most part although years of disuse had left a permanent damp coldness which no fire could quench. He made his way to the royal apartment half dreading what he might encounter.

'What is this place?' The King paced his chamber. 'Is it to be my prison? Is it to be the place I meet my maker? I cannot be here. I must be away. I must be somewhere the ghosts of the past do not haunt me…'

'Majesty.' Argyle knelt but the frantic pacing did not subside.

The royal room was a stark contrast of dilapidated walls and dirty windows and few pieces of bright furniture and tapestries that had been hung in a hurry. Everything underlined its inhabitant's current state.

'Ghosts. I cannot sleep. I cannot think. Would that I had good council, and yet, I have sent away those most dear to me. Now that I think on it, it was wrong of me. I should have parted with someone of less import. I should have sent no emissary at all. We could hold out for months on end at

Conwy.' The King's lamentations skittered to the vast beams overhead, his clothes rustling. Without looking up, Argyle knew that he was pulling at his hair. 'Oh, why did we ever quit Conwy? I did not want it to be so. I wanted the kingdom to expand, I wanted to subdue the Irish, bring them to heel, include them in my kingdom, make them safe. Now look at me… Look at the company I keep. Traitor's son. Traitor soldier.'

The King's feet finally stopped in front of Argyle, the worn tips of his expensive leather boots in full view. 'What?'

'You sent for me, Majesty.'

'Did I?' Uncertainty crept into the King's voice. 'Did I really?'

'Yes, Majesty,' Harry's voice interceded from somewhere in the shadows. Half the time, he was locked up in his chamber, the other half he was forced to suffer his uncle's increasingly volatile company. 'You asked for Sir Argyle.'

'What did I want from him?'

'I know not uncle since you tell me nothing.'

'Stop your moping, boy.' The King's feet disappeared, resumed their pacing, tips dragging across the ancient floors. 'This is no time for self-pity. It is not you whose crown sits askew. It is not you who constantly fear for your life, who cannot sleep for worry that traitors roam the halls outside your room, honing their blades, spiking your wine, poisoning your food.'

'No uncle, I beg forgiveness.' The fatigue in Harry's apology told Argyle that this was a conversation they had had many times.

The King's ranting was bound to set his teeth on edge, and in this remote land, it was also bound to unwind him.

Deciding to speak before he was bid, Argyle said, 'Any orders, Majesty?'

'What? Why are you here, Sire?' The King's pacing paused once more. 'Oh, do get up.'

He rose, locking his hands behind his back. Now that they were face to face, Argyle could tell at once that the King had not slept for nights.

'You sent for me, Majesty.'

'It is true,' Harry piped up. 'You issued the order not half an hour ago.'

'Eavesdropping, eh?' The King leapt and Harry retreated. 'See there, Sire, see how my own flesh and blood flees before me. Would that his wretched father would do the same. How I would jeer if Henry had the good sense of his son.' He turned away and slogged to the window. 'Go away, you tiresome miscreant. Go pack something. That is all you know how to do.'

Once Harry had escaped the room, Argyle watched for some time as the King paced, muttering to himself. Since they left Conwy, and before then, the King's mood had become ever more bizarre. Anger and fear entangled, sparks of mad confidence and cheer surfaced to stutter to a halt on his face. The King's hair was the colour of dead straw, left too long in a dark corner of a barn, his cheeks rough with stubble and his clothes stained with dirt. If he had had a mirror of polished copper at hand, he would have cried at his own appearance, but it seemed he had tipped beyond the point of personal vanity.

'Look at the state of this place.' The King rounded on Argyle, fists clenched, eyes red. 'Who in their right mind would seek shelter here? No furnishings, no fire in the kitchen stoves, not even enough kindling to warm these measly rooms… I am reduced to sleeping on straw. What make you of that, Sire? Straw for a King. What madness is this? It is a dream, is it not? Soon I shall rise anew, home in Chester, a healthy fire in the hearth, mulled wine to steady my worries, warm clothes to drive away this incessant cold.'

'The walls were built to impress power, Majesty, not to provide comfort.' Argyle tried to ignore the tears of damp that rolled down the castle's stone cheeks. 'If we had known we were coming here…'

'They would have dug out the bedding? Swathed the walls in curtains and bright hangings? Left more wood for us to fire, more water to drink, more food to consume?' The King's sunken cheeks proved that he too was feeling the meagre meals. 'No! They would have me come here to this shamble of a place to take away my wits. This I know now, Sire. This I know and they will *not* succeed. We leave for Conwy as soon as my horse is saddled.'

'Yes, Majesty, I have already given the order. They are putting on the saddle even as we speak.'

The King dropped onto a wooden chest, his head in his hands. 'Have you? Have we talked of this already?'

Swallowing concern, Argyle touched the hilt of his sword. 'The order came from Sir William just moments before your summons.'

'Do you long for home as I do, Sir Argyle?' The King sought Argyle's eyes, looking for comfort. 'Do you yearn for a warm bed, a kind smile from your wife?'

'Yes, Majesty, and I hold faith that soon I shall have both again.'

Looking about, the King seemed suddenly shocked at his surroundings. 'I miss Anne. Her face and smile keep me sane when I am pulled in all directions, worn thin by the worries of government. Why did we come here, Sire? Why?'

On your orders, he thought and donned what he hoped was a comforting smile though the mention of the King's long deceased wife riddled his soul with worry. You are unravelling before my eyes and you do nothing to hide it. If I see it so do everyone else and they are left to wonder if they owe you loyalty when a strong man of sound mind awaits their coming with open arms.

'We shall return to Conwy, Majesty, where certainly a comfortable bed and a warm meal are sure to welcome you.' Argyle skirted the King's question.

'To linger there awaiting the return of my nephew and brother.' The King bit his lip. 'They do not know to find me here, thus we must return to Conwy do you not agree?'

If Bolingbroke has any wits about him he will have taken them prisoner by now. Since such talk would not move the King to action, Argyle smiled again. 'Yes, Majesty. We must return to Conwy that they know where to find you and convey good news.'

'It will be good news?' The King had the look of a gullible child.

'No doubt, Majesty, it will be news that takes all of us home.'

'Home…' The King resumed his pacing. 'How I long for home. For the comforts of Anne. I shall make her a new set of earrings and a necklace when we return. The gems will match her eyes. She will like that. It may even set her in the mood of making a child. We need a child. Anne's own child… She will like that.'

Argyle did not bother to wait to be dismissed. As he closed the door on the King, he wondered how little it might take for the last thread of sanity to unwind.

CHAPTER 17

13 August 1399 – Conwy Castle

'My father asks that you meet with him, your Majesty,' Harry knelt before the King. 'Alone.'

'What is this madness?' The whisper crept round the room, enveloping all those present with its cold tentacles. 'Alone? After what he has done to me?'

'He says it is a family matter and that together you can right a wrong.' Harry's voice was flat.

The return to Conwy had indeed offered a respite from the rough life of run down castles that afforded no comfort. Though the food was better and more plentiful and the castle itself in much better condition it was not enough to disguise just how dire the situation had become.

'A family matter? A *family* matter?' The King rose on legs that shook. Today, he was wearing a regal an attire as could be provided since his coffers had been looted while he was in the south, mustering men in vain. 'He dares speak to me of family? When he has incarcerated my own blood, punished my brother and nephew in unspeakable ways, I have no doubt. If he is anything as his accursed father, his veins will flow with ice and he will stop at nothing to ensure all shall cower before him.'

Harry drew back, his eyes on the floor. Vengeance and fury reached their sticky tendrils around the room. The news of Huntingdon and Surrey had brought with it a new bout of madness. Yesterday, the King had cried until his eyes were raw, tearing at his clothes and calling for Anne. Today, he was burning with hatred. There was no telling what he might do in an hour or two.

'I will make him crawl on his hands and knees from here to London. I will make him surrender my kin, and if he has harmed them, I shall do to him what he has done to them. I will hang his traitor body from the walls of the Tower to leave his flesh to fall from his bones, and every day, I will stand across the yard and laugh at him. That is what happens to traitors!' The King drew breath.

'So, tell me now, sweet Harry, what are you?' His whisper was more menacing than all his shouting and roaring. Harry trembled and dared not speak.

'Well?'

'Majesty…'

The King slapped Harry across the face, and Argyle sensed the mood of the room waver. If this continued he would be forced to intervene and then where might happen?

'Know this, *Harry*,' the King said with a strange calmness. 'You are *my* prisoner. Until your father begs my forgiveness and returns my nephew and brother to me you shall be treated as a prisoner. Sir Argyle. Put little Harry in a cell. No better yet, put him in the stocks.'

The King's cold smile made Argyle want to argue, instead he merely nodded. 'At once, your Majesty.'

'No, let him wait.' The King looked Harry up and down. 'Now you know what happens to those who defy me. I have loved you, but now my love has grown to disgust.'

Harry's lip trembled. Perhaps he had believed that Argyle could protect him, but the King's moods were so unpredictable that if Argyle put a foot out of place now, he too would be in the stocks and there would be no one to change the course of events.

In the silence, the King stared down the men in the room. 'Well? You are here to council me, so get on with it.'

'Let us not be hasty, Majesty,' Salisbury ventured and ducked just in time for the pewter cup flung at him to clatter against the wall rather than his face. 'We must at least hear what Lord Bolingbroke …'

'Lord? Lord! The moment Henry left these shores he forfeited his titles. His father knew as much. He pinned his hopes on this creature that now trails my every step, sniffing up my leg, licking my boots to make the most of his destitute situation.' The King grabbed the back of his chair, his fingers digging into the ragged padding. 'What little hope you had of my benevolence, Salisbury, you must surely know that it has quite gone. You can hope for little more than that I keep you alive.'

Argyle folded his arms and watched the King fail to master his temper. In the past week, even more soldiers had abandoned the King's side, either to return home or to join Bolingbroke who had advanced from Chester and now dwelled near Flint. Every day, Argyle walked among his own men, listening to their concerns and attempting to alleviate what problems he might. His own troops were depleting and he found he could not bring himself to hunt them down. Rather they return to Beauworth and relieve Bolingbroke's men, perhaps they could take back control of the estate, though he held only such hopes in the night when he dreamt of being home once more. He had sworn that he would do right by Isobel be a proper husband and turn his attentions to his family. Whatever Bolingbroke demanded he would deliver as long as he was permitted to stay at Beauworth far away from court.

'If you agree to his terms, he shall come alone with no weapons, your Majesty.' Harry steeled himself, he had nothing left to lose. 'He asks only that you bring me.'

The King's high-pitched laugh bounced off the walls. 'Of course he does. He wants to see that I have not harmed you. Well, I might go – alone. I am no fool. I shall never part with you until your father is subdued and order restored to the realm.'

Next to Argyle Salisbury moved, a pale, yellow bruise visible above his collar, evidence that he had taken the brunt of a tantrum the other day. 'Majesty, let me go to the enemy camp.'

'And do what? Change bend the knee to Henry as so many others have done before you? No, my dear John. You lost me my White Harts; who knows what you might lose next time?'

Salisbury's face turned red. 'I have always been loyal to your Majesty, I offer to broker some other arrangement, surely you …'

'Sir Argyle will go.' The King returned to his seat taking the measure of Salisbury's long face with calm. 'I will lose no more men to Henry. And I need you here, Salisbury. Go, Sir Argyle, do not return unless you carry with you terms of Henry's surrender. I shall accept nothing but his unconditioned submission. And the return of my brother and nephew.'

Finally, finally the wheels are set in motion. He bowed low and turned for the door. The sooner he could be away the better.

'One more thing,' the King said. 'I put Harry in your care, Sire. And I believe you will agree that it is best that he stays here. Beware you come back directly. I must interpret a prolonged absence as treason.'

Grasping Harry firmly by the arm, Argyle made for the courtyard wondering if his sudden appearance in Bolingbroke's camp might prompt him to issue the command and force a change of sides. Since he would not be able to bring Harry, would the battle for the Crown prove more important to Bolingbroke than his son and heir?

'What happens now, Sire?' Harry was on the brink of tears, no doubt remembering what happened to the servant who was sent to Argyle not long ago. Harry shuddered. 'Am I for the stocks? Will you have me whipped?'

'It is not my decision.' Argyle's words rang hollow.

'What happened to him? The servant? After …'

Nodding to two of his own Beauworth men, Argyle leaned in. 'He died. I will not let the same happen to you.'

'The whipping or the dying?'

Gesturing for his captain, Franklin, to come close, he muttered, 'Either. I cannot keep you out of the cells, but perhaps it is the best place for you to be. Our King…'

Harry stiffened. 'I can fend for myself.'

'Franklin.' Argyle turned away from Harry. 'The King has ordered that Lord Monmouth be taken to the best of the cells and made comfortable there. I leave you to ensure he is cared for as befits his station.'

He left Harry to Franklin and called for one of the stable

boys. 'Saddle my horse and four more for the men riding with me. We leave as soon as the horses are ready.'

The stable boy ran across the courtyard and Argyle turned to his squire who had been waiting in the sunlight. 'Peter, fetch four of my best men. We ride for Flint and have not a moment to lose.'

Peter jumped to and vanished in the chaotic courtyard where soldiers, cooks and servants were coming and going, swerving to avoid bumping into one another. Argyle thought of Jeremy, the squire who had run into the heat of battle with his horse and who had now abandoned the cause. And of the spit-boy with the broken tooth who had died from the kick he took from the dray horse in Kells. His father, the cook, was still in camp, but his spirit had gone and his remaining son was a shadow in his father's wake.

A stable boy walked past with Argyle's horse, it whipped its tail and shook its head against the bridle. He brushed a hand down its neck and stepped from the mounting block into the saddle. His men gathered around him, their faces set, hiding any questions that might stir within.

'Open the gate!'

Argyle grabbed the white cloth and held it high above his head, glancing up in time to see the King flanked by Salisbury on the rampart. Both nodded grimly. Behind him, his men mounted their horses and fell in. Spurring on his steed, he ducked under the portcullis and only tucked the white cloth away when the King could no longer see him.

He would raise it once more when they arrived at Bolingbroke's camp and then let matters unfold. Fleetingly, he wondered if he would be allowed to return or if this was the last he saw of Conwy.

ADRIFT

A small flickering light dissolved the horse beneath him and replaced it with soft bed, cushions, furs and blankets piled around and on him. He was sweating though not from a fever.

Argyle blinked at the tight bandage around his head, seeing only one side of the room was a terrifying shock. Then he remembered that he had been seeing with both eyes on the beach and relaxed. His head might be bound, but both his eyes worked. He licked his lips and tested if he could lift his arm without making the view swim. It seemed to work. Noticing a small table next to his bed, he attempted to grab a cup, but using only one eye made it difficult to calculate distance. He missed and knocked over a small flask sitting next to it.

'All hells!'

A helping hand came into view, offering him the cup. Grateful, Argyle took it and drank with care. He still remembered retching from the last sip he had and did not want to soil himself a second time. Moving made him realise that his stiff, saltwater soaked clothes had been replaced by soft fabric.

The sweet relief of cold drink restored his voice. 'Thank you.'

The hand took the cup and put it down. Argyle studied the gold band on one of the fingers; it was broad and ornate, the tiny red gemstones embedded in the gold glittered. 'Do you feel better?'

Argyle recognised the soft female voice and tried to recall her name but failed. Struggling to string together the words, he managed to rasp, 'Battered and bruised. Better.'

The silence that followed was long and yet comfortable. Argyle could hear the woman walk around the room and closed his eye. When he opened it again, she had moved a chair close to his bed and sat in plain view. She smiled a little. 'You are a little warm.'

'A nice change,' Argyle said and cleared his throat. She offered him more water, and he accepted it with a sigh. 'Thank you…'

'Marie.' She took the cup and filled it. 'And you are?'

He paused, and she gave him a puzzled stare.

'You do not remember? Grand-Maman said I was not to speak to you; it would tire you and your head has been injured.' She blushed. 'She said maybe there were things you could not remember.'

'Ah.'

Without knowing it, Marie had given him an excuse not to give his name. Until he knew more about where he was and with whom, Argyle decided to let her believe he suffered from loss of memory. He had heard that sometimes people who hit their heads hard experienced such affliction.

For once, time might work in his favour.

Turning his head from her quizzical gaze, he let himself drift back to a place where time had played a trick on a disturbed man.

ꙮ

CHAPTER 18

13 August 1399 – Flint, Wales

Bolingbroke's emissaries were awaiting the King's messenger at the crumbling city walls outside Flint. Behind them, his mighty camp sprawled up the countryside, the Lancaster banner streaming from the castle at the heart of the city.

When Argyle approached, he recognised Bolingbroke's half-brother the Marquess of Somerset, John Beaufort, sitting astride a brown hunter, his head cocked to one side. Next to him, the King's defected adoptive brother, Albemarle, loomed. It was as they had feared, he had been a traitor all along. Argyle wondered if Bolingbroke trusted Albemarle or kept him close because he did not.

'Sir Argyle.' The rest of Somerset's greeting was carried away by the wind.

'My Lord Somerset.'

'I wonder if my cousin Henry will give you another title

soon,' Albemarle said, his signature smirk fixed in place. 'Since I have learned that you too are rallying to our cause, Sire.'

'My Lord.' Argyle gave a curt nod to the miscreant and turned his attention to Somerset. 'I bring a message from the King.'

'This way.' Somerset let Albemarle lead the way and rode next to Argyle. 'Is Harry well?'

Argyle acknowledged the genuine concern in Somerset's eyes and made the only answer he could without revealing that the King had put Harry in a cell. 'When last I saw Master Harry, he was safe. He sends his regards to his family.'

'Will he back his father?'

'I cannot say, my Lord.' Argyle's steed side-stepped and he tightened the reins. 'He has been at his uncle's side day and night.'

Somerset looked ahead at Albemarle's back and lowered his voice. 'There is a man who believes he is destined for greatness. What luck that my brother is wise and knows that his cousin cannot be trusted.' His cloak snapped in a kick of wind. 'After all, if Edward here had not spoken out of turn, my brother would never have been exiled in the first place.'

The ride from Conwy to Flint had been tense, presenting a stark contrast to the fields of ripe crops and the calls of farmers working their fields, boys tending sheep and girls and women washing clothes in the rapid streams that criss-crossed this part of the realm. Daily life was lived with little regard for what the rich of this land were doing. If the call came to muster, the men would pick up what arms they had and join as was their duty. Until such a time occurred, they simply lived their lives. Argyle envied them their simpler, if harsher, reality.

Somerset's revelation cooled Argyle's blood. 'Albemarle is to blame?'

'It was he who spilled poison in the King's ears about your brother and mine alike. He was certain the King would reward him with the Lancaster estates for his information. As we all know, he did not. It was Albemarle who betrayed my brother – and now, it is he who betrays the King.' Somerset's face mirrored the disgust in his words. 'If he believes that Henry will reward him for his loyalty, he is mistaken.'

'And yet, he is here, roaming free. I take it you find him to be useful?'

'For now.' Somerset stood up in the stirrups and called out, 'I shall take Sir Argyle to my Lord Bolingbroke.' When the Duke turned an expression of loathing on Somerset, he gestured. 'You are needed for the counsel.'

Loathing turned to self-importance as greed bled into Albemarle's smile. 'Of course. How they make any decisions without me, I shall never know.'

Somerset watched him turn left and waited until he was out of earshot. Although the weather was brisk, the sun was out in force and Somerset's brow glistened. 'Even his horse's arse looks arrogant.'

Despite of the dire circumstances, Argyle snorted a laugh. 'Perhaps they are of the same stock.'

'You may tell the King that his uncle, the Duke of York, has had many qualms about the role he played.' Somerset dismounted and held open the outer flaps to Bolingbroke's tent. As ever, it appeared he preferred being among his troops rather than lounging in a castle though one was readily available. Somerset paused. 'Lord Edmund is still torn, just as he was when his older brothers were alive. He was ill-suited as regent in the King's absence, which he did state beforehand, only the King ignored him. York wishes to live a life of peace but has lived on the main in strife. He is an old man and cannot be condemned for his choices.' Shaking his head, he gestured. 'I have said my piece and you will hear no more of it. From here, you go on alone.'

Argyle ducked through the opening and relished in the respite from scorching sun. His garb stuck to his back but there was nothing to be done about that. Pushing through the second pair of tent flaps, he was met with a familiar sight.

'Sir Argyle.' Bolingbroke's voice held no surprise. 'My cousin sent you. In the end.'

'My Lord.'

Bolingbroke was alone in the tent, several braziers glowing and, for a moment, a dry, burning desert wind caressed Argyle's brow, dragged from the depths of memory's deep well. 'I come bearing the King's command.'

'And what does my cousin want?'

'He is prepared to meet with you, my Lord.' Argyle watched Bolingbroke put down his quill. It seemed a great labour. 'But he will not bring your son.'

'Ah.' Bolingbroke folded his hands. 'It is as I feared. Harry is a prisoner.'

'No, my Lord, he is quite free,' Argyle lied.

'What does Richard propose?'

'A meeting alone. Just you and his Majesty.'

Bolingbroke stroked his beard. 'He truly believes that I will agree to such an arrangement?'

'He is willing to come without a guard. It is no more than you offered. He is accepting your proposal.' He was well aware what danger the King was placing himself in and yet, there was nothing else to be done. 'It is his understanding that you are to discuss terms.'

Bolingbroke rose and leaned on his desk. 'Terms for me or him?'

'For peace, my Lord, is that not what you both seek?'

'And what do you think, Sire?' Bolingbroke wore a grim expression. 'Do you think there can be peace between us? Do you believe my cousin will bestow upon me my rightful inheritance and accept that I have broken exile and retuned? Will he let me stay?'

'No, my Lord.' Argyle earned a curt nod. 'You and I both know that if the King decides to award Lancaster lands to anyone it will be to your son. Though I would not count on it, and nor do you. If Master Harry is lucky, he will be able to persuade the King to let you return to exile. If not…'

'I am for the Tower.' Bolingbroke shrugged. 'No, I see in your eyes that the King has other plans for me. The hangman's noose then, to be treated as a common criminal? It matters not. I accepted my fate the moment I decided to set foot on the ship that carried me back to England. I have since discovered that the lords of the land hanker for a different kind of solution.'

It was as Argyle had thought since the boy, Felix, nearly had his throat slit before he could deliver his dark message. Bolingbroke was here for a crown. 'You would break your father's promise to the King?'

Once more, he stroked his pointed beard. 'My father declared his loyalty to England. He promised only that I would support the rightful heir. You know of my grandfather's will. If the King neglects to father a male heir, the reign of England shall revert to Lancaster.'

'You had this planned all along, you and your father.' Acceptance slid along Argyle's words. 'Well played.'

'I am merely seeking to fulfil my grandfather's wishes.'

Bolingbroke sighed and moved to stoke the brazier closest to him. The late summer heat could not penetrate the thick canvas. 'Until the Queen comes of age and the King can father a son by her, he is in want of an heir.'

'He has chosen the Lord of the Marches, as you well know.' As ever when Argyle was in the presence of any courtier he was playing their game, trying to decipher why all of these empty words were necessary.

'A child.'

'The King is in his prime, the Queen will come of age. If you came for a crown, you come in vain. There are many years for them to produce an heir. Breaking exile seems reckless and excessive, would you not agree, my Lord?' Argyle sought another avenue without waiting for a reply. 'If the King should decide to be generous and bestow the Lancaster inheritance upon your son, then surely…'

'Surely I should be content? This is what you propose; this is the King's grand offer?' Bolingbroke held his hands over the glowing embers. 'Let me assure you that had Richard made any such declaration I should indeed be content. Only now that I am returned, the veil of court torn asunder by my year in exile, I see for myself what kind of a King rules England. I see the misery and dejection and I hear the rumblings around the land. Tell me true, Sir Argyle, would Richard survive another revolt?'

'Another revolt, my Lord?' Dejection prickled Argyle's neck. The King had survived the peasants rising against his council when he was just twelve years old, back then he was a golden-haired boy, beloved by the people. Time had since washed away his charm.

As soon as Bolingbroke clapped eyes on the King, he would know how unfit he was to rule and it would be all too easy for the Lords of England to choose another heir.

Not a child, as Edmund Mortimer the little Earl of March, but a man grown, skilful and politically adept. A man mentioned in a will penned by one of the greatest kings of all time, Bolingbroke's own grandfather. Against such odds, the King would be helpless.

'Richard stopped one once. It cost my father his London home, The Savoy, although it saved the land.' Bolingbroke scratched his neck. 'If only my cousin had not decided to administer some harsh justice, as his father once did – I believe your master was present at Limoges?'

'La Fontaine never spoke of it.' Argyle had once asked about it at a feast and gotten nothing in return but a searing glare.

'My father mentioned Limoges once. That was enough for me. In the end, witnessing that such cruelty had supplanted from father to son was what drove him to leave our shores after the fiasco in Scotland, so many years ago. You were there, I believe. You know how close we came to outright war. Would Richard have survived if the Scots rose up in earnest?'

In the stark interior of Bolingbroke's massive tent, the painted poles that held up the canopy were a splash of jarring colour. The rest of the furnishings were simple and dark from wear. Bolingbroke mimicked the gloom as he eyed Argyle. 'What the King did after the peasants' revolt has never been forgotten. He believes himself safe, but no man wearing a crown is ever safe. The people who farm the land are not blind to Richard's faults, to his spending, his taxes. How they hate taxes.'

'He has a kingdom to manage. How might you do things?' Unease stole into his question, rendering it poison.

'What I might do remains, for the time being, unimportant. Richard has forgotten how to be a king. That is all that matters.' Bolingbroke stepped close. 'Search your heart and tell me that you do not believe the people might once more rise against him. And win.'

'You would induce revolt?'

'If he sends me away a second time, it will come on its own. For the love of God, Sire, even my own uncle York supports my claim.' Bolingbroke's usual calm vanished for a moment. 'England needs a King who understands the needs of the people, who can balance the factions at court and ensure that the land prospers. England needs a King who will give it new purpose.'

Argyle considered his words. 'A King who will revive the war on France.'

'I am no fool.' Bolingbroke snapped. 'I have been a guest at the French court and I shall not revive any war with France. There are other enemies about, Sir Argyle, the Scots and the Welsh. You are recently returned from Ireland and know that they too are up in arms. I come here in such force not only to impress upon my cousin the import of his setting England before himself, but because I know what the Welsh are capable of. To hide here is clever on Richard's part, if not foolhardy. The Welsh hold no love for us.' Bolingbroke paused. 'On one point, we do agree, my cousin and I. We must broker a peace.'

Acknowledging the wisdom of his crass words sat as a band around Argyle's chest. 'Will you meet the King alone?'

'Yes,' Bolingbroke said. 'I task you to convey an offer in return. I suggest we both bring five men whom we would trust with our lives. Richard and I shall speak alone. The men will be present to witness what we agree upon. As a sign of good faith, he must come to me. We shall meet here, in Flint.'

'What happens if he agrees?'

Bolingbroke returned to his seat, his eyes once more trained upon the maps before him. 'In two days' time, I shall send Henry Percy to escort the King to Flint. Richard will fly a white banner from the top of the castle to prove to Percy that he is ready to accept my invitation. He must bring Harry, and as a token of good will, I shall hand over the King's brother and nephew once our talk is concluded.'

Eager to get underway without knowing whatever ploy Bolingbroke was sure to instigate, Argyle almost sighed a breath of relief. 'I shall deliver your message, my Lord.'

Rustling with his papers, Bolingbroke spoke to his inkwell. 'You will leave on the morrow. It is late in the afternoon and we can make accommodation for you and your men. We have unfinished business, you and I, and will speak again this evening at the castle. But for now, I must turn to other matters at hand.'

Pushing through the inner flaps, Argyle nearly trampled Albemarle and the rest of Bolingbroke's advisors. It was odd to see all these noblemen gathering around a traitor, ready to turn traitors themselves. While Argyle agreed that England was in need of an amenable King, he was much less certain that the process of gaining such a King would be simple. When Thomas Percy strutted by it took all of his self-restraint to keep from wiping the smug grin off his face. The whole Percy clan was despicable, but none more than the Earl of Worchester, and yet, if Bolingbroke was to succeed, he needed the Percy funds.

Outside the tent, Somerset and his black mare awaited Argyle's return, his horse's reins loose in Somerset's hand. 'Success, Sire?'

'Of sorts.' His thoughts ran dark. 'I have been invited to stay for the night.'

'My brother is kind to his guests.' Somerset led his horse

towards the castle road. 'To some of them, if he thinks them useful or perhaps even prepared to heed his advice.'

'He mentioned Surrey and Huntingdon.' Though the King had been specific that they be returned, Argyle hoped he knew better than to believe it might actually happen. 'Are they here?'

Somerset made a noncommittal gesture. 'Surrey is at Chester Castle enjoying the pleasures of some room or other. Huntingdon was taken for a ride to Holt Castle. I believe he was instrumental in ensuring that my brother now has money to pay his men.'

Though he should not be surprised, Argyle regretted that the King's treasure had been seized by the enemy. All he had left was the regalia, and in due course, Bolingbroke would pry those from him as well. What was done was done.

'What will he do to me? I too am here on the King's business as well.'

Smiling, Somerset draped his cloak over his arm and led the way towards Flint Castle. In the distance, the clang of steel and general din told Argyle that the men in Bolingbroke's camp were kept busy honing their skills.

'I am told that you have long since made a clever decision.' Something in Somerset's tone made Argyle wary. 'Your stay here will be the first of many occasions on which we may enjoy your company, Sire. I shall have my squire find quarters for you and your men. You have already met one of them I believe. Felix? He was sent to find you and deliver a message from the Duke of York. Though Lord Edmund is not here at the moment.'

'Felix is your servant? He told me he was in York's service,' Argyle said though it mattered little. 'I often wondered if the boy made it back safely.' He caught the glint in Somerset's eyes. 'He should not have come. We none of us should be here.'

'I envy not the messenger who was sent to see Salisbury, for that one never returned. Though even you must acknowledge that we all need to be here.' The castle came ever closer, revealing the watch on the walls, the snapping standards that flew from the towers. Somerset's boots scraped against the cobbles. 'Whether or not we want to. No matter what side we back, this is exactly where we should be. England is suffering and when the cousins meet we shall see who will be the one to mend her wounds.'

Argyle looked at the sloping hills spreading around Bolingbroke's camp. 'What does Lord Bolingbroke mean to do?'

'My brother likes to keep his own council. Not even the Duke of York knew exactly what was to come. He knew well enough that Henry did not come solely for his lands, as you must have guessed.' Somerset gave his reins to a squire with the Lancaster crest on his chest. 'Take Sir Argyle's horse too and make sure it is watered and fed. Stable it with mine and gather the horses of Sir Argyle's men. Same treatment for all of them.'

The squire led the black and brown destrier away and Argyle looked after them. Was he an honoured guest or was he a prisoner? He could not tell.

'Why does Lord Bolingbroke not keep his council in the castle?'

'He enjoys camp life as you well know and often speaks with great fondness of his pilgrimage to Jerusalem.' Somerset studied Argyle. 'Such adventures you have already had, and now, you are thrown together again. I must confess – as he never will – that when Felix returned with your avowal, my brother was quiet for a long time. I do not think he imagined that he might pry you from the King's side.'

'He had leverage.' This irked.

'Beauworth.'

'My children, and my wife.' Argyle wondered if the entire Lancaster line was only interested in material wealth, if they were incapable of feeling as he did that family was all that mattered. 'What is a man to do when his loved ones are in the hands of a traitor with an army?'

'You must know that my brother is not unreasonable. Henry would never let any harm come to your family,' Somerset said and gave a strange lingering smile. 'He is not a monster.'

I have seen your brother at his worst, and he is as much a monster as his cousin. They are brought up to be ruthless, and so they are, when it suits them, just as they are amiable when that will award them what they want, Argyle thought. They do not distinguish between the one and the other, they do not need to.

'If you ever tire of Beauworth,' Somerset continued. shall happily take it off your hands, Sire. It is a pleasant place though the master of arms is a prickly bastard, I hear.'

At the mention of Stephen, Argyle's dark mood brightened for a moment. He was still at Beauworth and the notion brought more consolation than any reassurances.

'He too knows Lord Bolingbroke.'

'So I gather.' Somerset crossed the courtyard and two soldiers opened a door. 'Sometimes, I think I missed out on something not going on the pilgrimage with my brothers. Though I did not stay idle while they were away.'

'You had your father to serve, no doubt.' The long ride was beginning to take its toll and Argyle wanted a little time to himself to prepare for whatever the feast might bring.

Felix appeared with two servants in tow. He looked in good health, no fear dancing in his gaze or cautioning his step. 'Sir Argyle, I have secured rooms for you and your men. This way.'

Somerset nodded. 'We will meet again tonight. I shall come for you when dinner is served, and afterwards, you will get some time alone with my brother. If he is so inclined.'

ꟸ ꟸ

CHAPTER 19

13 August 1399 – Flint, Wales

The great hall rang with voices, servants scuttling between the tables carrying pitchers, platters and bowls of water for the men to wash their hands. Argyle twirled his knife. He held a place of honour a few seats to the right of Bolingbroke, a Beaufort on either side for company. The dais stood empty. Bolingbroke had the good sense to be seen as a peer to his men, not as a Lord. In his mind, Argyle acknowledged the deft move.

'To think we are once more united,' Thomas Beaufort said, half a sausage skewered on his knife. 'It is almost as if we are young and bound for adventure again, is it not, Sire?'

Argyle stuffed a piece of bread in his mouth. Better not to say anything than to speak out of turn. He had been locked in his rooms until Somerset had come for him, and now, he was stuck between what increasingly felt as his jailors. Bolingbroke's half-brothers were good company if not for the sidelong glances and the whispers exchanged before they were seated.

The younger Beaufort took his silence as agreement and blundered on. 'John here envies us, you see, for he was forced to stay in our father's service and that was not nearly as interesting as what we lived through. I am certain you miss the warm desert wind, the exotic animals – and among many other creatures.' Humour sparkled in Thomas Beaufort's eyes and Argyle tried to return the smile, the bread turning to clay in his mouth.

Somerset set down his pewter cup. 'My brother loves to jest.'

Finally, the bread slid down and he could speak again. 'In this case, he is correct. I do miss the warm wind and the exotic creatures. For a while, Jerusalem was a place of peace and wonder for me.'

'Then something happened,' Beaufort chimed in and chased the sausage with a chunk of cabbage. 'Something very strange that made our brother cut short our stay.'

'Something of which he never speaks,' Somerset said with a trace of threat in his voice.

'Oh come now John, Sir Argyle was there.' Beaufort waved his knife and some cabbage flew from the tip. It tumbled down the table, making little greasy stains on its way. 'He and I share this…'

'We are not alone now, Tom,' Somerset hissed. 'What our brother does not even mention in private, certainly should not be enhanced by your stories when in public. No matter what the two of you share.'

Beaufort leaned in with an intimate smile. 'John here thinks we are constantly surrounded by enemies, that our halls are filled with traitors, thieves and turncoats.'

'There is wisdom in silence, my Lord.' Argyle pushed away his bowl.

'If you say so,' Beaufort looked disappointed only to light up. 'Is it true you are to go with Percy and secure the King's surrender?'

Although Argyle kept his eyes on Beaufort, he sensed Somerset tense up. 'If that be the case it is news to me.'

'I am certain that is what Henry wishes to speak with you about once the meal is at an end. He was best pleased that the King finally sent you to our camp. He had hoped it was you who came to Chester, for then we would not have had to come all this way. You would have made the King see reason and surrender much sooner, I have no doubt.' Beaufort paused to drink deep, wine beading at the corners of his lips. 'At least, the food and drink are plenty here. If you are in the mood, I can send a woman to your rooms? The King's worn castles make for dreary places and I hear tell that company is scarce.'

'That will not be necessary,' Argyle said with little effort to disguise that he was tiring of the company.

'Come now, Sire, I know the English wenches are not as fine as the women of Jerusalem, but they know what they are about...'

'Thomas.' Bolingbroke silenced Beaufort just by speaking his name. 'I shall claim Sir Argyle's company for myself now. Switch seats with him.'

Without another word, Beaufort stood, pulled back his chair and offered it to Argyle. Some things never changed, such as Thomas Beaufort's desire to please his older, royal half-brother. He was as much dependent on Bolingbroke as Surrey and Huntingdon were on the King. To be out of favour meant more than meals taken at the back of the room.

'Sir Argyle.' Bolingbroke's gesture was no invitation.

As soon as he took Beaufort's chair, Somerset moved up too and spoke through a smile. 'We keep Tom around for his easy manners, although with drink they may become a little rough.'

Before Argyle could reply, Bolingbroke spoke, his eyes fixed on the hall. 'It is time you joined our side.'

A single heartstring twanged. There was a little devotion left for the King after all it seemed. Reaching for his cup, Argyle said, 'Now?'

'I call on you to honour your pledge. It has been long enough in the making. You must have known that once you came here, the wheels would be set in motion.' Bolingbroke skewered a piece of meat and looked at the pink juices winding down the blade.

'What is your plan?'

'When you leave Percy will be hot on your heels.' Bolingbroke sipped his wine. 'It falls to you to ensure that he is successful. I mean to have my cousin here without delay. Look about, Sire, is it not obvious that the King can ill afford to decline my offer?'

The hall was crammed to the last seat with men eating, drinking and clearly thinking themselves on the winning side. Unlike the King's drab accommodation even at Conwy castle, Flint was equipped as a royal castle already, fires lit in every hearth, thick wall-hangings soaking up the cold from the solid walls. When Argyle had arrived it had not escaped his notice that workmen had been busy tending to the curtain wall. Allied with the Percy family, Bolingbroke had the money and the power to keep his men happy. The King had nothing but a skeleton crew at his disposal.

Argyle let a servant fill his cup. 'What happens if he refuses?'

'A siege is the last thing I need. Right now, the prospect of marching is enough to occupy my ever-growing army – and more men rally to my cause every hour,' Bolingbroke said, still with his eyes on the hall. 'Tell me true, Sire, would the King be able to withstand a long siege? Has he provision, water and food for the horses?'

'The horses would be turned into food within a fortnight.' Argyle cast a sidelong glance at Somerset who laughed without mirth at something his younger brother was saying. 'Still, the King has not nearly as many men to feed as you do, my Lord, and the forests, fields and barns have been picked clean by his men. The stores are brimming in Conwy.' A little lie to see how Bolingbroke might react.

'Is that so?' He raised his cup to Thomas Percy, the Earl of Worcester, with a sigh. 'He is a tiresome man.'

'Worthless.' Argyle suffered a glare from Worcester who was no doubt insulted that he was not sat next to Bolingbroke, whispering in his ear, invaluable to the conquering Lord. He turned his attention to his drink. The liquid shone silver in the receding light. He had not had a drop of wine for months and it was going straight to his head.

'I did not need him. However, I do need his brother and it seems they are a set,' Bolingbroke said. Next to Worcester sat a man of similar looks but his eyes were calculating and clear, where Worcester looked blank and self-important.

'Henry Percy will succeed in persuading the King to meet me, whether you choose to honour your pledge to me or not. Do you think I will take your words at face value? I know Richard struggles to keep his men as it is, every day new men arrive ready to join our cause if only we will feed them.'

Argyle leaned back and put his hands in his lap. 'I needed

to ascertain how much you know, my Lord. Would you have told me if I had asked?'

'You grow more like your brother every time I meet you.' Stroking his pointed beard, Bolingbroke watched two serving wenches trying to escape the groping hands of drunken captains. 'When you join my ranks I want you to keep my men in check. Rumours of your abilities have reached my ears and I like what I hear. They need discipline. So far, only I and my brother John seem put the fear in them.'

'I do not operate through fear. Your son will attest to that.'

For the first time that night, Bolingbroke fixed his eyes on Argyle for a moment, before his gaze slipped away. 'Fear is efficient. It is a lesson Harry must learn.'

'Fear is unnecessary.' For once, joy tickled from this game of saying much without revealing anything. Was this what Thomas had chased every second of every day? Some strange satisfaction in knowing that the opponent could not speak freely? 'I prefer to build loyalty through my actions.'

'Such as abandoning a losing cause?' Bolingbroke's knife scratched across the silver plate.

'You hold my family prisoner, no doubt you will admit that I had little choice in the matter.'

Bolingbroke laughed and half the table turned their gaze to him trying to assess if they should join in. 'There is always a choice.'

Argyle decided on a different approach. 'What is to become of your son, the King's ward?'

'He is no ward.' Bolingbroke sheathed his eating knife. 'As far as I can glean he is little more than a prisoner. I think you forget that many of *your* men have already joined my cause. They sleep in my camp, they eat my food, they take my pay. And they tell such interesting tales.'

'It changes nothing.' Argyle swallowed disappointment. He had hoped they would make for Beauworth not come here ready to serve. 'Before, your son was a favourite. If he is a prisoner it is because of your return. His safety relies solely on the King's regard which dwindles by the day. Had you not come, Master Harry would be free and happy.'

Bolingbroke's icy silence dragged on and from down the table, Beaufort's voice reached Argyle's ear. Somerset put a hand over his brother's cup when the servant came to replenish it and Argyle tried to recall if Thomas had been as fond of drink in the past as he seemed to be now. Was the happy appearance just that, an appearance?

'Is he unharmed?' Bolingbroke's question was more a breath than actual words.

'He was when I left.' Argyle looked out over the many men crammed into the great hall of Flint castle. He could not find his own guard of four anywhere. 'His condition depends on your actions, my Lord.'

'As is true of you, Sire.' Bolingbroke put a hand on his arm. 'We all hold precious pieces in our hands.'

'I hold nothing.'

I will not play your games, he thought. I will be home and with my family, and if needs be, I will leave England with them forever.

Pushing back his chair, Bolingbroke nodded to the men at the table. Without a word, he gestured to Argyle to follow him. As a distraction, Somerset called for wine and began an animated conversation with Albemarle who Bolingbroke had ignored throughout the meal. It seemed that even if you turned your cloak for Bolingbroke's cause, you should not expect to be awarded special attention.

The side-doors opened and a gust of air whipped

through Argyle's hair, cooling his brow. August was slowly turning to September and though Wales was not nearly as warm as the south of England it was still in summer's grip. How he longed for Beauworth.

'Your family is safe, just as I promised, for I honour my promises,' Bolingbroke said bluntly leading the way down the corridor without a backwards glance. 'It is up to you whether they remain so.'

Argyle followed, sliding his eating knife under his belt and securing the knot with a tug. 'You have my word, my Lord, what more do you want?'

Bolingbroke opened a door to a dark room, lit only by a low-burning fire. 'I want you to bring me the King.'

A figure stepped into the firelight. 'I believe that, together, Sir Argyle and I can deliver what you desire, my Lord.'

CHAPTER 20

14 August 1399 – Flint

Argyle woke early, listening to the castle come to life. Outside, the watch changed, captains calling orders to their soldiers, servants' steps rang hard and quick, everyone filled with purpose. His door snickered open and he closed his eyes. Someone puttered about and a fire sprung to life, a splash informing him that his washbasin was being replenished. When the door closed, Argyle got up and washed his face in the cold water.

He was dressing when the knock fell. 'Sire?'

'Come.'

One of his own men entered, his hair in disarray. He had no doubt enjoyed a night on a dry straw mattress and was struggling to remember why he wanted to return to Conwy. 'My Lord Bolingbroke…'

'I will go to him shortly. Pack what little we have and be ready to leave within the hour.' The soldier's face fell and

Argyle forced a smile. 'Rouse the others and get to the hall, there will be time to eat before we leave. Go by the stables on your way and hurry the stable boys.'

With a look of gratitude, the soldier closed the door.

You have to treat them with equal measures of kindness and discipline, La Fontaine whispered in the recesses of Argyle's mind. Then they will love you and be loyal to you. Only fools rule through fear, true power lies in devotion.

Argyle wondered if La Fontaine ever distributed the same advice to the King and if that was why he had finally decided to rid himself of someone, he had once called friend, someone whose death he appeared to have mourned for years.

The longer he was away from the King the more Argyle wondered if, in fact, the King was a great actor with a tentative hold on the world at best. What state would he be in when Argyle returned to Conwy? Would the King even know who he was?

Fully dressed, he searched for his sword but in vain. There was little in the room beside a bed, a chest and a few trunks, pushed into a corner, a thick coat of dust on their lids. He would have to return for it once his business with Bolingbroke was completed. Though what was left to say after last night, Argyle did not know. In the outer chamber, he came across his guard of four two of whom reeked from drink, all of them beady-eyed and rumpled.

'Wash in my basin,' Argyle said and added, 'a half crown to the man who finds my sword and saves me having to search for myself.'

'Yes, Sire.'

At the other side of the chamber door, a servant was shuffling his feet and fingering his emblem, Bolingbroke's golden fleur-de-lis on blue, squared with gold lions on red.

Catching his gaze, the servant's hands dropped to his sides. 'My Lord Bolingbroke requests your…'

'No time to waste then,' Argyle cut across. 'I want to be on my way as soon as our fast is broken.'

Perplexed, the servant sped down the corridor, taking him through a few wide hallways that led them into the courtyard where his horse was being saddled. Clearly, Bolingbroke wanted him gone as much as he wanted to go. What remained was to hammer out the final details.

'My Lord is in his tent.'

What is it with Bolingbroke and his tent? Argyle wondered. Is it because he wants to be near his men or prove that he does not suffer from pretence as some of his fellow lords?

Somerset had hinted it was because his brother preferred camp-life though Argyle doubted that very much. He puzzled with the idea as the servant weaved his way towards Bolingbroke's pavilion, perched at the edge of the camp with the castle at its back. The peaked canvas roof reached for the sky, the entrance shaded by a canopy held up by carefully crafted and decorated posts, subdued and opulent all at once.

Just as Argyle pushed through the inner flaps, Bolingbroke rolled up a sheet of paper and handed it to a squire. 'Pass this on.'

The squire scrambled by, giving Argyle the briefest glance before he was gone.

'You summoned me, my Lord?'

Bolingbroke leaned back in his chair, the leather creaking a little. '*Am* I your Lord? Am I the only man you will serve from now on?'

Argyle schooled his expression. 'You are, my Lord. Apart from God.'

Bolingbroke roared a laugh, pure amusement dancing on his words. 'God? What talks we had about God, Sire, when you were first knighted and went on a pilgrimage you did not want to attend, seeking a murderer. I remember well enough that you only went to the Holy Sepulchre once on my expressed command. Since then, you sought solace in other temples.'

Argyle's neck burned but he kept quiet as Bolingbroke snapped shut his inkwell. 'I shall accept your pledge of allegiance – once you swear fealty to me on bended knee.'

'You have my word, which must suffice.'

'I shall have your sword too.' Bolingbroke pointed at his ornate psalter. 'Swear upon God's holy scripture and I will believe you.'

Argyle put his hands on the Bible; this part was easy enough. He had no quarrel with God nor any great faith in any such deity. There was much truth in Bolingbroke's jape. Just as it was true that, in Jerusalem, Argyle had sought other temples, with goddesses made from flesh and bone who took his offerings of desire and infatuation. If it helped appease Bolingbroke, Argyle was fully prepared to swear upon the severed head of a clergyman.

'My Lord Bolingbroke, I offer my sword, my fealty and my honour to your cause.'

Bolingbroke half-smiled. 'Very well, I accept your pledge. The day after you arrive at Conwy, Henry Percy shall reach the town. You will ensure he gets safe passage into the King's chambers, and that he – and he alone – speaks to Richard. If need be, you may remain, but only if you are instrumental in convincing my cousin that he must release my son and come to me.' Rubbing his eyes, Bolingbroke leaned forward. Amidst the splashes of colour, he was a dark stain. 'Percy will arrive at the castle with just five men. It is up to you to open the gates and take him to Richard. Go against this and you will discover what else I have prepared. One can never be too careful.'

'As you command, my Lord.' Argyle drew breath. Only a fool would send six men to retrieve a King and Bolingbroke was no fool.

'Northumberland is now your instrument, Sire. Use him well.' Bolingbroke shuffled his papers into neat stacks. 'Get Richard to surrender and make sure he is not up to any tricks. Whatever he may say once Northumberland leaves, send word to my forces.'

'The trap is set,' Argyle said every word acrid.

'I look to you to spring it.' Bolingbroke nodded to the tent opening his attention already elsewhere. 'John will see you off.'

Outside the tent Somerset once more waited, reins in hand. Unlike his men, Argyle would have to leave with an empty stomach. As he mounted his brown hunter it bared its teeth and flattened its ears.

'Your horse is a vicious creature.' Somerset threw the reins to Argyle. 'Where did you get it?'

'It was a gift from the King.'

Laughing, Somerset turned his own steed and made for the western edge of the camp. 'Now it makes sense. It is nothing like its master, I thought, but now I take that back. It is exactly as its master.'

'If you say so, my Lord.'

Weathering the change of tone, Somerset looked over his shoulder. 'Everything is settled with my brother?'

'If the King agrees, Northumberland shall escort him here.'

Flecks of copper broke the smooth brown of his hair as Somerset fell in beside Argyle. 'And if he does not?'

'There was no talk of it.'

Somerset scratched his cheek absentmindedly. 'All or nothing then.'

'Let us hope, my Lord, that we shall not meet on the field.'

'Oh, I have no desire to meet you in battle,' Somerset said by way of farewell. 'I have heard of the havoc you can wreak against an enemy. And yet, I feel no fear anymore.'

Argyle fell in before his armed guard and raised his hand to Somerset, a thought settling within. Then you are a fool.

CHAPTER 21

15 August 1399 – Conwy Castle

'Henry Percy.' The King spat his visitor's name. 'Why are you here? Where is your traitor brother?'

Northumberland glanced at Argyle who offered a neutral nod in return. Until the King was on his way to Flint the agreement with Bolingbroke was that the King must continue to believe that Argyle was his loyal subject.

'He is with your cousin, Majesty.' Northumberland ignored the King's sharp words. 'I am here to ensure you that Lord Bolingbroke has returned purely to claim his inheritance. He is certain that your Majesty did not mean for the Lancaster estate to revert to the Crown and that there has been some misunderstanding or other. He is keen to see the matter to a close and then he is prepared to return to his exile, as you have commanded.'

Although the King tried to take the measure of Northumberland, Argyle could tell he was confused. Only a few hours ago, the King had been coerced down from the crumbling battlement where he had been tottering along, talking to himself in Latin and gesticulating to some phantom or other.

Argyle had returned to tales of the King unravelling. One moment, he called for the guards to release Harry and the next, he dragged the boy to the cells himself sputtering and screaming from the top of his lungs that Harry was a traitor and must sail back to France at once.

The night Argyle had spent in Flint, the King had picked three soldiers at random and had them flogged in the courtyard while he forced the captains to call out the cracks of the whip. One soldier had died, the other two were dragged back into camp. Argyle's men had told him that the two soldiers who survived had disappeared along with their rescuers.

At this very moment, the King looked and sounded himself as he sat on his makeshift throne, drilling his fingers into the holes that had once harboured his gemstones. The ancient great hall stood raw and tomblike with no adornments but the blackened stone carvings and massive hearths. The assembled men were the only splashes of colour in this drab cave, the King radiating brighter than the rest though his clothes were worn and tattered.

His gaze pierced Northumberland's who stared at his feet. 'Do you take me for a fool, Percy?'

'No, Majesty.' Percy's neck grew redder by the word. 'I am merely a messenger.'

'Why has Henry not come himself if all he hopes to gain back is his inheritance?' The King's fingers dug and dug, his nails scraping against the wood, expanding the holes as if he was making room for bigger stones. 'A letter sent from France would have settled the matter. No need for him to break his exile and come to England. No need at all to raise an army or call to him *my* Lords. The plain fact is that Henry overreached and now, he is afraid to face me.'

Northumberland was clever enough not to keep quiet.

The King flicked away a sliver of wood, aiming at Percy. 'He never thought to write to me?'

He did and you threw the letters into the fire, Argyle thought maintaining his impassive expression. He was here at the grace of the King to bear witness to how Bolingbroke treated his cousin, but also to ensure Percy did not overstep the mark. It would serve everyone if the King would grant his cousin's request. In his current state, it was impossible to decipher what he might do.

'I believe he did, Majesty,' Northumberland said. 'When he did not hear back he worried that the letters had gone astray and that perhaps your Majesty was in the company of ill advice.'

'So, he came to rescue me?' The King's voice climbed an octave. Argyle hoped he would not unravel just yet. 'He came to ensure I was in good health and of sound mind?'

'I do not presume to understand what prompted Lord Bolingbroke to return…'

Wrong choice, Argyle thought only seconds before the King exploded. 'Then why the *Hell* are you here if you know nothing? Am I to treat with a nobody? You were all he could spare, is that it? Does he think he has won already? Does he take me for a fool?'

I wonder what Northumberland will do now, Argyle mused. It was like being at a new play. No one knew the outcome; everyone kept rooting for a new hero, a new villain.

'Please, your Majesty, know that not an hour passes that Lord Bolingbroke does not struggle with his conscience.' Ever the great actor, Northumberland fell to his knees.

'As he should.' The King glared at Northumberland's bent head. 'Tell him that he can take his troubled conscience and return to his exile. When I have word he has left I shall revert his inheritance to his son and extend my cousin's exile to the rest of his natural life. He will know it as a kindness if he is clever enough.'

Argyle was impressed by Northumberland's restraint who knew Bolingbroke would never accept such a fickle promise. Daring to look up, Percy stayed kneeling, folding his hands in plea. 'That would appease Lord Bolingbroke most mightily, Majesty. That only leaves one other request…'

'What more can he possibly want?' Leaning in, the King's ragged cloak fell forward revealing dirty clumps of ermine sown haphazardly onto the faded purple velvet. 'Safe passage?'

'He asks that justice be metered out to the five men who procured the death of your beloved uncle Woodstock.'

Taken aback, the King rose from his seat and began pacing before the kneeling nobleman. In the eyes of everyone present, Percy was a traitor to the crown, but how many had received messages such as Argyle? How many were secretly supporting Bolingbroke?

Every few steps, the King stopped and tugged at his hair before resuming his pacing. Argyle wished for him to control his slippery mind a few moments longer. Just long enough to send Northumberland from the room without irrefutable evidence that the King was in the grip of madness.

'Woodstock? Henry ought let the dead rest.'

'Perhaps you would consider, Majesty, riding with your cousin to hold a parliament in London? If the parliament agrees, Lord Bolingbroke will regain his title as Duke and will be named steward of England. By proxy,' Northumberland added in the face of blooming rage. 'I understand you have recently knighted Lord Monmouth. If you are willing he may be allowed to act in his father's place?'

'Harry?' The King fiddled with a lump of shedding ermine. 'Harry as steward? I suppose…'

Northumberland produced a box covered in red velvet, the colour a vibrant assault on the senses in the dusty gloom. 'I am prepared to swear upon these holy relics blessed by God's emissary on earth, the holy Pope himself, that Lord Bolingbroke will honour the terms of the letter I have surrendered to your Majesty's own hands.'

Greed conquered the King's expression. 'Blessed by the Pope?'

'Yes, your Majesty.' Northumberland slid the chest towards the King, wood scraping along bare stone flooring. 'A gift to prove fealty.'

Rather than grasping the box as Argyle could see he wanted to the King pushed it back into Percy's grasp with his foot. 'Swear.'

Northumberland placed one hand on the case and raised the other. Locking eyes with the King, he proceeded to swear that Bolingbroke's offer was made in earnest and with a pure heart, that he would agree to let his son rule as Duke of Lancaster and Hereford and steward of England in his place until Bolingbroke had served the remaining five years of his exile.

'At which time,' the King added, smacking his lips with pleasure. 'He shall return and submit himself to my rule and swear eternal fealty to me and my heir, that he shall never again to rise up against his anointed King – and he will never take another wife.'

If Northumberland was troubled by his conscience, he kept it well hidden. His hand still on the box, Northumberland repeated the King's words. Only when his oath was complete did he rise and hand the box to one of his men. The King ogled him and Percy smiled in apology. 'Once you meet with Lord Bolingbroke at Flint, Majesty, the shrine will be yours.'

Licking his lips, the King made no effort to hide his disappointment. 'So be it. I shall be pleased only when that shrine is safe in London, resting next to my regalia. Unchallenged and safe.'

The audience thus concluded, Salisbury who had been posted along with Argyle at the door opened it and led Northumberland from the King's chamber into the cold reception rooms just beyond.

'When does Lord Bolingbroke suggest this meeting take place?' Salisbury's tone was measured, his expression taut.

For the first time, Northumberland's glance brushed over Argyle's face before it settled on Salisbury. 'As soon as can be. Lord Bolingbroke is eager to get the matter resolved and resume his exile.'

'Would that he had never come,' Salisbury said. 'We may be on our way at dawn.'

Henry Percy straightened his belt. 'Very well.'

Watching Northumberland walk away, his men falling in behind him, Salisbury turned to Argyle. 'Why did you let that snake into the King's chambers? You know the state he is in…'

'His Majesty wished to see him.' Argyle closed the door behind them and they made for the King's rooms. 'Was I to refuse his orders?'

'He is ill.' Salisbury pushed Argyle aside just as the chamber doors opened. 'I shall speak to his Majesty – alone.'

The King looked up, a whisper of confusion in his smile. 'What is it, old friend?'

'A word alone, your Majesty?'

'We can speak freely here.' Gone was the simmering rage. In the privacy of his own quarters, the King appeared almost content. 'If you are worried about Sir Argyle we have settled our differences. I have decided it is not his fault that we lost the southern force after all. It is Percy's brother's fault.' His smile turned wolfish. 'Worcester.'

Salisbury knew better than to object and only offered an angry glare before approaching the King. Argyle trailed behind marvelling at how easily he could accuse and acquit a man for a crime he had never committed.

'Once I meet with Henry,' the King continued and hooked his hand around Salisbury's arm. 'I shall persuade him to take the southern route through Wales.'

'Is that wise, Majesty?' Salisbury was silenced when the King's fingers dug into his arm.

'I still have loyal subjects in this wretched part of my realm, never forget. When we go south certain Welshmen will rise, capture my wayward cousin and send him back into exile. Or whatever they deem appropriate.' The King's words crept out. 'Does he think me such a fool? It is he who is a fool, my dear John, for underestimating me. He always has and at last, it will be his downfall.'

He released Salisbury and walked to the window facing the forest. The shutters were thrown wide and hooked on old, rusting catches that bled dark red tears down the grey stone. Resting his hands on the sill he looked afield.

'Henry thinks he is so very clever, he believes I will be simple enough to grant him even more power. Did you hear Percy's promise? That Harry will act in Henry's place? Do they not know that Harry loves *me*? He will do as *I* command. That is why we must be vigilant, we must take measure.'

'Yes Majesty,' Salisbury's voice betrayed his doubt and the King spun to face him.

'I swear to you that whatever assurances I may give him, he shall surely be put to a bitter death for this outrage and the injury he has caused me. Have no doubt, my Lord, that no parliament will be held at Westminster on this matter.'

He crooked a finger at Salisbury. 'Come with me. I want to discuss certain matters before we leave.'

Argyle opened the door for them to pass and thought he saw a sliver of self-satisfaction on the nobleman's face.

He does not trust me nor should he, Argyle acknowledged in thought.

As soon as the door to the King's inner chamber closed, Argyle lost no time in making his way to the stables. He had a message to convey.

CHAPTER 22

18 August 1399 – Chester, England

'Sir Argyle.'

Bolingbroke was surrounded by dozens of noblemen, all in their finest garb, whereas he was dressed in plain clothes his only ornament the glittering crest on his chest. He wore no rings nor any chain around his neck and his head was bare.

'I rode all night, my Lord.' Throughout, he had lamented that it had come to this.

'And?'

'Your plan worked.'

A small smile curled Bolingbroke's lips for a moment. 'Good.'

'My lord Northumberland is taking the King to Flint.'

'Just as we planned.' Bolingbroke turned to his waiting followers. 'We shall take the coastal road to Flint. Prepare my forces to depart at noon.'

A jumbled choir of congratulations flooded the room and the waves of joy crashed around Argyle. He did not hear their words he only saw the King before him. A frightened child in a man's body, a bird with broken wings that did not understand it could not simply fly away.

The capture had been easy, Percy waiting where he said he would, surrounding the King and simply declaring that he was to escort his Majesty to Flint. Gone was the stealthy certainty that he could trick Bolingbroke into taking a path south. Not that it would have made any difference since there were no loyal Welshmen waiting to ambush Bolingbroke. There never had been.

'Sir Argyle.' Bolingbroke's voice penetrated Argyle's contemplations. 'It was done without bloodshed?'

'Yes, my Lord, the King surrendered at once.' That old gnawing feeling of disdain Argyle had harboured many years ago when he had first travelled with Bolingbroke resurfaced. 'You have won.'

'Have I?' Bolingbroke's question betrayed no emotion. 'I am no fool, Sire, as you well know. I may have the King and I can make my own terms, in that sense, yes, I have won. And then what? My uncle and the lords I just sent from the room have made up their minds. Collectively, they desire me to take the throne of England.'

'Was that not always the plan?' Argyle could not help himself.

Stroking his beard, Bolingbroke appeared strained. 'No. I wanted my inheritance that much is true. I sent many a letter to the King…'

'All of which he received,' Argyle said. 'And burned. As far as I could gather.'

'Ah yes, you were absent from the King's side for a while, Sire.' Bolingbroke gave one of his rare smiles. 'And why was that?'

'Celeste.'

'You would risk everything for that tart?'

Argyle swallowed acrid spit. 'That tart was your cousin.'

'Half-cousin.' Bolingbroke gestured as if caught in a web. 'You should know better than to be ensnared by a woman, Sire. You are too prone to chivalry and it leaves you volatile. How am I to know you may not one day turn your sword on me?'

You will never know, Argyle wanted to say. The way this was going, he would once more be in the Tower, Isobel alone with the children, a guard at her door loyal only to Bolingbroke. There was no oath he could swear that would rinse the stain of betrayal. It would cling to him until his last breath.

'Know this, Sire, I shall never take my eyes off you.' Bolingbroke put on his cloak. 'I have learned my lesson. If only my cousin was not such a cretin he too would know of what you are capable. Fortunately, he realised his mistake too late. He should have let you stay in the Tower. I would have.'

'And yet, here I am.'

Smoothing the trim of his plain, black cloak, Bolingbroke looked up at Argyle. 'Yes, here you are. And now, you can come with me to witness what happens when a King refuses to listen to reason.'

The sounds of a vast army gathering, drums banging and trumpets sounded through the open door. Bolingbroke was going in force, bringing a hammer to the King's already brittle dreams and once and for all smash any doubt of the outcome.

In the courtyard, Argyle took the reins of a new horse, the ride through the night had worn out his hunter. He had left it foaming at the mouth when he entered Chester at dawn a sleepy stableboy taking it to the paddock behind the castle. By now, it would be fed and watered whereas he would go to the King hungry, tired and surrounded by enemies.

Overhead, Bolingbroke's pennant fluttered in the breeze, unfurling in a shimmer of blue, gold and red as it emerged from the gatehouse and disappeared into the light beyond the stone.

Argyle turned the beautiful, white horse and fell in. Soon, the King would know everything.

ꙮ ꙮ

CHAPTER 23

18 August 1399 – Flint, Wales

'The King refuses to eat, my Lord.' Henry Percy, the Earl of Northumberland, wrung his hands. He appeared to have slept but little, his skin sallow and his eyes beady. 'He has taken no food since he came into our custody.'

Bolingbroke was still in his saddle, his train of noblemen, knights and soldiers trailing behind him as a long, lethal tail.

Befitting, Argyle thought, here in Wales, the land of dragons.

'Sir Argyle.' Bolingbroke snapped his fingers and old rage rattled through Argyle. He cantered up to the castle gates.

'My Lord?'

'Go with Percy and see if your presence can persuade the King to take some sustenance.' Bolingbroke lowered his voice. 'I will not be remembered as the man who dragged a starving King from his prison and forced him to sign his surrender. You will ensure Richard is fed before I see him.'

Northumberland stepped aside as Argyle made to dismount and Bolingbroke caught his arm. 'You will ride in. Let the King see you.'

Without answer, Argyle spurred on the white stallion and rode through the gates into the courtyard. In one of the top windows, he caught a glimpse of the King staring into the distance. Drums, trumpets and cheers echoed around the enclosure and Argyle's heart sank as he dismounted.

'This way, Sire.' Northumberland led the way into the darkness.

Flint castle was cold and unwelcoming. Even though the King had only spent one night in this place, and yet, it seemed uncommonly cruel. He tried to take heart that since their return to Wales, the King had tasted a similar reality in the many forlorn castles he had scurried between trying to find sanctuary. Another ought not break what little spirit he had left and yet the fact that he refused food drove fear into Argyle's heart.

'I will eat with my fellow prisoners,' the King's voice travelled through the door to his chambers, high-pitched and wavering. 'Bring them here and we shall share a meal.'

Northumberland paused outside the door, a hand resting on the boards. 'He has used me as a taster since we took him, and since Rhuddlan, he has flatly refused to take even the food that I taste before him.'

'Can you blame him?'

Percy looked ready to snap. 'Can you make him eat?'

Argyle rubbed his eyes. 'No one can make a King do anything as you are living proof. Perhaps, if you let him eat with the other prisoners, with those he still counts as friends, he may take food.'

Snapping his fingers, Northumberland called over his shoulder, 'Fetch the Lords. Bring them here.'

A soldier disappeared down the hall and Percy pushed open the door. 'See here, Majesty, who I have found to keep you company.'

Forcing away the shiver Northumberland's words sent through him, Argyle stepped into the bare room. The King was seated at a long leaning table, plates of food perched at the end that seemed the most stable. A bowl sat before him, a trencher soaking up the steam. Argyle noticed that all the food had been cut up leaving no need for a knife to take this meal. Percy might be at his wits end, but he was cautious.

'Majesty.' Argyle wondered if this was perhaps the last time he knelt in the King's presence.

'What?' The King's gaze was slow to wander from the table to his kneeling form. 'Sir Argyle. I believe there has been some grave mistake. Percy has taken my acceptance of his pledge to be a hoax and he has brought me here without my cousin's knowledge.'

'I am sorry, Majesty,' Argyle said to stop the King. 'Lord Bolingbroke has come. He insists that you eat before you meet him.'

The King blinked. 'Henry is here? He knows?'

Behind him, Northumberland's boots creaked. 'Yes. He knows, Majesty, as I have…'

'Quiet!' The King's wide-eyed gaze lent him a strange childish air which was at odds with his commanding tone. 'You stay quiet. You are trying to poison me. You have taken something so that the food will not affect you, but I am greatly affected. Sir Argyle, do you think my cousin means for me to die? I shall not. I shall not eat.'

The doors opened once more announcing that the King's depleted council was approaching. Argyle rose and said, 'Majesty, I do not believe that Lord Percy, nor anyone else intends for you to die. And see here, your Lords are come to keep you company for your meal.'

Salisbury walked past Argyle disdain plain on his unshaven face. 'You are here?'

'My Lord.' He did not know what to say. He had warned Salisbury of his own decision, but words were worthless until they turned into reality.

'Salisbury, my dear friend, come sit here by me. Taste this food. It looks fresh but I am not sure…' The King's voice trailed off and his gaze wandered.

Once seated around the table the noblemen passed around bowls and platters. They ate what food was served, but the King's bowl remained untouched.

Northumberland whispered in Argyle's ear, 'Make him eat.'

'He is a man grown, anointed and untouchable,' he retorted, his words dropping as icicles. 'I cannot make him do anything.'

'Lord Bolingbroke…' Northumberland lost his nerve when Argyle shot him a piercing glare.

Still, he knew that he had to try, because beyond the castle walls lurked a dragon who would not suffer failure. 'Majesty, will you not take a little bread? You must preserve your strength as you are about to negotiate with your cousin. Build your stamina for the words you must exchange.'

The King turned a hazy gaze upon Argyle. 'Will I have to stay here long? It is so very uncomfortable. I should be kept in better chambers. A fire lit in every room. Truly, Sire, where are all my servants, do they not see that their King is in need of their care?'

'Soon, you shall be on your way to London,' Argyle promised and the King straightened a little. 'You need sustenance for the impending journey. Please eat, Majesty.'

'Yes,' Salisbury echoed, coddling the King in kind words. 'You must be strong for the journey ahead. We all must.'

Still, the King did not move. He took in the other prisoners eating and drinking in silence while his hands remained folded in his lap and Northumberland made a quiet groan, urging Argyle to retreat to the far end of the room.

'We cannot linger here forever,' Percy whispered and looked out of a gaping window at Bolingbroke's dragon's tail of men curling around the gates. 'What should we do?'

Summoning some semblance of calm, Argyle said, 'Send word to Lord Bolingbroke that the King is not interested in eating. He wishes to speak to his cousin and learn what is to happen. We cannot touch the King or force food down his throat. He must eat at his own accord.'

'What does he think to achieve?' Northumberland's patience was spent. 'Does he think Bolingbroke will forego all his demands and rush to his side pleading that he must eat and offer to return to exile for nothing more than to watch the King stuff his face with partridge?'

'Are you telling me you would not fear poisoning if you were taken captive?' Argyle closed his eyes and spots danced in the dark. When he opened them again, Northumberland's muddy brown eyes were slits in his face. 'I make no accusations, my Lord, however, it is not hard to imagine why the King asked you to taste his food. And why he is afraid.'

With a reluctant half-grin, Henry Percy sighed. 'Yes.'

He turned. 'Tell my Lord that he is wanted in the castle.' Watching a soldier leave the room to convey the message, Northumberland's shoulders slumped a little. 'I wonder what will happen next?'

They did not have to wait long before footsteps and rattling announced the coming of Bolingbroke. His herald called for all the unimportant men to exit and Argyle heard a brief exchange in French take place outside the door. Then Bolingbroke entered and bowed low before the King.

'Cousin, I welcome you to my chambers,' the King said, acknowledging Bolingbroke's deference with a wary smile.

'Cousin, I am sorry to hear that you do not trust my men to treat you as you are entitled.' Bolingbroke approached the table. 'I can assure you that the food is quite safe to eat.'

'You have hardly come here merely to reassure me that the food can be eaten.' The King made a sweeping gesture. 'As you see, my Lords have filled their bellies and are still fine. I have no such concerns.'

Acknowledging the King's words, Bolingbroke took a seat. 'I have come to lay before you the report from your people that you have governed them very badly and rigorously and that they are not content. If it pleases you, cousin, I shall help you govern them better than they have been used to for these past twenty years.'

Argyle watched the King's face as feelings ran across it faster than it could change to accommodate them. He was distraught, he was suspicious, he was enraged and desperate all at once. When Bolingbroke finished his, no doubt, carefully rehearsed speech, the King leaned back.

'Since it pleases *you*, cousin, it shall please me.'

Next to Argyle, Northumberland's breath caught. Could it really be this easy to take a King and mould him in new image, Argyle wondered. Could all this have been achieved with much less force? He had to wonder what the King was secretly planning, for it was not in his nature to accept the charge of others.

Bolingbroke looked to be deciding something, his eyes brushing over the lords assembled in the room before his gaze came to rest on the bishop of Carlisle. 'Bishop Merke, we have had our differences, but please believe me I mean no harm to come to England and her people. Rest assured that only necessary measures will be administered and that no one without fault will be punished, and that those punished will not be so beyond their crimes.'

From the bishop, Bolingbroke worked his way around the table addressing each of the men there. His words brought tears to some and haughty airs to others. Argyle felt the shift of mood in the room and exchanged a glance with Henry Percy.

'Sir Bastian,' Bolingbroke said when he reached Salisbury who sat by the King's right hand, his face white with anger. 'Please convey my message to the Earl.'

Sir Bastian, one of the oldest knights in Bolingbroke's keep stepped forward and cleared his throat. 'My Lord Salisbury, do not expect to be spoken to any more than you did speak to my Lord, Henry of Bolingbroke, during his stay in Paris. Know that my Lord Bolingbroke will spare no words for you, no solace and no assistance for you gave him none. You will be treated as he was by you.'

Salisbury's face remained white, unbridled fear dancing in his eyes. Argyle knew not what had passed since Bolingbroke was determined to debase the Earl in such a fashion. Knowing Bolingbroke, the cause was most likely just, but Argyle could tell from the King's expression that he too was puzzled.

Rising from his seat, Bolingbroke bowed once more to the King and then walked out of the room silence trailing in his wake. For a beat, no one moved, no one breathed.

'What now?' the King asked no one in particular.

Northumberland stepped forward and nodded for his soldiers to take the Lords back to their rooms. 'We ride for Chester, Majesty.'

'Oh,' the King said with some regret. 'Anne will be disappointed.'

CHAPTER 24

1 September 1399 – London

'Smile, Sir Argyle. You must play your part.'

Henry Percy, the Earl of Northumberland, waved at the nearest flock of Londoner's who cheered in return. In the distance, vicious hissing filtered through the happy greetings strewn before Bolingbroke's horse.

'God bless Henry of Lancaster,' the people shouted outside Aldgate. Even the thick defensive walls were not able to silence the cheering crowd all of whom had dressed the town in Lancastrian red, the women wearing red roses in their hair and on their dresses. All the banners were red, some lined with a deep green. Every guild must have worked day and night to ensure each was as opulent as the next in their welcome of England's saviour.

'Long live the good Duke of Lancaster.'

Bolingbroke raised his hands to the blessings and turned his face to the sky, completing the pious impression. His reception in London was even more impressive than his send-off had been in Dover. The English people loved him. They turned out for him and proved that he was right to return. Already minstrels were strumming their lutes and composing songs in his honour.

'We are victorious.' Thomas Percy, the Earl of Worcester, dressed in gaudy yellow trimmed with deep blue, rode next to his brother, Northumberland.

Behind them his son, Sir Harry "Hotspur" smiled at a group of young women who blew kisses and blushed. Of an age with Argyle, Hotspur had been knighted along with the King and Bolingbroke during the reign of King Edward, though any allegiance with the King had been washed away by Hotspur's newfound fame. On his broad chest, he sported his father's crest, a blue rampant lion on a field of gold. When he caught Argyle's eye, his smile turned into a self-satisfied smirk.

'You wonder about the King.' Northumberland grew sombre. 'I understand. You were with him for so long. Did you watch him unravel in Wales?'

'Vicious gossip.' Argyle forced himself to smile and the young women forgot all about Hotspur.

'You are very popular,' he commented from behind, a hint of bitterness in his voice.

Northumberland laughed. 'Beware, son, for our new friend here has something we all want for: a golden crown already on his head and a white stallion between his legs.'

Worcester howled with laughter and Hotspur joined in although his performance was less convincing.

The throng of people lining the streets forced them to continue two abreast and Argyle found himself riding next to Hotspur, behind the Percy brothers whose splendour was surpassed only by Thomas Beaufort and his brother

John, the Earl of Somerset, who had pride of place behind Bolingbroke's lone figure.

'Is there any truth to the gossip? We heard such conflicting rumours that we could not make head or tail of any of them.' Hotspur patted his horse and adjusted the gilded bridle. 'Did the King unravel?'

'It is as you say, rumours and gossip and nothing more.' Even now, Argyle could not bring himself to cast further shame upon the King.

'I would not hold it against him,' Hotspur said and bent to accept a red rose from the crooked hand of an old woman. 'Running from the ever-growing army Lord Bolingbroke amassed, seeing your own army flee in the night… It would drive any man mad.'

'Until I betrayed him,' Argyle said suffered Hotspur's intent attention. 'Before then, he feared no enemy. He had no cause to.'

'When you switched sides…' Disbelief lingered on Hotspur's comment. 'I have heard tell of your victory in Kells. Lord Monmouth sings your praises to all who will listen. Including his father.'

Argyle felt hands brush against his boot and tightened his grip on the reins. 'It was luck. The Irish underestimated us.'

'A force of three thousand to defeat twice the number.'

'Well trained soldiers against farmers and new recruits.' Toning it down was somehow paramount. 'We had archers. They made short process of most of the enemy. You have seen plenty of battles yourself, Sire, you know how it is.'

Sniffing the rose, Hotspur smiled, his face open and handsome. 'Yes. I have been blessed with much to do by way of Lord Gaunt. I can only hope that his son will continue to find use of me. This is all good and well, and I admit, I enjoy the adoration.' Sir Harry looked about. 'Although I am no use in counsel.'

Argyle forced himself to relax. 'A soldier not a courtier?'

Surprise crept into Hotspur's light brown eyes. 'That would be the measure of it.'

'I know how you feel.' Argyle ducked under a tavern sign and a burst of rosebuds and petals fell into his hair. 'Let me offer some advice, Sire. Now that you are close to Lord Bolingbroke you may have to train your courtier gallantry as you train your arm for battle.'

'You know what he intends?' Hotspur's voice dropped. 'You have heard tell?'

Argyle brushed red petals out of his hair. 'Nothing has slipped from my Lord Bolingbroke's tight lips.' He enjoyed the sight of Hotspur's cheeks burning. 'I am no fool, though many enough think so, and neither are you. The King is heading for the Tower as we speak. Do you think anyone will put him back on his throne?'

'Lord Bolingbroke will insist…'

When Hotspur did not continue, Argyle smiled at him. 'Yes, because he must. And then the noblemen of England will rise as one and demand that Bolingbroke claim the Crown. How can he refuse such a call?'

In front of them, St Paul's Cathedral stretched its white walls to the heavens. The crowd opened up and Bolingbroke's procession fanned out. Hotspur turned to follow his father, leaving Argyle's question hanging in the air.

'I must say, Sir Argyle,' Worcester said as Argyle's horse came to a halt next to his. 'I am pleased you came to your senses and changed sides in time. We were concerned you might play your own game.'

'Is that so, my Lord?'

Worcester turned an earnest expression to Argyle. 'Of course. I witnessed your victory in Ireland, I know how your men love you. Not one came to our camp without regret in his step and in his words. None of them wanted to leave you, all of them were pleased when you returned to them.'

'They should have let their regret govern them and obeyed my command,' he said. 'Perhaps we would not be here today.'

'Do you think Lord Bolingbroke would have received you if you did not bring one of the best trained contingents in all of England?' Worcester muttered. 'Your name might hold some small import, but your biggest asset was your men, equal only to your relationship with the King. Had you chosen to go back on your words much might have unfolded quite differently.'

'I came because Lord Bolingbroke dangled my family's lives before my eyes.' Argyle struggled to keep up an indifferent expression. 'If he had not, I would have died for the King.'

Before the cathedral steps, Bolingbroke dismounted, his silver and gold armour glistening in the sun. Worcester's horse lowered its head. The promise of autumn might enrich the air but summer held London in its grip still.

'Sometimes, I wonder why Lord Bolingbroke insists that you are clever,' Worcester said and swung from his saddle with little grace. Here was a man in dire need of a mounting block. 'To me, you rarely display any real understanding of the world we live in.'

Argyle dismounted with ease. 'Then you need fear nothing from me.'

The crowd grew quiet as Bolingbroke scaled the steps and the cathedral doors swung open to receive him.

Worcester and Argyle watched the Duke of York and his son, Albemarle, enter the cathedral in Bolingbroke's wake. United with what family he had left, he looked for once at ease, free in a way Argyle had never before witnessed.

'I know. Just as I know that I am free, but are you, Sire? Or are you chained to the next man who wears the crown?' Worcester sneered and walked ahead to join the long line of noblemen, churchmen, knights, ladies and high-ranking merchants waiting to enter the church.

When Argyle finally felt the cool embrace of the high-vaulted church, Bolingbroke was kneeling alone before the altar, deep in prayer. Rays of sunlight played on his armour setting silver and gold ablaze in the bright church-room, a jewel glistening at God's feet.

Hotspur pushed his way to Argyle and jerked his head towards the altar. 'See there?'

Argyle only had to turn his head to see what Hotspur was drawing attention to. A few paces from Bolingbroke, his Beaufort half-brothers knelt in unison, their heads tilted towards the stained-glass window above the altar. With their backs turned, Argyle almost believed they were as deep in prayer as Bolingbroke himself although they had never expressed much interest in divine matters.

To their left stood a massive stone tomb flanked by a lance and shield bearing the royal coat of arms. John of Gaunt's tomb. Bolingbroke rose and turned to it. For a moment, his face a study of serenity then it crumbled, his whole body shook and he fell weeping to the floor, his hands clutching the base of his father's final resting place.

If this is theatre, Argyle thought, then he is the finest actor there ever was.

CHAPTER 25

3 September 1399 – The Tower

'They called me a wicked bastard.' The King's eyes swam with tears threatening to flood his face. 'They called me "little bastard". How dare they? Do they not know who I am? Who my father was? My mother? My poor mother...' The King gave way and wailed. 'They tried to kill me. Me, their King!'

Disillusion and despair battled for space on the King's face and he pulled at his hair. He had been allowed a vast wardrobe, on Argyle's plea, and his rooms in the Tower were as comfortable as could be arranged, and yet, to the King this was the lowest he had ever been. He refused to bathe, refused to change his clothes, and so he sat in his chair of state in dirty hose and a tattered gown. The few remaining patches of ermine on his cloak were a murky grey-brown.

'Is it true?' The King turned greedy, wet eyes to Argyle. 'Did my cousin cry in the cathedral?'

Argyle fed the King's monster. 'Yes, he fell to his knees before his father's tomb and cried for all to see.'

'I would never act in such a disgraceful fashion in God's house.' The King's laugh came out soft and moist. 'Never.'

The late Lord Arundel might disagree. Argyle thought of Queen Anne's funeral and how the King had taken a stick to Arundel's face. 'No, Majesty.'

'Am I, Sir Argyle? Am I still your Majesty?'

'Tell me about the attempt on your life,' Argyle said to avoid the question.

In truth, no one knew if the King would be admitted back into Westminster castle or if he was finished. If Argyle was to hazard a guess Bolingbroke would never place a loathsome King on the throne again, the Lords of England would not abide it.

'Four men came at me, blades drawn. If not for the Mayor and his men, they would have slit my throat. I am certain they would.' The King's tears streaked his dirty cheeks. 'They meant to kill me, to kill an anointed King. What madness is coursing through my beloved city? What has happened while I was away?'

You gave the rule of England to a man who did not care for it, who wanted rid of it so bad that he gave it up on a promise, Argyle thought and shook his head. 'London is not what it used to be, Majesty.'

Before he had been allowed to visit the King, Hotspur had taken him aside, expressing concern about the King's condition. Although this was in some ways true, he was more himself in his London prison than he had been the past many weeks in his Welsh castles. His speech was clear, his mind lucid.

Now he stood and went to the window. 'No block.'

'No need, Majesty,' Argyle said though the King's words brought shivers down his spine. 'Lord Bolingbroke will be here to see you shortly.'

'Will he set me free?'

The dire subject was a sharp contrast to the gleam of plush furniture and carefully decorated walls. These were the very apartments in which the King had been held when Bolingbroke first rose to challenge his cousin. He had sworn it was never to happen again. How wrong he had been. Sometimes, Argyle wondered if this had been Gaunt's plan all along and he simply had not lived to see his son returned in glory. One thing he did not doubt, time was running out for the King.

'I cannot say, Majesty. As you might well imagine he does not share his plans and ideas with me, since he has little cause to trust me. Though I am here with his blessing he has given no indication of what is to happen in the time to come.' What was one more lie?

The King abandoned the subject and returned to his seat. 'What of my lovely Isabella? What has happened to her? Is she safe?'

At least today, you know whom your wife is. Argyle offered a consoling smile. 'Lord Bolingbroke has charged me with ensuring her safety, Majesty. She is to come to London.'

'Here?' the King whispered, his eyes big and dark. 'She is a child. She cannot come here, she will wilt, she is such a delicate flower, she cannot survive here. You must not send her here.'

'She is to stay with the Bishop of London. It is all arranged.'

'A pious man.' The King nodded his gaze lingering on

the locked door. 'Yes, he will keep her in good health, he will not harm her. It was a good decision, Sir Argyle, a very good decision. I am pleased she will not be sent here. When I am released I shall walk in the Windsor gardens with her and we will admire the peacocks I once gifted her and laugh at her little dogs.'

'She will like that, Majesty,' Argyle said.

She will not be allowed to bring her dogs, she will not be allowed to bring anything and you will never walk freely at Windsor together. Or Bolingbroke will be considered a fool and that he is not.

'For one thing I am grateful,' the King continued, scratching his neck. 'That my poor Anne is not here to witness my fall. I am fond of Isabella, but she is a child and knows little about the world. Anne would have insisted she come with me. She would never have left my side.'

At the mere mention of the King's first wife Argyle's concern increased and he tried to mask it. 'She was a fine woman, Majesty.'

'That she was…' The King went quiet, picking small pieces of fur from his cloak. 'Such a wonderful woman, so wise and elegant. She was my port in a storm. Why did she have to die?'

This was a dangerous road and Argyle decided to change the subject. 'Are you ready to meet your cousin, Majesty?'

The air soured. 'What do you mean, Sire?'

'He intends to meet you later today, Majesty. He sent a missive.' Argyle dared say no more. He did not want to ignite the King's temper nor did he want to push him over the edge of reason.

Shaking his head, the King looked down as if seeing himself for the first time. 'Then I must prepare. I must decide what to demand, for demands I shall make. I will make my case known to him and anyone with him. I demand that York and Albemarle be brought to trial. They are traitors to the Crown and deserve to be put to the sword.'

He paused and looked at Argyle, cunning glittering in his eyes. 'First, I must bathe and dress, for my cousin shall never outshine me in any way. He will know that he is in the presence of the one true King of England and he will grovel before my feet once I am done with him. Fetch me warm water.'

He turned to pass along the order. No amount of water would wash away the King's sins, but to see him once more full of purpose was compensation for the fear Argyle had harboured when he had entered the royal Tower chambers.

He could only hope and pray that the King did not sink into despair when he discovered how few options were open to him. Only one option to own the truth.

If he wanted to live, he had to give up his crown and pray that such an act was enough to save his life.

CHAPTER 26

16 April 1400 – Boulogne, France

'Where do you come from?' Marie's father gave Argyle a shrewd look. 'Maman says you cannot remember your own name. Perhaps you recall where you are from.'

Argyle was still adjusting to standing on his own and the swimming sensation in his head ebbed and flooded, broken pieces of last night's dream haunting the inner swell. Teetering before Marie's father Argyle knew better than to stall or concoct a story. Here was a man who would settle for nothing less than the truth. What remained was for Argyle to decide just how much to divulge.

He swallowed against the heaving feeling before he answered. 'Hampshire in England, my Lord.'

'Hm. And how did you come to be here?'

'I went to Calais to survey some horses I was considering buying.' Argyle tilted his hip to spare his injured leg. The calf was healing very slowly and somehow during his time in the water his old injury from Jerusalem had torn and the skin was reluctant to close.

'Did you strike a good deal?' Marie's father looked keen. 'I breed horses, the finest you will ever see. They are of Arabic descent.' His pleased smile bore witness to his pride. 'When you are better, perhaps you would care to see them?'

Argyle tried to smile back. 'It would be an honour …'

'Jean-Pierre de Reines. Lord de Reines to you.'

'Why are you tiring our guest?' Grand-Maman's angry question preceded her appearance. 'Jean. I told you…' The threat hung heavy in the air as she marched past her son and pushed a chair behind Argyle. 'Sit.'

Obeying, Argyle slumped while de Reines stood, his expression hard. 'Maman…'

'Non, Jean. You may be the Lord of our lands, but I will not allow that you neglect your duties as a host.' She never even glanced at her son, her sole focus was on Argyle. 'I apologise for my son's lack of civility. How are you?'

'Dizzy, my Lady.'

Grand-Maman turned on her heels. 'Jean, how can you let a wounded man in my care stand here? He has only just left the sick chamber.' Her seething glare made her son cringe. Though she was half his size and as bent as an old oak branch, she was formidable and clearly not used to being gainsaid. 'I must go and get more herbs from town. You will ensure that our guest is not worn out by your speeches of horses or your impertinent questioning.'

She left without waiting for a reply. Jean de Reines might be the lord of the manor, but against his mother, he had no say at all. Sighing, he rubbed his neck. 'She has a mind of her own. And the servants all love her.'

'My aunt was much the same,' Argyle offered. 'She cared for me and my sisters when my parents died. Some women it is best to simply obey.'

De Reines looked up. 'Strange that you would remember all that and not your name.'

'It comes and it goes.' Argyle bit his tongue. In the stifling room, it was easy to slip and trap himself.

'What are you doing out of bed?' Marie's voice demanded, echoing her grandmother's malcontent. 'Father, have you ordered him here?'

'Marie.'

She shook her long light brown hair, little bells jingling from the elaborate braids that held it back from her face. 'Grand-Maman said that I am to be in charge of the patient until he is well.'

Argyle thought he heard a note of pride and rebellion in her voice. 'I am much better, my Lady. And your father has been very kind.'

De Reines shuffled the papers on his desk. Although they were in his study, surrounded by missives and heavy, masculine furniture, two women had just put him in his place. 'Very well, if you think a grown man should spend his days in bed surrounded by women so be it.'

'He is not well.' Marie grabbed Argyle's arm and forced him to get up a little too quickly because the floor to disappear beneath his feet and he tilted to lean against her.

Outside the door, she winked. 'He is a good man, simply uneasy that he does not know who you are or why you are here. He is looking out for us.'

'You can hardly blame him.' Argyle closed his eyes to steady the world.

'Oh, I do not.' Marie's warm hand grabbed his arm. 'And I am a fool. I should not expect that you are well enough to storm out just because I am.'

Argyle cautiously opened his eyes as the hallway stopped

moving. 'Will this feeling – this shifting of the ground – ever stop?'

'Grand-Maman says it will, though she cannot say when. You suffered greatly in the sea and perhaps before…' Marie's voice trailed away and Argyle thought he saw distrust steal across her fine features.

'I do not remember how I came to be in the water. If something happened, it must have been in Calais.'

'Calais?' She stopped fidgeting with her sleeve. 'But that is miles and miles away.'

'How far?'

'Thirty miles if not more. Have you floated in the sea all the way from Calais? Surely you must have made some of the journey in a boat or on a ship. No one can survive in the sea for days.'

Argyle shrugged and was rewarded with a shooting pain in his neck. 'No. I remember going from England to Calais. To inspect some horses. Since then, nothing.'

Best to keep to the same lie. He had enough trouble remembering the bare essentials. Weaving a web of lies would only serve to get him caught before he was well enough to leave.

'Father breeds horses.' She gestured towards a window with a splendid view of vibrant green fields, spring bursting through the dark soil. 'Do you feel well enough to walk to your room?'

'I am imposing…'

She slapped his arm. 'Do not speak nonsense. You would be fish food by now had we not found you. We shall walk slowly. If Grand-Maman finds I have not cared for you properly, she will stop teaching me.'

'What is she teaching you?' Argyle let Marie guide him down the hallway, marvelling at how much she reminded him of his sister Joan. His many troubled dreams had restored his family to him and now, he yearned to be with them.

'She is a wise woman,' Marie said and turned into a small gallery, the walls covered with elaborate tapestries, aging wall-hangings and elegant paintings. Everywhere the eye rested offered a certain brand of subdued luxury. 'She has been helping people rid themselves of disease or mend injuries for as long as anyone can remember. She is a known as a great healer.'

A woman physician. I knew a young woman once in Jerusalem who aspired to be one too. Argyle was startled by the onslaught of fragmented memories that broke before they made sense. He could not even remember the girl's name, only that she had saved him from something and later paid a hefty price for her kindness.

Marie seemed to take his silence as a sign of fatigue and pushed him down onto a bench. 'Are you unwell?'

'Tired,' Argyle half-lied. 'Perhaps your father is right I have been in bed too long.'

'What does he know?' Marie's mischievous grin was infectious. 'I do love my father, but he knows little about healing and even less about having to stay in bed to get well.'

'Then I will take the advice of your grandmother and you.' After a few shallow breaths, he felt as if he might be able to resume walking. 'You say Calais is very far from here, might you tell me where I am?'

'Just outside Boulogne.' Marie offered a steadying arm.

That was why de Reines had given him a hard time when he had disclosed that he was from England. The city of Boulogne as well as the surrounding area had taken the brunt of some hard English reaping during the war of King Edward. Argyle remembered hearing the tales from both minstrels and tutors, all of them impressing that the King had merely done what needed doing to keep the French in check.

It was little wonder that the population felt more closely connected to the French throne than the English and Argyle knew that from now on he had to be careful. He was an undesirable houseguest in the home of someone who most likely wanted to see all Englishmen dead.

Marie chattered, her air slightly affected, until they reached Argyle's rooms and she excused herself, leaving him to the care of an elderly servant who grunted when his charge tripped and leaned heavily on his crooked shoulder.

Once perched on his bed, the servant left Argyle to his bleak musings. There was no doubt in his mind that the more he healed, the harder Jean de Reines would push for straight answers. How long before he decided that Argyle had lounged far too long upstairs and decided to throw him in a dungeon instead?

As his eyes slid closed, Argyle acknowledged that he had to get word back to England. He could not let matters slide as they once had.

CHAPTER 27

28 September 1399 – London

The light inside made the windows of the Tower glitter in the dark. Argyle shuddered at the memory of the damp cell he had once occupied, and could so easily return to if Bolingbroke took a shine to the idea.

The Queen was safe with the Bishop of London, and the King kept in state in the Tower. Although Bolingbroke held the commoners and most of the Londoners in the palm of his hand, Argyle never doubted that there were still plenty of able men who would rally to the King's rescue if they learned that he was a prisoner. And so, the imprisoned King would have to suffer a heavy guard outside his door and next to no visitors.

Argyle turned his horse towards Westminster, the summons from Bolingbroke weighing heavily upon him.

Behind him, two of Bolingbroke's men followed. Since their return to London, the permission to live in his own house he had enjoyed was not rescinded. Bolingbroke and his council feared that Argyle would be one of the able men willing to risk his life for the King, although Bolingbroke held all the trump cards. Beauworth was still under guard and so it would remain until Argyle had proven his loyalty beyond doubt.

The chill of autumn crept through London, sneaking from the riverside and up the streets to the heart of the city. Once they left behind the last estates along the Strand, the air curled its cold fists around Argyle's chest and squeezed tight. Ahead an orange glow on the grey sky revealed Westminster before the palace came into view. He had suggested taking a barge, but Bolingbroke's men had their orders. They were to go on horseback.

He had grown used to his white hunter much quicker than he had anticipated. The stallion was well trained and strong, it never tired and had a way of nuzzling his hand that was very reassuring. The irony of Bolingbroke's gift was not lost on him. A knight on a white horse, the legendary King Arthur returned from myth. Except that Argyle had betrayed his king and pushed England into unrest. If anything, he was Lancelot without the love affair.

'Who goes there?' The call came from the castle wall.

'Sir Argyle, on Lord Bolingbroke's business.'

The big gate opened and he cantered into a torch-lit courtyard, scullery maids and servants scuttling about. Before he reached the mounting block, a boy grabbed the reins, ready to lead his horse away to the stables. Lucky beast.

'Sir Argyle.' Harry waited with a servant carrying a torch.

'Lord Monmouth.'

Some of the warmth left Harry's eyes. 'I am no longer Master Harry to you?'

'If you wish to be I shall be proud to call you Master Harry,' Argyle said and watched the stable boy walk off with his horse, silver tail swishing in the twilight.

'Then that is my wish.' Harry took the torch from the servant. 'I shall take Sir Argyle to my father.'

They walked across the courtyard and through a vaulted gate into a small garden, iron links protecting the array of late blooming flowers from being trampled by busy feet.

'How is the King?'

Argyle looked at Harry's neck, the torch dancing before him. 'You have not visited?'

'He will not receive me.' When Harry stopped Argyle almost bumped into him. 'He calls me a foul creature. I think he hates me. He must think I am to blame for his capture.'

He placed the torch in an iron grate and sat on a low stone bench. Argyle breathed in the floral scent, for a seductive moment, he was back in Framlingham's safe haven. Then he went to sit by Harry.

'If he does it is because I have been a coward.' Argyle sighed. 'I have not told him that it was I who betrayed him, I who ensured that Northumberland would intercept him, I who told your father of the King's plan to travel south. You are not to blame, and those words must come from me.'

Harry drew a hand through his dark hair. 'My father had already laid plans of his own. You were a means to an end, nothing more.'

'Perhaps someday I shall believe you, Master Harry, for now, let me own the fault that is mine.'

The sweet scent of flowers hid unpleasant rot. London in September. Even here behind thick walls nothing can erase the stink of too many people crammed together in too little space.

'My father has his reasons. At least that is what I keep telling myself, for otherwise I shall never be able to forgive myself.' Harry's face had aged well past his thirteen years, as had his voice. 'I gather he has something of yours.'

'In a manner of speaking,' Argyle said. 'I must admit, Master Harry, I cannot criticise your father for his precautions. After all, we have known each other long and have rarely been on the same side. If he does see me as a means to an end, I understand.'

Harry kept staring into the increasing darkness. 'Should I feel the same? Should I forgive him for leaving me to whatever fate the King saw fit to bestow? If not for you I would have been flogged and left to rot in the stocks. That is what the King wanted, and only your presence stopped him.'

'His love for you…'

'Was it love? Is what I feel for my father love? Devotion? Or simply duty?' Harry's questions came out in dull punches. 'Does *he* love me?'

'Sometimes fathers have to make decisions that seem unreasonable, unfeeling even.' Argyle saw little Edmund's bright blue eyes in his mind, the child confused and petulant. 'Love is a strange thing, Master Harry, for it rests in the hands of others, and we are helpless in their grasp.'

Harry rubbed his eyes and stood. 'We should not linger here.'

'If you need anything…' Argyle did not know how to continue.

'Yes.' Harry picked up the torch and led the way through the maze that was the palace of Westminster. 'I know.'

The silent walk was as uncomfortable as the half-spoken words that hung between them. Argyle looked away as they passed the rooms that had once belonged to his brother, Thomas. The Mowbray crest still adorned the stone above the door. He wondered what state the rooms were in. Could Thomas come and go even now without anyone knowing? Or were the piles of paper weighted down by dust? No, most likely they were taken away or burned. For a fleeting moment, he sensed Thomas' eyes on his back but resisted the urge to turn. If he wanted to see a ghost he knew how to summon one.

Two guards stood watch by the door to Gaunt's apartments. Bolingbroke's now. They acknowledged Harry and pushed open the door for him. Argyle passed behind Harry, steeling himself against another wave of memories, but none came. The room was transformed. Where piles of paper, dark wooden furniture and closed shutters had always surrounded Gaunt, Bolingbroke had transformed his lodgings.

The wood was washed with lime, the shutters removed and the windows sparkling clean. The desk was the same, though the top had been sanded down and only a few neat stacks of paper were visible. Most of the tonic bottles, trinkets and other effects were gone and the tapestries looked to have been washed and mended.

'My Lord.' Argyle swept a bow.

'Sir Argyle.' Fatigue rode on Bolingbroke's voice. 'Harry.'

'Father.'

Something passed between father and son that Argyle only noticed because of the underlying hostility in Harry's greeting. He left as soon as Bolingbroke nodded assent.

'I went to the King today,' Bolingbroke said. Argyle kept quiet. 'To make terms. To ask him to resign his crown before parliament assembles.'

He turned from the fire, flames leaping in his eyes. 'As no doubt you can imagine he was less than accommodating though he never said as much. He asked merely to study our terms.'

Did he expect a reply? Advice? Bolingbroke could not possibly believe that Argyle would hold any sway with the King. He could not ask the impossible of him merely to prove what? Loyalty?

'I thought you might know he is safe and out of harm's way. Though that is not why I called you here.' Bolingbroke sat down. 'There is perhaps a handful of men at court whom I trust less than you. I need to know that you will be loyal to me.'

'I am, my Lord.' Argyle could not even muster a flicker of anger. At most, he felt dismay. 'Have I not already proven as much by delivering the King to you? And the Queen?'

'If you should attempt to free the King or even speak for him tomorrow know now that I have prepared cells for those who might oppose me.' Where Argyle failed to ignite his wrath, Bolingbroke succeeded. 'You can have the one in which Richard found you.'

The prospect of once more being in the Tower filled Argyle with an odd sense of calm, but he wanted to remain free. 'I go where you command, my Lord.'

'Will you continue to do so if I release Beauworth to you? If I call off my soldiers and let you re-join your family?'

His blunt words cut deep. 'How can I know if I can trust you, Sire, when I have seen how far you will go for the King? How can I believe that you no longer feel loyal to my cousin?'

'How can you know that the lords of England will stay loyal to you, my Lord?' Argyle asked before he could stop himself. 'The King spent the better part of five years doubting my loyalty and had no cause to until you lay a siege to my home and threatened my family. Had you not done so I would have fallen on your sword to save the King.'

Bolingbroke got up and leaned forward, resting his hands on the desk. 'Therein lies the problem, Sire. For I have no wish to lay siege to your home for the rest of your life. I need all my men where they do most good. Keeping watch over you and your family is hardly worth the effort. And yet…'

'I will sign whatever papers you wish, whatever commands, orders, terms you desire.' His patience slipped, rage and fear gnawed at his guts. 'Lay down my sword and never pick it up again. Give up training men for the Crown to use. Offer my life in return for the freedom of my wife and children. Whatever your terms, I shall accept.'

Picking up an ivory knife from his desk, Bolingbroke turned and stared out the window. 'Promises are easy to make. And you are right, how can I trust the lords of England? The difference between you and them is that they came to me out of free will. You came on a threat.'

'You issued that threat. You gave me no choice.'

'Very well then, I shall lay bare my terms. You will be present in the great hall two days from now. Until that time, you are to stay here in the palace in rooms prepared for you. You will not interfere with whatever transpires.'

Although almost a head shorter than Argyle, the fierce expression on Bolingbroke's face rendered him formidable. 'If you wish to remain free you shall heed any command I send, any order I issue. Or you will discover just how loyal my friends are. How willing they are to stretch even farther for me than you ever did for Richard. Until such a time as I see fit to trust you, *Sire*, you will be a breath away from the fate from which Richard saved you.'

The threat of the Tower would loom over his head until his dying day. It was fast becoming hollow whereas the idea of having to stay in Westminster palace tied a claustrophobic string around Argyle's neck.

'Yes, my Lord.'

'For twenty years, I have watched my cousin squander away his natural position and lay waste to a land I dearly love. I have seen him fail, time and again, to take sound advice. I have seen him send people to the gallows when he could have been benevolent. I have witnessed his erratic behaviour and strange affiliations to unsuitable upstarts. I have had enough. England has had enough, Sire.' Bolingbroke took a step back. 'So have you.'

'I am at your command, my Lord.' The words stuck in Argyle's throat and when he forced them out, they cut like glass. 'I once swore fealty to the Crown. La Fontaine warned me that with such an oath came great responsibility. I stand by my oath. I am loyal to the Crown.'

'The Crown…' Bolingbroke resumed his seat behind the desk. 'Not to the man wearing it.'

'Kings come and go, my Lord. The country must survive.'

In his customary fashion, Bolingbroke stroked his beard, new threads of white gleamed through it. 'Tonight, Sire, it appears we finally agree upon something. I pray that we can continue to do so.'

ꕥ ꕥ

CHAPTER 28

30 September 1399 – Westminster Palace, London

From the back of the great hall, Argyle had an excellent view of all the lords and commoners assembled. The atmosphere was one of excitement and joy. Argyle spied the Earl of Somerset shake hands with his brother, Thomas Beaufort, both of them no doubt expecting a reward for their loyalty. At the very front, Harry and his three younger brothers shimmered in their Lancaster colours, for once secure in their supremacy.

In Wales, Harry had asked Argyle what to do if he had to choose between family and loyalty, and he knew now that the love Harry felt was that of a child revering his father from afar. The love he felt for the King was much more present and tangible. This was a dire time for the boy and Argyle doubted he would ever truly forgive his father for his actions.

Harry turned his head and Argyle followed his gaze. At the very end of the hall stood the King's empty throne draped in cloth of gold. Argyle would have sworn that it had been taken down several steps for it looked nothing like the ominous throne upon which only months ago King Richard had sat in judgement of all who grovelled at his feet.

Vivid images of his own humiliation under the watchful eye of all the mighty men now assembled raced through Argyle's mind. Most clear was the memory of him kneeling before the King apologising for leaving England without permission to seek a happiness that was forever denied him. He also remembered Thomas kneeling next to him, a satisfied smile playing at the corner of his mouth. Now, even court gossip was silent on the topic of Thomas Mowbray.

Argyle's haunted visions subsided as the hall hushed. The archbishop of York, Richard le Scrope, stood before the crowd and unfolded a vast piece of parchment, his every move reverent.

Clearing his throat, he intoned. 'My Lords, fellow Englishmen, I, Richard King of England do freely and with love in my heart renounce my title and crown. It has been my great misfortune to be an inadequate ruler and, in the sight of God and men, I assert that I am worthy to be deposed.'

The Archbishop folded the document and sat down and Thomas Arundel, the former Archbishop of Canterbury, rose. 'My Lord Langley, Duke of York, do you accept?'

York, about to depose one nephew and place another on the throne of England, put his hand on his heart and spoke clearly. 'I do.'

'My Lord Arundel, Earl of Surrey, do you accept?'

'I do!'

Stone-faced Argyle watched as all the assembled Lords accepted the King's admission and renouncement. While his heart was hardened where the King was concerned, the enormity of what transpired left cracks in his resolve. His eyes strayed to Bolingbroke who stood at the end of the line of Lords with his back turned to the crowd. It was impossible to guess what might be going through his mind.

'My Lord Bolingbroke, do you accept?'

They omitted his title, Argyle thought as Bolingbroke turned to the assembly and mimicked the rest of the noblemen. 'I do.'

Promptly, Thomas Arundel turned to the commons his gaze commanding. 'I now ask the assembled Commons. Do you accept?'

With the voice of one, the answer rose to the vaulted timber ceiling. 'I do!'

Argyle had never seen the terms the King had been forced to accept, but the words read by the Archbishop were too foreign to ever have passed the King's lips or emerged from his quill. It mattered not for everyone in the hall from the greatest Lord to the lowest commoner were well pleased.

The assembly hushed once more as Bolingbroke rose from his seat. The Lancaster crest towered above his head when he turned to look at the Lords and commoners as if recording who was present and who was not.

'In the name of the Father, Son and Holy Ghost.' His voice rang through the room. 'I, Henry of Lancaster, do challenge this realm of England and the Crown with all its members, as I am descended by the right line of the blood and through that right that God of his grace has sent to me to recover it.'

With a flourish he pulled out the King's signet and Argyle's blood froze. Bolingbroke held the signet high and turned slowly affording every single man in the great hall to see for himself what he was holding. Last to cast his eyes on the signet was Thomas Arundel who offered up his hand.

Arundel led Bolingbroke to the steps before the throne and there, he knelt in silent prayer. All around, Argyle witnessed men with tears in their eyes look down at their folded hands most no doubt sending up prayers of their own for a realm of peace and prosperity. England had been mismanaged, he would not deny it, but this was a steep price to pay.

Argyle looked up at the Lords and noticed Salisbury staring at the floor his face as grey as the marble beneath his feet. He was not attending as a free man. The only reason he was present was that Bolingbroke needed the support of every last noble family. Salisbury lived under house arrest his fierce loyalty to the now dethroned King a noose around his neck.

When Bolingbroke finally roused, Arundel and le Scrope stepped up either side of him, took his arms and offered him the throne. Though Arundel was not yet reinstated as Archbishop of Canterbury, for all intents and purposes, two Archbishops had placed Bolingbroke on the throne rendering his action doubly blessed by God.

For a just a moment no one moved, and then the roar of the assembly washed over Argyle applause ringing in the great hall making the many flames flicker and dance. It boomed to the rafters and sang against the stone drowning in its own echo. The people had spoken a new King was crowned.

Thomas Arundel stepped forward and declared that for the benefit of England King Richard's shortcomings as ruler should be set down and confirmed. He gave his place to a small, sallow man who unfolded a large document.

'Against the former King Richard, England lays the following charges before the people…'

In quiet protest, Argyle pushed through the crowd eager to escape. He was outside the Westminster walls before the sound from the great hall disappeared. Although he was pleased to be away the errand that awaited him brought him no pleasure at all. The letter from Thomas' wife Elizabeth rustled inside his shirt.

When he had first read it he had been inclined to ignore her, but after meeting with Bolingbroke two nights ago Argyle had changed his mind. There had been an altogether forlorn feel to her words:

– Brother, if it pleases you, I ask that you pay a visit as soon as may be. I have news of a most discomforting nature and ask your presence that I might be consoled. I have no one else to whom I dare turn. I am alone. –

Free from his promise to Bolingbroke to stay in Westminster until the last day of September, Argyle felt he was going from one trap to another. In all things, Elizabeth had been her husband's equal. Her letter might have an air of loneliness about it, although to take it at face value was something only a fool would do.

London's rank and dirty streets offered little comfort. Although a sudden bout of rain yesterday had washed away much of the filth in the gutters, the city clung to the stink of decay. He pulled his cloak over his nose and pushed his horse into a canter. Best get to this business settled without delay.

It was a short ride before he could hand the reins to a stable boy, his gaze drifting to the candlelit windows of Thomas' magnificent London house. 'Water him, do not put him up.'

'M'lord.' The boy took the stallion and Argyle scaled the steps as a steward appeared, ushered Argyle inside and closed the door with a snap.

'I shall see if my Lady is still up.'

You know full well, she is up. It is not yet time for supper, and I can hear her and the children in the parlour.

He sidled up to the hall's open hearth and untied his cloak. Little warmth escaped the big fire bolstering the sensation that uncertainty had seeped through stone and wood.

'Lady Mowbray will be with you presently,' the steward said in his high-pitched voice. He stood beside an open door that led to a small chamber off the hall. 'You may wait here.'

Argyle offered a curt nod in the face of impertinence. 'Please inform my Lady that I shall not stay long.'

He took in the thick and luxurious tapestries that hung heavy on the walls and the well-fed hearth. There were silver candlesticks all around and plenty of golden trinkets on the tables but most impressive was the set of shelves in opulent, exotic wood, weighed down with massive leather-bound books. Argyle let his fingers glide over the intricate binding. It reeked of good quality and many of the books looked new.

'Argyle.'

He turned to face Elizabeth. 'You summoned me.'

Her hands trembled as she held them out for him to take. 'He is gone.'

Argyle paused before brushing a quick kiss on her dry

skin. 'Truly gone?'

'How many kinds are there?' She snatched away her hands.

'A few more than I bargained for when I saw off Thomas,' Argyle said. Elizabeth wore a rare look of panic and he softened. 'I understand that these are trying times for you since you were no doubt charged with silence whenever his name was mentioned. I had assumed he would have left long ago and so your letter unsettled me. Where is he?'

'If I knew would I have asked you here?' Even exasperated, Elizabeth was cold and terse. 'It must be the King who has sent him away. Which is why I trust that you know what has become of your brother. After all, you are such a great friend of the King.'

You take much for granted, Argyle thought as he led her to the only chair in the room positioned directly before the hearth. 'Which King?'

Elizabeth's eyes widened in an unspoken question.

'Yesterday, King Richard gave up his claim to the throne and relinquished his crown, I heard his words read out not half an hour ago. Now, his crown adorns Lord Bolingbroke's head. I should not wonder if he is anointed before the week is out.' Argyle scoured her shocked expression. 'You did not know?'

'I have no links to court anymore. It is as I wrote to you. I am alone.' Her admission came out on a hard breath. 'What happened?'

'Bolingbroke's claim was accepted by Lords and commoners alike. High and low, they cheered him on.' He stepped away from her chair and edged closer to the fire. It was as if Elizabeth's very nature froze the air. 'When did Thomas leave?'

'A servant in royal livery called on us a week ago. It was a brief meeting before Thomas left. He was awarded no time to pack or even send word to anyone. Had I not been present none of us would have known.' Elizabeth's voice faltered. 'My sons… they are fatherless.'

'This is nothing more than what his peers have believed all along – that he is exiled.' Argyle mustered some sympathy. 'I am sorry, Elizabeth. Thomas saved my life once.'

'And what did he get for his troubles?' Her sharp words nicked and cut. 'Nothing.'

'He got my silence,' Argyle said. 'I told no one he was back not even you, because he wished it so. Whatever he did after that night I never knew. He made no contact and I did not reach out for him. How could I when, to all the world, he was lost somewhere abroad?'

Which was not entirely true. In Argyle's mind, Thomas had been with him since Kells. It was as if Elizabeth's claim rammed its head against an unbreachable wall built inside Argyle's head.

'If you must know his visits here were erratic. He came and went as he pleased with no concern for me or his children.' Her admission wore no passion, no pretence. 'The boys have not seen him since the day you sent him out to sea.'

'I doubt anyone has ever made a shorter journey than Thomas. He was back before you and I left the harbour. Perhaps he witnessed the tears in our sister's eyes as he returned to shore.'

'I might have known he would not truly leave.' A note of uncertainty skewed her admission. 'I swear that was the extent of it. You must believe me. He told me no more than was necessary and he never told me he would return, break his exile before it had truly begun.'

Argyle worked his hands inside his cloak. Despite the intense heat of the cramped, over-stuffed room his fingers were cold. 'What he did, he no doubt did to keep you safe.'

'He was always so full of secrets and so distant, always at court. My father told me to be grateful that the great Lord Mowbray would consider me. In the end…' Elizabeth turned her head. 'He was in such a state when he left.'

'I can imagine.' Argyle had sympathy to offer.

'Can you?'

More than you know, he thought but kept it to himself. He knelt before her and waited for her to look at him. 'Why did you write to me?'

'I want you to find out where he is gone,' she said. 'I must know.'

'I cannot.' Her face fell as he continued. 'The King was brought back in chains. What we are to call him now that he is dethroned, I know not. Bolingbroke will have some idea or other but for now, no one is even to speak of him. The King has not been permitted to speak to anyone since he fell into Bolingbroke's hands in Flint. There is no way he could have ordered a servant to leave his side without everyone knowing.'

'If you are anything like Thomas you will have been clever enough to back both sides.' Elizabeth's voice had taken on a strange, pleading quality.

'I went with the King to Ireland. I sealed my fate to save my family, my sons.' Sweat beaded his brow, made the tips of his short hair damp. 'I hold no sway over Bolingbroke.'

It is he who holds sway over me. Argyle welcomed the ache in his heart as an old friend. Our new King holds my fate in his hands and will do so until my dying day. I have no choice but to obey him and hope that my future actions may keep my children away from the poison of court.

Elizabeth started. 'How can you know? Perhaps he will listen to you if you go to him…'

'And say what? The Lords and commoners alike love Bolingbroke. The joy with which he was received when he entered London must have carried all the way here. The cheers that rang to the roof today were such as I have never heard before.' Argyle sighed and rose, his knees protesting. 'But he harbours no love for our family. There is nothing I can do to persuade him that, from today, I am his loyal subject. I have made my attempts and they were thwarted.'

'Your family…' Elizabeth's objection was silenced by a gesture.

'He holds their safety in his hands.'

How many nights had Argyle woken from a chilling dream that Beauworth was overrun by Lancaster men? His wife defiled, his children carried off to certain death.

Fear tugged at his heart. 'We must accept the new order of the land, Elizabeth. You are the wife of a traitor and I his brother. I have supported a ruined King. I can only hope to slip into oblivion if I do nothing. You ought to do the same. Send the boys home. If you feel you cannot leave London then you can come to me. I advise you to leave at once. From now on, life will be difficult for you.'

Elizabeth rose and grabbed his hands, her pale eyes roaming his face. She wet her lips. 'I beseech you, Argyle. Go to him, for my boys if not for me…'

'I will not sacrifice the life of my children for anyone,' he whispered in her ear and she jerked back as if burned.

Ignoring her pain, he said, 'Had our situations been reversed nor would Thomas.'

CHAPTER 29

28 April 1400 – Boulogne, France

Betrayal is a strange thing, it lures you in with a sweet scent, though behind it lingers a bitterness deep and dark.

Last night's dream of Elizabeth's despair clung to Argyle's mind and he had to grab the rail tight to ward off unwanted memories. Next to him, Jean-Pierre de Reines paused in his recitation of his horses' attributes.

'Your horses are exquisite.' Argyle said to ease the awkward moment. He followed a mare and foal both a startling gold colour as they careered around the pen. 'How much for the foal?'

'He is the finest one I have and I plan to keep him for breeding purposes. I doubt you could afford him even if I wanted to sell him on.' De Reines turned and pointed at another pen. 'This colt is more your style.'

Argyle gave the two golden horses one last look before turning to follow de Reines towards a pen with a large grey colt. His mane and tail were jet black, reinforcing his agitated stance. 'He seems untamed.'

De Reines laughed. 'You do not strike me as a man easily intimidated.'

'Once that might be true,' Argyle said. 'But that was before I took a beating to the head. As I am still adjusting to the ground not moving under my feet a bucking horse would be a poor choice of steed.'

'Maman says that you are much improved. You will be able to travel soon.' De Reines nodded at his master of horse to steady the colt and bring it closer. 'Where will you go?'

'South.' Argyle watched the master grabbling for the short rope that dangled below the colt's solid chin. 'I was looking for my brother before… all this happened.'

'I thought you were inspecting horses.' De Reines held out a palm of grain and the colt nuzzled around it. 'Does your brother have a name even if you do not?'

'Thomas.' Argyle cursed himself for being caught in a lie. 'And I am Argyle Mowbray.'

'Ah.'

'I am not here on my King's orders…'

De Reines never took his eyes off the horse. 'Which King?'

'King Henry.'

The colt suddenly bolted and the master of horse lost his grip, stumbling in the pen as the beast whirled and kicked up sand. The big muscles worked tirelessly under his shiny hide. A magnificent animal if only it could be broken to ride.

'What of your other King? The one our beloved Princess

married?'

Argyle wiped some sand from his chest. 'King Richard lost the love of his people. It would appear that such loss is a greater sin than deposing your own kin.'

'Even so, your allegiance lay with him.' De Reines leaned on the wooden rail, worn smooth by years of wear. 'So did ours. France agreed to a peace with King Richard only because he married our Princess. Now that he is King no more – and your words reinforce the news flooding in from court – well, we want her back.'

'France would break the peace?'

'I am a humble servant of the King of France.' De Reines appeared to enjoy the struggle between the master of horse and the colt although his comments betrayed his true state. 'And I cannot imagine that King Charles would allow for his daughter to be kept in England much longer. If she is not free to return the war may well be renewed.'

Argyle considered the impact of de Reines' words. With a new King of England, the country was fragile. Add to that Argyle's sons lived in the south where the French fleet were most likely to make port before marching on London. If they brought the war to England, Beauworth would take the brunt of invasion.

'You maintain that you are not here for the King?' de Reines asked, yanking Argyle back to the present.

'No. I am here on a personal errand. Or rather, I was in Calais on a personal errand.'

De Reines opened his mouth only to be interrupted by a servant whispering in his ear with animated urgency. Nodding, de Reines turned on his heel. 'We are not done, Sire, though I sense we make progress at last. I shall send for you when I am returned and then I shall have the truth.'

These last weeks, more pieces had begun to fall into

place. Argyle remembered how he had traded his loyalty for empty words, desperate to keep what family he had left safe. When last they had all been together it was to share bad tidings. Bad tidings that had turned into dangerous conjectures.

Dread resurfaced along with another disjointed memory.

ꙮ ꙮ

CHAPTER 30

12 October 1399 – Argyle's London house

Margaret shook the letter. 'Surely this is a joke?'

'Why would you say that, sister?' Eleanor asked. 'We all knew…'

'Knew what?' Elizabeth's shrill voice cut through the air. 'None of you knew anything, save perhaps Argyle.'

Margaret and Eleanor looked at Argyle, brows raised at the sudden familiarity with which Elizabeth spoke of him. None of the family had ever been close to Thomas' wintry wife. Argyle had himself been surprised when she had arrived at his doorstep a week ago informing him that the boys were sent to Framlingham and that she would accept his offer to house her.

He was still not allowed to return to Beauworth and his house arrest was proving lonesome. Even Elizabeth's curt company was better than nothing. No news reached him from home and he could not send word to Isobel about what had transpired. When Elizabeth arrived with her servants, clothes and possessions, he had welcomed her at the door, carrying her luggage to her rooms himself.

They had spent a few tight-lipped evenings together and for the most part, Elizabeth preferred to keep to her rooms. She deigned to join him for breakfast if only to sit in silence and suck yolks from soft-boiled eggs keeping her own counsel and asking for nothing more than wood for her hearth and some sewing to keep her hands occupied.

Then the letters had arrived. Thomas' ghost reappeared hungry for revenge.

Now, Elizabeth's gaze made Argyle uncomfortable. He turned from her to face Margaret. His eldest sister had a worn look about her though her garb and other adornments were as rich as ever. She flicked her hand. 'What do you know?'

'Thomas left England less than a month ago. He may or may not be dead. One thing remains certain, he cannot possibly have made it all the way to Venice.' Argyle had this conversation with Elizabeth so many times it had lost all meaning.

'You would know.' She sat down interlacing her fingers to stop her hands shaking. 'I am told you once rode hard for England taking a similar route to that of my husband.'

Eleanor and Margaret exchanged a confused glance. It appeared that Thomas had kept Argyle's return from Jerusalem a secret from their sisters, just as he had asked. Instead, he had confided in Elizabeth.

'How can we know that he is not dead?' Eleanor sounded exhausted and slightly annoyed. 'Why should I trust your word?' She sat on the edge of a chair, her fine gown gleaming in competition with her golden hair which was, today, caught in a net studded with blue gemstones.

Argyle interfered before the look of disgust on both women's faces could turn into something more vicious. 'When first I sent him into exile, Elizabeth knew he was coming back as soon as we had turned away from the dock. She housed him for several months before he visited me in the Tower, as *you* are well aware. Let us have no more secrets.'

'What are you talking about?' Margaret demanded. 'I was certain…'

'That only you knew Thomas never left?'

Argyle had long suspected that she had known of their brother's return. Of all of them, Margaret and Thomas shared as many traits as Argyle did with Eleanor who wore an appalled expression. Apparently neither Margaret nor Thomas had believed she could be trusted with such a dark secret, and perhaps they were right. After all there were rumours that Eleanor was a frequent visitor at court. She and her husband were said to be cultivating a relationship with King Henry.

'He visited me after my brawl with Grenteville when I was locked in a cell.' Argyle exchanged a wry smile with Eleanor and suffered Margaret's angry huff. 'For some time I thought it had all been a dream brought on by loss of blood. Until Elizabeth summoned me.'

'Elizabeth?' Eleanor picked up a trinket and turned it in the waning daylight. The big windows offered a pleasing view into a walled garden and his sister was unusually interested in the vista. 'Why is she here anyway?'

'I am a guest,' Elizabeth's triumph drowned in a snort of derision. She turned her attention to Argyle. 'Though perhaps I mistook your invitation?'

He shook his head at her and poured the wine before he passed the tray around, having dismissed his servants, and held out the last cup to Margaret.

'Elizabeth *is* here at my invitation. For one, I am glad that she was not alone when the news reached her – us.' Argyle stared into his cup. He was also glad she was here because the news had torn away his weak grasp on reality and if she had not slumped across the table he would have gone mad.

'As his wife, you have as much a right to be here as any of us.' Margaret inclined her cup before drinking. Eleanor made to protest and Margaret brought her to heel. 'Oh, do be quiet. If we have all received the same message that Thomas has died in Venice we may well trust that he is at least dead. Though not where we are led to believe. It suggests whoever is trying to fool us is a fool himself.'

'Who knew?' Eleanor fiddled with her necklace. Being cowed by her eldest sister always left her frantic. 'Thomas hardly knew a soul outside England and certainly no one in Italy.'

'Never underestimate our brother.' Argyle brushed off the strange detachment with which they were discussing the news of Thomas' death. 'If indeed he left when Elizabeth claims…'

'He did – under a cloud.'

Irritation rode on his next comment. 'Then it would be impossible for him to make it to Venice before meeting his death. Which proves Margaret's point. Someone is trying to deceive us, to make us believe our traitor brother died far from England.'

'Why?'

Eleanor's innocent question made Margaret sigh. 'Because they do not wish for us to know the truth. I think someone close to Bolingbroke – King Henry – issued a spy to follow Thomas. I know I would, for it was impossible to determine where our brother's loyalties lay and there has long been bad blood between the two.'

Margaret put aside her cup. 'If you were to carry out such an order, Argyle, what would you do?'

'I would seek to get him out of the way for good.' The words tasted bitter in his mouth, as the truth often did. He looked at Eleanor and wondered what she was thinking. 'Bolingbroke has been surrounded by loyal friends since the moment he set foot on English soil. Now that he wears the crown of England, any one of these loyal friends might seek to curry favour with their new King by doing away with an enemy.'

'My God…' Elizabeth's composure crumbled. Perhaps for the very first time, she understood the true nature of the man she had first married and since followed as he rose and then fell from grace, relying on her to keep him hidden and safe.

'I loved my brother, but I doubt that God would help him.' Margaret dabbed the corner of her lips and pushed the silk handkerchief back into her tapered sleeve. 'There are many in England who would prefer our brother dead. And even more who would prosper by it.'

'Why Venice?' Eleanor appeared somehow uplifted by Margaret's comment. 'It seems strange for anyone to assume that none of us knew that our brother never left the country.'

Argyle leaned back in his chair. 'Whatever the cause, I imagine the solution would have presented itself as follows: If he had left England as he was sentenced to do and if he had not disembarked and crept back onto land when we turned our backs then he would have come across

Bolingbroke somewhere in France. Since it is well-known that King Charles took in Bolingbroke, Thomas would have had to make his way through France in all haste for he would not be welcome there. To someone who did not know that Thomas returned to England the choice would then be a simple one: Either our brother would go to Spain or Italy.'

'Italy would have suited Thomas best.' Margaret paused to cough into her sleeve. 'He might even have given the illusion that he wanted to go on pilgrimage.'

Elizabeth gave a leaden laugh. 'No one who truly knew my husband would have believed he would care for pilgrimage.'

'Being so far from home no one did know him.' Eleanor glanced quickly at Elizabeth. 'When he wanted to, Thomas made friends easily. Many found him pleasing. Perhaps he…'

'We are speculating.' Margaret coughed again. Argyle looked at his eldest sister. Did she have a whisper of pallor about her? 'We know that he stayed in England, do we not Argyle? Elizabeth?'

'Yes.' His voice mixed with Elizabeth's. She rested her hands on the back of his chair. Argyle spoke first. 'I believe he is dead just not as far afield as Venice. It must be in a place much closer to our shores. If I am not much mistaken Thomas would not have made it further than Calais.'

'Calais?' Eleanor appeared bewildered while Margaret nodded.

'He would not have been able get out of England without encountering someone in Bolingbroke's pay.' She picked a new, embroidered handkerchief from her neckline. 'By that time, everyone in England knew that Bolingbroke was set to take the throne. Most of his supporters would be eager to prove their loyalty to him. Thomas' death would be a good way to prove commitment and an even better way to secure a handsome reward.'

'Exactly,' Argyle said and felt Elizabeth lean against the chair. Beneath her silken dress he could feel the rise and fall of her bones where her chest pressed against his back. 'By the time Bolingbroke decided to return to England, he may well have known that Thomas was still in the country. If he is anything like his father he has spies at every port in France and beyond. He has most certainly left instructions that if someone matching Thomas' description was found in Calais – or anywhere – he was to be detained. At best.'

Eleanor began pacing the room her heavy skirt rustling. 'You are saying that Thomas died in Calais? That he had no friends left who might come to his aid?'

'He had changed allegiance so many times. Have we not all?' Argyle clutched the armrests as Margaret nodded assent.

Though the news of Thomas' death was shocking, it was not so much that his brother drew breath no more that set his teeth on edge. It was the lie they were being fed. He did not need to look at his sisters to know that they shared his unease. A part of him had waited for this news for months on end and now that it was here, whoever was spinning a web of lies would have been better off simply stating that Thomas had drowned off the coast of England. Why conjure up such an elaborate story? It would only be done by someone who thought that the Mowbray family was ignorant of Thomas remaining in England. To Argyle there was only one explanation. Such a tale would be thought up by someone who had himself been exiled.

Elizabeth was the only one riddled by genuine shock though he would have thought her to be least affected of all. Perhaps she had loved Thomas in her own way. The tears that rolled down her pale, narrow cheeks were a testament to her emotions, although there was something calculating in her eyes.

'To survive we must at times make unsavoury choices.' Margaret's voice was calm. 'Should we ask for his body to be sent home?'

'Bolingbroke would never allow it.' Argyle was certain.

Elizabeth wiped her cheeks and stepped away from the chair. His back grew cold where her chest had rested. 'Not as a nobleman, but as the King? Who would stand against him?'

'He does not need any enemies in England. The murder of one of their own, even one believed to be in exile would irk many a noble family.' Margaret sniffed and crossed herself. 'Lest you forget, neither of us are in a position to ask favours of King Henry. He does not need us.'

Throughout this exchange, Eleanor was oddly silent. She might be the only one who could approach the King and demand answers, especially if de Welles was high in favour as rumours suggested.

'The crowd cheered him on as if he was a hero not a man who had been exiled for his offences to the King. It is my hope that he will forget about us, allow us to sink into obscurity. Such absolution can only transpire if we make no noise, ask no favours beyond our reach.' Argyle rolled his shoulders. 'I hope to return to Beauworth soon. London holds nothing for me.'

'First you must attend tomorrow's ceremony, Argyle. It will be such an occasion.' Elizabeth's cheeks flushed unnaturally rosy.

Bitterness marred Margaret's expression, she did not like to be overrun by anyone. Inside he cursed having told

Elizabeth. It seemed loneliness could make you do strange things. The invitation was issued and accepted on her advice.

Argyle breathed deep. 'Yes, I am to be present at Westminster.'

'He is to represent the house of Mowbray,' Elizabeth continued. It was the only sore point for her. 'My sons are not old enough to be of any real importance, it seems.'

'Be glad if they never have to come to court.' Argyle did not want to ignite another heated discussion with Elizabeth. Already they were beginning to sound like an old married couple, and if he were to have such discussions he would have them with his own wife who waited for him at Beauworth.

He turned his attention to Margaret. 'You are welcome to join me, sister, if you wish. Though I warn you that almost everyone present loathes the sight of me. It will not be pleasant.'

'I know none more disinclined to be singled out by the royal family than you, dear brother.' Margaret turned her head for another cough. 'You may find that many others believe it a great honour to be asked to attend Westminster.'

'Tomorrow will be a grand ceremony and an even greater spectacle, though you need not doubt that he is King already, dear Margaret. Surely you will be there too with Sir Reginald.' Argyle rose. 'Sit here for a while, Elizabeth.'

'If you think for a moment I believe she ever loved Thomas…' Eleanor's argument died on her lips.

Placing a heavy hand on Elizabeth's shoulder he felt trapped in a coop of chickens spoiling for a fight. 'There is no need to be insolent, sister.'

'I am sorry, Elizabeth, forgive me.' Her sugared words fell to the floor.

'You are forgiven,' Elizabeth said, and Argyle eased his grasp. 'We are all weighed down by the news.' Elizabeth turned her face to Argyle. 'I wish to return to my rooms. I feel unwell.'

Argyle escorted his sister-in-law to the door and closed it behind her. 'You overreach, Eleanor.'

'Oh please, do not take her side now.' Eleanor tucked her hand into the crook of his arm and smiled. 'You never liked. And since she is no longer family, what obligation do we owe her? I still cannot believe you are housing her. Is it because her sons do not wish her return to Framlingham? It is very harsh that they should have our childhood home. No, we cannot trust her, she is here to make mischief.'

'Would you wish the same treatment from your husband's family?' Argyle put his hand on hers, offering no smile in return. 'She is alone. Imagine how she suffered at the hand Thomas had in the death of her father. Throughout, she remained loyal to the Crown that condemned him to death. She watched him beheaded. She stood by Thomas when he was exiled…'

'… and when he returned, she housed him. Yes, yes, brother,' she said and rested her head on his upper arm. 'Whatever you say she makes my skin crawl. You cannot force me to trust her, please do not try.'

Can we trust you? he thought while he tried to read his sister's expression. All he saw was a mirror image though her cheeks had filled in of late and her hair had lost some of its lustre.

'Care to share your thoughts, Margaret?'

'Elizabeth is of little matter. Thomas is dead, of that I am certain. There would be no point in sending us this message if he was not.' Margaret had taken the seat by the fire and was clutching her embroidered handkerchief. 'Someone does not want us to go in search of our brother.'

'You are right,' Eleanor said, her hand still resting on Argyle's arm. 'Thomas is dead and most likely by order of the King. King Henry. Oh, how bothersome. What are we to call the other King? King Richard? That sounds too odd. Argyle, what will happen to him?'

'For all their enmity, I do not believe King Henry will harm him,' Argyle said. 'Our new King will want to make a public display of mercy. I have heard that he will endow the King's former title to him and that he shall once more be known as Lord Bordeaux. Still, he cannot allow for him to return to court. There are limits even to King Henry's mercy.'

'Mercy?' Margaret rolled her eyes and stifled a cough with some effort. 'If King Henry is merciful, I am a beggar.'

'Be careful what you say, sister,' Eleanor said with a little malice.

'Neither you nor I are invited to attend tomorrow,' Margaret shot back. 'Since you are, Argyle, you must go and be our eyes and ears. Perhaps after the official ceremony someone will let slip a truth or two that might help us decide what to do next.'

'You may not be invited, dear sister.' Saccharine triumph coated Eleanor's words. 'But I am.'

Margaret suffered another fit of coughing and Argyle filled her cup with wine, awarding Eleanor a sinister glare. It did nothing to wipe the exultant smile off her face.

'What do you mean you are invited?' he demanded.

'My husband backed King Henry when he first returned to England, is it such a wonder that we are to attend his coronation?' Eleanor snatched the pitcher from him and replenished her own cup. 'You see, we are not all so foolish as to declare openly whom we support until we are certain of the outcome. You should learn from that, Margaret.'

Incensed, she rose and left the room. An aroma of rose petals with a vague sickly scent trailed behind her.

Argyle sighed. 'Eleanor…'

She put down her cup and pulled his arms around her. Every time he looked into her eyes he saw his own reflection, enhanced by the similarities they shared. It was eerie to find her entirely devoid sentiment, her care for others skin deep. They might look alike, but that did not make them two of a kind. Far from it.

'Oh come now, brother.' Eleanor kissed his cheek. 'It has always been the two of us against the rest. Even you cannot deny that.'

CHAPTER 31

13 October 1399 – Westminster

'It is a year to the day that my father left England.' Harry stared at the procession forming outside Westminster Abbey. 'You know that only too well.'

Argyle shook out his new cloak, the dark blue wool turned black by the rain. 'I do, though it is not a fond memory for me – no more so than it is for you.'

'You will call me a fool, Sire,' Harry said, 'but I wonder if my father will make me Prince of Wales.'

'Why should he not, Master Harry?'

To get out of the downpour, Harry stepped under one of the low marquees that had been put up all around the Abbey courtyard to offer a little shelter.

'He thinks I did nothing when he first returned. He thinks I was disloyal. He does not understand that I was torn. He asked me to turn my back to my King, the man who took me in and provided for me, while he… for most of that year he spent away, I had no news. And when he finally did arrive, he… he must have known what danger his actions put me in. Or was I wrong to hesitate?'

'Time will lend perspective,' Argyle said in a vain attempt to soothe. 'If nothing else, he understands that you could not leave your uncle for I explained that you were only safe as long as you stayed with him. Your father knows that.'

'And now he is our King.' There was a hint of hurt in Harry's voice. 'He will not tell me what is to happen to my uncle. He says only that Lord Bordeaux will have his title.'

'Until your father is anointed today he must be careful.'

Harry looked up, his eyes sharp with pain. 'I am his son… How can I convince him to trust me? I see the way he looks at my brothers, as if he is deciding to cast me aside and choose a new heir. He did not accept my uncle's heir, why should he accept me? Why should England?'

Increasing desperation made Harry curl his fists around the hem of his cloak. Argyle put a hand on his shoulder. 'You have long been separated, Master Harry. Once you are together again there will be time to speak of what is important. This is a tense time for us all, other things weigh heavy on your father's mind. Allow him some time to settle.'

Why am I defending Bolingbroke? Argyle thought.

Of course, he was not doing it out of loyalty to the new English King, he was doing it because he recognised the pain in Harry's eyes. It was the same pain that Argyle had toiled with all his life, because he could never tell if Thomas had loved him or not. Harry deserved to know if his father loved him – and how much.

'Let him go to church and don his crown?' Harry's short laugh brought Argyle back to the present. 'He displaced me for his brother Thomas. He is to carry the Lancaster Sword into the church. The sign of my father's heritage – of mine – carried by a man born a bastard. I will carry the Curtana, while Somerset and Warwick will carry the two swords of justice.'

Four swords, Argyle thought, a novel idea.

King Henry was looking to make a statement. From today, Lancaster came before all others.

'Tonight, he is to create the Order of the Bath and knight my three brothers. Humphrey is *nine.*' Mastering his temper, Harry nodded at a couple of priests carrying a shrine between them. 'He even rooted through my uncle's possessions and found the oil of St Thomas He will be anointed with it, snotnosed little brat.'

In silence they watched the gathering grow for a while. Argyle wondered what else Bolingbroke might have in store for his spectators and when he might begin to name Bolingbroke King Henry in his mind. Harry chewed his lip and brushed raindrops from the white and black ermine on his cloak.

'Will you attend the feast tonight, Sire?'

'Your father has been gracious in his invitation. We must all come to terms with this new arrangement.' He turned his head when the crowd began to part. 'Best take your place, Master Harry.'

'I pray you will always speak my name with such affection, Sire,' Harry said and began to make his way to the head of the procession. 'And that you might forgive my father his theatrics.'

Argyle looked around for Eleanor, but his sister was nowhere to be seen. The doors to the church were eating up visitors by the hundreds; soon he would have to go in too.

'I did not want to disturb.' A bony hand snaked around his wrist. 'No doubt you were ingratiating yourself with the new Prince. Tell me is he as amiable as they say?'

'I thought you decided to stay at home and mourn the death of your husband.' Argyle took in Elizabeth's silk dress and the obsidian lace in her hair. Even the silver-crusted teardrop pearls around her neck were black.

'I mourned him when he left. I knew this time he would not return.'

Argyle stepped into the rain. 'You should have taken to the stage.'

'I would never be able to upstage the greatest actor of all,' Elizabeth's dress rustled as they crossed the yard. 'He who is about to be anointed.'

At least you did not mean me, Argyle thought and let her walk in front of him. His wife should have been here, not Elizabeth, but Isobel remained incarcerated at Beauworth. If he played his part these coming days, she might soon be released. It was a petty solace and yet, it was all he had.

'When do you return to Framlingham?'

Elizabeth gave a faint smile. 'When I tire of your company, brother.'

The abbey doors opened, letting in the outside damp. King Henry entered his bare head dripping with rain, his coat of ermine and purple drenched. The procession took its beginning.

Through the opening, Argyle spied the scores of men who followed their King on this day. It was said there were six thousand, though it looked more like three thousand to Argyle.

Then the doors closed and all eyes followed King Henry as he proceeded to the high altar where he first knelt and then lay down as a pilgrim would before a holy shrine.

Next to Argyle, Elizabeth made a sharp intake of breath when Thomas Arundel, the newly reinstated Archbishop of Canterbury, stepped forward holding the oil of St Thomas ready to anoint the new King of England.

Argyle found himself thinking of the King who sat in the Tower.

CHAPTER 32

27 October 1399 – London

'Richard of Bordeaux, you are sentenced to perpetual imprisonment at the King's pleasure!'

The court applauded the swift verdict with a fervour that suggested they had just been informed that they were to receive a grant of a thousand crowns a year for the rest of their lives.

Locking his hands behind his back, he acknowledged that if Thomas had still been alive he would have been cheering with the rest of them. Argyle, however, could not.

'Take the prisoner away,' Henry Percy, Earl of Northumberland declared. Even from afar, it was evident that he enjoyed being at the centre of this particular spectacle.

Four guards stepped forward, dressed in chainmail and blackened plate, two of them wearing helmets and all of them heavily armed. They seized the King, now once more known to the world as Richard of Bordeaux, and led him through the crowd which parted so slowly that most of the men had time to stare the former King in the eye.

'Now, there are two living Kings.' John Beaufort, the Earl of Somerset nodded at the armed guard that pushed through the sea of people. 'He may have lost the kingship and now be a mere Lord, but he is still anointed. My brother should have taken up the commoners on their proposal of a trial.'

'And try him for what? Having been the rightful King of England?'

Argyle's sarcasm was not lost on Somerset. 'I know not the particulars, though I do know that he is to move around the country until such a time as my brother finds he is no longer a danger to the Crown. Fifty-eight lords set their names to the judgement. He is to be isolated.'

'What more could you want?' The bitterness of being kept in London had taken permanent residence, souring his mood. 'What of his request to be sent to a monastery?'

'Anyone can access a monastery.' Somerset studied his nails. 'You, for one.'

There it is, Argyle thought, the truth behind the judgement. 'Is our new King fearful of the future?'

'The Lords and commoners agreed that the measures enforced are to keep Lord Bordeaux safe. It is certainly more than our King got.' Somerset shook his head. 'Besides it could have been much worse. He could have been tried for treason against England.'

Argyle looked at the Earl. 'He has done nothing treasonous.'

'Since when has that ever been an issue in the royal family?'

Argyle decided it was best not to answer the question who knew how many were listening even if the room vibrated with emotion and commotion?

'When is Lord Bordeaux to be moved?' Surely King Henry would want his cousin out of sight and soon.

Somerset smiled. 'If our new King did not deign to tell you, Sire, nor shall I. Some secrets we must keep from you at least until we are satisfied that you are no longer a threat. Just between us, my brother will never live down the fact that Richard is still an anointed King. You will understand that he cannot stay in the Tower. The Londoners are a volatile lot, for now, they love their new King. What happens once the novelty wears off? No, he is right to make arrangements. He must ensure that Lord Bordeaux is far away from London – that he is forgotten.'

'What does he hope to gain?'

'That the people will find him merciful – something Bordeaux never was.' Somerset pulled on a pair of leather riding gloves while they let the wave of courtiers and lords swallow them up and carry them towards the doors of the throne room.

'For how long?' Argyle wondered aloud as the crowd began to disperse, the new King's council filing out of the room by a side door, preparing to assume their duties.

'Time will tell.' Beaufort inclined his head. 'Henry will not be rash.'

ꕥ

CHAPTER 33

28 October 1399 – Argyle's London house

Argyle looked up from his desk at the sound of voices coming from the hall. He heard his steward's shuffling steps hurrying towards the study. Without much thought, he pushed the letter he was writing under the stack of papers next to him, smudging the wet ink.

A single knock came.

'Yes?'

Mills, his steward, opened the door and stepped aside without announcing the visitor. There was no need.

'Sir Argyle.' Harry was pulling off his gloves, a broad smile on his face. 'How are you?'

'My Lord, what an honour.' He gave Mills a quick nod. 'Refreshments.'

Harry looked after Mills who shuffled out the door, slow as always to close it behind him. 'I cannot stay long. I have come to you with an offer.'

Argyle proffered Harry a chair by the hearth and he held out his hands to the flames with a sigh of contentment. 'Do you know where they are taking Lord Bordeaux?'

'No, Master Harry. Your father thinks it too great a risk to tell me anything these days.'

Harry's cheeks flushed. 'I keep telling him he is too cautious but he will not listen. Even I am not privy to the entire scheme although I know where Bordeaux' journey will end. As you may have guessed, my father is keen to keep me from my uncle.'

'It is only natural that he prefers you stay in London. You are needed in his council if you are to learn how to govern.'

'I have watched my uncle at work for years, Sire,' Harry said dismissively and looked about. 'This is a comfortable room. Are you happy here? Well, I suppose you are not. Are you at least comfortable? I hear your sister-in-law keeps you company.'

Argyle sat at the desk. 'She lives here though I would not call her company. She keeps to her rooms and has her own servants to tend her.'

'Was she at the coronation?'

'Yes. She did not attend the feast.'

He turned a quizzical expression to Argyle. 'One more would hardly have made a difference. They say that we fed six thousand men and almost as many ladies. Nearly twice as many as my father could fit into the church. My feet are still sore from standing behind him with that wretched sword.'

'I believe Elizabeth should have enjoyed the experience,' Argyle said and decided to test his luck. 'She is in mourning and so found it tasteless to indulge in a feast.'

'What does she mourn?'

'My brother's death.' He watched Harry for any sign that he knew something and saw only pure surprise. 'It seems he died in Venice.'

'I am sorry to hear of it.' Harry crossed himself. 'I know you pleaded with the King for your brother's exile to be revoked or at the very least reduced.'

'We lived in hope.' Argyle was interrupted by a couple of servants carrying a small pot of mulled wine and a tray of glasses. The warm spices filled the room with comfortable notes. Once the tray of cups, bread and other treats were arranged, Argyle dismissed the servants. 'Will you take some wine?'

Nodding, Harry contemplated the fire. 'Venice? Did you know he had gone there?'

'No. Not even my sister-in-law knew where he had gone. It must have been almost impossible for him to send word. Perhaps he did not want to be a burden to his children.'

Again, Argyle examined Harry who tasted the wine and sighed once more. 'A sad business. I am sorry if I have come at a bad time, Sire. As I said, I have some news to share. I know you will be pleased.'

He offered the silver platter of bread and sweetmeats and Harry picked a few pieces. 'I might not be able to tell you where my uncle is at present. Instead, I can tell you that once he is delivered safely to Pontefract you may visit him. It is all arranged with my father.'

'How generous,' Argyle said and thought, what is the price of this favour?

'In return, my father would like to visit your estate. Beauworth.' Harry sniffed the wine. 'He cannot remember ever being there before and he is eager to visit all of the south to let himself be seen by his subjects.'

Chewing a piece of dried apple, Harry surveyed Argyle's desk. 'I have been hard at work trying to convince my father that you are loyal to us now. I have vouched for you but…' He picked a piece of apple from his teeth. 'Well, if you agree to this arrangement you can visit Lord Bordeaux and perhaps convey a greeting from me?'

Sometimes, I forget that you are still a child, Argyle thought and fixed a smile. Isobel would be furious to play hostess to the King, but if it would get Argyle out of London and on the road home, he would agree to walk barefoot through a fire. A royal visit seemed a small price to pay.

'I shall be honoured.' He took a swig of wine and let time stretch. Best not to seem too excited. 'Do you know when I might go to Pontefract?'

'Father must sign letters of safe passage to ensure that you are admitted. In return, you must publicly swear never to take up arms against any Lancaster soldier, guard or servant – and that you shall return without delay to court once the visit has been completed.' Harry's voice wavered. 'As you are not to stay at the castle you must make other arrangements in case you need to spend the night. And you are to publicly invite my father to your estate.'

For every time they met, Harry looked ever more as his father, thick dark hair, grey eyes, lean frame. He would grow to be a handsome youth and in time, his physique would match his mature expression.

'How public must my invitation be?'

'Before the court should suffice, I believe.' Harry gave an apologetic nod. 'Along with your pledge to serve the King of England.'

Acknowledging the shrewdness of the plan, Argyle asked the only question that mattered. 'When might I return to my family?'

'Once you have recounted your visit with my uncle to my father.' Picking up another piece of dried apple, Harry dipped it in his wine. 'He shall call off his guard as soon as you have presented your pledge at court, Sire. When you return to Beauworth your family will be free, as will you.'

'Thank you, my Lord.' Only a glance from Harry stopped Argyle bending his knee right there and then.

'You need not thank me, Sire, and please do not call me a Lord,' Harry said and stood. 'I had little to do with any of it.'

'You spoke up for me, for your uncle, when no one else would.' Argyle did not care that his words carried a choke.

Emptying his cup, Harry gave the room a final cursory glance. 'Someone once taught me that it is better to be generous than petty. That more could be achieved by being visible and sometimes fighting a cause others had abandoned. That to be a true leader you have to dare to take the first step. Thank that man, for he taught me something very valuable.'

Argyle opened the door and Harry preceded him into the hall. 'Come at my father's invitation, make right what can be righted, Sire, and you will find yourself with your family before long.'

Harry turned his back to Argyle and left the house, three guards in tow. He might feel safe but only because his father was cautious. As the door clicked shut, letting in a breath of icy air, something rustled behind him.

'You are leaving London?' Elizabeth stood at the top of the stairs, her face a startling white against her glum widow's garb. 'When?'

'I do not know.' Argyle held out his hand. 'Will you come and take some warm wine with me?'

She brushed past his outstretched hand and walked into the study. 'How can you leave?'

'I have not seen my family in many months…'

'What of me?' she cut him short. 'Am I no longer family? Is Eleanor to be proven right?'

You eavesdropped.

Argyle poured a cup of wine. 'You are here at my invitation, Elizabeth. Beware you do not overstep your position within our family. I have spoken in your favour more than once. I should hate to think it a wasted effort.'

'Your sisters always hated me.' Elizabeth gulped the wine and made a face when she burned her tongue. 'Is this what you serve our future King?'

'He did not complain.' Argyle left her by the fire and leaned on his desk. 'King Henry will soon release me from my current ties. I am to make a short journey, return to court and then I shall leave to be reunited with my family.' He locked eyes with Elizabeth. 'Perhaps it is time you went home to Framlingham.'

'That is not my home.'

'It is where your sons are,' Argyle said and continued his silent battle with her cold gaze. 'You can make it your home. I shall do all I can to ensure that your sons do not lose their inheritance though you cannot imagine they will keep all of my brother's titles. Thomas will be Baron Mowbray, it is an inherited title. As for the rest, time will tell…'

A lesser woman would have argued or wailed and cried, Elizabeth just glared. He watched her come to terms with her situation. 'Until Tom is of an age I shall be his ward. He will want for nothing nor will John or my girls. That is my wish.'

'I shall do what I can.' Argyle did not want to commit to fighting her battle when he had not yet won his own. Freedom for his family, Beauworth entailed to Edmund at all costs.

'And what of my poor husband?' Elizabeth put down her cup and rose. 'The lie we were all fed? What will you do about that, I wonder.'

Argyle watched her leave and pulled a half-finished letter from the pile. Although the words were smudged they were still legible. He dipped the quill and continued:

> – *Expect me home before the year is out. God willing, I will have secured all of our freedoms and we will live in peace.* –

He folded the letter and warmed some wax. This time he did make his mark. A prancing unicorn glistened in the dark blue puddle. He looked at it for a long time making up his mind.

The ghost of La Fontaine needed to be put to rest.

CHAPTER 34

28 April 1400 – Boulogne, France

'Two men brought me a message from the Countess of Auvergne and Boulogne.' Jean-Pierre de Reines chewed on a straw.

They were walking back from the horse pens, having spent the better part of an hour discussing the foals. The de Reines estate was nestled in a valley, surrounded by rolling hills that were already rich with grass and flowers. Argyle wondered if perhaps, the same was true of Beauworth, after all spring in the south was often weeks ahead of the rest of England. Still, the fields in the distance were dark green with crops and he knew that his tenants would not enjoy such a sight for another half month or more.

De Reines seemed to decide something. 'Around the time Marie found you on the beach, a fisherman had rescued a man, badly injured and unconscious. The Countess has taken in the man and made him as comfortable as possible. She sent word to me that I might send Maman to see the unfortunate soul.'

'Did she?' Argyle kindled a small hope that this man might shed some light on the dark patches that still riddled his memories.

'She had her hands full with you – and she is not a young woman anymore.' Scratching his cheek, de Reines aimed straight for the stables. He was almost more fond of his horses than his family as his daughter often reminded him. 'Maman met the messengers when they left my rooms and demanded they tell her what the Countess wanted. You may guess her reaction once she learned that I had said she was not to go.'

Argyle smothered a smile. 'She went.'

'In a state, too. When she returned, she would scarce speak to me about the man. Perhaps she will be more inclined to tell you.' De Reines stepped into a stall. 'When you are well enough we shall talk about how to get you on your way.'

'If the offer still stands I might just buy your silver colt.' Argyle had watched the master of horse tame the beast and was satisfied that by the time he was well enough to sit a horse, the colt would suit his needs. 'He is a fine horse.'

'Yes, but can you afford him, Sir Argyle?'

Before he could commit to anything, the stable master claimed de Reines' attention and Argyle decided to take a stroll near the house and enjoy the fine weather. Who knew when dark clouds would amass anew?

He came across Grand-Maman in the garden behind the house. For a while, he watched her, her hands working tirelessly at the many beds, cutting herbs, pruning flowers and tending to her pots. There was something serene about the sight.

'Have you come to ogle or assist?' she asked without turning around.

Argyle felt as a child caught spying. 'What do you need?'

'Water and the two small pouches over by the bench.' Grand-maman waved a hand. 'You can begin by pouring water into this hole.' She straightened her back and began picking out little seeds from the linen pouch. 'Plenty of water.'

Splashing water into the void, Argyle examined the garden. It was so unlike any found at an English manor, it almost looked as if it belonged in a convent. A fountain tinkled at the far end hidden from view its sound permeating the distant warble of birds.

'Good. Now step aside, I need space.' She nudged him and threw piles of dry dirt into the hole. When it was half full, she churned the dirt into a slosh of mud, pushed an arm into the mix and began stirring. She let the little seeds drip into the wet dirt. 'There, all they need now is plenty of sun and moisture. Perhaps you can help me – until you leave?'

'With pleasure.' Argyle put down the pail and offered Grand-Maman an arm. She took it but gave him a knowing smile. Not too long ago, it was she who had supported him and she watching her work he knew she did not need any aid.

'Let me look at you.' She pushed Argyle onto a bench. 'The wounds are healing nicely. Though you still look frightful.'

Argyle felt stronger, the shifting had almost ceased and his appetite had returned. Since Grand-Maman had said that his body would heal faster if he slept a lot he did so without qualms.

'Blue and purple.' Grand-Maman prodded his cheek. 'The pain has subsided?'

'Yes.' Argyle winced when she poked his calf. 'Except my leg.'

'Give it time, dear boy.' She settled next to him, her gaze bounding from one blooming bed to the next. 'Jean wants to know when you can leave. He is uncomfortable putting up an Englishman in his own house.'

'He told me that you have been to see a man at the court of the Countess.'

'Did he tell you that he did not want me to go?' There was an edge to Grand-Maman's voice. 'That he thought I was far too old to go the few miles from here to serve the Countess? Luckily, I met the servants and made them wait. Some days I think he has lost his mind – sending away the servants of the Countess. We need her patronage – and I helped her mother birth her…'

Ah here it is, he thought, the reason Grand-Maman is snappish with her son.

Donning his most innocent expression, Argyle asked, 'How is the man they found?'

'He is as well as can be expected.' She appeared unfazed by his question. 'Just as you, he was badly injured, but he is healing fast and he knows what happened to you.'

Argyle's blood ran cold. 'Has he told you?'

'No. He will not even tell his hostess although she tries by any means to extract the tale from him. Therefore, she asks that you come to see her as soon as you are able to ride.' Grand-Maman put a hand on his chest when he made to stand up. 'You can go tomorrow. I will take you personally. When Jean hears that the Countess has summoned you he has no option but to let me go too, and he must allow you a horse from his stables. I hear you have taken to the grey colt?'

Returning Grand-Maman's knowing smile, he patted her hand the skin dry and caked with mud. 'I shall pay handsomely for it. Though I must insist the master of horse keeps working with it until I am fit to ride and I shall let you decide when that might be.'

'Wise decision. You are so unlike my son. Jean would take a hit to the head and jump on a horse the moment he saw one.' She waved him off with a crackled laugh. 'Go rest and I shall see you tonight.'

For another couple of hours, Argyle explored the gardens, winding his way down paths and sitting down whenever he came across a bench. He had much to ponder and though his body still tired quickly, his mind was not so easily calmed.

In the end, he returned to the house and spent the remainder of the day lying on his bed, staring up at the brightly coloured canopy. When Marie came to call for dinner, he was happy to let her carry the conversation from his room to the hall and for most of the meal. Occasionally, she would glance at him, but for the most part, she simply kept his plate full and his cup within easy reach.

It was late before Argyle could retreat without anyone noticing and he went to sit by the little desk in his room. The quill floated above the paper as he tried to decide what might be safe to write.

De Reines needed to be paid for the colt not to mention that he would need to pay for food and shelter no matter if he decided to return to England or continue searching for the truth of Thomas' death.

In the end, Argyle simply penned:

– Elizabeth

The journey has been prolonged. Please reimburse Lord de Reines for a colt of the finest quality. I believe it will aid my future endeavours and ensure my success. Cover any other costs sent to you. –

He put down the quill. Long-winded explanations would put both of them in danger and she had expressly asked to know nothing.

If Elizabeth was called upon by King Henry to appear at court it was better she be kept in the dark. She had to protect her children first and foremost, even if she had to give up Argyle in her attempt.

Tomorrow, he would see this Englishman who claimed to know him. For some reason, the notion drew fear into his heart but he had to know what had happened. The splintered pieces that came to him in his dreams were driving him mad. And he knew what madness might do to a man.

When he closed his eyes the world turned grey.

CHAPTER 35

10 November 1399 – Pontefract Castle, England

The castle loomed overhead teasing memories of a time long ago when a summons from Bolingbroke had sent him on a hard ride to reach these walls. Back then, Argyle had been left waiting in a cold hall for hours. Now, he wondered if he would receive a similar welcome.

Spurring on his white stallion he made for the drawbridge that led to the inner courtyard of Pontefract. Once he had made a public pledge of allegiance to King Henry, witnessed by the court, the message Harry had promised had arrived without delay. The King offered Argyle free passage to visit Lord Bordeaux, the only condition being that he was attended by six men from the royal guard. Now, they clattered down the road towards the castle.

'Who goes there?' The shout from the tower guard woke Argyle from his thoughts.

He held out a document bearing the royal seal. 'Sir Argyle Mowbray, I bring a royal decree allowing me safe passage.'

'Proceed.' The portcullis creaked on its cold hinges as it lifted. When Argyle looked up, the glint of the spikes told him they had been recently sharpened. Riding in ahead of his guard, he was greeted by a few stable boys and the castle chaplain.

'I had word a visitor was coming,' the chaplain said as Argyle dismounted. 'The King sent a messenger yesterday though I confess I had not believed you would be here so soon.'

'And why not, Chaplain?' Argyle handed the hunter's reins to a scrawny boy with blue-tinted lips.

Confusion stole into the chaplain's rich voice. 'Several messages have come of other visitors. So far none have showed up.'

'Well, I am a man of my word. Take me to the prisoner and take care of the men if you will. The journey was gruelling in this weather.'

The chaplain led the way into the great hall where Argyle stopped to shake his cloak. Stomping his feet on the bare, stone floor, he took in the bleak interior. 'Why is there no fire? This is a cold season to save on wood, Chaplain.'

The chaplain shook his head. 'When the King's family is not here we do not keep a fire in every room, my Lord.'

'I would have thought that with such an important prisoner you would at least keep the hall fire going.'

'There is merit in your concern only King Henry has requested that we save on wood for the time being.' The chaplain kept up his chatter as they crossed the hall in the direction of a wooden staircase. 'There is so much being done to the castle that we must save where we can. If we warm the whole place the wood will be gone within a few weeks. After all, is it not better to keep the wood for when the snow arrives as it always does a month or so from now?' He paused at the top of the stairs. 'The prisoner is down here.'

'Down?'

'Yes, my Lord. The King left instruction to fit a room for my Lord Bordeaux in the cellar.' The chaplain lost a little of his nerve. 'I would have chosen some of the upstairs apartments, but the King…'

'Never mind, Chaplain, just lead me there.' Argyle followed the aging man down the creaking wooden stairs.

At the end of the passage, two flickering torches lit up a plain door hung on massive iron hinges. The smell of oil filled the passage and assaulted at Argyle's nose. The chaplain took out a wad of keys and searched for the right one. Argyle wondered why there was no guard on the door, no jailor to keep the keys.

When Bolingbroke took the Crown, England had been quick to settle and peace had been restored, no doubt King Henry was well-informed of any unwelcome visitors. After all, the battlements were manned and very few people knew where Lord Bordeaux was kept. Even most of the court believed he was still carted around the country perhaps locked up in a monastery or the like.

To own the truth, most court gossip these days centred around the possibility of a royal wedding – or more. An embassy led by Thomas Percy, the Earl of Worcester, had been despatched to France to negotiate a match for one or more of the Princes. The idea of Worcester in Paris had made Argyle laugh.

'A visitor, my Lord.' The door swung open on well-oiled hinges. Some expenses it appeared should not be spared. The chaplain lingered in the corridor. 'It is my Lord Mowbray.'

'Lord Mowbray?' A cracked voice repeated. 'I thought he was gone?'

Argyle stepped past the gaping chaplain into a dimly lit room. 'It is Argyle Mowbray, your… my Lord.'

'Ah… now I understand. For a moment, I feared I had died and all my old enemies were now coming forth to gaze upon me in Purgatory.' The dethroned King stood and opened his arms. 'Come, let me look upon my first visitor since I came to this appalling place.'

Argyle bowed low before approaching. Bordeaux was a pale rendition of his former majestic self. Until he spoke. 'And you, Chaplain, you can leave us.'

'My Lord…' The chaplain made a weak protest.

'I may just be a prisoner, but I still have some say in how I entertain my guests – and about who is allowed to stay when I speak to them?' Bordeaux waved off the chaplain. 'Go and fetch us some wine and something to eat Sir Argyle shall stay for some time.'

Muttering something not quite audible, the chaplain closed the door.

'And there is no need to lock the door, Chaplain.' Bordeaux sighed when the key turned. 'Alas, you may find yourself imprisoned with me, Sire.'

'My Lord, how are they treating you?' Argyle asked though he could make his own assessment.

'I still struggle to understand what has happened to me. Every dawn, I wake here and am once more reminded of my demise. Though even now I cannot regret my reign nor my actions when I was King. I am given to believe that people wish me to be penitent. I cannot be. Only God can judge me and it seems he will be waiting for some time.' Bordeaux gestured around the room before taking his seat near a banked fire. 'As you see, I have all the comforts a prisoner could ask for.'

Argyle sat down on a low stool facing his former King. It would be a long time before the urge to kneel before him would subside. 'It is sparse, my Lord.'

'What could I possibly desire now that I am no longer a King? That was what that traitor cousin of mine asked when I said very much the same to him. And as you see he had already decided I needed nothing more than a bed, feather of course, a table, some books and a couple of instruments. Nothing to write on, naturally, and a couple of chairs in case I should chose to try sitting to the left of this paltry fire rather than the right. I do not believe he ever thought I would have any visitors and so, he did not feel I required anything else.' Bordeaux shook his head. 'Still, I cannot complain. The chaplain is hardly good company. At least, he keeps all the regular church hours and comes for me that I may attend mass at the castle chapel and receive Holy Communion.'

The sound of footsteps rose from outside and Argyle turned to the door as a young girl of ten or eleven slipped in carrying a tray with a carafe of what appeared to be wine, some bread and a few other dishes. Bordeaux nodded to the girl and she slipped out of the room again locking behind her. Argyle listened to the receding footsteps until he felt sure they were alone.

'My Lord, I am appalled at your conditions, truly I am. I cannot imagine that Bol… that King Henry would want you to make do with so little. Imprisonment is one thing, but to put you in the cellar when there are plenty of rooms above ground that would suit the purpose…'

Bordeaux silenced him. 'I am well treated and, on the whole, I want for nothing. I suppose the food could be better and there could be more dishes, nevertheless they bring me something to eat and for that I must be grateful.'

Where was the angry King who would not be appeased? Who was this modest creature? Had King Henry managed to break his cousin before he sent him away to this forlorn place? Argyle could not tell.

'Tell me, my Lord, is there anything I can do for you?'

'Short of getting my crown back, beating Bolingbroke to a pulp and return England to me?' A glimmer of the King he used to be was lost in a cough. 'When I first came here I was still furious at Henry's betrayal and I could not believe the court and all the lords had turned against me. I confess, sometimes, I still find myself contemplating what I will do to them once I am freed. None of that is what keeps me awake at night.'

'What is it, my Lord? Tell me and I shall attend to it immediately.' The damp space was already irking.

'Now, now, we have plenty of time I should wager. Why not enjoy whatever the cook has conjured up for us while we speak?' Bordeaux pointed to the tray and Argyle rose to fetch it. Placing the tray on the spindly wooden table he poured the wine, which appeared watered down, and set out the pewter bowls.

'One thing causes me great grief,' Bordeaux confessed. 'Since I was a boy God has visited me in my dreams, always guiding me.'

Argyle remembered the hours spent waiting for the King to return from the shrine at Milford Haven in Wales. Long before then he had laid every action at God's door, claiming that he was directed by divine intervention. He had sent Thomas and Bolingbroke into exile on the word of God. Now, one was denounced as dead and the other was King of England. Such was the turn of fortune's wheel.

Fat tears suddenly spilled down Bordeaux's hollow cheeks. 'Not once since my imprisonment has God shown himself to me. I fear He is displeased in me that He thinks I am a weak man and not the rightful King He tried to mould in his own image. Judgement is perhaps upon me and I am too blind to see.'

Agitation made Bordeaux fidgety, his voice climbing. 'God has abandoned me. I know that He has abandoned me and that, on the final day of judgement, I shall not be welcomed me into Heaven. I am bound for Hell, Sir Argyle. *Hell*.'

Cups and scraps of food spilled onto the floor when Bordeaux leaped forward from his seat kicking up the dirty old rushes. He grabbed Argyle's collar and shook it with great force.

'God has forsaken me, because He finds I did not heed his advice, He believes I listened to devilish council. He believes me a weak King!' His last word dissolved into a screech, spittle flying, raw madness lacing the walls.

Argyle tried to pull away, but Bordeaux's grip tightened his jagged fingernails dug into Argyles neck, drawing blood as they scraped away skin.

'My Lord, I am sure…' His half-hearted argument fanned Bordeaux' temper.

'*Sure*? Of what exactly? That I was a weak King? That God has forsaken me? I am a descendent of the Hammer of Scots. A grandson of the greatest King, England ever saw. I am the son of the Black Prince. What do you know of my misfortunes?' Bordeaux was lost in his rant. 'I shall redeem myself. I shall redeem myself to God and to all of England; you just wait and see. When I return to my rightful throne I shall not be weak, I shall punish all those who stood against me. All those who were disloyal and corrupt. I shall conquer them all and my lineage shall rule England forever!'

Argyle tugged hard and sent Bordeaux sprawling. He looked up, tears and sweat smearing the dirty rushes that clung to his cheeks and forehead. Shock battled rage. 'You dare lay hands on your King?'

'What use am I to you if you throttle me, my Lord?' Argyle's throat burned.

When Bordeaux sat up and brushed the rushes from his shirt, something flittered across his face, changing his expression in an instant. 'I *do* have use of you. You must intercede with Henry, you must make him see that I cannot be trapped here as some lowly beast. If he is determined to rule in my place, so be it – for now – but I cannot sit idle here. You must convince him that I can go to a monastery. I can live a holy life among monks, doing God's work. Once I am surrounded by godly men, I shall once more speak to God.'

Helping him to his feet, Argyle winced at the feel of bony arms through the tattered shirt. 'I have already made an attempt.'

'Yes?' Bordeaux' eyes had an otherworldly shimmer. He turned and gestured towards a corner, his voice suddenly soft. 'There you see, my dear, Sir Argyle would never abandon me. He understands that I must be nearer God. What chance do I have of convening with the Lord when I am halfway to Hell? Now that Sir Argyle is here he will put things right. I shall redeem myself. And I shall be free.'

Argyle swallowed back a potent mix of fear and pity. 'My Lord.'

'I can be ready within the hour.' Bordeaux grabbed a couple of books then threw them down on the bed. 'To Hell with it, I can be ready to flee now. Take me away from this hole and you shall be richly rewarded. I will call back your brother. There. That would please you I am sure? Yes, yes, I see it in your eyes. Oh, you are a sly creature. If that is to be your payment I am willing to make it. As soon as I am free, your brother will be on his way home. You shall see him much sooner than you might imagine…'

He is dead, Argyle's mind reeled, he is dead, we all know it. I felt it, I felt the truth of it when the letter arrived. How can he not know that Thomas is dead?

Argyle opened his mouth to say so, but the words would not come.

When Bordeaux leaned in the fever in his eyes scorched. 'He never left. I would not let him, you see, he was of too much use to me.'

Turning on the spot, Bordeaux sent Argyle what was no doubt intended as a meaningful smile. 'What say you to that? I had to send him away there was nothing to be done. I could not be seen to prefer him to my own family. That was God's order. However, he did not stipulate how long your brother had to be gone for, so I sent word with his wife – that scarecrow of a woman – that the captain would put him in a little skiff as soon as could be and provide oarsmen to row him back to shore.'

Bordeaux picked at a piece of bread, all the crumbs falling to the floor. 'Your brother was magnificent. He made his way back to court without anyone knowing. If it had not been for that little misunderstanding... He had to make himself known to you. He feared for your life.'

'My Lord,' Argyle tried to interject. 'Thomas...'

'Is my fiercest champion. Not on the surface, oh no, never on the surface. He was as sly and slick as a snake, but then you have to be if you are to survive court. It will not do to be kind or soft. La Fontaine knew too, he taught him well.'

He threw the rest of the bread under his bed. 'They keep food from me. Anne and I have spoken of it often enough and she agrees that we must save what we can and keep it hidden. She says they put poison in the stew and I think she is right. It is foul and it has her on her knees moaning at all hours of the night. Anne tastes all my food. She will not have me fall ill.'

It was much worse than Wales. Finding an escape in his cup, he wondered if this was why King Henry was willing to let him visit? Perhaps he wanted Argyle to see that there is no King to restore should he wake one day and decide that once more he would change sides. The bitter liquid bit into his cheeks, drying out his mouth. Could the deposed King be right?

'We have little time left, Sire,' Bordeaux said with a maddening smile. 'You must fetch to me Thomas so that we can make our case, so that we can plan my succession. Anne is pregnant, you see. Is she not radiant?' Once more Bordeaux gestured to the darkest corner.

'Yes, she truly is.' Argyle suppressed a shudder, there was nothing left to do but play along. He would never be able to convince Bordeaux that Thomas was dead. 'What do I do if I cannot find Thomas, my Lord?'

At the prospect of having no sly champion to ride to his aid Bordeaux began to pick at his dirty shirt. 'I must have my regalia. I must be seen to my best advantage. In these threads no one could recognise me. Procure a bath and clothes, and my crown. When the people see me with my crown they will know me, they will love me again.'

'My Lord.' Argyle made one last attempt to push past the insanity. 'It may be some time before I can return.'

'I understand, there is much to do,' Bordeaux skirted Argyle and knocked on the cell door. 'You are right. We must be tactical. For the time being, ask my cousin that I might retire to a monastery. You will make my request known?'

'Yes, my Lord, if that is your command.'

Sensing Bordeaux return to the present, his feverish behaviour was replaced by a lucid mind. 'It is. It will not be permanent. I must leave Pontefract. I have this burning sensation in my gut that Henry has sent me here to die and I cannot die in his prison. I must be free.' He stopped to listen for the echo of footsteps in the corridor, although everything was quiet. 'One more thing, Sir Argyle.'

'Yes, my Lord?'

'Keep the Queen safe. Declare for her. Keep her safe and away from those vipers who call themselves my cousins. In her condition, she must be surrounded by people who love her,' he urged. 'Take her now. They let her come and go it is quite remarkable. One moment she is there, the next…' He glanced at the corner. His shoulders dropped.

When he turned back, his cheeks were pale and wet. 'What… How did you come to be here?'

'King Henry allowed for me to visit, my Lord.'

'King Henry,' Bordeaux sneered. 'You are here to do his bidding. Am I to lose my life to your traitor sword?'

'No, my Lord.' Argyle looked into Bordeaux' eyes and saw only suspicion. 'I asked to visit you and had to make certain… admissions. Do you have a message for the Queen?'

'The Queen?' Bordeaux looked lost for a moment and then his face lit up. 'Isabella. Yes, how is she? Is she safe? Dear child, how I miss her. Life with her was easy, she is so kind and sweet.'

'A message, my Lord?'

The chaplain's heavy footsteps echoed down the corridor, growing ominous as they neared.

Bordeaux appeared restored to the present. 'Isabella is fair game now, Sir Argyle, and Henry has Harry in his claws who could sorely use a Princess to affirm his right to the throne. They must not have Isabella. She is not just a Princess, she is my Queen, my wife. I hold it to you to keep her safe until I escape. If needs be convince my cousin that I am prepared to live on a modest estate with her, far away from court. We shall be husband and wife and nothing more.'

'I shall do my best, my Lord.' Argyle's loyalty and love to the little Queen was unchanged by what had come to pass these past months, and she had seemed pleased to see him when he had brought her to London at King Henry's command.

The key turned in the lock and the door creaked as it flew open, the chaplain's round face red from running down the narrow staircase. 'You called, my Lord?'

'Yes.' If Bordeaux was perplexed to see the chaplain, he hid it well. He waved at the mess on the floor. 'Take my visitor away and send someone to clean this up. The food is getting worse, Chaplain. I trust you will see to it that a new cook is sent for. It would not do that you end up starving me to death for surely my cousin would not want that on his conscience.' The last words dripped with malice and threat.

'I shall see to it at once, my Lord.' The chaplain grabbed Argyle by the sleeve. 'You seem to have tired our guest, Lord Mowbray…'

The disgruntled prisoner cut him short. 'Lord Mowbray is in exile. This is his brother, Sir Argyle. Do get your titles straight, Chaplain, or I shall be forced to start calling you a choir boy!'

Argyle turned to look at Bordeaux, who had a vicious grin plastered on his haggard, dirty face. For the moment, he was back in the present, but for how long, Argyle wondered.

'I thank you for your time, my Lord Bordeaux.' He bowed and Bordeaux made much of their farewell, pushing breadcrumbs into the palm of his hand with a knowing smile before he turned to his portly, squat jailor.

'Now, Chaplain, I should like time for quiet contemplation. You can call for me at Matins, I think. I shall do the rest of my praying alone before my little, wooden cross.'

Argyle trailed in the chaplain's wake down the passage towards the stairs and fresh air. As soon as he was in the courtyard, Argyle called for his horse and the six guards spilled from the gatehouse to join him.

As the forest swallowed up Pontefract Castle, Argyle brushed his cloak and hose as if the insanity would somehow travel with him.

CHAPTER 36

2 May 1400 – Château de Boulogne-sur-Mer, France

'I understand from Madame de Reines that you were found on the beach not long from where a fisherman found my guest.'

Argyle pushed the eerie whisper of a deranged King from his mind and looked at the Countess. She was an impressive woman. She held a title in her own right, was twice married and in complete command of the lavishly decorated, bright room.

Her dark eyes searched Argyle's face. 'You wish to meet him?'

'If it pleases your Grace,' Argyle said. 'I hope perhaps the man you house might help me recreate what happened from I arrived in Calais and until I washed up on your shores.'

The Countess was still a young woman. He had no difficulty imagining half her servants to be madly in love with her, just as Grand-Maman had told him while they rumbled along the road. She had decided that he was still too weak to sit a horse and so, de Reines had readily agreed that the carriage was the right means of transportation.

As soon as they arrived, she had been ushered away somewhere and Argyle had been left to meet the Countess alone.

'You suffer the loss of memory.' She offered a sympathetic nod that made her diamond necklace glisten. 'As soon as Johanne told me, I knew I had to meet you. A man washes up on a beach with no recollection of either his name or history. Such a tale stirs my curiosity and now that you are here, it demands satisfaction.'

In the opulence of a royal family member, he was hard pressed to do anything but accede her demand if he was to avoid being sent to Paris as soon as she saw fit.

'I am fortunate that, under the watchful care of Madame de Reines, I have mended well and find much of my memory restored.'

'You still do not remember what happened?'

'Fragments, disturbed images.' Argyle tried not to sway with the wobble of the floor under his feet. After almost a week of steady footing, the return of his nausea was as unwelcome as it was unhelpful. 'Nothing I dare trust to be the truth.'

The Countess rose from her throne-like seat underlining her descent. When she reached Argyle, she took his arm. 'I am given to understand that you have been a loyal servant to my nephew's daughter since her arrival in England. She is sorely missed at court.'

'The Queen is a great patron.' Argyle paused when something akin to concern flickered across the Countess' fine features.

'I believe she regards you as a dear friend,' she said as she guided him to a window overseeing a splendid park. 'For that reason alone, I shall assist in any way I can. My nephew is very fond of his daughter as you well know. Since her hardship not a day goes by that some measure is not taken to ensure her safety.'

There it was, the real reason she was so kind and helpful. She desired some way to King Henry. There was but one problem with her plan and Argyle was not going to foil his chance unless he had no other option. 'I do not know that I can assist, your Grace, but upon my honour, I shall make an attempt.'

'Honour will not buy you safe passage through France,' the Countess said and lowered her voice. 'I can.'

'You are most kind.' Argyle kept his gaze on the view.

'My kindness comes at a price as you are no doubt aware. That is a matter which we shall discuss later.' She gestured for a servant to come closer. 'Sir Argyle will see our guest now. You shall both dine with me tonight and delight me with the true and full story of how you came to wash up in Boulogne.'

Argyle left the hall wondering if anyone ever contradicted the Countess. He had yet to meet her husband and, for some reason, he suspected that she preferred to keep some guests to herself.

'Sir Argyle,' the servant announced as he opened a door.

'Thank you.' The hoarse voice was unfamiliar and Argyle's hopes shrunk. The servant turned and gestured for Argyle to enter. The door closed with a clink.

Staring at the battered man on the cot all the missing

pieces fell into place.

Part II
Deceit and Death

CHAPTER 37

20 November 1399 – Beauworth

'Why are they coming here?' Isobel still had that wide-eyed fearful look about her, a stubborn hesitance in her manner. Argyle knew she would care nothing for his news and, therefore, had not broached it upon first arriving home. Unfortunately, it was news that could not wait.

Now, she was shaking even more than she had been when he had reached Beauworth just two nights hence. She had tumbled into his arms and he had kissed tears from her cheeks. Her reaction in the courtyard had whisked away any concern he had felt on the journey south. Whatever she might have felt during his long absence, she forgave him then and there.

It had taken him less than a day to wreck their brittle happiness. And now, her words tripped on a rush of dread.

'What is happening? You have only just returned to us. Have you not made enough sacrifices? Proven yourself to him?'

More than you will ever know. Argyle tried to calm Isobel down by taking her hand in his. Standing just outside the great hall where men were still breaking their fast, calling for bread and discussing the day ahead, Argyle did not want to say more than bore overhearing.

'This is a final act of deference, dear wife. It is what I had to agree to, to ensure that you and our children were set free. This removes the Lancaster guard from our gates for good. We must make a public display of loyalty to the new King. It is no more than custom dictates.'

'Did you not attend his coronation? See him anointed? Hear the bishop speak the words that makes him our King?' Her words lurched on her tongue. 'For so you said last night. You swore to me.'

'Yes, and afterwards I went to see Lord Bordeaux.'

She pulled away the shock in her eyes enhanced by her dark garb. 'Why would you do that? Why visit *him*? He who publicly renounced his claim to the throne. He is deposed, he asked for his cousin to take the throne. We had the news by messenger. He is nothing to us anymore, he deserves your loyalty no more. We do – your family does. That is all you should concern yourself with. I do not understand why you would do such a thing?' Every question was a stab of accusation.

'To make sure he was dealt with properly. It is one thing to say he is safe, quite another to show it.' Argyle neglected to tell her that he feared not only for Bordeaux' safety but also for his sanity.

The bloom on her cheeks told him she was furious and barely able to check herself. She opened her mouth just as a few Lancaster guards filed past, their expressions vacant, their ears no doubt trained on what was said in this house until the King arrived himself to release them.

'I would have a private word, wife.' Argyle pulled her into the parlour, coloured light falling through the doors leading into the great hall. He kicked the door to the outer hall closed. 'King Henry sanctioned my visit. He sealed the papers that gave me safe passage to see his cousin.'

'Clearly King Henry was testing your loyalty. Is that why you did not return sooner?' Isobel crossed her arms. Just last night, she had given him her body, now she refused his touch. 'Are you going to attempt to save Bordeaux from some awful fate? For I admit, I imagined you were done doing anything for a man who put you behind bars.'

Argyle shot her a dark look and sat on one of the chairs, pushing cushions out of the way. 'Lord Bordeaux is still in prison. I did nothing to save him and I do not intend to start plotting now, Isobel. It is as you say, I am done.'

'Then why go to him, Argyle?' She spoke his name as if it was a curse. 'Why not return to us as soon as you were able?'

You did not see him in Wales, Argyle wanted to say, you do not understand the beast I unleashed when I put him into his cousin's hands. What betrayal I had to commit to come home.

'Well?'

'I understand.' Argyle grabbed Isobel's arm when she turned away, the stained glass twisting her reflection. 'I do understand that you felt abandoned and that you still do. If I might offer a better explanation than that I did all I could to return to you – to our children – I would, but I have no other explanation.'

Isobel did not turn around, nor did she attempt to free

herself from his grasp. 'They whisper that you are a traitor. That that is why you were thrown in the Tower.' Her voice teetered. 'Is it true?'

'I…' Releasing Isobel, Argyle ran a hand through his hair. He wanted to wash away the betrayal, madness and newly brokered deals. 'I am home now. Can we not leave it at that?'

'I have lived nearly half a year under guard, Argyle. I gave birth with strangers standing outside my chamber. They came in as soon as Thom was born and snatched him away. They employed a nurse I had never seen before and put her in charge of my children. Our children.' Isobel made an effort to still her hands. 'You left me alone. To go and fight a war for a man who could not keep the love of his people. And now, you serve his conqueror. How am I to react? Tell me that, for I am at my wit's end.'

Rising, Argyle wrapped his arms tight around her. Isobel was worn thin from worry and she had a new frail quality. Perhaps his mind simply refused to remember what it was like to touch her. They had been apart for too long and he was determined to stay by her side in years to come.

'No matter my actions everything I have done since Ireland, I did for you, for our family,' Argyle whispered into her hair. 'We have a new King and must all make our peace with it. Yes, I rode into London with him and yes, I attended his coronation. I can attest that he is beloved by lords and commoners alike. I was his enemy's fiercest protector. It is only natural that King Henry demands more from me than most others.'

Isobel wet his garb with her silent tears. 'But no more. Once we have entertained the King then no more?'

'Not if I can help it.' He kissed her forehead. 'We are at the mercy of King Henry now.'

'As we were once at the mercy of another King.' Isobel looked up at him, her cheeks wore a pretty wash of pink highlighted by the gleam of tears. 'What other news do you bring?'

'Thomas is dead.'

Isobel's breath caught and then she exhaled. 'I am sorry.'

Relishing the scent of freshly churned butter and heavy spices lingering in her hair Argyle released her. 'We got the news a few weeks after I returned from Wales. It appears he died in Venice. Elizabeth was distraught.'

'You saw her?'

'Her, Margaret and Eleanor. In London.' Argyle knew how little Isobel thought of her sister-in-law and decided not to tell her about his invitation or Elizabeth's attending the coronation ceremony, hooked to his arm. 'They were all at court.'

'Making new alliances no doubt.' Isobel fiddled with the ends of her thick woven shawl. 'And what about you? Were you making new alliances too?'

'I am not my brother.' Argyle's words hung between them suspended in time. They drained the parlour of colour and dragged warmth from the wall-hangings and thick rush matting.

He drew breath and shook his head. 'I will apologise for my own actions as long as you need me to, but I will not accept that you continue to dangle Thomas' misdeeds over my head. Others may do so that is something I cannot control. But I will not have my own wife constantly reminding me of a brother who is now lost to me forever. For though we were never close it is as if I have lost a part of myself. You of all people should know what it is like to lose a sibling.'

It was a low blow to remind her of her sister who had

burned as a witch although she was innocent. Still, if it served to impress his feelings on her, so be it.

Isobel chewed her lip. 'Whatever you might think of me I am sad to hear of his death. Did you get any word on how he died?'

'No.' Isobel's question tugged at a loose thread in Argyle's mind. They never had heard how Thomas died, only that it had been in Venice. If you were to lie about a man's death why not give a cause for it?

She busied herself straightening her shawl, pulling it tight around her shoulders. No matter how warm it was, it seemed she was perpetually cold and November did nothing to alleviate her shivers. 'Do you think it was the mortality?'

'Perhaps. The letter did not specify.' Argyle sat back down in the chair, it felt strange, as if it did not belong to him. Before he had left for London last, she had asked if she could turn his study into a parlour. It overlooked the gardens which she loved and he had accepted, his mind on other matters. Now, his study felt dark and cramped. It was Isobel's, not his.

'Odd.' Isobel warmed her hands by the hearth. She sighed. 'So, we are to entertain a King once more.'

Looking into her eyes, Argyle could almost deceive himself that she genuinely loved him. 'Yes, we are. At least this time, we can be certain he will not keep the house up at night screaming at his wife.'

Isobel bent and kissed his hair, the whisper of a smile on her face. 'He will marry, you think?'

'He has heirs, but yes, he is a man in his prime and the King of England. Surely someone will want to be his wife. And he needs to forge alliances.'

'Perhaps he is travelling the land to see if anyone takes

his fancy?' Isobel played with his hair the sensation intensely intimate. 'For certainly he will not take a foreign bride?'

'He has sent an embassy to France though I believe it is to negotiate brides for his sons.' Argyle closed his eyes. 'Whatever else happens his first priority must to keep the peace with France.'

'What will happen to the Queen?'

Isabella might be the one safe topic for them to discuss. Isobel adored the young girl and had rarely argued when he was called to serve her. Now, Isabella was to be Lady Bordeaux and was not allowed to see her husband, a punishment Argyle felt was more a blessing than a curse. While she was strong-willed and determined to see a once strong man broken and forlorn might break her spirit.

'There has been no decision on the matter.' He leaned back against a firm, silk covered cushion. 'For the time being, she resides with the Bishop of London. She enjoys as much freedom as might be expected and sent word just before I left that Master Harry was in constant attendance.'

'Surely they cannot expect her to entertain his attentions? Her husband has been usurped and put in prison.' Isobel paused, considered something. 'They would not go to extreme measures to ensure a match, would they? She is married. She is anointed…'

'She still signs her letters as Queen of England.' He had been torn between shock and pride when he had heard of her audacity.

'Daring.'

'Or to prove a point.' He half-smiled when Isobel made a face. 'Come now, wife, you cannot put anything past the Queen. It is hardly her fault that her husband was captured.'

'You told me that he agreed to meet Bolingbroke – King Henry – oh, for God's sake what are we to call them all?'

These are confusing times, he thought.

'We must call them by their current titles. Which makes Bolingbroke King Henry from now on.'

When Isobel sniffed, he finally saw through the thin veneer of calm. 'Something is troubling you?'

'I feel as if we have been apart for a lifetime. Now that my prayers have finally been answered I scarcely dare say anything for fear you will disappear. Already, your attention is turned from me, from us. Is it greedy of me to want some time alone with you? Free from concern and worry, safe from the world.'

From the moment he dismounted in the courtyard yesterday evening, captains and servants had swarmed. Even Stephen had claimed his attention. It had been well into the night before Argyle had joined Isobel in her chambers. They had not wasted time speaking.

With a smile, he offered her the chair opposite him. 'You have me now. Command me.'

'Tell me about Ireland.' Isobel stretched her feet to the fire. 'Did you give battle?'

'I was sent to Kells.' Finding it hard to speak of a victory that felt as if it was decades gone, he kept his narrative succinct. 'There was a battle. We won.'

'Is that how you related the news to your King?'

Surrendering, Argyle pulled his chair closer to hers. 'Very well. The King sent me to Kells with three thousand men. MacMurrough was rumoured to dwell there and the King wanted to teach the rebellious man a lesson. When we arrived he was not there though other Irish nobles and knights were. When the gates to the city opened more than five thousand armed men were ready to give us an Irish welcome.'

Argyle watched the flames lick against the grate. He had

not enjoyed a proper fire since returning from Ireland. 'We struck a deep wound into the centre of their first wave of attackers. Our archers made short process of the flanks.' He closed his eyes, felt her hand on his arm. 'To go into battle is to see the world through two tiny slits. It is a strange mixture of fear and arrogance. It is as if I forget that I can die, as if I know that I will survive and perish at the same time. It mattered not that I took a lance to the shoulder. All I had eyes for was the enemy.'

Her hand meandered to his shoulder, probing the skin through his woollen gown. 'Go on. I am a woman and shall never see a battlefield. You must take me there even just for a moment.'

When her fingertips caught the edge of the scar, he twisted to catch her hand, pressing a kiss into her palm. 'Before long, I was fighting without my helmet. I think I threw it aside because my enemies' blood burned my eyes blurring my vision. When the second wave of soldiers fell upon us, I could taste victory. They outnumbered us but they were farmers with pitchforks and recruits with dull blades. The King had sent with us some of the best trained men in his army.'

He let her go and rubbed his temple. 'It was a massacre. The blood spilled churned the dry ground to mud.'

'What of the city?' Isobel appeared mesmerised.

He remembered the other commanders' desire to raid Kells. 'It stands to this day.'

She shifted in her seat. 'Why did you not put it to the torch? Is that not the way?'

'No wife, it is not. The city held only women and children, a few old men… Innocent souls. It was punishment enough that they watched the English army lay waste to their future, kill their husbands, fathers, sons without remorse. I shall never put innocent people to death.'

'*You* gave the order to spare them?'

Did she want him to prove he was no monster? Argyle sighed. 'There was no need to sack the city. There were no men left to protect those within the walls.'

'How long did it take?'

'I cannot say.' Argyle closed his eyes again and Coxcombe's limp body swam in the darkness. 'It was swift. We lost four hundred men or thereabout. We buried more than five thousand bodies.'

'I do not understand?' Isobel's whisper made him open his eyes.

'We buried the dead. All of them.'

Drawing her shawl close around her shoulders, Isobel gave him a strange, cold look. 'Why? If you did not sack the city you should have let the women bury their dead.'

'There was little time to spare and they were frightened. Who would leave the city to face an enemy clad in steel and blood?' Argyle recalled the long, warm, stinking days. 'The sun was relentless. It cooked the bodies until they bubbled in the sun. I had no choice. If we had not buried them my men would have fallen sick and died. Thomas Percy asked me the same question as you did. He wanted to let their own kin do that. But their kin had watched us slaughter their men. Why would they trust us not to do the same if they came for their dead?'

Isobel stared at his hands. 'You handled the dead?'

'What would you have me do, wife?' He suddenly wanted her to understand the pressure he had been under, the reek of decay, the men's lives, the King in his might, the terrifying prospect that Argyle might never return to Beauworth but be thrown in the Tower no matter if he lost or won a hundred battles.

'I needed to prove to myself that I am no barbarian.' He resisted the urge to rub his hands to rid them of the stain of death. 'I sent all my men to dig graves and I went myself.'

'Why? No one would expect you to, surely?' Something about the idea repulsed her, discomfort dancing on her face.

'I could not ask them to do something I was not prepared to do. No one wants to return to a battlefield. Many of the men were frightened that the ghosts of the dead would haunt them. I was more concerned that the dead would contaminate the air and water and kill us without grace.' Unable to stay in his seat, Argyle went to stare out of the window at the bare fields that stretched towards the distant forest. 'Master Harry asked much the same question you just did.'

Isobel straightened. 'Harry?'

'The Prince of Wales as it is now.' Argyle thought he saw something flicker across her delicate features.

'He was with you?'

'Sent by the King to keep me in my place.' He leaned against the window sill. 'You must remember where the King found me.'

'The Tower.' Her expression hardened. 'No. I do not care to know why you were there. I saw the wound yesterday, husband. It is still red and raw and when I touched it you shied away. None of that matters anymore for you are here now. And here you must remain. That is the agreement with King Henry, is it not? Stay here and be a loyal subject?'

Argyle could only nod. What good was it to tell her that he must obey the new King in any command? If he summoned Argyle to go to London, he must go. What little freedom he had enjoyed before it was gone snatched away by fate.

'Tell me about Prince Harry.' She picked up an intricate embroidery and set about threading some red silk. 'He must be happy his father is returned?'

'The time in Ireland taught him something about leadership, I believe. The time in Wales, being dragged from one castle to the next, the constant flight, no messages received or sent, no way to know what might happen… It was hard for him.'

She paused, the needle halfway through the cotton and he continued. 'Harry went from being beloved nephew to being a prisoner. At the very end, the King… Lord Bordeaux demanded that he be flogged and left to die on the stocks.'

Isobel threaded the silk anew, turning the frame. 'The poor boy.'

'Lord Salisbury prevented the disaster.' Argyle swallowed. 'I was sent away to treat with Bolingbroke on the King's command. That was when I…'

'Whatever transpired next I trust your actions heralded from love.' Isobel stabbed the taut cotton, embellishing the embroidery with more red.

Argyle had tried to convince himself that it was so, but it had been more than love of his family it had been something that he could not quite define.

'So much was done for love in those days. Bolingbroke's return – I hope was not pure ambition. I pray that he thought about his sons too. Harry stayed with the King…'

Her sewing pace increased. 'He loved his uncle?'

'He still does. Even after all that happened he loves him and has worked tirelessly to keep him safe. Keep in mind that Harry revered his father from afar while he lived in the royal palace for years. Although he may have accepted his fate I wonder if he is altogether happy. While he may have gained a father he lost an uncle whom he loved as a father.'

Argyle's gaze strayed to Isobel. Should he tell her that Lord Bordeaux had gone mad? How could anyone who did not witness it ever grasp what he had seen? What Harry had experienced? How bruised it had left the boy instilling doubt that love even existed.

'Harry looked to me for reassurance that his beloved uncle had come to no harm.' He desired her approval above all else. 'Now, do you understand why I had to visit Lord Bordeaux at Pontefract?'

Snipping the thread, her eyes never strayed from her work. 'If you did it out of duty then I do not. But if you did it for love of our new royal family… No, I confess I believe you should not have gone, not even to please the Prince. It does not matter what I think. We are free. Our children will not have to grow up under the watchful eye of a royal guard. We must take heart in small favours.'

The watchful guard will never be far from us, he thought and shook the ominous feeling from his bones. 'We must prepare for a royal visit, my love. There is much to attend to and I want you to help me.'

'Before we do, let us go to the nursery.' Isobel sent him one of her rare, satisfied smiles that put dimples into her cheeks and took years off her haggard expression. 'You have yet to meet your son. Thomas.'

Argyle's heart skipped. Why had she chosen the name of a man she detested? To please him?

'Thomas?'

'I thought you would approve.' Isobel put away the embroidery. 'He is a fine little boy. Please, Argyle, let Edmund and little Thomas be balm for our coming ordeal.'

He followed her out of the door and up the stairs.

Yesterday, Stephen had tried to warn him that Isobel had made decisions that might have his hackles up. For her to name his second son for his exiled brother was a surprise. What might have possessed her?

Argyle suppressed an urge to spit to ward off evil. Would his son grow up tainted by the mischief and malice that Thomas had lived with? Surely a name in itself could not place upon the bearer all the aliments of the past.

Isobel opened the door to the nursery spreading her arms wide. 'Meet our sweet Thomas.'

She picked up the babe from the cot and earned a wide, toothless grin. The crown of his head showed wisps of copper hair and his eyes were that washed-out colour of all new-borns. He looked like his mother with a lick of something familiar that Argyle failed to place.

'Papa!'

He turned at the tug on his shirt. 'Ned.'

He still marvelled that the dark hair Ned had been born with was now a crown of golden curls. He also praised himself lucky that his first-born did not look one ounce a Mowbray with his bright blue eyes. Argyle hoped Ned would never have to go to court. He deserved a quiet life as a landowner, not the turbulent life of a courtier.

As the son of a knight he might just be passed over. As the son of a Mowbray he might not. At least Ned did not favour the dark and sombre look of his cousins. More than anything, Argyle hoped that his sons would grow up to form a strong and honest bond with each other.

He lifted Ned from the floor and pointed at the babe in Isobel's arms. 'Come see your brother.'

The boy hid his face in Argyle's hair and wailed.

CHAPTER 38

31 November 1399 – Beauworth

The minstrel finished his tale and the musicians struck a jaunty tune that soon filled the floor with dancers. Argyle noticed the minstrel glance at the dais where Isobel was left to entertain Harry.

She was staring into space while he clapped along to the tune and made eyes at a fair young maid from the royal retinue. There had not been many moments to spend alone, but he appeared in good spirits and that was enough to satisfy Argyle that the Prince was easing into his new life.

Argyle nodded at Margaret who had come only reluctantly at his request, her husband not in tow. She acknowledged him with a grim smile before emptying her cup. From a distance her skin had the quality of old wax.

'This is a fine feast, M'lord.' The minstrel sidled up next

to Argyle. 'It's been long since I've last been invited to entertain such guests as these who adorn your halls. What a great honour it is to be minstrel to a King – however late he might've come to his crown.'

'I should thank you for your excellent stories. Master?'

'Jasper.' The minstrel smiled once more, a soft and comfortable beam that surely many a woman would enjoy. 'Believe me, M'lord, the pleasure is all mine.'

Inclining his head, he looked at the guests dancing. It had been a scramble to find enough gentry to fill the hall, but with a push and a few invitations for people living farther afield he had managed. Now, the great hall of Beauworth brimmed and sparkled, everyone decked out in their finest garb, the ladies with gemstones in their hair and sewn onto their gowns, the men sporting elegant belts and pins.

'You tell a fair tale, Master Jasper.'

'Oh, I have so many to tell, M'lord. After all, that's what I do. And I confess I'm most pleased to see a familiar face in the crowd although I wonder if the feeling is mutual.' Jasper was leaning on his lute, a sneaky glitter in his eye. 'But then she mightn't remember me, it has been long.'

'You do not sound to be from around here?' Argyle wondered how a minstrel of Jasper's talent chose to travel the roads rather than take a permanent position in a great house. 'Who might you know?'

'The lady of the house, M'lord.' Jasper smiled in the face of Argyle's curious glance. 'When I knew her she was, of course, much younger. Now hers is an interesting tale.'

'Is that so?'

'I'm sure you already know it, M'lord.' Jasper's eyes swept the room.

To Argyle the minstrel looked almost nervous. 'Of her

first husband? Yes, I do.'

'She was married before? That I didn't know. No M'lord, I was thinking about her childhood. That's when I knew her. It's not often you hear of a bastard girl rising so high above her station as she has.' He dipped his head hastily when Argyle cleared his throat. 'Begging your pardon, M'lord.'

'Bastard girl?' The question was out before he could stop himself.

'Pay him no mind, husband,' Isobel said at Argyle's elbow. Her voice was silken, her words deadly. 'What is the purport of a minstrel if not to tell tales that warp mind and truth alike?'

Jasper smiled, but Argyle noticed that, this time, the smile did not reach the minstrel's eyes and Isobel shook in silent anger, her fingers digging into his arm.

'Too true, wife.' He touched the pearl-drop earring to ease her manner. 'I thank you once more, Master Jasper, for your service. Come find me in the morning and I shall pay you.'

Argyle watched Jasper walk away, his lute carelessly perched on his shoulder. When he passed the maid Harry had graced with his attention, the minstrel ran his hand up her arm and leaned in to say something that made her blush. They disappeared in the crowd. Here perhaps was the reason Jasper held no permanent position.

'You ought not pay him a groat.'

'Whyever not?' He turned his attention to Isobel who had wiped any sign of emotion from her expression. 'He delivered a grand tale and amused the King.'

'Is that rare?' Isobel ground her teeth in a stiff smile. 'Too much of anything can turn even the sweetest experience sour. Beware King Henry does not find out what

Jasper is for then he will not thank you for inviting him to entertain the royal court. Did you not see him just now? That girl will never be the same again.'

Argyle squeezed her hand and lowered his voice. 'If you have something to tell me, my dear, this is not the time. Rest assured that he will be paid for his services and then he will leave as was ever the arrangement. If King Henry takes an interest and invites him to court it is out of our hands. I for one was amused by his tale.'

'Oh, he tells the most enchanting tales. It is his gift. How much of it can be trusted is another matter entirely. Know only that once he enchanted the wrong woman – charmed his way into her bed.' When she pulled away, her hand was red from his grasp. 'Best you keep an eye on the ladies here tonight, the maids especially. We would not want any of them defiled.'

She dipped her head. 'I want to be present when you pay him.'

'If it pleases you.' Argyle watched Harry dance with a dark-haired woman his eyes scanning the hall, a dutiful smile fixed in place. 'Though I cannot imagine why you find it necessary.'

'No, and that is exactly why I intend to be there.'

As Isobel turned and left Argyle noticed King Henry following her progression with a thoughtful expression.

Not wanting to be caught in another bout of watchful silence with his King, Argyle spied Margaret and crossed the floor, dancers parting for him until he reached her secluded spot in one of the niches. She put away her kerchief, but he noticed the feverish burn of her eyes and the sickly-sweet whiff on her breath.

CHAPTER 39

1 December 1399 – Beauworth

'I believe you were about to tell me something yesterday.' Argyle was tired, he had had too much wine and was in no mood to take King Henry hunting at noon. 'I would know what it was.'

'It seemed to upset your wife, M'lord,' Jasper said slipping the fat purse inside his robe. 'Better…'

'Better you tell me here than in the presence of our guests, I have no doubt.' Argyle had not called on Isobel before going downstairs. His curiosity would not be satisfied if she were present. 'And be quick about it. As you might imagine I have much to attend to today.'

'I worked for a long time in the household of a great lord, one of the greatest in our kingdom.' The minstrel's voice changed as if to captivate an audience. 'He had a fierce temper and a great thirst for all things worldly. Including women. Young women.'

'What is that to me?'

'One of the women he courted was to be the mother of a fair girl. The woman worked first in the kitchens and then served the tables where she turned the heads of many a man. Then the Lord noticed her. He made certain she became a maid to his own wife and then, he began his pursuit. Day and night, he'd haunt her steps.' Jasper wore a thin smile. 'What woman could refuse him?'

'I assume you are not speaking of my wife for she is somewhat younger than you.' In the bright December light Jasper looked older than Argyle had believed last night.

'Oh no, not your wife. Her mother.'

He was in no mood for a fairy story. 'She is long since dead.'

'Yes, and her husband remarried. The whole county wondered why he took her in, so I heard tell when I passed through the village many years later. It intrigued me even more that he kept her daughter in his household. How many men would take in a woman spoiled?' Jasper's eyes strayed to the array of pitchers, but he knew better than to ask for refreshment. 'I went to the castle and offered my services. The Lord was away and his steward received me with every curtsey, employing me without delay. There in the kitchens I saw for myself the child.'

'There is no need to spin a tale, Minstrel.' Argyle's head pounded. 'Speak plainly and let us have done with this.'

'I suspect most men didn't see what the farmer did – that there might be profit to be made, lands to be had or money at least. If you cared for the Lord's child as if she were your own.' His voice had a devious undertone. 'While the nobleman might be a vicious creature, foul-tempered, petty and vindictive – as all men of his family are – he also knew the value of loyalty. He blessed the match since the maid was a maid no more and most likely his wife wouldn't suffer her return…'

A glance in Argyle's direction had Jasper pick up his pace. 'The farmer told me all of this, one night in the tavern, looking to unload his fears and concern. I was happy to lend an ear. After all, that's how all minstrels work. We take the tales of common folk and transform them into epic fables that'll entertain and fascinate the lords of the land. It's strange, M'lord, how little the women and men in castles know of the lives outside their high walls. And how easy it is to mould a tale to bewilder and enchant.'

Argyle worked his jaw, he did not like where Jasper's account was going. Mighty men had seduced women since time immemorial and some women had even won their freedom this way. However, such a ruse could go wrong. Celeste called at the back of his mind and he pushed her away. She had died for bedding the wrong man, but more than anything, she had died because of her bloodline. Anyone affiliated with the royal family was under constant scrutiny and one false move could send you to the scaffold.

'Who was the lord?'

'A man of royal stock.' Jasper sniggered. 'A royal uncle, although back then he was a King's son. He died a traitor. At your brother's hand if I'm not much mistaken. Though perhaps not at his command.'

Argyle's mind went blank just as the door smashed open.

'Liar.' Isobel came hurtling into the room, her eyes black with rage. 'You are a foul, despicable liar!'

Jasper sidestepped just in time and Isobel's hand missed its mark. He bowed low to her. 'I'm many things, M'lady, but a liar I am not.'

'Do not believe a word he is saying, husband. Has he told you what he is called?' There was disgusting triumph in Isobel's voice. 'Jasper the castrate.'

'By the hand of your own father, M'lady.' Jasper snarled. 'He caught me stealing a few pieces of silver and decided to make sure I never spawned any thieving children. Isn't that the story you chose?'

'He is a thief and a liar.' Isobel's initial resolve trembled.

'A thief does not a liar make, M'lady.' Jasper gave Isobel an insolent look. 'Had your husband or any other of his household asked before they employed me I would've told them the truth. I've mended my ways. I steal no more, I am not capable.'

Isobel turned to Argyle anger blooming on her cheeks. 'My father loved my mother. There is no truth in his words. He may say he is a thief no more but who will trust such a culprit?'

'Perhaps the same man who trusted a witch's sister?' Jasper retorted.

'Enough!' Argyle beat his hand on the table hard enough to make the inkwell wobble. 'Master Jasper, you have upset my wife and are no longer welcome beneath my roof. You are paid for your services and free to go. I urge you not to linger. You are on my land and in the presence of a King. A wise man knows his place. Leave us.'

Jasper patted the purse under his shirt and made a mocking bow to Isobel. 'I beg your forgiveness. The truth is a harsh master…'

'Out.' Argyle silenced Isobel with a glance. 'Your tale here is at an end.' Argyle fixed the minstrel with a glare. 'If you value what life you have left no tales will be told that in any way can be traced back to Beauworth. None. Or you will find that the last thing you feel is cold steel slowly piercing your throat.'

White-faced, Jasper left the room, the door gaping behind him. Argyle closed it, cutting off Isobel's escape. This was not her parlour, there was no stained-glass door to take her to safety.

She plucked a little courage from thin air and smiled. 'Thank…'

'Is it true?' Argyle leaned against the door keeping his shock in check. 'Are you the child of Thomas of Woodstock? Are you related to the King?'

Isobel went white. 'I… He…'

'No lies, Isobel, that is what we promised each other on our wedding day. No lies only truth. It was your dearest wish if I am not much mistaken.' Argyle tasted the depth of his own deceit and swallowed acid. 'This is not a tale he tells to entertain people. I believe he has never told it before. Now is the time for you to speak in your defence.' He paused but she kept quiet. 'The truth, wife.'

Pale as the ice crusting the windows, Isobel said, 'I told you that my father interfered. That he was instrumental in my first marriage. How could a farmer ever hope to sway a lord? Imagine my surprise when you did not even ask about the circumstances.'

'You could rival Jasper as a minstrel.' Argyle threw her spite back in her face. 'How many times have you used the tale of a violent husband? Is it even true, Isobel? Or have you deceived me to your own advantage? Do you think no husband would ever do what you dreamed up to ensnare me?'

Her strained face stopped him and she poised herself. 'Geoffrey was real. And I did kill him. Just as I said. You are the first man I have ever trusted with my true story…' Isobel grabbed the back of the nearest chair her gold marriage band stark against her pale skin. 'If you knew the whole truth would you ever have married me? Or just sent me away with a look of disdain?'

Argyle refused to take the bait and waited for her to continue. Their wills battled and, for once, his won. She resigned. 'My father – the farmer – he was distraught when I told him what had come to pass. At his wit's end, he turned to my natural father and pleaded for him to…'

'Make the alliance.' Argyle sat at his desk, a lead wall rising between them. 'He used you. You were a means to an end. Nothing more. Another alliance, however small, would be a gain for Woodstock. Doubt not that he took a goodly sum to hand over his natural born daughter to the son of a minor lord.'

Isobel shrunk back, shaking her head. 'No…'

'He sold you off to a man who almost killed you. I wonder how he reacted when he heard that your dear, young husband had died before his time?' He had seen enough of Woodstock to know that part of him would have been proud. To acknowledge her in the first place must have come at great cost.

'He did nothing. I went to stay with my father – the man who raised me as his own,' Isobel said. 'He took me in but did not speak to me. Perhaps he guessed what I had done, though he never asked. His wife was the only bulwark between us.' She snarled. 'And then news came of Tilly and her bastard of a husband.'

'And you arrived here. Saw me.'

She nodded. 'I met the golden lord of Beauworth.'

Dread seeped into his veins. 'Did you tell him who I was?'

'Who do you think paid for my return? Me?' There was something incredulous in Isobel's voice. 'As soon as he heard your name he sanctioned our match. For the first and only time, he held me in his arms and kissed my head and told me that I was fulfilling my destiny. That he was pleased my first husband had died because now… Now, I could be of use to him.'

'Did you spy on me?'

Rubbing her dry eyes, Isobel stared at the floor. 'Yes. Until you stopped telling me things. Until you shut me out. When my words dried up so did his interest.'

I was right to keep secrets from you, Argyle thought as years of doubt evaporated. You cannot be trusted. If you had known about the warrant you would have warned Woodstock and he would still be alive.

He would be alive, but in all likelihood Isobel would be twice widowed and Argyle would have been killed for carrying out a royal order.

'And when he died?'

'I needed to find a new protector.' Isobel twisted her wedding band. 'By then, it was obvious that your own family meant more to you than I ever could. I turned to the two remaining brothers, my uncles. I knew both of them were looking to secure their positions at court and that they believed your brother was becoming too powerful. Whispering in the King's ear, feeding him lies. I could be leverage, a spy in a Mowbray household. Except you told me nothing of consequence though I did not know it at the time. This I learned only later. Much later.'

'Who took you in?' Blinding rage turned his gaze red. The sting of deceit and truth in her words fed his fury.

'John of Gaunt.'

The earth shifted beneath his feet. 'You warned off Bolingbroke? You told him the King was away in Ireland and that England was ripe for the picking?' Who was this woman? Realisation hit as lance at full tilt. 'You created a new King.'

'My cousin promised to reward me.' Satisfaction stole into Isobel's voice. 'All he required was your loyalty. He offered to protect us, protect your children, until you accepted his rule. Once he governed you I would be free. He was true to his word. The moment you surrendered Lord Bordeaux he sent word and dispersed his guard.'

Sour vomit bit the inside of his mouth. 'You have been free for weeks?'

'I was never a captive.' Isobel shook back her hair, her triumph hideous. 'You were. Anything can be bought, even loyalty. Your brother taught me that.'

'Who knows?' Argyle shook from anger; his fingertips bled from gripping the table to keep from striking her. Somehow, she knew he never would, even now. 'Who besides me knows what you are? Tell me!'

She had slept with him, given him children, dined with him and fed him lies. The depth of her deception cast his study into gloom.

'His position at court is secure. He will not betray my secret.' Her words slashed open his chest. 'If only I could be sure of you.'

When Argyle rose, Isobel flinched. Could she tell that he was moments away from reaching for her neck? He knocked the inkwell off the table. It crashed into the wall bleeding black blood onto the floor.

'Your distress when I told you that King Henry was to come here?' Argyle pushed out the question.

'A show.' Isobel eyed the door. Before she could move, he caught her arm, making her eyes brim.

'I suppose, I should congratulate you on your performance. It was worthy of court itself.' Iron laced his tongue. 'What would you have done if Jasper had not revealed your secret?'

'Kept quiet, perhaps tried to win you over. make you mine. I tried you know. I wanted you to love me.' Hurt and fear flickered in her voice and her eyes. 'I wanted you desire me as you did that French whore.'

'That French whore was your cousin.' Argyle enjoyed Isobel's shock. His fury took root, blotting out what little compassion he had for her. The situation would be laughable if it was not so dangerous.

'If she had been free I would be in exactly the same position as you have put me in.' The memory of Celeste dying lodged in his mind.

Isobel backed away, both hands at her neck. 'You lie. It is a lie. She is not what I am, she is not… You lie…'

'Careful, *wife*.' Her horror cooled his temper. Clarity descended. 'You are in no position to accuse me of anything. And you are forgetting something.'

'What?'

'By your devising our children are part of the succession.' His words turned into shards. 'King Henry would be a fool if he does not see them as threats and an even greater fool if he lets us keep them here. If he can take the throne then so can they. In time.'

'No.' Isobel fell back into the chair. 'No…'

'Your actions have served only to put them in harm's way. You have condemned them to a fate worse than death – you have condemned us. When the knock comes, when you have to turn them over to strangers to live out their lives as hostages in a rancorous house, know that you alone are responsible. You who claim to love them. You will be their destruction.'

Tears streamed down Isobel's pale cheeks. 'He would

never…'

'You are right about one thing. Loyalty can be bought.' Argyle struggled to keep his voice low, inaudible to the scurry of servants and guests in the hallway. He pinned her in place with a cold gaze. 'I only hope you think it a price worth paying.'

Isobel's hands slid down to cover her belly. She finally looked him in the eyes, swallowed her tears.

'You are pregnant?' Argyle's world crumbled.

Isobel cowered as he raised his hand. 'Leave me, you cursed woman. Get out!'

CHAPTER 40

7 December 1399 – Beauworth

'Tell me how it all came about.' Argyle's request was toneless and strained. 'I need to know.'

He had spent the past week prowling the halls at night, stirring old ghosts. Every evening, when they sat at the high table presiding over dinner, he would push his food about and drink too much while she would stare into space before slipping away early.

He could not forgive Isobel the secret she had kept from him, she who had asked that they always be honest with one another. She remained a stranger to him, a viper in the nest.

Last night, a message had arrived that forced Argyle to make a decision. At first light, he had asked a maid to fetch Isobel and bring her to his study where she now stood rigid before him as a child waiting for a scolding.

'You will not like it.' The faded bruise on her pale cheek held a pinprick of crust in the centre that had yet to come off. It reminded him of what he had done, the shame he felt whenever he glanced in her direction. No matter their discord he should not have resorted to violence.

'I will have the truth. You owe me that much, wife.'

'Very well.' Isobel swept an angry gesture. 'I sometimes wonder if it is possible that you can think even less of me than you already do.'

'If I do, you are to blame. Get on with it.'

Isobel's furious glare dissolved. Despite her many lies, despite her falseness and pretence, she was the mother of his children, his wife before God. Above all else, he looked for a path to take him out of the murky darkness. If she hoped that he would forgive her for keeping from him her true ancestry she was gravely mistaken.

He would never again trust her with any information including the letter that lay, just now, in the small chest on the table behind Isobel. The message it contained would drive him from the house on the morrow and if not for the children he would be happy to go never to return.

'My natural father was a simple man in many ways,' Isobel began, her hands folded before her stomach. 'He was fiercely devoted to his family, determined that his wife never look at another man while he should be allowed to frequent other women.'

She let the sentence linger spite dripping from her lips. Was it possible that she believed Argyle had strayed while he had been away? Could he blame her if she did?

'I spent much of my youth in his household,' Isobel said, yanking him back into the present. 'Perhaps my mother had told him about me, perhaps because they were always short a scullery maid or two. It is possible he had no idea who I was. What care has a nobleman for scullery maids?' The bitterness in her tone was unmistakable. 'I was there when Jasper arrived, a strapping young man who knew how to turn women's heads and convince them he only had eyes for them. He was charming to all even me at my tender age of twelve. He was tall and handsome and when he smiled the whole world stopped moving.'

Isobel sat down on the edge of a low chair. 'This was shortly before I met my first husband, Geoffrey. Perhaps my father – not Lord Woodstock, I knew not of our affiliation then – caught wind of my fascination with the young minstrel for he was most adamant that I be removed from the house.' When she spoke of the man who had loved her as his own, her expression softened.

'Jasper was never interested in me. He had an altogether different objective in mind. One night, Lady Woodstock was entertaining a large party.' Isobel sniffed. 'She had Jasper play songs which had a bawdy edge to them. Many of the women present blushed and all the husbands frowned, but Lady Woodstock ignored them. She was smitten with the young minstrel and blind to the disapproving glares.'

'Why were you there?' Argyle tried to envisage a young, innocent Isobel and failed. In the flicker of a few lit oil vats, her features appeared washed out, foreign.

'I was asked to wait on some of the lower tables. Fetch wine and make sure the guests had what they needed. I was young and eager to please and my mother could hardly refuse Lady Woodstock's request.'

'Lady Woodstock requested you?' Argyle struggled to accept the story was to be told at Isobel's pace. He would suffer her company until he had the truth.

'Yes.' She smoothed her dress. 'By now she must have

noticed how I resembled her husband. Perhaps he told her of me. Whatever the reason, I was in the hall when she called upon Jasper to sit on the topmost step of the dais and play a song just for her. He jumped at the opportunity eager to please her. It was clear to all that he meant to have the lady of the house in her husband's own bed by the end of the evening. Even I knew, although I could not put words to it and the kitchen buzzed with gossip each time I returned for another pitcher of wine.

'I was too young to imagine that she might entertain the same idea, although life since has taught me differently. I know now that women are as salacious as men. And why should they not be?' Isobel's words dripped defiance. 'When men are so often away?'

She drew breath. 'Jasper flirted openly with Lady Woodstock and she received his attention with much joy. They forgot the world around them. Some of the women began voicing their opinions of the lady's behaviour while several of the men looked ready to send messengers to Lord Woodstock. Somehow, she regained her composure and sent Jasper from the steps – reluctantly, I suspect.'

Isobel reached for the pitcher on the low table next to her and poured a cup of wine, but did not drink. 'He rejoined the musicians and the guests seemed more at ease several of the ladies ready to stand a dance or two before Lady Woodstock. Her husband was high at court at the time, do not forget, so entertaining her was important.'

Isobel was right. This would have taken place while King Richard was young and in the grip of his uncle Thomas of Woodstock. Around the time when the blank order that later took La Fontaine from this world, was first created. However much Argyle struggled the memory of La Fontaine was not laid to rest. He suspected it might never be.

'Late that night, I was walking back to the kitchens.' Isobel hesitated, as if sorting through her memories. Argyle wondered if at last she would tell him the truth? How would he know if she lied, she had so much practice keeping secrets from him.

Her eyes betrayed raw fear. 'The party had run late and we were still about the hall clearing the tables and refreshing the rushes. Lady Woodstock hated getting up to a soiled great hall. She always had her servants work till the early hours to ensure that when she got up the next day all was back to its usual state.'

Isobel twirled her cup. 'I was carrying a pail of dirty water or some such, something heavy, when a senior servant hailed me and offered to take my burden if I would deliver some wine to Lady Woodstock's chambers. I remember wondering that she was still up, but my arms were sore and I agreed. I should not have.'

A noise in the hallway caused her to stop and Argyle listened with intent. Footsteps ran past the door and disappeared. 'Go on.'

'They are all dead now. What does it matter?' Isobel put the cup down hard, wine sloshing over the side and dripping to the floor.

'I shall be the judge of that.' He splayed his hands on the desk, the wood smooth under his palms. 'Go on.'

She eased into a more comfortable position, setting the now empty cup on the floor beside her chair. Spilled wine bled into the hem of her dress, the wool drinking it up with greed.

'I knocked on her door, but no maid came to open it. When I knocked again, I heard her call out from inside the room. I was concerned that she had been left alone with no one in attendance. So, I opened the door.' Isobel's eyes glazed over. 'She was not alone.'

'Jasper?'

'In her bed.'

Argyle could tell that Isobel was reliving the scene. Her eyes sought the floor, her hands opened and closed. 'They were naked. He sat atop her, facing me, a raunchy smile on his lips. Her eyes were closed, her mouth open… I do not think she realised I was there – not that it was I. And Jasper. He wore such a cunning expression.'

Her words were distant, forced. 'The pitcher slipped from my hands, and clattered to the floor. I turned and fled.'

'You had already seen too much.' Argyle knew where her tale was heading. The vision alone might not be traumatic but what came next would have been. 'You were a witness to her seduction. A witness she did not need.'

'The next morning, Lord Woodstock arrived back,' Isobel continued as if she had not heard him at all. 'If his wife was surprised she did not let on. She greeted him by the door, led him to his room and ordered food and drink to be fetched from the kitchens. I delivered it.'

She turned her eyes to the tapestry on the wall behind to Argyle's chair. 'When I arrived he had sent her from his study. After I had set out the meal he told me to stay, said he needed confirmation of a certain matter. Some gossip that had prompted his return. He asked if I had heard anything untoward in the kitchen. I said nothing. He asked me about the party the night before. Wanted to know if anything was amiss. I told him no. He pushed, I insisted.'

'He would have had spies in his household. We all do.' She still would not meet his eye. Argyle flexed his hand. 'He must have ridden all night for Pleshey Castle to arrive the next day. He knew.'

'He was supposed to have been in London for at least another month.' Isobel picked up her cup. Turned it with stiff fingers. 'You met him, you know his anger knew no bounds. He came around the table and grabbed me by the arm, squeezing it so tight I thought it would break. He demanded I tell him all that I had heard. Had seen. He pushed me against the wall, knocked the wine from the tray, shouted at me. So, I told.'

You delivered Jasper to a man many would not hesitate to call the devil to his side, Argyle thought and prompted her. 'What of Jasper?'

'He was already taken.' She wet her lips. 'Caught sneaking out of her rooms at dawn by some of the guards Lord Woodstock had no doubt sent ahead. He was dragged to the cells. I never saw him, only heard that his face was bloodied and one of his arms broken.

'The servants' quarters buzzed with rumour that Lord Woodstock had approached his wife and asked that she measure out the minstre's punishment. I suspect she told her husband that Jasper had forced himself on her, climbed into bed with her that night and done unspeakable things. That she had tried to resist.'

Hugging herself Isobel droned on as if desperate to be done. 'I saw her the next day, her steps pained but her face unmarked. Perhaps it was the only way for her to keep herself safe. God knows I understand now what the desire to survive can make a woman do.'

'What punishment did he receive?'

'They do not call him the castrate for nothing.' Isobel turned a defiant expression on him. 'It has a fitting rhyme to it, do you not think?'

Argyle ignored her jab. 'Why would she choose castration?'

'You of all people should have learned long ago that gossip has only elements of the truth in it.' Isobel shied away when he leaned forward. Even with the desk between them, she feared him now. 'I doubt she had any hand in his sentence. Woodstock metered out the punishment. He wanted to ensure that Jasper would never again pleasure a woman. She had no choice other than to obey her husband, in that and all other decisions.' Regret riddled her confession. 'Just as she was forced to suffer me as her lady-in-waiting. I stood behind Lady Woodstock when they cut him. There was so much blood…'

Although he resented her, he pitied Isobel's younger self. Jasper was no longer important. His tale was nothing more than the opening to deeper, darker secrets. Deep inside Argyle craved an explanation that might in time enable him to forgive her.

'You were in the employ of Lady Woodstock?'

'No doubt my natural father considered it a fitting punishment. She would have to suffer the constant company of the girl who betrayed her secret and caused her pain. She would have her husband's bastard child brush her hair and string pearls around her neck.' Dismay gave way to cold calculation. 'In turn, I was to spread the tale that Jasper was a thief. Woodstock was a cruel man and for that, I do not miss him. Still, he was my father. Somehow, I understand him – I understand both of them.'

Argyle leaned back in his chair. The low winter sun sent skittering rays through the slats that covered the window as if it could burn away the sense of betrayal. In this room, his desk and chair appeared giant, imposing. He did not doubt that, at this moment, he cut a similar figure to his wife. Isobel seemed subdued, but not defeated.

'How did Jasper know who you were if you did not?'

'As he said, he met my father – the farmer – at the tavern. My mother had died and he could not mourn her in the company of his new wife.' Her words rode on a grim wave. 'It matters not, the deed was done, the story told, the minstrel cast out bloodied and dejected only a few days after his punishment. No doubt he was released from his prison in the hopes that he would die from loss of blood. Lord Woodstock would have distributed decrees that Jasper was banned from his lands. A guarantee that he would never be employed in any great household.'

Isobel's tale left Argyle empty. The truth was never as satisfactory as he hoped. He wondered if Lady Woodstock had a hand in Isobel's first marriage if she had pushed the young man in her path knowing what he was.

What cut deepest was Isobel's use of the word "father" about Thomas of Woodstock the most notorious of the King's uncles. The pride with which she lay bare her affinity, heedless of the price of her tainted blood.

'What are the chances that you should randomly meet Jasper and hire him to entertain our King?' Her voice brought Argyle back.

It was Stephen who had employed him, though Argyle had never told her. He picked up a quill. 'He is a wandering minstrel. Perhaps chance sent him my way.'

'Will you deny the possibility that he learned of my presence here and came to stir up trouble?' She rose and folded her hands over her stomach again – a gesture impossible to misunderstand. 'I wonder who found him out and sent him here. Who would stand to gain from our discord?'

Argyle refused to speculate, refused to even think about it. Happenstance had crossed the paths of Stephen and the minstrel in a village tavern not long before King Henry was due to arrive. Had not Argyle himself requested entertainment to be found? Isobel was seeing ghosts. When he paused, her expression changed and she withdrew into herself.

He pulled out a piece of paper. 'I leave tomorrow.' Snapped open the inkwell lid.

Isobel's thick woollen skirt flicked around her ankles. 'What?'

'What is there to hold me here, wife?' He heated the inkwell between his hands. 'I have had your tale, but I will never know if it is true. Everyone involved are either dead or cast aside. Marked as liars themselves.' When her eyes flooded, he felt nothing. 'I have had a message that takes me to London.'

'Then it was a horse I heard last night.' Isobel tugged at her sleeves. 'What is it this time? Is my cousin desperate for your council? That cannot be. King Henry does not trust you.' Her voice turned cold, snide. 'Why should he?'

'Why should he trust you?'

'I am loyal to my family.' The disgust on her face turned into a plea on her lips. 'Please…'

'You have had your say.' He dipped the quill and pressed the tip into the paper hard enough leave a stain. 'Now go.'

'I can…'

'There is nothing you can do.' Argyle looked up to find her gaping, shock mingling with raw rage. He dismissed her. 'Except pray.'

ꕥ ꕥ

CHAPTER 41

12 December 1399 – London

Margaret's breath rattled. The chamber was stifling hot, the walls wept with damp that the tapestries could not soak up.

Swallowing against the stench, Argyle slipped inside. 'Sister?'

'Thomas?'

'No, sweet Margaret, it is Argyle,' Sir Reginald said from his seat by the bed. He held a skeletal hand in his, his cheeks sallow. 'Your Thomas is dead, remember?'

Even at this dire moment, the depth of Sir Reginald's affection surprised Argyle. He had always thought the nobleman was caught off guard when he was married to Margaret. That she had been able to conjure up love from the reclusive knight was a miracle.

'She is very weak, Sire.' Despair lingered in Sir Reginald's voice. He appeared dishevelled, as if he had slept in the chair by his wife's bed for days. 'Today, my physician informed me that he can do no more for her. All is in the hands of God now.'

'Perhaps you wish for a quiet moment to pray for my sister's recovery, Sire?' Argyle wanted a moment with Margaret and hoped that she might not be as far gone as her husband dreaded. 'I shall sit with her for a while and join you when I have spoken with her.'

Sir Reginald tucked Margaret's hand under the covers before he rose. 'You are kind, but I fear she is at death's door. I doubt she can speak at all.'

As if to prove her husband right, Margaret issued a rattling cough. Sir Reginald fell to his knees beside her and held a handkerchief to her mouth. It came away bloody. He stared at it with fearful eyes.

Argyle seized the opportunity. 'Perhaps you can spare a moment for me, Sire? Let one of my sister's ladies attend her while we speak?'

'Yes…' He got to his feet, steadying himself on a bedpost. 'Yes, a lady…' His eyes flicked to Margaret and away, his words broken.

'I shall call for one and come to you as soon as she is here,' Argyle said and put a comforting hand on Sir Reginald's shoulder, steering him towards the door. 'You look in need of rest and perhaps a bite to eat?'

'No…' Sir Reginald looked up at Argyle and seemed to make up his mind. 'Yes. Yes, you are right, I must pray. I must secure her recovery. It is in His hands. You will come and pray with me?'

'As soon as can be.' He had no real desire to kneel before an altar and plead with a god he had no reason to trust. Still, if it got Margaret's husband out of the room, he would promise to dance with the Devil if needs be.

'We must not tire her.' Sir Reginald sent his wife a watery smile, tears glistening in his eyes. 'Must we, my dear? You need your rest and to regain your strength.'

Margaret turned her head to his voice and the faintest of smiles crossed her gaunt face. 'Leave me with Argyle, husband, I know him now.'

Sir Reginald pulled Argyle to the door and peered at Margaret over his shoulder. 'She is frail. I hope you are not here to add to her burdens.'

'I am afraid I bear ill tidings, Sire.' Argyle was worn to the bone, his heart broken. 'I have to tell her that our sister Eleanor is dead.'

'Oh dear.' Sir Reginald slapped a hand to his mouth. 'She was so young, so full of life…'

Biting down on his grief he put an arm around Sir Reginald's shoulder. 'I think it better my sister hears the news from me than you. You must see her well again. I shall bear the yoke of bringing bad tidings. I shall be gentle when I tell her.'

'Is there a gentle way?'

'She needs not the details of our sister's death.' Argyle ushered Sir Reginald through the door. 'If you wish to hear the full account I shall tell you later.'

'No… No, you are right, I need not know. I shall weather this storm for sweet Margaret as she has weathered many a storm for me.' Sir Reginald's slight form drowned in the gloom of the corridor. 'I shall find a lady and send her at once.'

'Have a care that she knocks before entering.' Argyle gave what he hoped was a reassuring smile. 'We must not tire my sister with too many people at once.'

'Yes, yes we must ensure she knocks, Margaret must be allowed to rest. Yes…' Sir Reginald tottered away on stiff legs, the ceaseless vigil no doubt taking its toll. 'Yes… I shall see to it.'

As soon as Argyle was alone he threw open the shutters and let in the crisp December air. A thick carpet of snow had obliterated the sharp stench of London and left the city beautiful and near odourless. When he rode through the streets this morning he had revelled in the solace that at least the smell of death would not haunt him into Margaret's home. How wrong he had been.

'Brother…' Margaret wheezed and struggled to sit up. Argyle helped her settle against the pillows, her arms brittle in his grasp. 'You should not be here.'

'Where would you have me be, sister?' He plumped another pillow and pushed it gently down her back, but even with his efforts to be tender, she winced. 'You sent for me and I came without delay.'

Margaret nodded and another fit of coughing rattled her frame. Argyle poured some spiced wine from the pot over the fire and held the cup for her to drink. 'If you cannot speak, I shall not ask it of you. I can sit here and hold your hand if you prefer.'

'I have no need of a nursemaid.' Margaret's cheeks blossomed as she swallowed the mulled drink. 'I have things to say before I die.'

'Margaret…'

'Do not argue with me.' Margaret put a handkerchief to her mouth and fought an oncoming fit. 'I shall die soon and I have made my peace with it.'

Realisation grabbed hold. 'You knew in October.'

'Of course I did. It is only Reginald who will not accept it. When he is not here on vigil he prays in his chamber. I can hear him placate God at all hours of the day. It is tiresome.'

'He loves you.' Argyle offered Margaret a little more wine. This time she took the cup for herself and drank the contents in small sips, her shoulders shaking when the cough tried to grip her.

'He does,' Margaret conceded when she had finished the wine. 'And I am lucky, for he has never strayed from my side. I know I can be difficult and he has borne my ways with angelic patience. That is why I could not tell him about Eleanor. I sent word to you on a day when he was at court. It was the only way.'

Argyle steeled himself. He could not roar at Margaret in this state, though he was both heartbroken and furious that he should learn about Eleanor's death in a short, unfeeling letter. It was as if no one in the family understood the bond he shared with her, the sense of intense loss he felt at having lost forever his mirror image, the only one who looked as he did, gold and blue where the rest were brown and slate.

'Tell me, sweet sister, what happened?'

'Before Thomas was sent into exile – the first time…' Margaret coughed and Argyle grabbed her flailing hand. 'Eleanor began to think too highly of herself. She was never a match to Thomas and I, although she believed herself to be when he put her into play.'

'As the Queen's lady.' Sitting on the edge of Sir Reginald's abandoned chair, Argyle ground out the words. 'Eleanor had her secrets. We all do.'

'Yes. Only she was careless with them. Especially the ones Thomas shared with her in a moment of indiscretion.' Margaret's lips were caked with dried spittle and her nightgown was stained. 'After Thomas was exiled and before he came to you in the Tower – for which you have never properly thanked me – Eleanor began to play her own game.'

'I never knew you had a hand in his appearance.' The hole in Argyle's heart expanded, all jagged edges and dark emptiness. 'Thomas told me that she might be the one to secure a physician for me.'

'And so she did after a little prompting on my part.' Margaret smiled, a ghost of her former self. 'The reason why King Richard accepted her request was that he believed he could trust her. She had endeared herself to him and his little wife and brokered a peace between them. Bridged whatever gap had divided them.'

Argyle put another log on the fire and stirred the mulling wine. In the flames, he saw Celeste die again. Eleanor had replaced her at the Queen's court no doubt by Thomas' design. King Richard had commanded Thomas to find his way back into England well before Argyle put him on the ship. How much of this did Margaret know?

'Her efforts kept her in favour for some time. Long enough to ensure your survival.' Margaret slid down a little and slapped away Argyle's hand when he tried to help her. Her voice was strong but broken. 'Is there more wine? I shall have to muster all the strength I have left to tell this tale. Best you listen carefully I doubt there will be a chance to ask questions once I am done.'

He felt four years old again, Margaret bestowing her final words on him before she accepted the master of horse's hand to ride pillion with him to Sir Reginald's home. Gone forever from Framlingham and a rare visitor in Argyle's adult life.

Would he miss her now? As a child he did not. The world was so much smaller and more dangerous now than it had seemed then and too many of his family had been casualties.

'Eleanor fell from grace.' She heaved for breath. 'I know not the full circumstances, though I suspect her carefree way of handling secrets must be to blame. For whatever reason, she was not sent to Leeds with the Queen when King Richard left for Ireland.'

Margaret lost her battle against her cough and Argyle knelt by her bed, holding a new handkerchief out to her when the other was drenched.

'Disgusting.' Margaret spat into the little ornate bowl Argyle offered her. 'Where was I? Eleanor… She came to me complaining that the Queen no longer desired her company. I tried to tell her that she was only ever welcomed into the Queen's retinue because of you. She served as a reminder to the Queen that, somewhere out there, you were defending her and keeping her husband safe.'

'I failed.' Argyle choked back surprise as Margaret put a comforting hand over his. The skin was drawn tight over her bones, her wedding band loose around her finger. A strange belated caress.

'That is one failure we cannot own. It was all his own doing.' Her stern look made Argyle want to tell her that it was Isobel's doing. He settled on the chair again, watchful of every little spasm that coursed through Margaret, marring her features and tugging at his heartstrings.

'By then Eleanor had turned her attentions elsewhere. She sought the favour of Lord Bolingbroke when he first arrived in England, inflamed by righteous indignation and thirsting for revenge.' Sweat beaded her forehead. She looked so frail in the big, canopied bed, the carved bedposts standing sentry over her final hours.

'Bolingbroke?'

'Eleanor was among the first to realise that the King was heading for a fall and that Bolingbroke would replace him. In a way, she was wise to advise her husband to back Bolingbroke's claim.' A whisper of pride rode on Margaret's harsh words.

'I heard de Welles accept the claim at Westminster Palace. I watched him bend the knee in Westminster Abbey.' He had also bent the knee on that day and avoided his brother-in-law afterwards. De Welles had brimmed with satisfaction where Argyle had brooded.

'These are trying times, brother.' Margaret wiped her brow with the handkerchief, her fingers trembling. 'You had to declare for King Henry. We all did. You had to protect your family. I like to think it was prompted not just by your boys, but also by us, your sisters.'

No mention of my wife, he thought. If only you knew, Margaret, what a traitor I have housed and fathered children on.

On the ride to London, he had wondered if he would have made the same decisions had he known the magnitude of Isobel's betrayal. If it would have mattered. If Bolingbroke had not managed to sway him, one word from Isobel that he would never see his children again and he would have crumbled.

'Eleanor did more than curry favour with King Henry.' Her voice was little more than a rasping and he had to lean in to hear her. He tried to ignore the sickly-sweet scent. 'She bedded him.'

He jerked and knocked the spit pot from its precarious place on the small table by the bed. A timid knock on the door sounded as he was drying up the slimy fluid. 'Come.'

'I am not done…' Margaret's protests drowned in another fit.

'Find something to clean this up.' With an apologetic smile Argyle gestured to the woman hovering just inside the door. 'I was clumsy and knocked over the bowl… And bring some more spices for the wine.'

The lady bustled from the room relief plain on her face. Margaret smoothed the furs and blankets and turned a red-rimmed gaze on him.

'I sometimes forget that you run your own household. I almost went to scold you, but you are a man grown. The only one left in our family. If chance and happenstance would have it differently, you should have Framlingham. You should have it all…'

Unease stole through his body at the dreamlike quality of her scratching voice. He shook his head. 'Margaret, surely this can wait.'

'It cannot.' Her eyes were alight with feverish determination. 'Eleanor did what I could never imagine. What she hoped to gain, I know not. Her time as his mistress was short-lived. She travelled with him while he gathered men and strength on his way to London. There he left her and she came to me. Triumphant.'

Margaret must have spied his disbelief. 'She believed she was in the right and had secured some kind of power by being his bedmate. She was wrong. Once Bolingbroke was assured that the Lords of England would rally to his side, his determination grew and Eleanor's temptation waned. He had no need of a mistress. I believe he was desperate not to repeat his father's indiscretions with Lady Catherine. He had to seem clean – pious. A worthy king.'

'It worked.' Argyle refused to imagine his sister in Bolingbroke's bed.

'My only regret in life is that I was not present at his coronation. Sir Reginald was adamant we stay out of this particular power-struggle.' Margaret's bird-like chest rose and fell under the heap of blankets. 'I cannot say if de Welles knew of our sweet sister's indiscretion. Perhaps he even encouraged her. It would not be the first time a man has offered up his wife to promote his own fortune. Whatever the case he welcomed her back into his arms when she was spurned by her royal lover.'

'And now she is dead.' Tears spilled down his cheeks. He had not wept for his sister until this very moment, but hearing Margaret speak as she did about Eleanor broke some dam inside him. To lose Margaret would be to lose an absent mother-figure. With Eleanor he had lost another piece of himself.

'I want to know how.' Margaret coughed and slid further down weakness was catching her up. 'When last Eleanor visited she was the very image of health. If it was a sudden illness de Welles would have informed us – me…' She filled the handkerchief with foaming red spittle. 'I worry that our sister was poisoned. That whoever took away her was also responsible for Thomas' death. Please, Argyle, do not let me pass from this world in despair. Promise me you will discover what happened to him. Redeem him if you can, but find out the truth.'

A knock on the door startled Argyle. 'One moment.'

She grabbed his hand and squeezed it with superhuman force, her bones drilling into his palm. 'Promise me. Find out what happened to Thomas. And Eleanor if you can. The greatest secret lies with our brother – I know it.'

'You loved him.' It broke his heart to say the words.

'Yes. I loved him above all others for we were two of a kind.' Margaret closed her eyes and her face collapsed. 'What we did, we did to keep you safe. If Eleanor had kept to our plan she too would have been safe.' Her voice fluttered, caught in her chest. 'Find out, Argyle. For me…'

Argyle kissed Margaret's limp hand. He put the ruined handkerchief on the table and took a deep breath. He could not bring himself to tell Margaret that he was no longer safe. That Isobel had ruined any hope he might entertain of being left alone.

'I shall discover the truth about Thomas,' Argyle whispered to the room before he rose, his legs weak. 'Come!'

Margaret's maid entered with two servants in her wake. At her silent command they began cleaning up the mess Argyle had made next to Margaret's bed.

The intricate filigree silver pot replaced the small brass spit-pan and the rushes were swept aside, lavender water sloshed onto the shiny wooden floor to remove some of the stench. The maid closed the shutters and instantly, the room turned into a tomb.

'Sir Reginald is in the chapel at the end of the hall, Sire.' She brushed back Margaret's hair, an affectionate gesture. 'She seems at peace.'

Argyle wished relief on Margaret, though a little part of him resented her for her final appeal. How could he refuse her?

He left the room and passed a door. Behind it, Sir Reginald pleaded with God. Argyle wished him success even if his sister had been adamant that she was dying. Sometimes miracles did happen.

He walked blind into the pale sunlight, the looming decision pushing its talon's into his mind. No matter the outcome, he would never escape peril. Why not unearth the truth about Thomas? Why not grant Margaret her dying wish?

As he swung into the saddle, Sir Reginald cried out through the second story window.

CHAPTER 42

30 December 1399 – London

The Queen stood near the high altar as the Bishop of London performed the service. She was a dainty splash of rich purple against the worn imagery on the walls that reached to display a stirring fresco high above.

Since Margaret's effigy was underway, Sir Reginald had chosen to display a magnificent portrait of his beloved wife above her coffin. The church was crammed, leaving no room to move let alone exchange a quiet word as the sermon drew long.

'She would have hated the fuss.' Joan wiped a tear from her cheek and clutched Argyle's arm. 'You should have sent for me sooner.'

'I knew not how ill she was before she summoned me.' For the third time, Argyle caught himself looking for

Eleanor only to be reminded by raw sorrow. 'Was there a ceremony for Eleanor?'

'How would I know?' Joan hissed and then checked herself. 'I never hear from anyone. I should probably thank my husband for keeping me out of trouble.'

'Where is Sir Thomas?'

'He cares little for church as it is,' Joan whispered with a faint smile. She was still enamoured by her husband, the sombre Thomas Grey. 'I believe he is currently attending King Henry. He has much to concern himself with as you may have heard.'

Rumours of rebellions in the north and west were trumped only by the recent report that Lord Bordeaux had escaped his captivity. Some said he had gone north into Scotland, which Argyle found very hard to believe. Others insisted he was last seen rallying forces near the Welsh border. Neither scenario seemed very likely. If Richard of Bordeaux, dethroned King of England, remained in the state Argyle had left him, he was most likely surrounded by waddling, fat mice which he would feed believing them to be his children.

King Henry had dreamed to rule peacefully and, so far, all he had on his hands were threats of war and uprisings. He had assumed his cousin's seat and inherited all of his troubles. Nothing had changed.

Joan pushed back her black veil, her dark hair catching the steady flames of the massive church candles and elaborate oil vats. 'More dignitaries than I had ever imagined would attend any woman's funeral.'

'Margaret was hardly any woman.' Argyle earned a stern glance from the man standing next to him. He bent to whisper in Joan's ear. 'Though you are right. There are far more people here than I would ever have dreamed. Either Sir Reginald is better connected than we believed…'

He ducked when Joan laughed into her gloved hand. He shook his head. 'Or our sister had more allies than we knew.'

'The latter.' Joan folded her hands around Argyle's arm. The layers of rich fabric were not enough to ward off the insistent cold. 'I am surprised that the Queen… or Lady Bordeaux, is that how she is styled now? Either way, even she has come out of her sanctuary.'

'Or prison.'

Reaching up to tidy Argyle's hair, Joan put a hand on his cheek. 'Best we do not discuss the lady's arrangements. We might be seen to favour her.'

I still do, he thought and looked at the little Lady Bordeaux once more noting her strained and pious face. Next to her, one of her maids, Catherine, if memory served, wore an indifferent expression her hands folded into the holes in her cape. When she looked up, he offered a discreet nod and she returned it.

'… strange that no one told me.'

'What?'

'I understand that, as sisters go, I am the least interesting.' Joan did not bother to harness her displeasure. 'More is the pity that I am the only one left. Is it too much to ask that you pay attention to me while we pay our last respects?'

'Then perhaps we should heed the sermon.' Argyle felt the man's eyes on him once more and shot him a dark glare which plucked the self-righteous frown off his puffy face.

'Nonsense. I had hoped the Bishop of London might be a tad more interesting than is the case. Truly, Argyle, my own chaplain would do a better job of this funeral. I did not know that you had to be dull enough to make half the congregation fall asleep to be named Bishop.' Joan sniffed. 'No wonder Lady Bordeaux looks exhausted, she suffers the tedious man all of the time.'

Argyle smothered a smirk and enveloped Joan's folded hands in his own. 'You may not believe me, but you always were my favourite sister…' Prompted by her suspicious glance, he continued, 'For you are never shy to speak your mind.'

'I should hope not. In that, at least, I do not resemble either Margaret or our fair Eleanor.' Joan crossed herself when the Bishop turned to the congregation and bowed her head in mock devout salute. 'What I say is always exactly what I think.'

'At least she gets a funeral.'

Joan glared at Elizabeth. Although she was here at Argyle's invitation, they had managed to ignore her until now. Little though he liked it, he needed Elizabeth if he was to carry out Margaret's dying wish.

'What do you mean?' Joan's hushed question carried a dangerous undertone.

'You mourn Margaret, yet you shed no tears for my husband.' Elizabeth grabbed Argyle's other arm her kidskin gloves creaking in the sudden silence after another lengthy hymn. She glared. 'You were strangely absent when the news of his death reached us. Did you care so little about Thomas who now lies dead in some unmarked grave most likely killed by our new *King*?' Disdain dripped as autumn honey, slow and sticky. 'You would have me unravel at the funeral of the woman who devised most of his schemes with him? What do all of you take me for? A fool?'

Her last words climbed an octave and the man who had been pushed aside by Elizabeth's tall, slender frame frowned once more. This time he earned an apologetic expression from Argyle and the man looked from Joan to Elizabeth before he returned the glance with a tired nod. Next to him stood a stout woman balancing a small child on her hip, gripping the hands of two white-haired boys who looked to be twins. The man looked down at them and back at Argyle and shrugged. His children were quieter than the two fighting hens locked either side of Argyle.

'… not invited.' Joan tugged at Argyle. 'Did you tell her to come? Was it not enough to offer her shelter? Do you have to parade her around? Where is Isobel? Why is she not here instead of this… this scarecrow?'

'Joan. Elizabeth.' Argyle gave them a warning look. 'I will have no more quarrels in God's house. We can speak of this after the ceremony. For now, we are here to pay our respects.'

Elizabeth clutched his arm with great intensity. 'I wonder why he is so distraught?'

At the altar, Sir Reginald fumbled with his wedding band before placing it on the coffin. His eldest son, Walther, supported his father when he turned to leave, the younger children trailing in their wake. There was something forlorn about the little procession.

The Bishop offered a benevolent nod and gestured discreetly at Lady Bordeaux before he stepped behind the altar and out of sight. Two guards appeared at either side of her and marched her from the church room.

Argyle decided he would apply to Harry for an audience with the former Queen. Her dejected air tugged at Argyle's heart and he took a step in her direction.

'Argyle!' A cry in unison from Joan and Elizabeth brought him back to the present.

'Where do you think you are going?' It seemed Joan had already taken over Margaret's role as the petulant older sister.

'Yes, you promised to see me safely back home.' Elizabeth sent Joan a triumphant smirk. 'Since you have been so kind as to offer me shelter once more.'

'Do you not have a London house of your own? As I recall none of your property was taken away when Thomas died.' Joan's eyes welled up. Argyle suspected they were tears of rage rather than grief.

'We are all that is left of our family now, sweet Joan,' Argyle said and wiped a tear from her plump cheek. 'You, I – and Elizabeth. Whether we care for it or not we are the last three souls who care an ounce about what happened to Thomas and Eleanor. We cannot afford to be enemies, we must …'

'Rub along …' Joan finished his sentence.

'Come to terms.' He glanced from Joan to Elizabeth. 'For now, we mourn the passing of Margaret. In due course, we must decide what to do next.'

'Do next?' Joan stepped back. 'What do you mean?'

Elizabeth's triumphant smile returned. 'I knew you would decide to help me.'

'I am not helping *you*. I am honouring a pledge to my sister.' His words wiped the smirk off Elizabeth's face. He turned to Joan. 'It was Margaret's dying wish that I unearth what happened to Thomas. I made a promise. How can I run from it now that she has passed?'

'Quite easily.' Joan's words came out in puffs of white. She clutched her thick cloak. 'She is dead and I am not. I cannot endure any more pain, Argyle. If you have any pity for me you will not let me stand here in due course to bury the last of my family. For surely that is the only outcome if you chase this mad notion. You cannot abandon me, not when you have only just returned. What of your children? What of Isobel? Honour *my* wish. Let it be, little brother. For once in your life choose the living over the dead and heed my advice.'

'Someone has to be the voice of those who were robbed of life. You cannot want this to be the end,' Argyle tried.

Around them, people were quickly dispersing, the dry cold breeze wafting in from the Thames driving all souls indoors. Already, the sun had dipped behind the rooftops, heavy clouds amassing overhead.

Joan's eyes were as dark as the sky. 'Do not come to me until you have given up this foolish notion, Argyle.' She turned on her heel. 'You shall find no sympathy here.'

Elizabeth watched Joan stalk off and then looked up at Argyle, her little white teeth glittering against her blue-tinted lips. 'Good riddance. For a moment, I worried you would be swayed by her little tantrum. It is a relief that you were not.'

'I may yet change my mind, Elizabeth.'

'I think not. Thomas always told me that once you made a decision, you stuck to it. There might be little he admired about you, but that was a trait he appreciated and often brought to my attention.'

She pushed her hand into the crook of his arm and headed for his house, the snow creaking under her leather boots. 'You have made up your mind. I can tell. So could your wretched sister. This was her final bid to make you change your mind and she knows she failed. Otherwise, you would have gone after her.'

How right you are, Argyle thought and matched Elizabeth's pace. And how sad that a near stranger knows me better than my own sister.

ꕥ ꕥ

CHAPTER 43

2 January 1400 – Windsor

The standards snapped in the sharp January wind as the grounds around Windsor slowly filled with people come to see their new King. It only added to the sense of joy that they were to celebrate the Epiphany and experience some of the greatest knights and nobles at play. King Henry had spared no expense to impress his subjects and, judging by the milling crowd, he had succeeded.

In pride of place, the Earl of Salisbury's distinctive green fable bird on a gold background squared with red diamonds on white flickered at the centre of the line. Unlike many of the other knights eager to prove their loyalty to their new sovereign, Argyle had no intention of entering the lists and he knew that quite a few were as relieved he had declined as they were that King Henry would not joust.

The first event of the day was the traditional mêlée and most of the participants were already mounting their horses ready to line up against each other in hopes of claiming glory and money.

Prince Harry walked by surrounded by men in royal livery. He raised a hand to Argyle who bowed in return. He thought that if anyone was plotting against the King, and rumours said that there was, they would never get away with their plans. Even when King Henry was still Lord Bolingbroke, he had been a careful man, and after he placed the crown on his own head, he had exercised extreme caution.

Argyle still remembered his large retinue of able-bodied soldiers sporting the Lancaster emblem when he had visited Beauworth. No doubt many of the men about to fight each other with blunted swords kept their honed steel nearby in case some trouble might arise.

Harry gestured to a couple of young men his own age and then veered towards Argyle, thick woollen cloak flaring to reveal a red silk lining and thick, fox fur edging. 'Sir Argyle, I hear you have not entered?'

'No, your Grace, I leave that to the young men,' Argyle said. Harry had been the bait in a tug of war between his father and beloved uncle. He had struggled when Richard of Bordeaux was thrown down, torn in his adoration. Now, he was next in line to the throne.

Shielding his eyes against the low sun, Argyle asked, 'Have you entered?'

'My father thinks I should wait.' Harry clearly wanted to succeed his father on the field and claim new fame to Lancaster, eager to assert himself in his new position. 'It will be quite a spectacle if only the weather holds.'

'A suitable celebration of Christ.' Argyle said noncommittally.

King Henry had declared that the tournament should be a celebration of the Epiphany. The religious message at the core of this great feast was not lost on anyone. King Henry meant to be seen as both devout and inspiring, a beacon of hope in a desolate world.

Harry smiled in earnest. 'I dare say so, Sire, and a suitable way to celebrate my father's accession and the coming of the new year. I would have liked to see you on the field tomorrow, but since that is not to be I wish for you to join me on the stands. We can make wagers and you can point out to me who is the greater swordsman. Together, we will win the day.'

Argyle bowed once more and watched Harry walk towards Windsor Castle, his guard in tow. Deciding that he had seen enough of the grounds for one day, Argyle headed towards the stables, the steely song of sparring knights a lively backdrop to his dark mood.

'Sir Argyle.' A man in Salisbury's livery stopped him. 'My Lord would have a word.'

Would he now? Argyle followed the servant to the edge of the woods. John Montagu, the Earl of Salisbury stood with his back to the festivities viewing a couple of adolescent squires trying to rein in a massive, silver destrier, its nostrils flaring.

'A fine day, would you not say, Sire?' Salisbury did not turn. 'A fine day indeed.'

Argyle looked into the woods when he heard dogs barking. 'Are you preparing for a day of hunting, my Lord?'

'Not I. The King has taken the hunt for himself and will invite the winners to join him.' The Earl tucked his hands under his richly embroidered cloak, his breath little puffs of white. He waved away his servant.

'Can I trust you?'

'Lady Bordeaux does, my Lord.' Everyone knew where Salisbury's affinity rested. Argyle wondered if he would be surprised that in this, they agreed. 'If that will suffice?'

'Then you will have heard the news?' Salisbury began walking along the fence, a few of the horses looking up as he passed. 'That no one knows where the King is these days. Even you cannot deny that it is high time to act. The longer we dawdle, the greater the risk of foul play.'

Argyle glanced around. It was unwise to speak about such matters when the squires were still in the enclosure. They had managed to soothe the destrier and led it to the far side where slender willow-trees made a natural barrier.

'Since my visit to Pontefract, I believe they moved him again though I am not in a position to glean more than gossip, much as yourself. He is in the wind. You can hardly resent King Henry for taking measures.' He kept his voice low and his eyes on the squires who had called for assistance, a couple of stable hands racing across the frozen ground with a leather halter in hand.

'You would have us do nothing?' Salisbury almost spat out his words. 'Our rightful King is gone and you expect me to sit by, to play at swords with the very men who have disposed of him? Men who loathe me and wish me dead?'

Argyle remembered his whispered conversation with Lady Bordeaux only yesterday. She had assured him that loyal Lords had her husband in safekeeping. If so, no one had thought to tell the Earl.

'Why risk your life if you do not have Bordeaux in hand? No, my Lord, I believe you are on a fool's quest. Enjoy the freedom you have for you will never be awarded with more.'

And if you saw him as I did, you would never take up arms to defend his claim, Argyle added in thought. A madman who stored bread under his bed for his pregnant, dead Queen. Even if the uprising was a success, Richard of Bordeaux could never live up to their expectations regal might and level-headed kingship.

'Lord Bordeaux.' Salisbury sneered. 'He is the *King*.'

I prefer my head on my shoulders, Argyle thought, I would call him the court jester if it were required.

When Salisbury turned away from the pen, Argyle continued, 'Having two Kings makes matters difficult.'

'There never should have been a second King.' The Earl's face betrayed his confident tone. 'We have the support of many men and we will free the rightful King to place him once more upon his God-given throne.'

'I wish you would not.' Argyle earned another hard look. 'You may think me fickle, but if you cannot produce Lord Bordeaux how long before people begin suspecting you might want the throne for yourself, my Lord?'

'Madness.' Shock travelled slowly across the Earl's features, lending years to his already advanced age. 'I would never.'

'That was what Gaunt said about his own son only days before his death.' Argyle kicked the frozen ground. 'Do nothing rash. That is my advice whether you care for it or not.'

Considering him, Salisbury shook his head. 'You are so unlike your brother.'

'I am still alive,' Argyle said and bowed to excuse himself. 'Make of that what you wish.'

He could not support a lost cause, but he could convey a warning. All that was left was to decide whom to warn.

More than ever, he wished he was more like Thomas, even if that meant he would spend the rest of his life looking over his shoulder.

CHAPTER 44

8 February 1400 – London

Little dots of light moved in the tavern windows when he turned his horse down the street. He had grown so used to the white stallion as his only companion beside the royal guard behind him that he was startled when a voice called out.

'A knight. Look children! A true knight on his white horse.'

Donning a smile, he waved at two scrawny children clutching the hands of a dirty young woman There was something familiar about her face although his fleeting glance was not enough to tell him what. He dismissed it, dropped a couple of coins on the ground and turned the corner, his house in sight. Inside, he would find the solitude he craved.

'M'lord, I'll take him.' A timid stable boy reached for the reins and the stallion nuzzled his hand. He muttered, 'When'll you name him, M'lord?'

When Argyle offered what he hoped was a kind smile, the boy shirked. With a sigh, he dismounted. 'What might you call him?'

The boy fiddled with the reins, his eyes on the ground. 'Whitey.'

'It is a good name.' Argyle managed to choke back a laugh. 'Easy to remember.'

'For his colour,' the boy said growing a bit bolder. 'He's white as snow. Perhaps you'd call him something with snow? Or ice?'

Heading for the open front, he said. 'We must think on it, Adam.'

The boy gave a grave nod and tugged for the stallion to follow him across the yard. Naturally, the horse already had a name. Virtus. Another jab at his honour and a name he could not abide.

Wickers greeted the stable boy as he passed into the sweet-smelling comfort of the stables. Other horses? Scaling the steps, voices floated towards him, too faint to make out. Had Elizabeth returned?

Entering the front hall, Argyle found two servants with the royal crest on their chest warming their hands in front of the roaring fire. They flicked a cursory glance in his direction and then returned to their pastime.

'M'lord.' Mills came shuffling into view, his grooved face brimming with concern. 'M'lady is in the parlour and so is the Prince…'

'Which lady?'

'Your wife.' Stephen appeared from the shadows, mittens still on his hands, his hair in disarray and dew beading his beard. 'You didn't expect us?'

Trying to regain his footing, Argyle turned for Mills to take his cloak. 'So much is happening these days, Smith, it must have slipped my mind.'

'Best not let your Lady wife know.' Stephen nodded for Argyle to retreat to the furthest corner. Turning their backs to the royal guards, Stephen muttered, 'We arrived just as Prince Harry was dismounting in the yard. She wasn't best pleased.'

'The Prince may do as he wishes.' He was not about to let Isobel's sudden arrival unseat him. 'His father governs England and holds all our fates in his hands. Besides which Prince Harry is a friend.'

Stephen tucked his gloves into his belt. 'A friend?'

'Of sorts.' The parlour had gone quiet. 'Best not keep them waiting. Mills, bring refreshments. And make the meal stretch to feed our guests.'

Without waiting for the steward to accept, Argyle made for the parlour with Stephen at his heel. The two guards kept their place by the fire and their voices low. Upstairs, scraping and bustling suggested more guests, Argyle could only hope that Elizabeth had not returned. One resentful woman at a time was more than enough with which to contend.

'M'lord…'

'Not now, Smith.' Dismissing him with a curt nod, Argyle entered the well-appointed chamber, chairs set by the hearth, a fire consuming pinecones and good wood, oil vats and candles illuminating the simple yet elegant décor of wood panelling and bright patterned paint. Harry turned and behind him, Argyle spied Isobel perching by the fire. He bowed. 'Your Grace…' He glanced at Isobel. 'Wife…'

Harry greeted him with a firm clasp of hands. 'Sire. I am sorry to turn up unannounced, but I come bearing news…' He stopped, trying to hide his discomfort.

'You are always welcome in my home, your Grace.' Argyle went to Isobel, brushing his lips over her cold hand. 'Perhaps you will let us speak in peace, wife? You must be tired from the journey here. I saw no wagon?'

'I am not yet so far gone that I cannot ride, husband.' Isobel cupped her belly with a proud smile. She knew full well that in company he had no option but to remain civil and play the doting husband of a pregnant wife. 'I should like to freshen up. You may call me when the meal is served. I have much to convey, but it can wait.'

She dipped a curtsey as she passed Harry, triumph lingering on her smiling lips. Argyle closed the door behind her, careful not to betray their little show. He turned to the Prince. 'I did not know she would arrive today.'

'Your wife was full well surprised to see me.' Harry's cloak was still slung around his shoulders, pinned in place by a large ruby brooch. The stone looked familiar, as it seemed so many things did these days.

Offering his best chair to Harry, Argyle sat down across from him, the fire filling the room with a happy crackling. 'Even after all these years, Isobel struggles to understand how my life works.'

'Does she?' The question revealed just how much Harry knew.

'Your father has taken you into his confidence on the matter?'

Staring at the fire, Harry nodded. 'In so many words. Your wife was more outspoken today than when I met her at Beauworth. A wonderful home you have created in the south, Sire, although I gather you are rarely there?'

And happiest when I am away. If not for my children, I would give it up for her to rule as she sees fit, he thought and roused himself. 'I am often called to court, you know how it is to be dependent on the crown. Such it was in the reign of Lord Bordeaux, and it appears that my attendance is to continue.'

'My father…' Biting his lip, Harry paused. 'I am here on his behalf. I am to secure further assurance that you played no part in the plot to… To kill him and capture me. To reinstate Lord Bordeaux. You see my father has had some troubling news of late. That you were… that Salisbury secured your backing and…'

He waited for more to come, but it did not. Instead, Harry glanced at the door although all was quiet. Argyle wondered why the refreshments he had ordered took so long to arrive and then dismissed the concern. Better to not have Mills wander into this conversation.

Leaning towards the fire, Harry scratched his chin. 'I know you are innocent. I know you would never rise against my father, against me. Not now, not when… If I was in a position…' Picking at a nail, he shook his head. 'He is sending me from court. Under the guise that he is eager I assume my place in Wales. I am to take Sir Harry Percy – Hotspur. Do you know him?'

'He was part your father's retinue in Wales. Hotspur is a practical man, well versed in warfare. The Percys are important allies and you may learn much from him.' The idea of Harry leaving for Wales made Argyle's skin crawl. The boy had only just escaped one jail to be put in another, albeit gilded and provided by his own father.

Brushing his dark hair from his forehead, Harry nodded. 'I am given to understand that he was made a knight of the Garter along with my father. I am told his military prowess is outstanding. I wonder if he shares your ideas of leadership? I suppose, I shall find out soon enough.' He turned a pained expression on Argyle. 'I tried to…'

A knock on the door cut him short and Argyle called for the servant to enter only to find Isobel balancing the tray of wine and spices. 'Wife?'

'They are preparing my rooms.' She put down the tray and spiced the wine. As she stirred, the spoon clinked against the sides of the flagon creating an angry melody. 'I did not want to get underfoot and decided to aid the preparations since no arrangements have been made for *my* arrival.'

'You are fortunate to have such a pleasing wife.' With grace, Harry ignored her snide remark. 'Beware you appreciate her as she deserves.'

Argyle took a cup from Isobel. 'I shall.'

'If I interrupted I can leave?' Her words cooled the warm room. 'Husband?'

'We will not be long.' He forced a smile. 'I would ask that you oversee the dinner arrangements. After all, you will know how many mouths we have to feed and make the most of my larders.'

'As you wish.' She curled her hands into little, white fists but her smile never faltered as she turned to Harry. 'I hope you will join our feast, your Grace, it will not be long underway now that I am here.'

'I thank you…' Once more, a knock on the door interrupted Harry.

If he ever wondered why his father put a guard on me, this must be proof that he is in the right, Argyle thought and turned as Mills opened the door and Elizabeth brushed past him, her cheeks pink and eyes glistening.

'Argyle, I…' Elizabeth caught sight of Isobel and plastered on an impersonal smile. 'Isobel? What a pleasant surprise. I did spy new horses in the stable, although I was led to believe you never travel this far north.'

Isobel returned the smile. 'Nor I that you travelled this far south, Elizabeth. Not these days at least, since you will have nothing to do in London. As you see, my husband is engaged with more pressing matters…'

'I have come at his invitation.' Elizabeth straightened her back and smirked as she pulled off her gloves. 'Perhaps you will be kind enough to show me to my rooms? They are kept ready for me. After all, it is not long since I was last here enjoying your husband's good company.'

Argyle ushered the ladies through the door, turning his back on Harry's curious glance. Once in the hall, he blocked the opening and fixed each of them with a scathing glare. 'As long as his Grace is here you will be on your best behaviour. Isobel, I already told you to make sure that the hall is prepared to seat everyone and that the kitchens stretch the food.' He turned his attention from her before she could argue and shot Elizabeth a tense look. 'Your rooms are ready for you. Go there and await to be summoned. Do not impose upon my wife to find that which you know very well how to locate yourself.'

He left them in the hall and closed the door hard enough for the latch to clatter. Closing his eyes for a moment, he summoned what threads of patience he could.

'What a commotion, Sire.' Harry's voice was thick with amusement. 'Is this common?'

'To own the truth, I wanted a quiet night in my house – alone.' He could have bitten off his own tongue. 'Naturally, your company is always welcome. As for my other guests…'

Harry sipped his mulled wine. 'As I tried to tell your wife, I am afraid I cannot stay. Though now that another visitor has arrived my curiosity is peaked. She is your brother's wife, is she not?'

'His widow, yes.' Argyle nursed his own cup. 'I was rash to invite her a while back and since then, she has adopted the habit of coming and going as she pleases.' Something he should have ended after Margaret's funeral but had avoided. Now, it appeared, he would pay the price for his faltering courage where his sister-in-law was concerned.

'Perhaps your wife can set her straight?'

Grateful that Harry had managed to relieve a little tension, Argyle snorted a laugh. 'In Elizabeth, Isobel may well have met her match. But let her try for I tire of my sister-in-law's company.'

Twisting his cup, Harry looked long at Argyle as if deciding something. 'Once I leave for Wales your life at court will become difficult. I urge you not to pay Lady Bordeaux any more visits. That is why I am here. To ask that you burn my letter. The one that grants you access to her.' Harry breathed deep. 'I would have to do so before I leave. I am sorry. I know you care for her.'

'She was just a child when I first met her, but there was something so pure about her that I cannot imagine anyone would not love. She has often been a good friend. Though she is still a child, living here has forced her to come of age before her time. For that we should all care for her.' Pulling out a small box, Argyle produced the letter of passage. 'That is why it grieves me to see her so diminished. To see how ill she is treated by the Bishop. You have often enough paid a call, cannot you impress upon him his responsibility? She was a Queen. Now, she lives as pauper, subject to his scorn and ignorance.'

Harry drew breath and Argyle threw the letter into the fire. It spat out lumps of wax to melt into the woven rush matting. He stomped out a few rogue embers before the matting caught fire. 'I overstepped. Forgive me, your Grace.'

'I miss the days when I was Master Harry to you, Sire.' He gnawed at a cuticle. 'Lady Bordeaux must make do with what she has. She is still suspected of knowing of the failed attempt to restore her husband. Of instigating the uprising and thereby sentencing many Lords to an untimely death. There is nothing I can do to improve her situation. She is fed, clothed and allowed to pray. That must suffice.'

The pain in his voice made it obvious that these were not his own words. As he rose from his seat, Harry pulled at the ruby pin, and Argyle recognised it as the stone that an English King had once placed upon the tiny finger of a French Princess promising her a life of prosperity and unadulterated devotion.

When Harry turned the pin the stone gleamed like freshly spilled blood. 'Loyalty is a strange matter, Sire, it makes men act in unimaginable ways. I hope you are not planning a great escape for her.'

Argyle wanted to laugh, but it stuck in his throat. 'No, your Grace. Is that why you came?'

'That and to tell you that if Lady Bordeaux asked a favour of you, please do not act on it.' Harry searched Argyle's face and, he hoped, found nothing. 'She is grasping at straws. Her husband is safe in my father's custody. Nothing will come to him as long as there are no more attempts to free him. Once the people have forgotten about him – and her – it is possible my father may accede that they be reunited, though it will not be for many years.'

'Might she be returned to France until such a time as the King is prepared to release Lord Bordeaux? She is a child and if she must suffer a life in captivity for such a duration, I fear…'

'Impossible.' Harry pulled his sleeves out over his fur-lined leather gloves. 'I have often taken your advice. Now, I offer you counsel in return. Go back to Beauworth as soon as can be and stay there. Come to London only on my father's express command. Do nothing rash, nothing irresponsible. Stay out of my father's sight and train what men he sends to you and all may yet be well.' He looked to be in agony. 'If you act out of turn, the Crown will know. Your wings are clipped, Sire, but you are allowed to live with your family. Watch your sons grow up and make peace with your wife. If you let her, she will be your salvation. If you agree, I will release you of your guard.'

Harry paused at the door and read Argyle's expression. 'What other choice do you have, Sire?'

Isobel joined him on the steps outside the house, the dank hand of February weighing them down. When Harry was gone, she turned to Argyle and looked up into his face. 'Elizabeth must go.'

'She is a guest.'

'She is a ghoul.' Isobel checked herself. 'Let her stay in her own house. As I recall, the it is as fine as any and much better situated than yours.'

'It was seized by the Crown.' Argyle bent to whisper in her ear. 'Hear me now, wife. Elizabeth stays until I see fit that she leaves. I will return to Beauworth only on Prince Harry's advice. You are never to meddle in my affairs again – ever! You shall never come here unannounced, you shall not go to court, and you shall do as I say. No more secret letters to your kin, no more spying. On the morrow, you shall leave to prepare for my return to our home. You will be an obedient wife and I shall be a doting father and fair master. That is to be our arrangement.'

He turned away from her aghast expression. 'Begone. You have spoiled my appetite.'

CHAPTER 45

9 February 1400 – Argyle's London house

Triumph danced in Elizabeth's eyes. '*She* was quick to tire of London.'

Argyle raised his hand to Stephen who returned the greeting before cantering out of the yard making up the rear of the Beauworth retinue. If his Master of Arms was perplexed at the order to return, he kept it to himself. They had only exchanged a few words last night. The meal had been meagre and the atmosphere toxic. Isobel had retired early complaining that the pregnancy left her exhausted whereas Elizabeth had outstayed her welcome at the table, sucking the marrow from bones and dipping dried apple skins into the honey vat until the very notion made Argyle sick.

'I believe she sent word only her letter never arrived. How was she to know that I plan to return to Beauworth within a few days?'

Elizabeth followed him into his study. 'I thought …'

'Close the door.'

She did as she was bid with an angry push. When she turned a cold smile curled her lips. 'Argyle. You cannot leave until you hear me out.'

'Very well.' He offered her a seat by the fire. 'Now that we are alone tell me why you are here, Elizabeth. No more games, I am in no mood. Begin by explaining why have you not brought my nephews with you? They are as welcome here as you are.'

'Or more so, I should wager.' A fleeting glimmer of malcontent crossed her pointed face. 'Being your brother's widow is even more difficult than being his wife. In death, Thomas has left me a challenge I find hard to meet on my own. Now that I know you can command a Prince, perhaps…'

'He commands me.' Argyle placed another chair opposite hers. 'Last night, he came only to order my return to Beauworth. King Henry plans to send a large contingent of men to be trained. I must return to my family and serve at the King's pleasure. And it is his pleasure that I provide soldiers for his army.'

Elizabeth's skirt rustled as she smoothed it. 'What of your promise to Margaret?'

'I was mistaken in taking you into my confidence,' he said and a little of her confidence faltered. 'Elizabeth, I can do nothing without it being reported. I have a royal guard at my door and no means of any kind to make enquiries. If I set one foot amiss, the consequences will be dire and I am not given to placing my family in the path of danger.

However much I should dearly wish to honour my promise to Margaret, I must, for the time being, turn my attention to the world of the living.'

'I want him restored.' Elizabeth dismissed his warning with a gesture. 'Post mortem. For my children. I wish for Thomas and John to advance in life. My sons deserve more than the meagre leftovers from their father. Margaret told you that…'

'She was dying.' Argyle suppressed the memory of his sister's bloodied handkerchief, her rasping voice. 'Who is to say she was of sound mind?'

Elizabeth twitched. 'When was she ever not? She and Thomas were so alike that sometimes I found them to be one and the same. If she says he left with a secret that might restore my sons and change their fate, I believe her. You should too.'

No doubt because you want for money and power as much as my brother ever did. You need something to believe in, a cause, a cross to bear, he thought. In that we are alike.

When she put her cold, bony hand on his, he let her. In one aspect she was in the right. Thomas and Margaret had always been two sides of the same coin. It simply was not the kind of currency in which Argyle wished to barter.

'What you ask of me is impossible.' Argyle placed her hand back in her lap. 'For now.'

Elizabeth raised her pale eyes to meet his. 'For now?'

'Prince Harry ordered me to return to Beauworth and so I shall.' He reached for the pitcher only to find it was empty and dregs at the bottom of the cups on the tray. Nothing had been cleaned since last night. 'For the time being, neither of us can do anything. It would be most unwise to stir up trouble this early in a new King's reign. Especially since we are both cursed with a family name that invokes immediate suspicion. I must impress upon you to do and say nothing that might upset the delicate balance in the land. Time must journey on for a while before we can hope to achieve anything.'

'You intend to discover what happened to Thomas?' Her eyes burned. 'When the time is right?'

In truth, he yearned to know what secret his brother had unearthed that warranted it leaving England with him. However much Argyle had tried to bury the ghost of Sir Alan Coxcombe, dismembered and dying, his words came stuttering back in Argyle's dreams and haunted his nights. He had to discover what Thomas knew. What his connection was with La Fontaine. Another ghost not laid to rest. Some days, he feared that he would run mad with all the voices in his head.

For a long time, he had refused to acknowledge the stark truth of Coxcombe's last accusation, had not wanted a disgraced knight to be right. He thirsted for the truth. What secret might be so dangerous, so terrible, that it had sent scores of men to their graves? That Margaret and Lady Bordeaux had asked him for much the same thing was of little consequence. Their words might cushion his own desire, but they only served to keep him awake at night. He had to know. Itched to know. To close the door to the past – once and for all.

'When the time comes you must play your part.' Argyle leaned back and looked at Elizabeth who sat tight-lipped and severe. 'You have means that I can never hope to match. The King may have stripped your sons of their inheritance, but your father was a wealthy man and upon his demise, you inherited his fortune. If I am to succeed, I may well find myself in need of funds and unable to extract them from my own estates.'

'You mean to leave without a royal permission.' She locked eyes with him, sly comprehension evident in her tone. 'And you mean to leave without telling your wife. Now that… is interesting.'

The smile she wore was enough to confirm that she was ready to meet his demands. 'I find she cannot be trusted.'

'Oh? Why?'

Argyle praised himself for having a ready answer. 'I fear that my children will suffer for my disobedience. Isobel is an innocent soul if she is asked to answer for my disappearance I know she cannot keep it secret. It is best that she knows nothing. You, on the other hand…'

'You are right to trust me above all others, my dear Argyle.' Elizabeth flashed another heartless smile. 'You may think Thomas never spoke well of you, but you are mistaken. He often owned that you have certain – obvious – virtues, to which he could never aspire. You needed each other and I see now that you have taken lessons from him too, though reluctantly.'

Her words unsettled Argyle and the feeling increased when she continued. 'You possess something all the other Mowbray's lack. You possess kindness. You strive to live an honest life. While admirable to be sure, you know by now that it is impossible for life is full of misdeeds and dark corners in which people whisper lies into your ears.'

'Your husband was one such man. In the end it became his undoing.' Unwanted grief surfaced in Argyle's voice, and he saw that Elizabeth had heard it too.

'That may be, and still, I need to know. If your intentions are to redeem Thomas so that my sons can once more be proud to bear the name Mowbray. That they might rise high in their own right, then I shall support your endeavours by any means necessary.' Everything about her little speech seemed rehearsed, controlled. 'In return for your services, I shall keep your secret from that woman of yours. That will be my own personal treat.'

Argyle cared not. 'You once said you knew not who warned Thomas that it was time to leave. I believe he took something with him, some collateral of sorts…'

She picked up an empty cup and twirled it between her fingers. 'My discretion comes at a price. Let us call that collateral too. Whatever you find on your journey, I forbid you to tell me. Write to me for money or other such favours, but keep whatever you discover to yourself. If it will restore my boys then I shall be satisfied that you will whisper your findings into those ears that need hearing it. I leave it to you to ensure your nephews' future is secure.' She slammed the cup down onto the spindly side table. 'I find I have grown weary of Mowbray intrigues.'

You are in the midst of one, Argyle thought and nodded. 'If you insist. What *do* you know?'

'The servant who warned my husband wore a white hart. Not prominently on his chest which was probably wise. It was stitched into the lining of his cloak.' Elizabeth tipped over the cup. 'He handed over a leather pouch and Thomas looked to know what it contained. He never told me what it was. He merely packed a few things and left within the hour. No word of goodbye, but then we had our goodbyes two years earlier – you heard them no doubt.'

'I always wondered if your argument was a charade,' Argyle admitted and earned another of her ruthless smiles.

'It was, all the while we shouted and threw things, he penned me a message. Just a few words "I shall return".' She rose and turned her back to Argyle, the garnets in her silver hairnet glistened. 'And he did. Not days after you sent him off.'

'That was why you shed no tears at his departure.'

'Easy enough to explain away if I was asked, after all, none of you ever believed there was much love between Thomas and I.' She turned around. 'And you were right. We had our children and I love them fiercely, but ours was a relationship based on mutual rise and power, not passion. I accepted that on my wedding night. There are other things in life worth fighting for, greater prospects. Love is for fools.'

How could he argue with that? 'Tell me what was in the pouch.'

'As I said he never showed me, although he told me that it had to be delivered to the King's father-in-law. When Thomas left he took only his favourite servant, Albert, who whispered to one of my ladies that if anything was amiss he was assigned to go to Paris.'

'Paris?' France had issued threats of an act of war if Lady Bordeaux was not returned to her native land. Though Argyle had no fully formed plan as of yet, he knew he could not go into the heart of enemy territory. It would be a surer way to find his death than if he was to plot the liberation of Lord Bordeaux himself.

Elizabeth turned a silver ring on her index finger the movement idle and yet tense. 'A few days after he left, I received a scrap of paper with some warbled words about Italy and nothing more. It was a crude imitation of his writing.' She tugged at the ring. 'When we received word that he had died, it was in the same hand. I would know it everywhere.'

'You made a great show of shock upon learning of his death. I have given you too little credit for your ability to play act.' He could muster no emotion. Had he not been overtaken by incredulity rather than shock when he received word of Thomas' death? Was he not every inch as fickle as her? Once he found his brother's final resting place then – perhaps – he might feel the loss and believe it to be true.

'It merely served as proof of what I had long suspected.' Her eyes betrayed a hint of true grief. 'I was alone for weeks unable to share my fear…'

'You were not alone. You lodged with me.' Argyle dismissed her plea. 'You could have told me.'

'He told me to trust no one. No one.' Elizabeth was as pale as a dusting of fresh snow by moonlight. 'I know full well that Thomas had many enemies, here and abroad. If that pouch contained some secret bound for Paris it would also hold a letter of safe passage. Which means the French would be too interested in what he brought to risk his death. And you know your brother, once he had the ear of the French King, well… he would know how to broker a deal to keep himself alive.'

If Elizabeth was right, Argyle would have to be even more careful from now on than he had imagined. But then Thomas had always said, he lacked imagination. Argyle tried to wrap his head around Elizabeth's words.

'You think he was killed by Lord Bordeaux' enemies?'

'No. He died by the hand of his *greatest* enemy.' She rose, layers of silk, cotton and wool hanging from her lithe form. 'You know who returned before Thomas fled with only the clothes on his back and that wretched pouch. Now, I charge you to uncover the truth – just as Margaret did on her deathbed. I shall be patient, but not forever. My sons deserve more than what I can give them at present. You can change that, but not if you insist on waiting for King Henry to forget your own transgressions.'

'You cannot stay here. It is not safe.' Argyle opened the door for her. However much he wanted her to be in the wrong, her point was valid. The longer he put off any investigation the more likely she might set and spring another trap. She had lived too long with Thomas to be wholly without plans.

From a darkened corner of the entry hall, a royal guard stirred. Argyle squeezed her hand lightly. 'I am certain your sons will rejoice to have you returned to them.'

She smiled without a single glance at their audience. 'I only called for a trifle that is now settled. I shall be leaving for Framlingham within the hour. If you need anything do not hesitate to ask.'

Halfway across the hall she turned. 'Do convey my regard to your darling wife. She must be thrilled that you are coming home. Just as you are delighted to return.'

Elizabeth's laughter rang in the hall long after she had gone.

ജ ര ജ ര

CHAPTER 46

21 February 1400 – Beauworth

– The Lord has seen fit to call my husband to his side. My grief is such that I could never have believed it if someone had told me it would be thus. My heart is broken and my soul is dark. I cannot eat nor sleep. I thought I had grieved before, but it seems sorrow is a pit without bottom. I pray that I shall soon be reunited with my family and that they might prove the succour I so desperately long for. My wishes for you remain unchanged.

Isabella, Dowager Queen of England –

Argyle put down the letter and stared at his hands. They were shaking.

For weeks, rumours had filtered from court and across the lands even as far afield as Beauworth, a place of exile and banishment. Rumours that the former King Richard had died. Some whispered of plots most foul while others shouted to the skies that he had taken an arrow to the heart when he mounted a rebellion to reclaim his throne.

Whatever the cause, the finality of her letter had crushed what little hope he harboured that all of the foul rumours were false.

He closed his eyes and tried to breathe. However shattered his loyalty to Bordeaux had been, however little faith Argyle had in anyone, he had never imagined that King Henry would order the death of his royal cousin. For surely, any such order must have come from him?

He picked up the letter anew.

Dowager Queen. Was her title self-styled? King Henry had forced Bordeaux to renounce his claim to the English throne. Was she to have an honorary title now that her husband was a threat no more? Would she be permitted to return to court, would the King use her as the pawn she had named herself when last Argyle had seen her?

Slowly, he rose to feed the fire. He felt as though he was a mirror of the cold castle walls. Last night's intense snowfall had left the world silent as the grave. Argyle pulled a chair close to the flames and tried to gather his thoughts. Isabella's letter had come in a bundle that included a royal declaration that Richard of Bordeaux had died on 15 February. In this announcement which bore the royal seal, it was stated that he had starved to death by his own design, something Argyle was all too happy to accept, even if the rest of the land might view matters differently.

Few enough had witnessed how deep Bordeaux had ventured into madness, and fewer still dared defy their new sovereign. Perhaps this might once and for all quell the insistent rumours that Richard of Bordeaux had escaped his prison and was amassing an army to march on London and take back his crown. No one would want a corpse for a King.

'M'lord, a word?' Stephen stepped into the room, startling Argyle. 'Is this a bad time?'

'Bad news.'

Stephen fetched a low stool and settled close to the fire. He did not say anything, just sat there, his feet stretched towards the flames. Argyle noticed new lines on his face and a bruise on his hand.

'What happened?'

Stephen followed Argyle's gaze. 'One of the horses was spooked by the snow. Didn't see the kick coming, silly beast.'

'Ah.' Argyle pushed another log into the fire, and they sat there for another couple of moments, staring at the flames.

'You said bad news, M'lord?'

'From Lady Bordeaux. Now she is to be known as the Dowager Queen.' He glanced at Stephen to find him stiffening. 'She grieves for the loss of her husband.'

Stephen shook his head. 'Poor child.'

Of late, Stephen and Argyle had spoken less than usual and it sometimes gnawed at him. To have such little response to the news of Bordeaux' death caused all concerns to stir and Argyle pushed it away unwilling to look too closely at what secrets might be harboured in his own house.

He stretched his bad leg towards the fire. The cold seeped into his old wounds and the ones he sustained in the heat of Jerusalem ached in constant protest to the English weather. Perhaps wounds remembered the climate in which they were inflicted?

'She would not like it to hear you call her a child.'

'She's seen more than most ought in a lifetime. She's only just ten, and so, she's a child if you ask me. A child living an adult's life.' Stephen shifted on the stool. 'Is she going home?'

'She does not say,' Argyle said, omitting the last sentence in her letter. He had told no one about her final command and was unwilling to put anyone at Beauworth at risk by divulging the secret. 'Only that she hopes to be back in France soon. I think she hopes in vain.'

'Why?'

Argyle had contemplated her situation since the first whispers about Bordeaux' death had surfaced. 'She is young, she is of royal stock, and she would be a perfect way for King Henry to secure peace with France. If she remarries.'

'I'd think King Henry'd learn from Bordeaux' mistake…' Stephen's objection stuttered to a halt.

'Prince Harry.' The cold left him numb to the world and its many grievances. Princes and princesses were pieces in a game. They were not their own. If he was in King Henry's position, he would attempt to have the two marry before the year was out to secure continued peace. Only a fool would disregard such an obvious solution.

More to the point, this latest news poked new holes in his resolve which was in tatters as it were. Twice he had decided to leave, ride away in the night, only for dawn to arrive and change his mind. Some nights he feared he had lost his nerve, had become an old and skittish man unable to do what must be done.

He shook his head. 'The Prince is a little older than the Dowager Queen, but not so much as to make it an imprudent match. And she has already proven herself a

Queen the English find easy to love. They would make a formidable pair.'

Stephen combed his beard with his fingers and winced when he hit a snag. 'Is that even allowed?'

'A papal dispensation should clear the path. The question is if King Charles will allow it. Such a union will be infinitely more attractive to King Henry than to the French.'

Stephen rose to fetch the pitcher and set it to heat near the fire adding a few cloves. 'You said she wishes to return home and her father wants her home. What'd change King Charles' mind?'

'That would prove hard. King Henry must offer something extraordinary to secure the match, though I still think he will press the matter for as long as he can.' Despite the gloom of this news he smiled. 'She will fight it. Ten years or no, as you said, she has seen more than most would in a lifetime. I doubt that she will go willingly to the altar.'

'She should fight it. Marrying into the family that took her husband's life…' Stephen poured the wine and offered Argyle a cup. 'She'd be mad to stay.'

'She may have no choice. When last we spoke, she repeated her words to me that she knows full well what she is to her father. He may love her, but in the end, she is a means to make alliances.'

Stephen swung his cup in despair. 'I'll say it again, poor child.'

They drank their wine in silence, Argyle briefly relaxing when the warm fluid made its way into his icy limbs. Even the pain in his calf eased a little. It felt good to share concerns with Stephen again, however, he could not afford to say too much. Already, they were treading dangerous territory.

'D'you think King Henry ordered the death?' Stephen asked at length.

Argyle wanted to lay the deed at King Henry's door, but he could not. If he wanted Bordeaux dead, he was more apt to have made a public show of it than let it happen in the shadows. In truth, if he had vied for his cousin's life, he would have had him killed in Wales and blamed it on rebel Welshmen. Something about Lord Bordeaux's death did not sit right.

'It appears it was not a violent death.' Argyle put down his cup. 'It is widely known that Bordeaux starved himself.'

He was prone to believe the story. After all, he had witnessed Bordeaux refuse to take food already at Flint well before he officially denounced his title.

'And what'd you say?' Stephen called him back to the present, to the comfortable room and warm fire.

'When I saw him in October I confess he was dishevelled. Why would he not be? He had been forced to denounce his throne, give up his claim and suffer imprisonment. If he was desperate he might try anything, but his survival instinct was extraordinary. The only reason he would choose starvation was to achieve something. Perhaps permission to enter a monastery, a wish he had expressed on several occasions.'

At Pontefract, Argyle had met a man frayed and splintered, speaking to God and fighting ghosts. Screaming about poisoning and debating with his dead wife. Perhaps Bordeaux had decided to starve himself to death just to unsettle the English noblemen? The truth rested somewhere in the shadows out of Argyle's grasp.

'A former King turned monk?' Stephen scratched his ear. 'D'you think he'd do that?'

'He was extremely pious. I believe that, given the choice, he would have gone happily to a monastery.' Argyle got up and fetched the Dowager Queen's letter. He crumbled it and dropped it into the fire. 'Better there be no evidence of our correspondence.'

'You're convinced King Henry believes you're loyal to him?'

'He has no cause to think otherwise.' Argyle thought of Isobel, most likely still feeding her cousin information on a regular basis. They lived as strangers by his command and while that meant that he was free from her constant presence, it also meant she was free to do as she saw fit. 'In time, he may realise that my loyalty is worth very little. But you came for a word and I wager this was not the topic of your choice?'

'Reginald Miller is coming this next Tuesday. It seems we might've finally found a new master of horse,' Stephen said. They had laboured for some time to find a suitable match for the position. 'You said you know him. Is he any good?'

Argyle smiled in earnest for the first time in weeks. 'If he has stopped throwing horseshit around then yes.'

In the silence after Stephen had left, Argyle picked up the letter that had accompanied the Dowager Queen's message. He grimaced at the royal seal and dreaded what the contents might say, what instructions King Henry might have included.

Standing by the fire, he contemplated dropping it in the flames.

'Do nothing reckless, husband.' Isobel's voice made Argyle start. 'I saw Smith leave.'

'We are looking for a new master of horse.' He did not turn. 'Smith was asking if I had any objections to the prospect.'

'Did you?' Isobel took his chair by the fire. So far, she played her part as he had wanted and went to bed alone every night to the sound of gossip outside her door.

'I know the man from my days of serving La Fontaine.'

Isobel ran her fingers over the embroidered border of a pillow. 'And the letter you look ready to throw into the fire – unopened…'

'No doubt you have seen it bears the royal seal.' He had never hated with such fervour. It was as if there was always a third person in the room, ready to reach out and stir what little peace he managed to find. 'Have you had any news of your own from court?'

'Who would write to me? If you think I am high in favour with King Henry, you are mistaken.' Isobel's voice trembled.

He turned the letter in his hand and broke the seal. The crisp snap of wax made Isobel look up. 'This may serve to set your mind at ease, wife. It is our beloved King commanding me to come at once to London.' His stiff announcement made Isobel stiffen. 'I am to escort the body of Richard of Bordeaux to St. Pauls where it is to be displayed to prove to all of England that the former King is at peace in death.'

'It seems only fair that he be displayed, though why he should be shown in state as a King, I shall never understand.' She turned a spiteful expression at Argyle. 'There is only *one* King of England. And never forget, husband, that you swore allegiance to that King when he accepted the crown. You bent the knee and offered him your sword.'

I remember him taking the crown from the Archbishop and placing it upon his own brow the hint of a smile on his face. He forced me to change my pledge, this time I gave it to the man wearing the crown. I paid for my former folly.

He looked at Isobel for a long time. 'I did what all English lords and knights did. We are sworn to the Crown and to England just as we ever were.'

'You are sworn to the King.'

Argyle slammed the letter onto the table. 'Then perhaps you would like to dictate my answer, wife? Above all others, you have the greatest need to keep in his good graces.'

'You know best how to heed a royal command, husband,' she returned, her voice as rigid as her posture. 'You have done so for as long as I can remember and you have never denied any King anything.' Her voice rose. 'Perhaps you would like to be alone while you make up the answer that would most please his Majesty? I know you will never take my advice.'

Argyle let her go, slamming the door behind her. When he was in London, he forgot about her. He longed only for his sons. Would he long for the unborn child once it was delivered to the world? Begotten by deceit, Argyle thought, but then so were our two boys and I love them without reserve.

Now, he was to leave them again to do King Henry's bidding and, for once, he was happy to go alone. He shuddered at the prospect of bringing Bordeaux to London of parading the corpse through the streets. Would the guilds be allowed to hang flags of mourning? Would women weep along the path? Or would they cheer now that the ill-fated King was no more?

Shaking his head to clear his mind he acknowledged that this order also presented an opportunity. All he had to do was reach out and grab it.

CHAPTER 47

12 March 1400 – St Paul's Cathedral, London

Argyle wiped his brow. March was proving hot and the streets of London had been teeming with people eager to look upon the corpse.

King Henry had been clever enough to let his cousin's body roll through the streets in a carriage that was open at either side. Slow enough for anyone to see the body and, in particular, the uncovered face. The King wanted to squash the budding rumours that Bordeaux had suffered a violent end by royal decree.

Lord Bordeaux looked to be asleep, peaceful in death. His face was gaunt and starved but otherwise intact.

Four royal guards were moving the royal remains from the carriage and into St Paul's Cathedral where it was to be exhibited until it was moved to King's Langley. Argyle knew that Bordeaux had requested a burial in Westminster Cathedral and had heard rumours that although Prince Harry had begged his father to grant this final wish, the King had been relentless. He would not let his cousin's tomb be turned into a shrine or a place of pilgrimage. He wanted to stow away Bordeaux and so it would be. Prince Harry had left his father in a rage, proving once more that his affection for his uncle was unwavering.

John Beaufort, the Earl of Somerset and half-brother to the King, stood atop of the steps leading into the enormous cathedral, surveying the guards. 'Put it in the preparation room. My brother does not want the body deteriorating and stinking up the place.'

'How considerate,' Argyle said in a tight voice. 'How long is the body to be on display?'

'A fortnight I believe. But not before he is encased in lead.' Somerset beckoned Argyle into the gloomy cavernous space. Low on the horizon, the sun could not reach inside. The guards moved down a side aisle towards a candlelit room framed by a thick wooden door.

'They are to keep the face visible.' Somerset tried to hide his discomfort. It seemed there were limits even to his adoration of his brother and all of his decisions.

'The streets were thronged with people.' It had been as Argyle suspected, the city was curious but not allowed to show any displays of grief. No mourners attended, no flags were hung from shops and windows. 'All of them wanted a last look at their King.'

'Former King.' Somerset's voice held no disdain. 'You know full well the rumours my brother hopes to put to rest. He will not have it be said that it was an untimely and violent end to Richard's life.'

Starving to death is not untimely then, Argyle thought and struggled to keep his voice even. 'His face does look serene.'

'Serene and unharmed.' The Earl sat down in a pew and gestured for Argyle to join him. 'Have you had word from the Dowager Queen?'

That *is* to be her title then. Argyle's hose clung to the cold seat when he settled. 'She wrote only to inform me of her husband's death. She seemed distraught.'

'She is keen to go home,' Somerset said in his usual blunt fashion. 'She says she has little interest in staying here and since she is out of favour she finds no reason to be detained.'

'It is natural that she longs for her father's court, for familiar faces and solace.' Argyle paused as the church choir began singing. A sweet, unbearable sound filled the cathedral's vaulted space.

When he turned back Somerset stared at him. 'Perhaps our King has other plans for her. She has lived in England for some time now and she must have made friends here. The people are fond of her.'

'They like her for the child she was when she first came here.' Argyle was keen to dismiss the notion. 'Once she is a woman grown they may feel differently.'

'Even you do not believe that.' The cathedral threw Somerset's laughter around causing the choir to waver for a moment. 'She may yet stand a chance of being Queen of England. Who could refuse such an offer?'

Argyle noticed the four guards returning to the centre aisle. They slouched and dragged their feet. 'She might considering what she has seen and learned in our land. What would she have to say about England that was positive when she and her husband were so poorly treated?'

'Prince Harry is of a marrying age and as likable as any she might have the fortune of meeting. Rather than spend time trying to find a suitable match far afield why not look a little closer to home?' Somerset dismissed the guards before they reached the pew and leaned in, lowering his voice. 'Harry was close to Bordeaux until the very end. He must have seen much of the Dowager Queen and she of him. What is to prevent them developing an attachment?'

Argyle knew it would never come to pass, no matter who or how many might wish it otherwise. 'She watched powerless as King Henry forced her husband to relinquish his crown. No matter what she might have felt about Prince Harry, I doubt she will accept such a union. She will, in effect, marry a royal family member who is close in bloodline to Lord Bordeaux. King Henry will have to gain not only a papal dispensation he must also convince the King of France that this is a fortuitous union. Truly, my Lord, do you see that happening?'

'My brother is used to getting his way,' Somerset said with a wry smile. 'I am sure the young lady will be no match for him. And she must know that she has a part to play.'

The cold air in the cathedral had chased the sweat from Argyle's brow. He wanted to return to the sunbathed streets and be away from this wretched church. He had much to do and nothing would be accomplished by exchanging words with King Henry's half-brother.

'She is a royal Princess as well as a Dowager Queen, I have no doubt she understands her position. What I am less certain of is her father's disposition to let his beloved daughter stay in England.'

'And why is that?' Danger laced the Earl's words.

'He was unwilling to part with her to Lord Bordeaux when he came to marry her. I was there, my Lord, and saw the pains it gave him to send her away. He travelled with her across France to ensure she was safe.' Argyle knew he sounded bitter. 'Now that she is widowed he may simply want her back at his own court because he loves her.'

'Love,' Somerset huffed. 'What kind of King accepts that his daughter has a say in any matter when there are alliances to be made? Advantageous alliances.'

'Some will benefit more from such an alliance as you suggest than others, I believe. But then, I am just a knight, I do not presume to understand how royal matches are made.' Argyle got up.

'No, you were spoilt when you married,' Somerset shot back. 'It was a match of love, was it not? For a while at least, though of late I have heard rumours. What luck that we are both too wise to listen to idle gossip are we not, Sire?'

CHAPTER 48

12 March 1400 – Argyle's London house

'M'lady sent me.' Stephen ran a hand through his greying ginger hair. 'She requests your return to Beauworth as soon as possible. As do I, M'lord, for King Henry's been generous and sent many new men our way and I…'

He had been waiting in the courtyard when Argyle returned to his London house. Was there never to be any peace in this hellhole? He held the reins of his stallion and felt the watchful eyes of his servants.

'As Master of Arms it is your task to handle such matters on your own. That is what I have entrusted to your care, Smith. You have never failed me yet and I do not imagine you should begin now.'

'M'lady…'

'She has the run of the household. Where the men are concerned, you are the one to make decisions in my absence. Between the two of you Beauworth is sure to prosper. Whatever your concerns surely it is naught that could not have been conveyed in a missive.' At Argyle's finality, Stephen scratched his cheek, a tell-tale gesture that he was unsure how to proceed. Patting the horse's neck, Argyle clicked his tongue. 'What?'

'Perhaps we might ride out of the city, M'lord? The London air's rank and I don't care for it.'

'You have only just arrived from Beauworth. How much more clean air can you want for?' The city did stink. The sudden change of weather had the filth of a long winter suffocating the streets. It had not yet been dawn when the first carts trundled through the streets carrying weary men who tied dirty scarfs over their mouths and noses before they began another day's arduous labour. When the sun set they would be drenched in filth, heads hanging as they returned to whatever hovels they had for shelter outside the city walls.

Another look at Stephen made Argyle relent. 'Fetch a fresh horse for Master Smith, Adam.'

The stable boy scurried from the mounting block towards the stables. Although the manor was a decent size the stable held no more than five horses at any time. The rest were set to pasture near the Abbey across the river, which was where Stephen's steed would be let loose once it was rubbed down and fed.

'All is well at home, Smith?'

'Yes, M'lord.' Stephen refused to meet Argyle's eye. 'Just wanted to nip into town and buy a few trinkets for Bessie and the lads.'

Quite a *nip*. It was a week's hard ride to get here and Stephen looked as if he had spent most nights sleeping rough. The spring had been unpredictable and the roads around London were little more than mud holes. Argyle shifted in the saddle and looked down upon his Master of Arms. 'How is Reggie settling in?'

Adam returned with a brown mare, tugging at the saddle padding as he went. The skinny boy had a way with the horses that reminded Argyle of Reggie. Perhaps he should bring the boy to Beauworth for proper training.

'He settling just fine, knows the lay of the land which helps.' Stephen groaned when he took his seat and turned the horse. 'He's not thrown a single piece of shit since he arrived. Fair to say, I'm a little disappointed.'

Laughing, Argyle surrendered to Stephen's easy company. 'He was a stable boy to La Fontaine. Whenever he was out of his depth he always resorted to throwing horseshit about as a way to win an argument. Only at the squires of course, he knew when to hold back.'

'So, if he ever throws a pile at me,' Stephen grinned, 'it's just because he thinks we're equals?'

'Consider it a sign of good faith.'

They rode along the street and turned left towards the bridge connecting the sprawling, overcrowded streets with the wide, green pastures of Southwark. Argyle rode ahead to steal a little time to sort through the jumbled thoughts running wild in his head. Stephen's sudden arrival had rattled his determination to finally get on with his own plans. Isobel he could easily ignore, Stephen was another matter. Even after all this time, he still viewed Stephen more as a friend than a servant, their common history left him feeling a little guilty for his deception.

Clattering through the first of the bridge gates, they were forced to ride single file in order to carve a path through the crowded bridge. Merchants were negotiating, store keepers were hawking wares and calling prices and half of London seemed to be out now that the weather had finally turned fine. Not that much light penetrated the two-storey houses with their overhanging balconies and attachments, linen strung out to create a bit of shade and keep goods from being soiled by the birds that circled above.

It was a while before they got out of the last gate and could finally ride abreast. By then, Argyle's ears were ringing from the bustle and his hair was sweaty at the nape of his neck. Letting his gaze wander to remark on any who might be following the, he was satisfied that they were as alone as they could hope to be in London. He leaned back against the high leather clad cantle, the reins loose in his grip and tilted his head towards the sky. Feathery clouds danced high above, chasing each other to cast spindly shadows when they crossed the sun.

Despite the relative calm of Southwark's expanses, unrest tickled in his veins. 'What is the true reason for you being here? If King Henry has sent as many men to be trained as you say, your place is at Beauworth. We cannot be seen to shirk our responsibilities. When I am not at home, you are in charge of the men and the training.' He gave a half-laugh. 'Hell, those are your duties even when I am at home.'

'It's just that…' Stephen fell behind as they passed a crew of young men filling holes in the road with rubble and sand. Once they were clear of the work, he rode up alongside Argyle again, his expression dark. 'I know it's not my place to ask, but what'll happen once you've completed your orders? You've already fetched the body, I know, I've heard the tales of the King entombed in lead.' He shivered. 'Still, you'll have to stay for the interment, I'll wager. And then what?'

'I need to make a short journey.' Argyle turned his horse towards Lambeth Moor. 'I shall be gone no more than a month. Two at most.'

'Where to?'

However much he wanted to share his plans he dared not tell Stephen. He had been in danger before because of Argyle and he would not risk it again. Also, if Stephen knew nothing, Isobel would gain nothing from pressing him for information.

'Wales. Prince Harry asked that I pay him a visit. He is finding it difficult to settle in the hostile region, so far from his family and friends.'

Stephen had to bridle his horse when a rabbit darted across the road. 'When'll you go?'

'As soon as Lord Bordeaux is interred. The Prince is coming here to attend the ceremony, and afterwards, he will once more journey to into Wales.' It was hardly a lie since Harry had indeed asked if Argyle might accompany him when the time came.

'You mightn't be going somewhere else?' Stephen's question was just, but it had an air of conspiracy about it that Argyle did not care for. 'It is only that M'lady…'

'My Lady what?' Argyle eyed Stephen, watching streaks of red creep up his throat. 'She has taken you into her confidence? Is that it?'

Stephen sighed. 'Bessie first, though she'd have none of it. Not her business, she says.'

'And she is right.' The mere suggestion of Isobel turning his servants against him fanned Argyle's rage. 'What has she told you?'

'Only that she worries you might do something stupid.' Stephen folded the reins in his grasp and shook his head. 'Though where she got that notion…'

'Perish the thought.' Argyle's light-hearted dismissal released some of the tension between them, even though he now knew that he had been right to feed Stephen a lie. 'I have only ever been rational.'

'As I told her.' Stephen brushed away a lazy spring fly and looked out over a flock of sheep tended by a couple of bare-footed, lank boys. 'It's just that you've been known to make certain unwise decisions when left alone in London too long.'

'Or anywhere too long.' Argyle changed topics. 'How are the new recruits? You say there are many? Have we room for them or must we build new barracks?'

'They're slow to learn, but I'll whip them into shape. A few'll take holy orders and I'd like them to do so soon. That'll clear up some space for those who stay. There's no need for more structures to go up for now, not if rumours are true and the Welsh are stirring. The Prince'll need reinforcements and we have men to spare. You can tell him that when you see him.' Stephen turned his horse towards the budding woods lining the north side of the moor.

For a while they trotted on in companiable silence, enjoying the chatter of birds and rustling of rabbits. This far afield the sounds of the city were muted and the air cleaner.

Eventually, Stephen cleared his throat. 'You'll not want to hear this, but M'lady is lonely. She's afraid that, well…' He gestured limply.

How much has she told you, I wonder, for you to be so invested in my wife's happiness and comfort? Argyle thought and spurred his horse into a trot, the new grass springy and soft.

They chased across the green, Argyle in the lead with Stephen at an easy distance, the quick breath of horses and dull echo of hooves tearing through Argyle's skittering thoughts. To know Isobel had sent Stephen away when he was needed at Beauworth irked more than it should. In truth, that she held any sway over him was disconcerting. Still, Stephen would fail in his mission. If Argyle had been inclined to share a little of the truth with him that last sliver dissolved and wafted away on the lukewarm breeze. Eventually, the ground began to give way under the horses and Argyle was forced to slow his steed to a trot and turn back towards the road. He looked at Stephen.

'You may inform Isobel that I shall accompany the Prince. That ought to bring her peace of mind.'

'Won't it get you into bad standing with King Henry?'

'I am visiting his son.' He teased a few knots from the base of the horse's sleek silvery mane. 'Perhaps I am not the friend he desires for the Prince, and yet, he must allow for some amusement to find its way even to Wales.'

'And this time, the King knows where you're going?' Stephen worked his shoulders. 'I needn't remind you what happened last time you forgot to tell a King before you left.'

'I am not leaving England, at least not truly, since I am going to his son's principality.' His lie was fast getting out of hand. 'I am sure a royal guard will be provided since I am never without one when I am in London. There is no cause for concern, Smith.'

'If you say so, M'lord.' Stephen cleared his throat. 'What'll you tell your wife?'

'Nothing. As I said, I shall return soon. If for any reason the Prince should desire I prolong my stay, I shall send word.' He shook out his cloak. 'I a well aware that it behoves me to prove my loyalty to our new regent and that, should I succeed it will benefit Beauworth and my sons.'

'What of the babe yet to be born?'

Any talk of the unborn child made him uncomfortable, but Argyle made an effort to smile. 'I shall be there for her birth.'

'You think it'll be a girl this time?'

'I live in hope. With two boys in the nursery, it would be good to have a girl.' Argyle leaned forward to pat the stallion's snowy hide. Sometimes, children and women would stop to cheer him on, as if he was the hero of a myth. Soon, he would not ride the white horse anymore. Virtus would return to the royal stables once he had left. As to the safety of his children and home, he trusted that whatever he unearthed, it would prove a guarantee that he might finally live in peace far from court.

'I have made the necessary provision. There truly is no need to worry, Stephen. As I say, Isobel should have this time to herself with nothing to distress her.'

Before he left for Pontefract to retrieve the body of a man he had once promised to defend with his own life, Argyle had written a short note to the Dowager Queen. He had asked that if it were within her power, she might keep King Henry from sending men to retrieve him, professing that she had sent him to broker some form of alliance.

Even the King could not refuse such an plea, not since he needed to keep the peace more than he needed Argyle's presence in London. If she was to agree, the Dowager Queen would prevent any unwanted interference from England while Elizabeth would pay his way. It was a dangerous scheme. Perhaps that was why he liked it.

'While I am gone, you will make any and all decisions. Isobel must not be unsettled. Tell her that I am well and that King Henry has asked that I remain in London, she may make of that what she can.' Argyle saw a trace of pain in Stephen's eyes as he nodded. 'I would not ask this of you if it were not necessary, Stephen. I shall return as soon as can be. Until then, you are to do anything to ease her mind.'

'You want me to keep her safe?' Stephen looked ill at ease.

'Yes.'

'Do anything I can to…'

Argyle turned his horse towards the bridge, a wagon loaded with last autumn's crops trundled by, the grain on it wet and sprouting. 'Whatever it takes. I rely on you.'

Stephen looked to be weighing his charge, and then he smiled. 'Very well. Just's long as you remember that I'm only doing what you asked.'

CHAPTER 49

3 April 1400 – Calais, France

Stephen had left for Beauworth two days after he had arrived, a strange smile playing at the corner of his mouth. Argyle was pleased to send away his friend. It was better to be safe at home than sail into danger. What Isobel had said upon his return, Argyle could only speculate for she had sent no word to him. He was nearly convinced that she had informed her royal cousin and, despite his feelings for her, Argyle found it hard to blame her if she had.

Of course, all this rested on Stephen betraying his promise to keep secret Argyle's intentions. Not that he knew the truth of them either, but Stephen was wily and had always been well-informed, it was entirely possible that he had gleaned the lie and simply decided to keep it to himself.

On the journey across the sea, Argyle had attempted to conjure up a plan of action once he landed in Calais. Elizabeth had been adamant that Thomas had gone there for the first leg of his journey, and since almost everyone believed Thomas had left for exile two full years before he did indeed leave England, Argyle had little choice but to follow her instructions.

If the situation had been different, Argyle might have gone straight to Paris and requested an audience with King Charles. Since he had heard nothing more from Isabella, the ten-year-old Dowager Queen of England, and had not been granted permission to speak to her after the funeral of her husband, safe passage through France was impossible to achieve. Calais was still English and so, he would make his start here and see what he might discover.

Despite the weak foundation of his pursuit, the distance from Isobel was a welcome respite. The more leagues he put between himself and her, the easier he breathed. He missed his boys and he worried about the unborn child nestled under his wife's heart. The children were his blood after all. Instead of dreams of home, he was often visited by vivid images of Margaret, Eleanor and Thomas playing with him when they were children. John was not even a faceless ghost lurking in the shadows anymore. Argyle had forgotten what his oldest brother looked like long ago and of late, he had forgotten him in his dreams.

Earlier this morning, Argyle had finally heard back from his little spies, a few children who had loitered around the harbour when he arrived at Calais, eager to earn a pittance. They told him that someone matching Thomas' description had been seen entering the castle of Calais. If it was as Argyle feared that single action had put Thomas into the hands of his enemies, though thinking thus would be to underestimate his brother. Looking up at the castle's imposing twin towered gatehouse, Argyle remembered a tormented time veiled in snow and shook his head. He could not afford to let in such bleak memories.

'Sir Argyle.' A young English soldier approached. 'You asked to see the Captain of Calais?'

'Yes.' It was a massive gamble, because Argyle knew not if King Henry had already sent a new warden to his overseas dominion. Calais had been without a captain for more than two years and Argyle was certain that the King was eager to fortify his hold of this most important port.

'I am sorry, Sire, he's not expected to arrive until next month.' The young man scraped his bootheel along the cobbled stone.

'Perhaps someone else can aid me?' Argyle was prepared to pay his way to knowledge. Elizabeth had slipped a fat purse into his hand before he left London along with a secretive smile. Turning his gaze to the gatehouse he said, 'I need to speak to anyone who guarded the prisoners some eight months ago.'

'Many soldiers've been shipped back to England on the King's orders,' the guard said. He was perhaps a full ten years younger than Argyle and seemed uncertain whether he should assist a stranger. 'You might speak to the prison warden? Master Windham.'

'Windham?' He inclined his head. 'I can find him myself if you would point me in the right direction.'

He had decided to pretend to be new to Calais, ignorant of the city's layout and the maze-like interior of the castle. After all it was long since he had passed through the town in the King's entourage when he brought home the Princess Isabella, and even longer since he had stayed in the castle during a frightful storm that claimed an innocent life and nearly had him in chains.

As in most outposts of a realm, allegiances changed rapidly and most men did not cling to positions of power for long. It was unlikely that anyone here remembered him or indeed thought it odd that he had returned.

'The warden's in the western most tower.' The young man looked relieved. 'He's been here these past two years and knows all there's to know about comings and goings.'

'Thank you,' Argyle pressed a few coins into his and left before the guard could offer to escort him. A good soldier would never let a stranger into the bowels of a seat of administration and control, but this time he counted it good fortune to encounter someone who was remiss in his duties.

The castle loomed over the harbour as desolate and haunted as it had when he had travelled back from pilgrimage as Bolingbroke's prisoner. At least, the last ghost of Calais, Coxcombe, had died at Argyle's feet in Ireland less than a year ago, spitting curses and spreading malice until his final breath.

'Where might I find Master Windham?' he asked a guard who poked his face out of a window opening in the gatehouse, the shutters hooked to the stone.

The guard gave him a hard stare. 'What's your business?'

'Inquiring about a prisoner.' Argyle glared back and the guard waved him through with a dour expression.

'The warden's expecting you, is he?' the guard yelled after him, but Argyle did not deign to answer nor did he break his stride.

'Master Windham?'

A lean, robust man with steel grey hair turned around. His belt was weighed down by a massive ring containing more keys than Argyle had ever seen before. Even the

Tower wardens did not carry around all the keys to the cells but it seemed that Windham was of a different belief. The man eyed him for a while before he turned and finished his order to two guards.

With a curt nod he sent them on their way and turned back to face Argyle. 'Who's asking?'

His accent revealed a Norfolk heritage. As most of the other soldiers in Calais, Windham had most likely taken his commission to protect the seaside city with stoic calm. It was just another assignment in another English city.

'Sir Argyle of Beauworth,' Argyle said. 'I come in search of a prisoner.'

Indicating that he follow, Windham walked briskly towards the tower. 'Important?'

'To me.' Argyle followed the warden into a small chamber which was surprisingly neat, the desk almost empty, a huge ledger lying on a reading stool next to the narrow window. One of the panes was broken.

Windham followed his gaze and laughed, an unexpected melodious sound. 'Seagull. I swear they're the dumbest animals alive. Smashed right into the window and flapped about in here, making a huge mess. In the end, we had to wring its neck. The cook made a fine pie of it.'

Argyle took the offered seat and studied the warden. Up close he was younger than his first impression, perhaps even younger than Argyle.

'You didn't come to hear about my bird troubles or get a recipe for gull pie though it was tasty. You say you're looking for a prisoner?'

Pleased with Windham's direct manner, Argyle nodded. 'He might have come here in September or perhaps a little before then.'

The warden reached for the pitcher. 'Drink?'

'Please,' Argyle said. 'It seems you have all the fine weather here, Master Windham.'

'How's it in England, M'lord?' Settling at his desk, the warden tipped his cup and drank deep.

'Wet, the farmers worry we will have another bad harvest.' Argyle took a healthy swig and rejoiced in the sharp flavour of fresh ale. 'We all pray that it will change soon, the fields should be green by now, but most are so wet they are blue.'

Windham laughed again. 'Aye, we'll pray for a change too. I'm off home soon, my appointment here's ending this summer and I can't wait to be back with my family. I'll not begrudge the poor fellow who comes to relieve me.'

'Who is to replace you?' After a week at sea with gruff sailors who swore more than spoke and another week holed up in a boarding house near the docks he rejoiced in having found someone with whom to exchange news and share a drink.

'Some follower of Lord Huntingdon or other,' Windham said. 'I confess I didn't make much of his name. S'long as he's here by July, I'll be content. There'll be plenty of changes made, no doubt, what with the new King and all.'

'What awaits you in England?'

'I came from a position in the Tower, I ain't going back there.' Windham put down his cup and scratched his stubbly chin. 'A man can only take so much of this life before he either succumbs to drink or grows unhinged. I've seen both things happen to good men and I don't fancy either, so I'll make my future some other way. Got a name for that prisoner of yours?'

'Thomas.' Argyle paused. 'He was exiled under the late King Richard, and so he may not have given his full name.'

'Thomas…' Bending over the reading stool, Windham flipped the ledger pages. 'There were many prisoners last year, unsteady times in England brought about a wave of crime here. It seems I might need a full name, Sire.'

'Mowbray,' Argyle said.

'Lord Mowbray? The Baron?' Windham looked up for a moment. 'Didn't he used to be Captain of Calais? One of his bairn came into the world here if memory serves.'

'That was a long time ago.' Argyle watched the warden flick through the pages, a furrow deepening on his brow. 'Maybe he gave another name.'

'If he looked like a lord, we'd have housed him according to his rank,' Windham said with caution. 'I treat my prisoners well.'

'I do not doubt it, but this man.' Argyle paused. 'He was fickle. He might not have revealed himself, he could have assumed another identity. Perhaps you had a prisoner by the name John Seagrave.'

It was an obvious idea once it presented itself for Thomas to claim their mother's maiden name of Seagrave and use their father's and older brother's given name, John.

'I have a Seagrave. Seems he came here in September.' Windham studied the ledger. 'He didn't stay long and his gaoler stayed with him. Two days, then they were out again. The entry ain't mine, it's hard to read but it seemed Seagrave was bound for England.'

'England?' That could not be Thomas. Not unless he had made his way to France by some other route and been intercepted. An unlikely scenario. 'Are you sure?'

'Says here they're waiting for safe passage to Dover.' Windham leaned on the ledger, fingers splayed over the page. 'Not what you expected, Sire?'

Running around in circles. Already it feels as if I am running around in circles. Why would anyone take him back the very moment he stepped foot in Calais? He shook his head at Windham who picked up the ledger and placed it on his desk.

'I don't often let others make entries, and even fewer get to read in this, but I've got to get back to my men, the watch is about to change and I've got a few new recruits who don't know their heads from their asses. If I'm not there, God only knows what'll happen. If you were to glance at it while I'm away, well, there'd be little I could do about it.'

Argyle gave a grateful smile and watched Windham leave the little room. He scooped up the ledger and carried it to the window; a gush of warm wind made the pages billow and when they settled, his breath caught. There on the page was the name T. Seagrave and a smudged entry did seem to state that the prisoner was bound for England. The pages billowed again.

His heart stuttered. T. Mowbray. The entry was not from September but November, a few days after they received word that Thomas had died in Venice. Whoever had brought him to the Calais prison had not believed anyone would come looking for him. Most likely, whoever had Thomas in chains thought it safe to enter his real name, certain that the Mowbray family was grief-stricken by the message that had claimed his death and unlikely to come asking questions. Argyle's eyes sought the far right column. A cross was sketched beside Thomas' name.

'What'd you make of it, Sire?' Windham leaned against the door frame, blocking out the sun with his square shoulders. 'Bound for England?'

Argyle closed the ledger and put it back on its stool. 'Yes, you were right. It seems I must journey back and seek him in England.'

'Sorry I couldn't be of more help to you, Sire.' The warden stepped aside to let Argyle pass.

'Not to worry.' He clasped hands with Windham, briefly grabbing his elbow. 'What would have happened if the prisoner had died while he was kept here?'

'Here?' Windham's eyes strayed to the ledger. 'He'd most likely be buried by the chapel. There was a bout of illness the summer before last that took out a lot of prisoners. We had to bury them in a pit. The mortality claimed its fair share that year. Nasty business.'

Argyle nodded and hoped he looked suitably disheartened. 'You have been of great help, Master Windham. Should you need me to repay you, I shall be in Calais another couple of nights.'

The warden walked Argyle to the gate and stayed there, watching him go. He turned a corner and leaned against the wall. His legs shook so bad that he feared he would have collapsed if he had to take another step. It was one thing to believe your brother dead, it was quite another to learn that he had still been alive when they had received word of his demise.

What if he had gone sooner to seek answers? Could he have prevented Thomas' death? The burden of guilt weighed down on him. What few hopes he had of a swift return to England were blotted out by one desire, to find his brother's remains and learn the truth of what had come to pass. If it meant travelling to the ends of the Earth, so be it.

'Sire?' A boy in dirty brown hose and a threadbare shirt looked up at him. 'Master Windham asks if you'll join him f' dinner t'night. The gate at seven?'

ꟸ ꟸ

CHAPTER 50

3 April 1400 – Castle of Calais

'I think you found more than you let on, Sire.' Windham picked his teeth with his table knife.

Upon learning that they were of an age, Argyle had wondered if, at first sight, he looked as old as the warden. There was something weather worn about his hard face and steel grey hair that lent years to his appearance. On the few occasions when Argyle looked into a polished mirror or caught his reflection in a puddle of water, his hair was as golden as ever and his skin smooth.

'You are right. It seems there was a prisoner by the name Mowbray in the castle. In November.' Argyle put down a chicken bone and wiped his mouth. 'I have lived too long with betrayal and deceit. I am sorry that I had to get you involved.'

'Not my point, Sire,' Windham said. 'I'd like to help any way I can.'

'Do you remember Thomas? Did you see him in November?' Hope flared only to gutter as he remembered the cross in the ledger. 'He had dark hair, grey eyes and a quick tongue.'

The warden nodded. 'Not an easy one to forget – I just never knew his name. He'd always have something to say, never lost for words. Until they came for him that is.' Windham offered up another drink. 'White Harts on their chests. I thought it strange since the crown had changed hands – or heads – by then. They told us to shut our mouths and we'd all go home. I should've done something…'

Accepting the flagon, Argyle gave a thin smile. 'What was there to be done? What can you do in the face of a royal command? I do not blame you for what befell him. If only I knew what happened to him.'

'I think he knew he'd never see daylight again.' Windham stoked the fire. Although his quarters were nestled in a corner of the castle wall away from the port, the spring evening had arrived with a chill. 'Something just didn't tally, so I followed them when they led him out of the gate. It wasn't long before I knew that they weren't taking him back to England. We get a lot of deserters, you see. You learn to spot those with something to hide.'

Although the parlour was plainly furnished it was welcoming the wooden panels limewashed and the floor planks polished to a shine. Off to one side a door led into what might be the warden's bedroom and on the opposite wall, a thick curtain hid an entrance to the servant's corridor, no doubt leading all the way to the kitchen. There was only one window, set high in the wall to afford a fine view of the town rooftops. The hearth was wide and the table set before it to keep the warden and any company he might have warm.

Right now, though, even the roaring fire could not banish the chill that ran up Argyle's spine. 'You said they did not take him far?'

Windham shifted in his seat. 'Only to the edge of the city. Out near the sludge fields, nothing grows or lives there. A small boat's waiting just off the bank, but they weren't taking the prisoner with them. Whatever they wanted to know he wasn't telling them nothing. One drew his knife and that's that.'

'They killed him.' Argyle envisioned his brother's gruelling death. 'Where is his body?'

'They dragged it into the water and left it. I couldn't go in after, they'd have known I was there and they didn't look as if it'd matter to take another life. I chose to keep breathing.' There was no apology in Windham's clipped report. He was simply a soldier delivering news in an efficient and detached manner. 'I saw it clear as day. They executed him. Sharp blade, swift move, he didn't suffer.'

'Upon arrival, did they present a letter?'

'Not to me. I didn't even know they'd taken him until my gaoler informed me.' He looked out of the window. 'I think the wretch's still in Calais.'

'He is no longer in your service?'

'He never came back,' Windham said. 'I supposed they paid well, though now you're here, I wonder if they didn't just scare him half to death. With no money he'd have no choice but to stay here. Getting a crossing's costly.'

'Can you find him?'

In the prolonged pause, Argyle wondered if perhaps he had overestimated their newfound friendship. It was possible that Windham was under orders to misdirect anyone who came asking the wrong questions.

In the end, the warden nodded. 'I'll let you know if I succeed.'

ꕥ ꕥ ꕥ ꕥ

CHAPTER 51

6 April 1400 – Calais Town

In the dead of night, Argyle woke in a cold sweat, skin crawling as he shook off the dream. Thomas had spoken to him from his watery grave, his face swollen and lips peeling, his warning dire.

To take his mind from the sinister ghost, he turned his thoughts to pressing matters. What were White Harts doing this side of the sea in November?

Most of them had backed Bolingbroke once they realised that King Richard would never take back his throne. They had discarded the emblem and assumed the Lancaster crest as soon as they swore fealty to King Henry. If there had been soldiers in Calais with the King's emblem on their chests, they must have been instructed to wear it for a reason. Thomas' wife, Elizabeth, had been adamant that the man who called at the house to warn Thomas of his impending fate had worn the white hart hidden under his cloak. She was certain that Thomas had been warned by the King himself to leave without delay. A final royal command that his brother had carried out without hesitation.

Could it be that King Henry had decided to dispose of an enemy, despite his grand speech of mercy and new beginnings? Or were other forces at play? King Henry had just one uncle left – York – and this was not his style. York favoured a quiet life of comfort. If Thomas of Woodstock, youngest son of old King Edward, had been alive this would have been his doing, but he had died at Thomas' hand, perhaps only a few streets from where Argyle now lodged.

Wriggling to find some comfort on the lumpy mattress, Argyle let his attention slip to another question. If Thomas had not come to Calais until November where had he been since he left England? If he had left at all.

Acknowledging that he needed more information, he scolded himself for not asking Windham how Thomas had looked. What if he had been locked away, tortured even?

Argyle got up and paced the floor, the bare planks smooth beneath his bare feet. His mind whirled with questions for which he had no answers. Looking out the window of his modest room he watched the sun cast its first rays on the rooftops. It was time to go.

Only one stable boy was awake when Argyle came in. Bleary-eyed the boy ducked out of sight and returned with the bridle and saddle for his horse. He struggled with the buckles, fingers no doubt dulled by sleep. At the sight, Argyle's thoughts finally came to rest. It was better to act than wait. Windham's message late last night had sparked renewed hope and when he swung into the saddle he felt a strange calm descend.

Outside the stables, the warden waited on a heavyset, brown mare.

Nodding a greeting, Argyle said, 'How did you find him so quickly?'

'I sent a couple of my guards to his house. It was abandoned.' Windham led the way, his voice hushed.

The city was quiet, only a few souls out and about, most of them destitute wretches, some staggering along drunkenly, lost to the world.

The warden turned down an alley. 'One of them went on to the taverns near the harbour and found him lurking in a dark corner. It took only a few drinks to persuade him to see us. I think he's hoping to be paid enough to board a ship.'

'If what he has to say is useful, I shall put him on a ship and pay for a cabin myself.' Though he knew better, hope soared. 'I meant to ask you yesterday, how did my brother look when you saw him?'

'Battered. One of his hands's bound and bloodied, his face bruised. I didn't think much of it at the time. You'd be surprised how many of our prisoners look like that. Bar-brawls, scrapes in alleys, fights on the docks. I thought he'd fallen into bad company and wound up in the cells because of it.' The warden stopped and peered down a narrow path. 'The man you seek'll be at the end. I've got to get back, the morning shift is about to begin and the night warden's a right old prick.'

Argyle grabbed Windham's arm. 'You have been a great help. Thank you.'

He tied his horse to a tree while the alley swallowed up Windham. As soon as he was gone, Argyle turned down the path, feeling strangely exposed although narrow two-storey houses obscured the pinking sky, casting ominous shadows in which it was easy to hide. The tattered building at the end of the path looked wrong somehow and Argyle's skin prickled. With each step, his sense of foreboding increased until he could barely breathe as he stole along the leaning houses.

Coming to a halt, he knocked lightly on the crooked door, the sound reinforced in the silence.

'Who's there?' asked an almost childish voice on the other side of the door.

'You were gaoler to Thomas Mowbray in November?'

A thin, sallow face appeared. 'Yes?'

'Warden Windham said you would meet with me.' Argyle stepped forward and the face disappeared.

Before he could push open the door, his world dissolved in pain.

ઇ ઊ ઇ ઊ

Part III

Secrets and Lies

CHAPTER 52

2 May 1400 – Château de Boulogne-sur-Mer, France

'It's you.' Windham coughed and held out his hand. 'When they threw you overboard I thought you lost forever.'

Reeling from the rush of sudden remembrance, Argyle let out a shivering breath. The floor lurched underfoot, sending a lick of bile up his throat. 'I… I had never… I had forgotten…'

Windham gestured to the cot. 'Sit, you look as if you've seen a ghost.'

'That was what I thought, for a moment. You look…' Argyle shook his head. 'You look well.'

'I'm healing nicely or so I'm told. It hurts like hell sometimes, but the pain's subsiding.' His hand slid up to rest on his throat. 'You on the other hand…'

'My saviour called me Monsieur Bleu et Violet until I remembered who I am.' By now Argyle's bruises had faded to a dull yellow and sickly green, the cuts healed to whispers of faint pink. 'They told me they had found me on the beach, thought me half-drowned. I have no recollection of how I ended up in the sea. I just remember crawling to escape the tide, sand scraping against raw wounds. They threw me overboard, you say? Who? How? Tell me everything.'

'You don't remember?' Windham's question was edged in worry. 'Madame de Reines said as much, but I wondered if perhaps she'd over-exaggerated or you'd kept the truth from her?' Again his hand strayed to the bandage around his neck. 'You don't even remember meeting me?'

'I did not even remember leaving England at first.' Argyle studied Windham. His throat was tightly bound, tiny, dark lines protruding from beneath the white linen. 'My memories are still shattered. Fragmented. Though I do recall how we met.' The relief on the warden's face was swift and Argyle relaxed. 'You remember everything?'

'Short of how I came to be caught in a fisherman's net, yes, I remember. Though most days, I wish I didn't.' He fidgeted with the neat knot at the base of his bandage. 'Madam de Reines says that they've fractured my Adam's apple. They certainly punched me hard enough.'

'I have only warped images.' Up close, it was evident that Windham had taken a beating and it pained Argyle to know he was the cause of it. 'I have no recollection of a ship or who might have taken us on board. It was only just now that I remembered it was you who accompanied me to the gaoler's hovel.'

'That bastard.' The warden's growl turned into a scratching cough and he reached for a cup of water. 'He must've warned them. There were four, heavily armed. One knocked you out – he was big as a bear, and the three others silenced me.'

Windham's blunt account was humbling. Argyle replenished his cup. 'You must have put up quite a fight.'

'I think they'd expected that you came alone. And you would've, except my horse was unusually skittish so I turned back. That's when I saw them bludgeon you. As soon as they discovered me, they made quick work of me and then they dragged us out of the gate towards the marshes. It was still dark and they made sure to shout and bawl about having to drag along a drunken friend.'

'Me.'

'Aye.' He leaned back to rest his head against the bare wall of his equally bare room. It was clean and bright with no adornments beside a cross above his cot, a small table, a stool and a washbasin which appeared to double as a side table. What little clothes he had been afforded hung on pegs opposite the bed. There were no rushes on the floor and no dried herbs to lend scent to the slightly stale air. It made Argyle wonder if Windham was a prisoner or a guest – or perhaps considered to be something in-between.

'Once outside the city, they forced us along the shore until we came across a small boat dragged onto the wetlands. Further into the sea a big vessel was anchored. I don't know who they were or how long they'd been waiting for someone to come and ask questions, but they were ready. No mistake.' This time, when Windham coughed pain spread on his face. His voice had begun to creak as if from misuse. 'I don't remember being put into the boat. I suspect they knocked me out too. Next I recall, we're at sea and they're hauling you onto the deck. They didn't waste any time, just punched you in the face until you woke.'

'What did they want?' Argyle's question came out as a whisper. How could he not remember any of this?

'Answers. They knew who you were. On board there were more men, at least one outranking the captain. Foul, great beast too. He liked to work with his hands' Windham reached to protect his throat. 'You weren't really coherent so they decided to see if I knew anything.'

'I am sorry.' Shame heated his neck. 'If not for me…'

'I'd have done it anyway.' He smiled and waved his empty cup. 'Pour me some wine this time and we're quits.'

Windham took small, careful sips. 'Madam de Reines says I mustn't drink deep, so of course that's all I want to do. Where was I? Ah, yes… When they turned on me you rallied and started shouting at them, tugging at your bonds. I owe you thanks, though it merely served to stoke the commander's rage. He gave my throat a final blow before turning back to you. I couldn't really see you – his back was so broad – but I could hear him trying to break every bone in your body. He'd drive each question home with a kick or punch.'

The notion about such abuse should have made him sick, but Windham's words did not spark a single memory. Argyle said, 'What did he ask? Do you remember?'

'It's about that brother of yours.' Windham took another sip, staring at him over the rim. 'About what you knew, why you'd come asking questions, who'd sent you? When you didn't answer, he lost it. Had to be dragged away before he killed you. Whatever their orders, it's clear they'd not benefit from you dying.' His raw voice was threadbare. 'I've never seen such rage. It took four men to hold him back. Once he calmed down, he drew his sword, swearing that he'd cut out your tongue if you didn't tell him the truth. By then, you were out again. I believed you'd died there and then.'

Argyle rubbed his calf. That was how his old wounds had ripped. 'I remember nothing of this, nothing at all. What was he asking for? Please be specific.'

'Something your brother'd brought with him when he left England. I couldn't make it out, I was wafting in and out of consciousness myself.' Windham looked at his hands. 'Seems your brother's hiding something, a secret that they're desperate to know. They thought you'd found out. That you'd trade it for your life.'

Argyle leaned over to clasp Windham's shoulder. 'I recall none of this. All I know is that if not for you I would not be here today. I owe you a great debt. For turning back, for attempting to keep me safe when I am the cause of your current misfortune. Name your price and it is yours.'

'You don't owe…' Windham stopped talking when the light squeezing under the door shifted, a shadow falling. 'We're not alone.'

'No one is ever alone in a great house.' Argyle watched the shadow for a while until it moved on and light crept in under the door once more. 'You have said nothing that does not bear repeating.' Except for the part about his brother, though Thomas' name had not been mentioned. He shook his head. 'You remember no more? No faces? No emblems or traits?'

'No. I'm sorry.' Windham's voice was reduced to a whisper. 'What'll you tell the Countess?'

'If someone was eavesdropping, no doubt every word will be repeated to her before the day is out. Leave it to me.' He hoped his voice did not betray the unease within and he poured another cup of wine to distract his whirling concerns. 'We need only tell her enough to gain safe passage through France to Venice.'

'Venice? What'd you want to do there? You know that your brother didn't make it past Calais. It was in my ledger… Or have you forgotten?'

'No, that I do remember. When news of his death reached us, we were led to believe he had died in Venice. I have always wondered why anyone would spin such an elaborate tale unless there is a grain of truth at its core. Perhaps news of Thomas made it there somehow. Perhaps he had an ally there. My brother was rarely caught without a plan in reserve. I must go there and see what I can unearth.' He caught Windham's gloomy expression and tried a smile. 'I do not doubt your account of what transpired in Calais, but there is more to the story than either of us can see.'

'You believe me then?'

'I believed you in Calais when you told me Thomas died and I believe now that the men who captured me – and you, regrettably – are the same. Or at least sent by the same foe. The question remains who?'

Argyle had spent many agonising nights pondering what his next move might be. Now he knew.

'There's more to the tale than meets the eye?' Windham sputtered when he drank too deep.

'Thomas was a master of secrets, whatever he left behind he will have gone to great lengths to hide. And there is something about his false death that does not tally. Something we were told in the letter we received, or rather not told. *How* he died. I must unearth the truth.' Argyle hoped his smile was reassuring. 'That does not mean you have to come with me. If you wish it I shall attempt to persuade the Countess that you must be sent home to England. As you told me in Calais, your term is nearly up. Who would wonder that you return a little sooner than anticipated?'

'You think she'd let us let us part ways?'

'What can she do once we are outside these walls?'

'She's the French King's aunt,' Windham said and a little of Argyle's resolve wavered. Her regal demeanour had not been a show. 'She's got more power than you might imagine. And she'll want something in return.'

'Whatever she might decide to claim as a fair price for letting two Englishmen go without informing her nephew, I shall pay it in full. None of this will affect you – whatever you decide to do.'

CHAPTER 53

14 May 1400 – Château de Boulogne-sur-Mer

'You understand that, even as the King's aunt, I do not enjoy unbridled power?' the Countess asked with a glow in her eyes. 'If I decide not to inform him of my actions, I will be held responsible in the event that you do something untoward.'

Argyle inclined his head. 'Yes, your Grace. I understand.'

'And you understand that I am concerned to do something that my nephew might find highly irrational? A betrayal even?' Her detached tone was almost unbearable. 'I have in my keep an Englishman of some standing it would appear, if you are to be trusted, and Madame de Reines claims that you are. My nephew would be most interested to meet you. To send you on your way without a word to him might be construed as unwise…'

The grand parlour somehow managed to give off an air of private intimacy though it was fit to seat at least forty and leave room for servants. It was decorated in a bold pattern of fluttering birds, oversized flower petals and vines heavy with grape clusters. One full wall was taken up by a spectacular tapestry depicting some ancestor of the Countess out on a hunt for a white stag. With the sun high in the sky there was no need to light the numerous candles sitting in extravagant candelabras and fitted in wall-mounts which were adorned with mother-of-pearl inlay and pieces of pink, yellow and green porcelain to mimic delicate flowers. It was in every way a chamber fit for its primary resident and the Countess' resplendent clothes fit the colour scheme and yet stood out, her dress a brilliant blue slit to reveal embroidered lilac silk. Her wide belt sparkled when she moved.

By now it was clear to Argyle that she was prepared to let them go if not at what cost. 'I hope I have not given cause for you to mistrust me. Please believe that I shall not be a disgrace, your Grace.'

'No, you shall not,' the Countess agreed with a smile. 'I confess I am curious to know what is in Venice that you must see or do?'

'I once went on a pilgrimage and though we passed through Venice I never experienced the city.' Argyle paused. 'I wish to make amends and visit it now. As my memory returns, I find that I have much for which to be grateful– and I thank God for this chance to achieve that which I skirted the first time.'

'A weak excuse if ever there was one,' Windham had said last night when they had toured the gardens a few guards stationed at the gates and along the castle walls. As Argyle now spoke the words he was tempted to agree.

The Countess flicked her wrist and the gold bands jangled. 'You expect me to accept such a feeble explanation? Really, Sire, do you think so little of me? After what happened to you I very much doubt that a pious act is at the foremost of your designs.'

He acknowledged the danger lurking in her light tone. 'There are some secrets best not spoken aloud. I wish only to keep you safe.'

'As safe as that poor man Windham? For you told him little enough about your true mission when first you met, or am I mistaken there too?' She shook her head. 'I have a mind to send word to my nephew at once.'

'I understand that you must inform your King. I merely ask that the news of my presence here is kept between as few as possible.'

'And if it is not?'

'I put my fate in your hands, your Grace,' Argyle said. He itched to be away, to chase a notion that had taken root in his mind and grew with every night spent in the Countess' opulent home.

No matter what she decided to do it was vital that no news of his survival and whereabouts reached England. Should she decide to send him to Paris in shackles he would have to plead with King Charles to be released. But if word travelled to the English court, all might be lost.

'My personal endeavour is of little matter to you and I cannot blame you – no matter how you choose to act.'

'No. Nor should you, for my conduct is not yours to judge. Let us be clear about that if nothing else.' The Countess seemed to consider something. 'Your man goes with you?'

'The matter is not yet settled…'

A sudden smile lit up her sparkling grey eyes. 'He might be persuaded to stay then? Only I know my maids find him very… agreeable.'

The wink she sent Argyle was unmistakable and he knew that if Windham had been in the room he would have cringed. 'Until I return to England I fear his fate is tied to mine, your Grace. I also imagine that, while he would be honoured by your offer, his heart would be with his family who no doubt misses him.'

'They would be fools not to,' the Countess said, her mischievous expression turning solemn. 'I must consider your request, Sire.'

Argyle swept a bow, careful to close his eyes against the surging feeling. He knew, as well as she did, that she was all that stood between him and any enemies that might have been informed of his survival. 'That is all I ask, your Grace.'

'Oh, I nearly forgot.' The Countess waved a servant closer. 'You have a visitor waiting in your room.'

Although she had been all grace and good mirth, Argyle's heart plummeted and brow beaded on his brow as he followed the servant along the long gallery that led from the main reception rooms and into the left wing where Argyle and Windham enjoyed her hospitality. At night, their doors might be locked from the outside, but apart from that small measure, they were visitors rather than prisoners and for that, he was grateful.

Thoughts whirled as they approached the stairs leading up to the first storey. He had sent word to Elizabeth. What if his sister-in-law had turned against him? What if she had informed Isobel of his whereabouts? Or worse still, King Henry?

He had once escaped a King's wrath, but only just, and this time his brother would not be there to wield his silver tongue and save him from a dismal fate. Moreover, he held no hopes that his new King would be lenient when he had often enough questioned Argyle's loyalty. To vanish without a trace would hardly prove that he was to be trusted.

When the servant reached for the latch, Argyle pushed past him and opened the door himself, his breath ragged and heart pounding.

'You look as if you have seen a ghost.' Grand-Maman's voice carried a tiny fleck of amusement. Studying him, she continued, 'Did you expect a much younger version of me? Ah well, Marie had to stay home, she is preparing for the arrival of her fiancée. She will be very busy these next many weeks.' She tilted her head to look past him. 'You may go.'

It was only then Argyle realised that the servant was hovering behind him and he closed the door on the man's curious expression. 'Thank you.'

'For what?' Grand-Maman tapped a crooked finger on the polished armrest of her chair.

There was only one in his room along with a table, a chest of clothes and his bed. On edge, he chose to stay standing, trying to calm his whirling min. His thoughts fluttered as swallows in spring.

'I did not know she was betrothed?'

'To a seasoned Lord,' Grand-Maman said. 'I dare say that is not what has you in such a state. Are you feeling ill? Have you exerted yourself? I left strict instructions that you were not to be overworked.'

'I have been as idle here as I was in your son's house.' Argyle forced a smile. 'You and Marie saved my life and I shall never forget either of you. I owe you my life.'

'Just mind that you do not stir up new trouble and I shall be content.' She twisted in her seat when the door opened.

'Monsieur Windham, you look much improved.'

'Thank you, my Lady, I feel it too.' Windham bowed before her and she ran her hands over his left arm nodding with satisfaction. 'You have healed better than this one.' She winked at Argyle who had to admire her blunt manner. 'He still hobbles around as an old man in want of a cane. I have a good mind to send him one of my own.'

'He took the brunt of it,' Windham said as susceptible of her wit as Argyle. 'I'm not sure I'd look as well in his place – if I'd had survived.'

'The story of two of you is still the most tasty piece of gossip in all of Boulogne.' Grand-Maman's smirk crinkled her face. 'And now, we are to lose you? We had only just grown used to you. Marie shall be disappointed that she was robbed of your company at her wedding feast.'

Windham glanced at Argyle who shook his head. He wondered how the old lady knew of their plans when he had told none but the Countess. Still, such a grand household had many ears and surely someone was bound to let slip a secret to curry favour with one of the great women of the land.

'I doubt our attending her feast would give rise to much joy. After all, we are Englishmen in the heart of France…'

'Pray our King never hears you say so.' Grand-Maman wriggled in her sat. 'He may well owe his life to his aunt, but his *court* is the heart of France even if he is abroad and he will not be told differently.'

She adjusted her shawl. 'My own son cannot wait to see you in the saddle, riding out of Boulogne. All I am left to wonder is where you are bound?'

Argyle eased onto the edge of his bed. 'We travel south. To Venice.'

She nodded as if to say she knew why and, not for the

first time, Argyle wondered how much he had said during his first, fever-riddled days in de Reines' home. 'You will need horses and provisions. What is being done for you?'

'Your son has kindly let me buy his grey colt. I am told it is ready to ride now.'

'He would have,' Grand-Maman said. 'He was white with fury when he found out that his stable master had it castrated. It would have been a magnificent breeding animal.'

'How does anyone make such a mistake?' Windham was leaning against the wall by the window.

'A head full of strong wine helped it along.' Grand-Maman's face wrinkled in a grin. 'If they had been alone, I doubt the poor man would have had a head to pain him much longer. As it were, there was nothing to be done save to send him away in disgrace. The horse was worth hundreds of francs.'

Windham whistled. Argyle admitted to himself that he too was shocked, particularly by the low price de Reines had asked.

'Without its most prized *possessions*...' She shook her head. 'Jean is happy to part with it. No one likes to keep a constant reminder of a future that is not to be. Nothing good can come from lingering in the past.' She fixed Argyle with a piercing gaze. 'As you will no doubt agree?'

'We shall find a mount for Master Windham in the stables either here or in the city,' Argyle said a breath too late.

'You will do no such thing,' Grand-Maman snapped. 'My son has plenty of horses. He can easily spare one more. Though perhaps not of similar value.' She tipped her head in Windham's direction. 'I doubt he would even dare mount such a costly beast.'

He smiled. 'You know me well.'

'You may boast the heritage of your fine steeds everywhere you go, though I suggest you refrain from doing so while you are in France. Let that be your payment for our hospitality.'

Grand-Maman got up and rummaged through her basket which sat beside the chair. 'Here are some herbs and ointments for the journey. I shall not visit again as I must help Marie prepare. It is in times such as these that she feels the loss of her mother most keenly.'

Argyle held out his hands to receive a collection of small leather bags, vials and a little earthenware pot sealed with wax. Some of had a strong scent that left him queasy.

'Be careful who you trust.' She squeezed his arm. 'Not everyone will settle for a letter of safe passage – even one signed by the Countess.'

As a last act, she adjusted Windham's bandage and told him not to overstrain his voice and gave him a pot of ointment to apply to his bruises. Once done fussing, she left, the click of her cane echoing through the corridor.

'She's well-informed.' Windham tucked the pot into a pocket in his garb. 'What was that nonsense about the letters?'

'The conflict between England and France is bound to make men do reckless things.' Argyle rubbed his leg. It felt as if a bruise lay underneath the skin. The hidden caution in her parting words was not lost on him either and it edged his previous concerns in new worry.

'You trust her?' Windham nodded towards the main building and the Countess' vast apartments. Her castle was built by several of her ancestors and sprawled as a mythical creature, curling around fair gardens and stretching towards lakes and forests and fields.

'I have no choice. I want to learn Thomas' secret and to do so I must go to Venice. If nothing else it is bound to put distance between myself and whoever wanted the truth so bad they were willing to kill me – and you – for it.'

Windham rubbed his throat. 'Then we go to Venice.'

'I have promised the Countess that we will tell her the tale of how we came to wash up on her shores.' Argyle rose and put a hand on the cold iron handle. 'We shall have to be careful how much we tell her. Though I believe she will enjoy every gory detail.'

'Small price to pay.' Windham paused by the door. 'She could've let the sea have me, you know. Or thrown me in a cell.'

'I have a feeling she is too fascinated by adventure and novelty for that,' Argyle said. 'We had best prepare for a long night.'

Once Windham left, Argyle lay down and stretched his aching body. He still had no idea if going to Venice was simply a diversion, a fool's quest, or if it might yield answers and if he might regret learning Thomas' secret. Grand-Maman's warning left him rattled and though he had no cause for concern part of him dared not trust Windham.

CHAPTER 54

16 May 1400 – Château de Boulogne-sur-Mer

The Duke narrowed his small eyes. They were set near his nose making his already fleshy face even more grotesque. Squat and rotund, he was the exact opposite of his wife though his attire was as opulent if not more so. Throughout Argyle's stay, he had seen the Duke perhaps a handful of times and had often wondered what made him so elusive.

'Let us have a little privacy, my dear,' the Countess said and planted a kiss on her husband's pink forehead. 'I wish to have a quiet word with Sir Argyle before he leaves us.'

He tried to imagine what any children begotten from this marriage would look like. All he could come up with was a cross between a pig and a nymph a laughable notion to say the least. He offered the Duke a submissive smile, remembering his initial surprise when he had first met the heavyset man. Although few noble marriages were made for love most attempted to find a way to rub along. Curiously, the Countess appeared genuinely enamoured by her husband though they could not be a more ill-matched pair.

Now, he looked even more upset than usual. 'Why?'

The Countess laughed, the sound musical and light. 'Oh, Jean, do be reasonable. You have so much to do. Were you not just telling me of all the plans and ideas you have?'

The Duke brightened. 'You should stay, Sir Argyle. I am planning a party and we are short of good men who may entertain the ladies.'

'He cannot stay, my dear. We discussed it at length last night, remember?' The Countess grabbed her husband lightly under the elbow and guided him to the door, planting another kiss on his glistening forehead. 'I am certain our steward will have some ideas on how to make the most of those we can rely on to participate. I trust you to find good musicians and entertainment as ever.'

The Duke departed with a sanguine smile on his fleshy face, his short stubby fingers laden with jewels glittered as he waved. It was almost impossible for Argyle to fathom that this was a man who had governed France during his nephew, King Charles' minority. Perhaps his brothers had been instrumental in many of the greater decisions although Jean de Berry had dealt with a peasants' revolt of his own at Harelle.

Argyle glanced at the Countess. It seemed more than plausible that she had played some part in ensuring her husband's success in such an endeavour, but then, looks could be deceiving and he might rise to the occasion if provoked. It was said that, at some point, the Duke fell out with another nephew, the Duke of Orléans, and that they could barely be in the same room as one another without spiteful accusations flying. Having met de Berry, Argyle struggled to fit this man into the figure painted by embassies and gossip. It was much easier to believe that de Berry simply sided with his brother, the Duke of Burgundy, who was, by all accounts an aggressive fellow.

At the door, the Duke barked at a servant who was slow to get out of the way and the Countess sighed. There had to be times when she praised her sovereignty of her lands, in Boulogne her word was law, no matter the elevated status of her husband.

She sat down, arranging her skirt. 'He is planning a grand party, something which he is infinitely better at than me – I am only good at getting matters settled.' Her veiled admission aligned with Argyle's own ideas of their internal relationship.

'You wanted to tell me something, your Grace?'

'I prefer to see it as encouraging you to do something.' She offered Argyle a seat by her side, the stool low but fitted with a large cushion. 'I know you are decided on going to Venice. However, it might prove useful to make a small detour and visit Milan along the way.'

'Milan?'

The Countess seemed to consider him for a while. Argyle tried to conjure what prompted this suggestion. No matter how he turned the idea in his mind he found nothing he knew to be connected to Milan.

'A certain lady lives in Milan who has been rumoured to be in love with your King Henry. Long before he was anyone other than a young nobleman eager to assert himself. It is said she was quite determined.' As understanding dawned, the Countess continued, 'Whether you visit there before or after Venice, I do hope you take my advice and go. I am sure she may shed some light on many things.'

'You are a very mysterious woman, your Grace.' Argyle was rewarded with a brilliant smile from the Countess. 'You leave me wondering how you came to the decision not to turn me over and now…'

She leaned forward with a serious expression. 'I do not often ask my husband to leave the room so that I might be alone with another man. Nor do I put up men who wash up on my shores without even an explanation of how they came to be bashed and beaten. I know danger is about and that you seem to have been caught in the thick of it.'

Pausing, she twisted the silver and pearl ring on her finger. 'I see now that this is not the first time you have been warned. It is said that your brother was a dangerous man to cross. Now, an even more dangerous man sits on your throne.' The Countess smiled coldly. 'My nephew is dangerous too. That is the trouble. Anyone who might sit on any throne will have to be ruthless. And the two of them are at each other's throats. Charles wants his daughter returned. Your King Henry wants to keep her. Some leverage is required and I believe you may find it in Milan.'

'Whom do you wish for me to seek out, your Grace?'

Though she appeared earnest, Argyle feared she was taunting him, teasing him into some trap he would only see once it was sprung.

'You told me once that you joined a pilgrimage that passed through Venice. It came to me that you might have gone with the future King Henry when he was still a Lord and not a contender to the throne of England.' Her concerned tone lent meaning to her words. 'The depth of men's desires are often lost on me, but I know well enough women's desires. Especially that of one who is famous for stating that if she had to, she would wait forever to marry the heir of Lancaster. Imagine what she might feel now that he is King.'

A fleeting memory such a story floated to the surface of Argyle's mind, but before he grasped the lady's name, it drifted away. 'How will I know where to find her?'

'I shall provide instructions, of course,' the Countess said, a soft smile pulling up her full lips. 'Though I have enjoyed your company, I am determined to have you off my lands. I cannot be seen to harbour an English fugitive much longer – not even one who claims to have lost his memory. In any event, it is restored now, is that not so?'

Her pause left Argyle with sweaty palms. She seemed to contemplate what to say next. 'You realise that I aid you only to help my nephew in getting back his daughter? I have often enough suffered his complaints that he married her off to the wrong man and now that this man is no more…' She smoothed her skirt. Today, she wore a pale yellow gown heavy with embroidery and beading. Pearl pendants dangled from her ears and her cuffs were crusted with gemstones. 'My nephew will stop at nothing to have her returned, Sire. I wish your King would see reason and that the two of them could broker some treaty of peace. It is a fool's wish for they are hot-headed and hanker for conflict.' She spoke the last words with disdain.

'You do not want England and France to go to war?' Argyle tried to imagine what role he might play if the two Kings did decide wage war.

'Of course not. My lands are some of the first to feel it every time our countries are at odds. I will not have my people harmed because my nephew and some usurper cannot come to terms over a *girl*.' The Countess' face had gone hard. 'I understand your desire to find the truth of your brother's death, and while I do not think you will find anything of use in Venice, by all means go there if you must. I urge you to visit Milan. I am certain you will not be disappointed.'

Argyle leaned back and eyed her for a while. He yearned to find out why Thomas had suffered such a dire fate. Her interest lay solely in preserving the peace. Still, both might be accomplished if he went about it the right way.

'Thank you for enlightening me, your Grace.' He inclined his head. 'I shall take your advice.'

The Countess rose and offered her hand to kiss. 'Good. Then I wish you a successful journey.'

'We shall leave as soon as possible.' Argyle brushed his lips against her scented skin. 'We may visit Paris upon our return.'

'I shall send word to my nephew.'

'If I may beg one more favour, your Grace?' He paused until she motioned for him to continue. 'That you do not tell King Charles that I am here. Not just yet.'

'Why not?'

Argyle looked her in the eye. 'I am putting my fate in your hands. You know as well as I that at court – any court – there are precious few whom you can trust. If you can tell me that no one at your nephew's court has any contact with the English…'

'You know very well that I cannot.' She tapped a finger on the carved armrest, her rings clinking. 'I can provide letters of safe conduct to see you across the country and onwards. Once you return, I have no choice but to inform my nephew of my little secret and for that he will not thank me. Should you take my advice there will be no need for you to visit Paris, and so, I have little reason to trouble Charles with news of your visit.'

'I can never hope to repay you for your kindness, your Grace,' Argyle said and prayed that her prediction might hold true. 'My means are limited. King Henry does not even know that I have gone, unless…'

'Unless?'

'My wife has told him. I left her no word of my plans.'

The Countess gave Argyle a quizzical look.

'There is only one who knows that I left and on what errand.' Argyle had often wondered if Elizabeth would betray him. 'Since she is my brother's widow, she might just turn her coat as quickly as he was known to do.'

'A strange confidante to choose,' the Countess said. 'And yet you trust her rather than your own wife.'

'My marriage is not quite as happy as yours.'

'You make your own happiness. If your wife has somehow disappointed you, most likely the fault is not hers alone.' The Countess waved her hand dismissively. 'Should we meet under happier circumstances, I shall demand the full tale and you will not deny me. Until such a time you have my leave to continue your journey.'

Biting his tongue not to spill his thoughts, he bowed and left. The Countess would never change his mind about Isobel. Their shared misery was all her doing and he would never forgive her.

CHAPTER 55

20 June 1400 – Outside Milan, Italy

The first weeks on the road had been hard on both of them. They had spoken little and grappled with staying in their saddles long enough to stumble into a tavern, staying awake only long enough to climb into bed.

Argyle had been haunted by miserable dreams and, though weary to the bone, he had often enough lain awake waiting for the sun to rise listening to Windham groan. Whatever had him tossing and turning, they never talked of it.

Little by little, Argyle's bruises subsided and his aches diminished. Without Grand-Maman's ointments and herbs he might never again have recognised his own features when they were cast back to him from a scoop of water or pane of glass. By now, he looked almost himself again, the cut of his jaw a little sharper and his body leaner, but on the whole he was recovered.

Windham had little in the way of visible bruises and, after a week, he had unstrapped the threaded and dirty bandage around his neck and declared that he was rather pleased with his new, rasping voice.

When they had both broken down laughing Windham had grabbed his neck hard and Argyle was sure not his tears were from amusement.

One thing Grand-Maman had not been able to cure was the dull pain in his calf. He had grown used to it cramping up at regular intervals and as long as he was able to drag himself up the narrow stairs of any odd tavern and fall onto a bed, he was no worse for wear.

'How much longer before we reach Venice?' Windham pulled up his collar, the sun hammered down upon them relentlessly as a fierce and angry God.

'If the tavern's mistress was anything to go by,' Argyle said and Windham snorted. 'It will be little more than a week.'

'Providing the good weather continues?'

'No sign of change.' Argyle wiped his forehead. He would not mind a quick torrent to wash away the stifling heat.

Windham rubbed his arm where it flaked. 'They must want for rain.'

'Only if their crops need water,' Argyle said and looked out over the vast fields lining the narrow road. They were startling green against the yellow tufts of grass dotting the road, which was barely a couple of dips in the dry soil. 'They must have crafted some rather ingenious methods to ensure their fields are watered.'

'I'm sure they did. I've not seen such lush fields near Calais.'

'And I have only ever seen the like in England.'

They rode on in silence for a while, the dry, hollow clop of hooves accompanied by the buzz of insects. Argyle wondered what he might find in Milan and why the Countess had urged him to go there. He had considered skirting the town and make straight for Venice, then again…

'That looks to be a mighty big city.'

Windham's voice made stirred Argyle from his thoughts. On the shimmering horizon strong stonewalls rose towards the sky, banners flying from each tower. 'Heavily fortified.'

'No doubt.' Windham looked over at Argyle. 'Where exactly are we?'

'Milan.'

He reined in his horse and Argyle had to follow suit. 'You took her advice? You said you wouldn't go. We agreed…'

'It was on the way.' Argyle earned a suspicious glance. 'I swear that this road will take us right to Venice.'

'If we ride straight through that city.' Surveying the walls that stretched for the skies, Windham scratched his stubbled chin. 'Somehow I don't think it was made with riding straight through it in mind.'

Argyle harked a laugh and covered his mouth with his sleeve as his horse kicked up dirt. 'Certainly not in warring times, but there is peace here. It is quite safe to enter the city – and to depart from it.'

'Did the lovely Countess ever tell you whom to visit?' Spurring on his sturdy brown horse Windham patted its neck. It seemed as reluctant to continue as its rider.

'She gave me a letter.' It was stashed in his saddlebag and he prayed that the lady was still in the city when they arrived. 'We may have to stay here a day or two.'

'I'm not the one desperate to get to Venice.' Reluctance danced on his voice as Windham clutched the knot of his reins.

Only once, since they set out, had Windham lamented that if he had never encountered Argyle, he would be on his way back to England by now. Ever since, he had trotted along without a single word as to this twist of fate. Perhaps he had simply kept any arguments in reserve.

'You will agree that we need to get out of the sun?' Argyle's forehead had peeled for two weeks straight and was now a deep golden brown. Windham's face was darker. In the burning midday heat it looked as if he had not washed for weeks on end, which was not far from the truth.

'Oh aye, I only worry that you'll ask me to spur this poor horse into a gallop. It'll drop where it stands and I'll be forced to walk the rest of the way.' He shielded his eyes. 'Unless you're going to offer me your steed.'

The silver gelding's muscles danced. It would have no trouble careering from here to the city gate and far beyond. Still, Windham was right. His horse might be willing and indeed able to overcome the midday heat, but Argyle was not.

'Let us rest here under this oak for a while and afford what shade we can for your poor horse.'

'I knew it. You're never going to let me ride that beast, are you?' Flashing a wide grin, Windham turned off the road, his horse sensing it was about to have a rest raised its head, pricked its ears and walked with new purpose.

'You cheeky beggar.' He clicked his tongue. 'There's nothing wrong with you, is there? You're just happiest when you're doing nothing.'

Argyle's horse turned its ears towards the road and Argyle glanced over his shoulder to watch a carriage rumble by, thick curtains closed against the dust and heat. The sides were decorated with large crests of blue and brown standing out against a bright backdrop. The motif was a man being eaten by a sea-monster.

He turned to find Windham had descended the soft edge of the ditch and followed him to the oak. 'I believe we may be in luck.'

'That'll be a first.' Windham picked through his meagre packs no doubt hunting for food. He seemed to suffer from constant hunger and had been quick to put meat back on his bones. 'How so?'

Climbing inelegantly from the saddle, Argyle gave the silver free rein and it joined Windham's brown mare by the muddy stream. 'If I am not much mistaken, the crest on the carriage that just passed by belongs to the lady's father.'

'Do we want him?' Windham slid into a seat and leaned against the tree trunk.

'It is widely known that as she is his pride and joy and he has endowed upon her the right to use his crest.' Uneasy energy tingled in his veins. 'She is also said to live here with her uncle, the Duke of Milan. The carriage is proof that she is indeed here.'

'I see. Then for what it's worth perhaps we're in luck.'

'Let us hope she does not live up to the crest or else we are about to be eaten by sea monsters.'

Windham closed his eyes and snorted. 'Too late. The sea monster already spat us out.'

Careful to spare his aching leg, Argyle laid down in the shade. 'Tonight, we shall sleep in a good bed and, who knows, we may even stay awake long enough to enjoy a meal.'

Windham folded his arms behind his head. 'I'll have a roast chicken, Sir Argyle, and you may fetch it for me.'

CHAPTER 56

22 June 1400 – Milan

The past is a double-edged sword, honed equally by truth and illusion and I will do well to remember that.

Argyle looked up at the marble carvings of the Virgin Mary holding the Christ child. It had the same awe-inspiring effect on him as it had years ago when he was travelling in Bolingbroke's wake and had passed through Porta Ticinese, the western gateway to Milan.

For once, he was alone as Windham stayed behind in their lodgings to rest his weary limbs. If Argyle could have done the same he would have, but fate would have it otherwise.

Not long after they had arrived in Milan he had learned that the woman he sought an audience with, Donna Lucia

Visconti, was about to embark on a journey that would take her from Milan for the rest of the year.

Rather than relax and regain his strength, Argyle had set about arranging a meeting with her, flaunting the Countess' letter wherever he went. By now, all of Milan would know that he was here and he was left to hope he had not spent all of his luck on catching a glimpse of Donna Lucia's carriage on the first day outside Milan.

This Sunday, she was expecting him outside the Basilica Sant'Ambrogio after Terce, which was, it seemed, the service she always attended. Argyle was relieved that she had not asked him to join in the mass. It was one thing to attend church in England and quite another in Italy, especially when his belief in God was tentative at best.

Riding along a long avenue where the houses were stacked side by side, he marvelled at the second stories that hung out over the street below and how several of the small balconies seemed tied together with string. He looked up in wonder just as a girl of seven or eight appeared carrying a basket with wet linen. She struggled with the first big piece and finally managed to tip over to the edge of the balcony and hang it over the string. The line dipped under the weight of water and cloth.

She pushed back a couple of stray locks of rich brown hair and when she caught Argyle's eye she offered a timid half-smile before returning her task.

The washing was a welcome cool drizzle as he passed. Although he had not been out more than a quarter of an hour, the day was already warm and his shirt was sticky from sweat. Last night, he had hardly slept at all he had been too busy worrying about his arrangement today. Windham had snored liberally and, in the end, Argyle had left the room to visit the stables and find a little solace with his horse, which Marie had aptly named Argent, the French word for silver.

Straight ahead, the Basilica's imposing presence provided some shade against the morning sun and Argyle relished in the shivers that ran down his spine where the wet bits of his shirt clung cold to his warm skin. The doors were already thrown open, bells tolling all over the city announcing that mass was at an end.

'Sir Argyle?'

'Yes?' Argyle turned to face a young servant wearing the Visconti serpent prominent on his chest.

The youth bowed and gestured. 'La Donna is waiting.'

Argyle had expected Donna Lucia Visconti to be attended by hordes of courtiers eager to please her. Instead, she stood in the shade of the Basilica with just one lady in attendance who was wearing a vacant expression.

He dismounted to a sharp pain in his calf and left the servant holding the reins. Biting down on the throbbing in his leg, Argyle forced himself to put more weight on it than he was used to. He did not intend to hobble along before her.

'Donna Lucia.' He bowed low.

The attending lady turned and sniffed haughtily before she curtsied and left disdain crunching with her every step.

'Sir Argyle. You have just witnessed a woman of unvarying loyalty who displays absolutely no kindness to strangers.' Lucia Visconti's words carried no apology.

'You are kind to afford me a little of your precious time.' Argyle was pleased to receive a warm smile. 'The Countess hoped I would find you well, my Lady. And I was happy to catch you before you leave.'

'Walk with me in the gardens where we may find some shade.' Rather than acknowledge the pleasantry, Donna

Lucia pointed to an opening in a low wall. 'Although the monks now live elsewhere, my uncle has kept the old monastery gardens in pristine condition and made it a communal area for all to enjoy.'

Argyle ducked under the low arch to a breath-taking sight. Colour and scents attacked the senses and, for a moment, left him speechless. The Donna studied him. 'It is quite spectacular. No matter how often I visit I am always delighted and restored even in my darkest moments.'

When she reached out, Argyle offered his arm. Her touch was as light as a feather. 'I hope you had time to read the letter from the Countess?'

'I did.' She glanced up at him, her dark hair glistening when a ray of sun perforated the lush canopy. 'You do not know what the Countess wrote?'

'No, my Lady. She did not see fit to inform me only bade me seek you out should my journey take me to your city.' Argyle was careful to be as deferential as possible a feat that was made difficult by his unfamiliarity of local customs.

The Donna was one of the most important people in Milan, her family ruled all of northern Italy and were very close with the Doge of Venice. Many of her sisters had made powerful alliances all over the continent and, no doubt, she too would make an important match.

'I once met the man who is now your King,' the Donna said watching a bird take flight. 'For a time, my uncle entertained the notion that I might marry him. I thwarted a suitor for him, did you know?'

'No, my Lady, I did not.'

'The negotiations were made in secret, as all good political transactions are, though I confess openly that I was smitten with Henry of Bolingbroke. He is the finest man I have ever met and any match that might be made for me would never suffice.'

'You might have been Queen of England by now,' Argyle ventured and she bestowed on him another smile. Though not a beauty in the conventional sense, she really was quite enchanting.

'Had he not fallen out with his cousin and been sent away in disgrace we might have married, it is true.' With a slight nod, she acknowledged a group of men bowing as they passed. 'Now that he is King I no longer harbour any illusions that we shall marry. Sadly, my uncle was most adamant that no further negotiations were to take place while Henry was exiled. If only my uncle had known then what we know now, Sire.'

'Might I ask, my Lady, when you first met King Henry?'

When she smiled, her eyes narrowed a little lending an air of mischief to her countenance. It was gone as quickly as it came. 'He visited my uncle on his way to Jerusalem. I saw little of him, but I could tell he was such a pious soul. Upon his return, he visited again and stayed longer.'

If she had been entranced by Bolingbroke, surely it could not have escaped her notice that the man who returned was not her heart's desire. Argyle hoped his concern did not show on his face. He had ridden back with Bolingbroke while one of his Beaufort brothers had pretended to be Lord Bolingbroke.

Secrets and lies, Argyle thought, there are always secrets and lies.

'I found him quite changed,' she said and gestured for a bench hugged either side by opulent bushes thick with bright, yellow flowers. They sat down and a sweet, sharp scent encompassed them.

'Of course, that was because it was not Henry who returned to us. I knew that as well as my uncle who had spent much time in his company. To anyone else, his brother looked much like him and had the same ease and affable manners as the Lord he impersonated.' Donna Lucia made no effort to hide her disappointment. 'I swore then that I would wait forever to meet Henry again. To marry him even if I only had days with him before I died.'

What surprised Argyle was not her blunt confession that she knew it was Beaufort who posed as Bolingbroke on the return journey, but that she could be so passionate about a man she barely knew.

'He must have made quite an impression for a young woman to swear such an oath.'

'He did.' She turned towards Argyle with a serene expression. 'I was honoured that Lord Beaufort confided in me. I believe perhaps he noticed that I was not fooled by his appearance. Or perhaps it was because my uncle saw it the moment he entered our house. No man can change that much in such a short span of time. To all others, Master Beaufort was Lord Bolingbroke and though he never told us exactly why he had agreed to be an imposter, he gave us to believe that it was Henry who had ordered him to do so.'

'It was, my Lady.' Argyle remembered Beaufort's consternation when he was ordered to impersonate his half-brother on the journey home, while the real Bolingbroke stole back to England in secret. 'I rode with Lord Bolingbroke back from Jerusalem.'

'Ah…' Donna Lucia picked a flower and held it to her chest. 'It must have been important for he seemed to me a serious man.'

'It was, my Lady,' Argyle said once more. Why did she not ask about the journey or demand an explanation now that he was here? He wondered if perhaps she knew more than she let on. It seemed so many did. Especially those who forgot to ask questions at crucial stages.

He cleared his throat. 'If you will permit, you have piqued my interest as to what the Countess might have written to you?'

Her rings glittered as she pulled a piece of paper from her sleeve. 'She writes that you are chasing the truth of your brother's death, a Lord Mowbray, I believe?' Argyle nodded and she continued, the letter still folded in her lap. 'The Countess believes that Lord Mowbray travelled with a great secret that was sent ahead of him at some point. Is it true that your brother is rumoured to have died of the mortality in Venice last fall?'

'That is what we are led to believe.' Argyle wondered how the Countess was so well-informed. Had Windham said more than he had owned to Argyle? Perhaps in the grips of fever or out of fear?

'How…'

'How is not important. What you plan to do with what I have to say next is.' Donna Lucia tucked the flower into her intricate hairstyle. It was a splash of bright yellow set off by a deep, dark brown. 'There was no bout of mortality in Venice last fall. Or last year at all.'

Shock stole the air from his lungs. What a fool would spin such a tale if it could be so easily unravelled. Shaking his head he acknowledged that it was perhaps not so easy, after all he had suffered a beating that should have left him for dead and happenstance had sent him to the shores of one of the few who might aid in his discoveries. Still, it seemed a hastily concocted lie perhaps born of a need to cover up an unsanctioned misdeed?

The Donna turned the letter in her hands before she tucked it into her sleeve. 'My uncle did not purely discontinue the negotiations for my marriage with Henry because he was exiled, though naturally, it provided a valid reason to recant.'

'Then why?' Argyle could hardly push out his question.

'It appears there is something in Henry's past too disconcerting for our family to accept any match between us.' Donna Lucia rose and brushed her pale blue silk skirt. 'We have been gone for a goodly amount of time, any longer would appear imprudent on my part. Please escort me back to the Basilica where, no doubt, my maid is eagerly awaiting my return.'

Crushing a wince, he rose and once more offered his arm. She took it with the same light touch. 'Before you ask, I know not what the secret is nor, it would seem, does the Countess. Although King Charles is a loving nephew, she could not speak of it with you even if she did. She harbours no doubt that he has placed spies at her court. It is the premise of all great houses.' Donna Lucia paused by a bush of tiny purple flowers. 'These few stolen moments with you are sure to be conveyed to my uncle without delay and he is not even in Milan these days. Should he arrive, I am prepared to face him. I shall simply say that I could not send away a servant of King Henry who was once proposed as my future husband.'

'Brave, my Lady.' Argyle picked a few flowers for her and she received them with grace. She might not be an obvious beauty, and yet, the warmth in her eyes and her easy nature made her very attractive. Argyle could easily imagine why Beaufort had decided to confide in her all those years ago. 'I wish to thank you for your time.'

They exited the garden and Donna Lucia grabbed the little bouquet with both hands. 'What I am most interested in, Sire, is what you mean to do next?'

'I shall go to Venice.' What she had revealed had only fuelled his intentions. 'If nothing else, it will be my alibi when I return to England. I went to see my brother's grave.'

'Even if the cause of his demise was a lie?'

He looked at her. 'There is no if about it, my Lady. My brother met his death in Calais. Venice is a blind, made up to ensure we did not look elsewhere. It is far enough afield that none would think we might investigate.'

Donna Lucia's face was immobile as they crossed the small square. When they reached the shade of the Basilica, her arrogant maid looked Argyle up and down, clearly finding him wanting in every way. 'We are late, Donna Lucia.'

'Please, Sire, if you need anything before you leave for Venice do not hesitate to write to me. My family is close with the Doge and I should like to ease your passing if I can now that you have come all this way to visit your poor brother's grave. If only I could have been of more use. All I can say is that if he passed through Milan it was without my family's knowledge.' Donna Lucia looked at her maid. 'A moment, Chiara.'

Chiara walked out of earshot her lips pinched in displeasure.

'She will not take kindly…'

'She will do as I command.' Donna Lucia was used to being obeyed, not instructed. 'It was the Countess' wish that you unearth what your brother knew. She fears that it might have a bearing on her nephew's daughter. Isabella is still in England, I believe?'

'Yes, the Dowager Queen was in England when I left.'

She looked about the square her hands clasped calmly before her. 'Let me secure you access to the Doge. And know that I do not approve of any involvement from my family or my family's acquaintances in any deception. If I find out that someone in our land has aided the shameful deceit you speak of, there will be consequences.'

'A letter from you will open the doors to the Doge's palace?'

She turned and gave a final smile, her hand briefly clasping his and pressing a square piece of paper into it. 'Keep this secret,' she whispered and nodded. 'Goodbye, Sir Argyle. May you find what you seek.'

'Goodbye, my Lady.' The rough edges of a wax seal pressed against his palm. 'Thank you for your kindness.'

Chiara stepped forward and flicked a wrist. The young servant who had taken Argent's reins returned with the colt as well as four beautiful mares. Donna Lucia accepted Argyle's aid to get into the saddle, her simple silk dress a cool brush against his skin. With a final disapproving glance from Chiara, Donna Lucia and her three companions turned for the Castello.

Argyle watched them go, Argent's reins loose in hand. Whatever the Countess had imparted, it had just secured him access to the Doge in Venice. It had also added to his burdens. Not for the first time, Argyle wondered just how far out of depth he was.

CHAPTER 57

22 June 1400 – Milan

'Fruitful morning?' Windham greeted him in the tavern's stables.

'Maybe.' For some reason, he was still reluctant to take Windham into his confidence.

Though they had shared misfortunes and now this long journey, and though Windham depended on Argyle to ever return to England, there was a rift between them that could not be bridged. Had Windham told the Countess more than he let on? On the way back from the Basilica, he had battled with his increasing mistrust. Why not just ask Windham what he had divulged? Now that they were once more face-to-face he found he could not voice his question.

Windham rubbed his mare's brown hide until it shone. 'I think this one's enjoying our rest even more than I am.'

His rusty voice, the gift of a common brute, reminded Argyle just how much he owed Windham. Not to tell him was a kindness not an expression of mistrust. Or so Argyle tried to convince himself.

'Donna Lucia was kind enough to afford some time in my company,' he said and noticed Windham hesitate before he continued grooming. 'She had some interesting tales to tell, not least…'

Windham held up the wad of straw. 'Don't want to know, Sire, if it's not too much to ask. It's just that knowing even one of your secrets's gotten me into more trouble than a lifetime serving as a warden and a soldier before then.'

'As you wish.' Somehow this small gesture served to comfort Argyle that, perhaps, there was no cause for concern after all. 'What is safe for you to know is that we leave for Venice tomorrow. The Donna was kind enough to ensure I can gain access to the right people once we arrive.'

'At least it's not a long journey this time.' Windham twisted another handful of straw into a wad. 'What'll you do once we get there?'

'You keep saying *we*.' Argyle let the stable boy take away Argent. 'You are not obligated to keep my company. You are free to go.'

'And how'd I get home?' Windham sat down on a bale of hay with a weary sigh. 'I'm English and last either of us were in France we were far from welcome. That letter of yours from the Countess is supposed to get us as far as Paris if you set your sights on it. And it's for you, not me.' When Argyle smiled an apology Windham shook his head. 'Without you, my chances of going home without seeing the inside of a French prison's virtually non-existent. Whether you want it or not we're stuck with each other, for now. I made my choice, such as it is, and I'm with you.'

'I will see you safely returned to England,' Argyle promised against his better judgement. 'On my oath.'

Windham watched the stable boy take the bridle off Argent at the far end of the stable. 'Either that or I'll steal that fine horse of yours and get as much as I can peddling it for my freedom.'

Making light of the situation, Argyle laughed 'You shall have to fight me for him and prove yourself a better swordsman than I.'

They made their way back to their rooms. Argyle had the larger at the back of the tavern with a fine view of the sprawling Milan landscape, Windham's small chamber sat next to it with a view to a clay wall.

Opening the door to his chamber, Argyle gestured for Windham to join him. 'I know you would rather I did not tell you and yet, there is something I must ask.'

'If I didn't know you any better, I'd think you were about to ask something I'd never agree to.'

Except you do know me, Argyle thought, just as I know what your answer will be.

ꕥ ꕥ

CHAPTER 58

5 July 1400 – Venice

The journey from Milan to Venice had been more arduous than Argyle had imagined. Sudden bursts of rain had left vast parts of the otherwise well-maintained, old Roman roads flooded in water the dry ground unable to drink up the downpour. A journey set to last a few days had now stretched for almost a fortnight.

Windham cursed and Argyle glanced over his shoulder. 'What is it?'

'It's thrown a shoe.' Windham let go of the horse's leg. 'I'll have to walk the rest of the way.'

'We shall still be there well before dark,' Argyle promised and got off his horse, groaning when he put his weight on his leg. As long as he was in the saddle, the dull ache subsided only to return more fiercely and fiery when he had to walk.

'You ride ahead. If it's that close, I'll make it on my own.'

Argyle found he was reluctant to leave Windham behind. 'The walk will do me good. We shall see the city soon enough.'

'You've been here before?'

It was probably safe to tell Windham a bit his past. 'It is almost twelve years past. I went on a pilgrimage.'

'Twelve years?' Windham ducked under his horse and a splash unleashed another curse. 'That'd have you here when King Henry was still a Lord. I remember hearing he'd gone on a pilgrimage after that failed attempt at taking some foreign city?'

'Yes.' Argyle tugged at Argent's reins. 'It was a long journey.'

They walked on in silence, mud clinging to their boots making it hard to keep a steady pace. Although the weather had improved, a storm never felt far afield and the skittering skies overhead left no doubt that there was still rain to be had.

'What'd you expect to find in Venice?'

Windham's question startled Argyle and he stepped into a puddle. 'God's blood!' Water seeped into his already soaked boot. 'I expect to find lies.'

'I've never met a man more pleased at the prospect of being lied to than you.' Windham stroked his horse's flank. 'We'll just have to stay out of sight, won't we?'

'And so you shall.' Argyle pointed to the looming grey horizon. 'There is Venice.'

'What'll we do about the horses?' Concern rode on his question as Windham stared at the lapping sea. 'And how'll we get there?'

'There are barges that can take us and our horses. Unless you prefer to stay on this side?' Argyle resumed walking and it took a while before the distinctive sound of hooves slogging through mud sounded from behind. He remembered the first time he had seen Venice. He too had been surprised by the seemingly floating city.

The heavens opened and carpeted them in water and Windham sighed. 'We'll sail though I've little love for it. Anything to get out of this rain.'

'It will be as wet in Venice as it is here.'

'But over there I'll have a roof over my head and a dry bed to rest my weary bones. I'll go far for that. Even if it means getting on a boat.'

Argyle smiled, he preferred them staying together. 'Good. I shall ride ahead and secure us passage. I will return and guide you to the docks.'

Windham was almost at the harbour when Argyle found him. He was troubled by accounts from sailors and merchants that there had been no bouts of the pestilence to speak of the past year. It was not uncommon that news of what passed in Venice travelled slowly, but for Donna Lucia's information to be so readily validated by total strangers was enough for Argyle's unease to grow. It remained to be seen if the Doge knew of the scheme to bury Thomas' ghost in Venice, or if he would refuse any involvement.

'We are this way.' Argyle dismounted and wound the reins around his wrist. 'They say the weather is fairer in Venice.'

Pushing his thick, soaked, grey hair out of his eyes, Windham snorted. 'Who? Blind seafarers?'

Reaching the wooden docks, Argyle turned left. Ships and barges tugged at their moorings, the wind strummed riggings and fishermen balanced the day's catch in baskets, crates and rolled barrels of salt along gangplanks.

'If you refuse to take my word for it then you must wait to trust your own eyes once we arrive.' He tossed a pouch to the bargeman and led Argent onto the barge, Windham hesitating on the docks. 'There is no two ways about it. If you want a dry bed best get aboard.'

Eyeing the bargeman, Windham dragged his horse on board, they both appeared reluctant to leave firm ground. 'How much English does that one understand?'

'None,' Argyle said, 'I contracted a translator at the harbour master's office to find passage for us.'

'Good, 'cause I'll be cursing quite a bit. I've little love for water.' Windham staggered as the barge pushed off. 'Bloody useless…'

Choking down a laugh, Argyle rested his hands on the salt-crusted railing. 'Best sit down and endure it for we shall have to return the way we came.'

'Who the Hell builds a city on water?' Slumping on the deck, Windham's face was greenish pale. 'It's madness.'

'It is also a spectacular sight,' Argyle promised. 'There will be much for you to see while I am busy.'

'It's an adventure I'd rather be without. And I'll be busy too finding a smith to shoe my horse.' Windham gripped the rail as the barge swung into the current. 'Would that we'd gone some other way.'

'And yet here you are, Master Windham,' Argyle said and drew in the reins when Argent side-stepped. 'Here *we* are.'

I wonder what I shall unearth once we are in the city, he thought, and how long I may have to wait for an audience.

There was no telling how many doors Donna Lucia's personal seal might open. She had been confident that the Doge would welcome him. Argyle had seen enough of the world to know that what was commonplace for some could be hard graft for others.

At the docks, he had learned that the Doge was not in Venice, which complicated his plans to get in and out of Venice within a week. Unless someone from the Doge's family might agree to a meeting, and Argyle was far from certain it could be arranged, he might be trapped on the floating city for longer than he wanted.

Windham groaned and Argyle glanced at his pale companion.

'A city on the water. Mad…'

'Do not worry,' Argyle said for comfort. 'Once we arrive you will find that the land of Venice is as sound and steady as that which we just left.'

Windham was too busy retching to pay attention.

Perhaps a little seasickness would ensure that he did not go poking his nose into things that were none of his business. Better to keep him in the dark as he had asked for than drag him all around Venice where the roads were made of water.

Next to Argent's big dark hooves, the warden curled up and hid his face in his hands, teaching the bargeman a few choice English phrases.

CHAPTER 59

8 July 1400 – Palazzo Ducale, Venice

The Dogaressa's face was so smooth that the light sprinkling of powder seemed unnecessary. Argyle was told she was older than fifty and yet, she looked much younger. She was startling in her plain black dress only a few, carefully selected, jewels emphasising her hazel eyes. Her composed manner was almost discomforting.

He bowed low. 'My Lady Dogaressa Venier.'

'Sir Argyle.' Agnese Venier extended a slender, fair hand, as smooth as her face. 'I am pleased to welcome you to my husband's house. Please, meet my son Nicolò and my daughter Orsola.'

Once more Argyle bowed low, catching Nicolò's eye for a moment. 'My Lord, my Lady.'

The Dogaressa gave a quick order in Italian and Nicolò

vanished from the room. 'My husband will be back from his journey within the week. Until then, I hope you shall come here for entertainment?'

'If it pleases my Lady,' Argyle said and Orsola smiled.

The Dogaressa gave her daughter a sharp glance. 'You may refer to me as your Serenity.'

Argyle bowed his head in embarrassment. He should have known what to call the most important woman in Venice. When last he had been to Venice the Doge had entertained Bolingbroke and a few of his most trusted men among whom Argyle had not counted. He was still not sure why the Dogaressa had agreed to see him when her husband was away. Donna Lucia's promise that her letter opened doors had held true.

'We do not usually allow foreign men to meet the Dogaressa while the Doge is away,' a servant had commented when he had ushered Argyle through the palazzo to the Dogaressa's apartments. 'This is highly unusual.'

Though Agnese Venier was a political figure she did not enjoy the same freedoms as the Queens of England. She was expected to live a demure life and only show herself when guests brought women whom she was expected to entertain. It made her decision to accept Argyle's visit even more curious, but then, perhaps her son Nicolò was there to take the place of her husband. He returned to the grand reception chamber with two servants in his wake. One carried a tray with small silver bowls and the other a large pitcher.

'Sir Argyle,' he said, his voice low and pleasant, his accent thick. 'While you are here I hope you will seek my company as much as my mother's.'

'I should be honoured, my Lord.' He hoped he had used

the right title. How was the Doge's son to be addressed?

'Now tell me, Sir Argyle,' the Dogaressa said, her skirt rustling as she moved. 'What brings you to Venice?'

Unlike its inhabitant, the chamber was opulent in every way. Marble, gold, murals and inlay gleamed and glistened in the light spearing through tall windows and falling from large, brass oil vats. Everything was polished to a high sheen and every surface meant for seating was furnished with embroidered pillows and silk throws. It was meant to impress and it did.

'I pursue news of my brother, Thomas, who was reported to have died here, your Serenity, from the mortality.' He almost felt bad for tainting the beautiful day with such a sinister lie.

'We have been greatly punished by God.' The Dogaressa's face darkened and behind her, Orsola nodded. 'If your brother found his death here I fear he may have suffered greatly.'

'We too have been touched by the pestilence, your Serenity,' Argyle said and glanced at Nicolò who was instructing the servants, his tone clipped. 'No country has been exempt from this divine punishment.'

'It is of little comfort that the world should be so sinful as to deserve such suffering.' Nicolò ran a hand through his raven hair. 'Our physicians are without remedy and our graveyards are overflowing. If your brother died here his remains are most likely buried on one of our islands.' His neck burned red, though it might simply be from the heat of the day. Even this far into the palazzo, the air was warm and moist.

'The illness does not distinguish between lord and peasant, all can fall prey to the sickness,' Argyle said and earned a smile from the Dogaressa. 'Still, I would like to visit the grave in which he is most likely laid to rest.'

'It must be the big one…' Orsola ignored her brother's warning glance. 'Nicolò and I can take you there. If we may, Mother?'

The Dogaressa nodded, she seemed deep in thought. 'If an English nobleman of your brother's standing was in Venice why did we not know of it?'

'He was exiled, your Serenity,' Argyle said blending shame into his words. 'The late King sent him from our shores in disgrace. It was a hard blow to our family.'

'Much the same is said of your new King who was once our honoured guest,' the Dogaressa said. Something lingered in her tone, a faint hint of malcontent. 'He was sent away in disgrace too, and yet he returned.'

The silence that followed told its own tale. The entire continent knew of King Henry's actions and of the death of the Lord of Bordeaux. If the English gossiped about the circumstances of his fate how much wilder were the rumours that had escaped the land? Whatever King Henry's intentions he had marred the beginning of his reign by his initial act, deposing an anointed King. It proved to everyone that even those under God's special protection were not safe from the ambition of lesser men.

Nicolò exchanged a quick glance with his mother while Orsola seemed to consider what she made of Argyle.

'My son will escort you to the cemetery tomorrow. I hope that you shall return tonight for dinner.' Orsola glanced at her mother, which the Dogaressa chose to ignore. 'I am certain the Doge will want you to stay in Venice until he has had a chance to meet with you himself, Sir Argyle. You shall be here as our honoured guest.'

Her meaning was plain. If the Dogaressa was to make special arrangements he owed her a debt which would inevitably have to be repaid. What this payment would entail remained to be seen.

Behind her, Nicolò glared at Orsola in a fashion that made Argyle pause. Did the family know more about the lie of Thomas' death than they were letting on?

CHAPTER 60

8 July 1400 – Bàcaro dei Orbi, Venice

'I'll just stay here then,' Windham said when Argyle told him about the dinner at the Doge's palace. 'I don't mind. You're right about the ground feeling solid. Perhaps I'll explore a little tonight.'

'I am sorry.' Argyle pulled off his tunic and winced as the cold water in the bowl hit his burning skin. In a few days, it would peel once more. 'The Dogaressa was adamant that I bring you.'

'How does she know about me?'

Argyle dipped his face into the cold water and drew away with a gasp. 'Her daughter saw us arrive.'

'There's a daughter?' As the weeks passed and he had been restored, Windham had shown an interest in all women they had met. Merchant's daughters, scullery maids, tavern wenches, he appeared to like them all. 'Fair, is she?'

'Dark, as most Venetian women are,' Argyle said and earned a gruff laugh and he relented. 'Yes, she is fair and well-mannered I have no doubt, though she said little enough today. Come tonight and form your own opinion of her.'

'As appealing as that sounds, I prefer leaving the pandering to you.' Windham rummaged around in his pack for a while before abandoning it. Whatever he was looking for he came away emptyhanded.

'Refusing an invitation to the most important place in the city will be considered a slight. And those in power are not used to being snubbed.' Argyle scraped back his hair and tied it with a piece of leather string. It had grown long and unruly and he was desperate to have it trimmed. However, if he wanted to fit in just a little, which was hard enough with his fair hair, it seemed he would have to wear it long for now.

Pulling on a tunic that had seen better days, he sighed. 'We must find somewhere to purchase proper attire. Not only to suit the purpose of our visit here but also for our journey home. Whether or not we go to Paris, the fastest route back to Calais is through France. I would rather be taken as an Italian merchant than an Englishman in tatters.'

'What's your plan? Am I to pose as your servant?' Windham gestured down himself. His shirt was bleached in an odd pattern from the beating sun of their journey to Milan. It could no longer be cleaned properly and the collar was fraying.

'You can pose as my lord and master for all I care.' When Windham snorted a laugh, Argyle grinned. 'Of course, you will be required to converse in Latin by tonight if not Italian.

Not to mention that the Dogaressa already knows I am a knight of the English nobility. Still, we can conjure up a title should you choose such a ruse.'

Shaking his head Windham pushed open the door. 'I'll stick to being a servant then. At least my clothes won't have to be as gaudy as yours.'

Stepping into the street, they turned right and walked at a leisurely pace towards the intersection. There, a wider avenue led to one of the many canals. Along the street were many trattorias offered a wide variety of meals and drinks to pilgrims and locals alike.

'Even the servants enjoy a splash of colour.' Argyle pointed at a table of men playing cards. 'You may have to endure being gaudy.'

'Your servant could fall sick,' Windham suggested.

As he passed, Argyle glanced at their cards. The one in the crimson waistcoat was bound to win. 'Then I must insist you ride in another barge.'

'I'll wear what you see fit. In these clothes the palace servants are bound to mistake me for a beggar and chase me away.' Windham shaded his eyes. 'I just don't see how we're going to find new clothes that we'll be able to wear tonight?'

'This way.'

When Argyle had left the palazzo, Orsola had lingered in the shadows of a grand, marbled hall eager to speak to him. It was she who had asked that he bring Windham and she who had told him where to buy garb. She was adamant that if he blended in whatever he hoped to achieve would come more readily to him. He had agreed.

After a few wrong turns, they found the tailor and once a wax impression of Orsola's seal was pressed into his hand, he was all ease and charm, pretending to ignore how his customers' ragged looks. Rather than reach for bolts of fabric, he pulled out an assortment of garb that he swore, would be ready for them before nightfall.

While his apprentice made his final measurements, Argyle paid a handsome fee and was promised delivery before the sun set. This afforded them a few hours to explore and they were quick to find some shade under a great olive tree outside a tavern not far from the canal. Tart wine brimmed in their cups, a bowl of salted olives sat on the table between them next to a nearly empty platter of smoked meat and a basket of freshly baked bread.

'I'll allow that they know how to make much of little.' Windham wiped his mouth with the back of his hand. 'If we'll eat half as well tonight I'll be all for visiting your Dogaressa every night.'

'Good. Because I need your help.'

Windham's hand hovered above his cup and he looked up. 'No.'

'If we are to get away from here as soon as possible…'

'I said no, and I meant it. I'll pose as your servant, but that's about the size of it.'

Argyle decided to push. 'You made your choice in Calais when you did not return to the prison. Instead you stayed behind in the darkness of the ally and saw what happened to me. You made your choice again in Boulogne after we nearly died at the hands of what I assume were our fellow countrymen. You made your choice when we left Milan and when you set foot on the barge that took you here.'

'Enough.' Windham avoided eye-contact. 'I've done much and more for you. That's my choice I'll freely admit it. But I won't be bullied into anything. The further we travel…'

'The further you are from your home. Do you not want to return?' Argyle acknowledged the the resentment in Windham's eyes. 'At least hear me out before you refuse.'

'What for?' He pushed away the olives. 'You run ever deeper into the shadows and you expect me to follow you? You know your brother died in Calais, at the hands of his own King's soldiers, perhaps even men you trained. Instead of going home once the Countess wanted you out of Boulogne you went further south. You're chasing a phantom.'

'You went with me. Why would you do that if you think me mad?'

'Don't you think it's a little mad?' Windham eyed him. '*Sire.*'

'How much did you tell the Countess?'

'Enough to ensure she'd not lock me up and throw away the key.' Windham drew a hand through his grey hair; it had grown long and unruly and he refused to tie it back. 'She's the aunt of England's enemy. What'd you have me do?'

'I only wish you had told me before we left Boulogne.' Argyle felt the deceit and wanted to know what Windham regarded as "enough". Instead of pursuing the topic, he pasted on a smile. 'I understand why you are reluctant.'

'I'm not like you. I don't know how to play the games that needs to be played.' Windham ran a finger around the bowl and it came away glistening from oil. 'I'm a warden – a soldier. All I know's I'm not going to get locked up if I can help it. What'd you think we did to the French prisoners in Calais? D'you think the French wouldn't return the favour? I know how gaolers are trained.'

Argyle remembered his time in the Tower and shivered against the afternoon heat. 'I too.'

Realisation dawned in Windham's eyes. 'You've been behind bars.'

'I broke house arrest and killed one of the King's most fervent servants.' It was not a memory he relished in revisiting. 'I was thrown in the Tower and it almost killed me.'

'Then you understand why I'm reluctant to know more than I need to.' Windham rubbed his throat, the bruising was gone but he had a permanent reminder in his raw voice. 'I've already taken a beating for you, and I did it freely – or just about. Don't go thinking I'll do it again.'

'This is why I wanted you to return to England when I left Boulogne.' Argyle stretched his aching leg into the ray of warm sunshine creeping towards their table. All around them life rumbled along as a cart drawn by an ox. 'I knew that, sooner or later, I would have to rely too heavily on you.'

'You've done this before – with someone else.' Windham was not asking a question.

He scratched his chin. 'Stephen knows that I never intended for him to get involved at all. Others changed the terms.'

'What happened to him?'

'He serves as my master of arms,' Argyle said and earned a little smile from Windham. 'Not all requests end badly.'

'It's my experience that most do.' Windham poured the last of the wine into his own cup. 'It's a nice place. A man could get lost here.'

'You would not have to board a barge again,' he agreed, and this time Windham laughed. 'I cannot ask anything of you…'

'But you're going to.'

'Just that you keep a sharp eye out tonight. If something strikes you as untoward tell me when we return to our lodgings. I may be too preoccupied to notice any strange behaviour, I look to you to be my eyes and ears. It may be nothing except that when I visited the Dogaressa today there was something about her son that felt out of place.'

Windham turned his cup. Though simple it was delicate in his big hands. Argyle let him consider in peace. He could tell that Windham would say yes in the end. He was a curious soul. Stephen's voice whispered in the back of Argyle's mind: Dangerous.

'Just watching.'

'Yes.'

'No getting yourself beaten half to death.' His tone grew hard.

'No promises,' Argyle said and tried to smile. It fell short. 'We are present at the Dogaressa's invitation. If you can keep your hands off the maids and I can keep to my courtesies there will be no trouble.'

'Can't make promises.' Windham washed down the rest of his drink. 'It's been a long time …'

Argyle rose and put a few pieces of silver on the table. 'Yes, it has.'

'That wasn't an invitation.' This time, Windham smiled. 'What'll I do if there's a willing woman at hand?'

'Tell her about your fear of water.' Argyle led the way towards the bácaro. 'That will put her off.'

'Some women're the maternal sort,' Windham said wistfully. 'If she is I'll not be able to resist.'

'If she likes a man who vomits at the sight of a puddle,' Argyle said, 'she deserves what she gets.'

CHAPTER 61

10 July 1400 – Palazzo Ducale

Argyle straightened his short jacket and adjusted the brooch at his chest. In the shadows, Windham's attempts not to look like a soldier were aided by his dark green cape made from coarse silk, which softened his features. A couple of serving women glanced at him and nudged each other.

'Your man is causing quite a stir.' Donna Orsola smiled at Argyle. 'He looks much improved since I saw him stagger off the barge.'

'No stomach for the sea, my Lady,' Argyle said and enjoyed her subdued laugh. 'He is best pleased on land.'

'How fortunate then that you are staying on our island.' Orsola looked down the table at her brooding brother. 'Or we would have been without his company tonight.'

The feast was set in what could only be the Doge's official reception hall, the décor distinctly masculine and every surface gleaming. Servants lined the wall ready to fill platters and bowls, replenish glass flagons and gem encrusted pitchers. The English court was magnificent, the Doge's palazzo was outrageous.

He tipped his glass at her. 'You mother was kind to extend the invitation to include both of us.'

'I know it is difficult to do without a servant.' Orsola turned her back to Nicolò's glare. It was obvious to anyone that he was far from pleased with tonight's seating. 'And I must confess, it was my brother's idea. He likes to think himself my father's substitute whenever he is not here.' She picked at the food on her plate. 'Mother indulges him too much.'

It gained me access, Argyle thought and inclined his glass towards Nicolò who reluctantly returned the greeting. He turned back to Orsola enjoying her easy manners. 'Tell me more about Venice, Donna Orsola.'

'You shall bear witness to it tomorrow, though where you mean to go there is not much in which to take joy.' She looked dismayed. 'The mortality has taken too many lives over the years, Sire. Still, I was surprised that your brother died of the sickness last year, since…'

'Yes?'

She leaned in her voice little more than a whisper almost lost in the clamour of a hall full of guests. 'No one died from the malady.'

'None at all?' Argyle was glad Donna Lucia had warned him during their conversation in Milan. He donned a surprised expression. 'But your brother…'

She twisted to face him fully. 'I fear my brother is not entirely to be trusted in this matter. That was why *I* offered to join you.'

'You appear concerned, Donna Orsola?'

She smiled. 'I like it when you speak my name. There is no need for a title tonight, you are among friends.'

'I must disagree, my Lady,' Argyle said. 'For if you believe your brother may not be entirely trustworthy is it not best I play the role of deferential guest to a fault?'

Under the table, Orsola grabbed his hand. 'They say you have been here before?'

I wonder who *they* are, Argyle thought and nodded. 'Yes. When Lord Bolingbroke – who is now King Henry – went on pilgrimage. I was fortunate enough to be part of his retinue and we dwelled on the shores of Venice for a few days. Though I never entered the city proper.'

'He came her twice as I recall. Going out and coming back.' Orsola kept his hand in hers the gesture strangely comforting and all too intimate. She smiled at her mother seated at the high table with her ladies, all of whom wore plain brown dresses. Only the Dogaressa's position and poise revealed her elevated status.

He felt his hostess's eyes on him. 'Why does your mother not…'

'When my father is not here she cannot be seen in the company of men as you may have learned this morning. After all, our servants believe themselves permitted to divulge whatever information they see fit. For you, she made an exception. One exception.' She released his hand. 'It is only because we are in the company of so many guests – all that she could muster on such short notice – that she is here at all. She may have issued the invitation, but it is my brother's feast.'

'Does the same rule apply to you?'

Her pealing laughter intensified Nicolò's glare. 'My mother is married to the Doge, not I. And his title is not hereditary though my brother is arguing hard that it ought to be. I am not restrained as my mother is, she is the figurehead, I am merely part of the furnishings.'

Her confidential smile had returned. 'Nicolò believes he is entitled to replace my father when his time comes. We all know that it will never come to pass.'

Argyle looked back at the Doge's son and wondered if that was the main cause of his irritation this evening. 'How can you speak with such conviction?'

'To be Doge is a political position. One must curry favour with all the most important families in Venice and beyond. My brother lacks certain obvious skills.'

Clapping her hands twice, Orsola looked at Argyle. 'How well do you dance, Sire?'

'As long as I have a good partner, I can manage, my Lady.'

In the candle light, she glistened and glittered, dressed in bright colours where her mother's garb was drab. 'Then I insist you show me your talents. I promise to prove a worthy partner.'

'What will your brother think?'

'As long as you do not grab me too hard he can say nothing.' Every word dripped mischief. 'He does not dance, although he knows the moves.'

Leading Orsola to the floor, Argyle noticed that Windham was gone from the shadows and tried to spot him without success.

Massive candles burned in dozens of candelabras down the centre of the table and in sconces along the walls and yet, there were plenty of shadows in which to linger.

CHAPTER 62

11 July 1400 –Bàcaro dei Orbi

On the cot in the corner, Windham groaned when Argyle threw open the shutters to let in what little breeze there was to be had. Although the day had only just dawned, the air was hot and salty.

'We need to speak.'

'Later…' Windham threw an arm over his eyes. 'Too early.'

'Nicolò Vernier shall arrive at any moment.' Argyle kicked and got another groan for his efforts. 'Our arrangement was for you to be my eyes and ears.'

Slowly, Windham sat up. 'The wine was good.'

'You were supposed to keep watch.' He could not say if he was more disappointed because it seemed Windham had

had a far more enjoyable evening than he had or if it was because he had failed his mission.

'Who's saying I didn't?' Windham's hair stuck up at odd angles and he had a distinct odour about him. 'I could do with something to drink.'

'You had plenty last night, actually, I am surprised you can make two words stick together.' Argyle kicked the cot for the second time. 'You would let me ride out with no notion if Nicolò is worth trusting or not?'

'Not. And you already know that.' He gave in and spilled out on the floor on all fours. 'Let me just get my head straight.'

'You think that there is something not right about the Dogaressa's son?'

Nodding slowly, Windham got up using the stand for the washbasin for support. 'There's plenty not right about him.' He plunged his face into the water. Dripping wet he flashed an unsettling smile. 'Nor would I put too much trust in the ephemeral Dogaressa.'

'What about Orsola?'

'Better than the rest if not a woman quite as fair or innocent as she might lead you to believe.' Windham dunked his face in the washbasin again. 'Still, she's taken with you and that's a good thing I'm told. It means she'll try to remedy whatever mischief her family's planning.'

'I can only hope that mischief does not see my head off,' Argyle said tersely and threw a cloth at Windham. 'Since you did do as I asked, thank you. Now get dressed you are coming with me.'

'Afraid not, Sire.' Windham mopped his face. 'Our agreement was for last night. That has come and gone.'

'I am extending it.' Argyle was fast regretting his promise to honour Windham's stipulation especially since he needed all the help he could get and his only companion was reluctant at best.

'And I'm refusing. Last night was a laugh and a difficult task. Today, I'm out and there's nothing you can do about it.'

Argyle put on his short jacket and eyed Windham. 'Then you may soon be all alone.'

'If they're going to risk killing you they'll not attempt it with Donna Orsola there,' Windham said matter-of-factly. 'And she will be. Her lady-in-waiting told me yesterday while I was helping her empty some wine pitchers.'

'It shows.' Argyle was pleased that Windham had indeed been his eyes and ears, at least until the wine took hold. 'You believe me safe?'

'If Donna Orsola's not with Nicolò, I'll be very much surprised.' Windham blew his nose into the cloth and tossed it into the washbasin before collapsing on his cot. 'We'll make this deal then since you can't do without me… If the Donna isn't there you whistle and I'll come running like a good dog. How's that?'

Perfect. Argyle gave Windham a curt nod. 'Very well.'

'Mind you it's the last time…' he began and Argyle closed the door on him. Best not to let him make his own terms until they were out of this city. Besides, Argyle was curious to know just how far the most important family in Venice was ready to go. And if someone might slip up if he kept needling.

At the stables near the tavern, Nicolò Venier and his retinue of servants and a few guards waited with what Argyle assumed was feigned patience. The Doge's son greeted Argyle with a nod as he mounted his horse and then swung out into the cobbled, dusty street. Although on an island it seemed that the fine-grained Italian dirt travelled everywhere and Venice was no exception. The day was still young and already dust danced on the wind.

Shielding his eyes, he noticed that there were no women in attendance. Rather than stick to the plan he had made with Windham, on a whim, Argyle decided that perhaps it was for the best. It might be Orsola was waiting for them somewhere along the route, perhaps she preferred lounging on a boat rather than sitting in the saddle. He fell in behind Nicolò and took in the sights.

'A fine morning,' the raven-haired man said over his shoulder. 'I must make my sister's apologies matters required her attendance urgently and she had to remain with my mother.'

'Please convey my regards to them both. The feast last night was very pleasant. It was most gracious of you to extend an invitation.' The tavern vanished as they turned a corner and aimed for one of the larger canals. A pylon of smoke caught his attention. 'What is burning on that island, my Lord?'

Nicolò did not even turn his head. 'That is San Lazzaro degli Armeni. The citizens call it the Leper Island. Whenever one of the men or women in the asylum dies, they burn the body.'

'Are they afraid the disease will spread?' Argyle had heard a little about the most gruesome disease and even seen a few men with the onset of it when he was in Jerusalem, but this practice was new to him.

'It is merely a practical measure.' Distaste marred Nicolò's expression. 'The families of a leper do not want the burden of having to find a priest to bury their dead relative.' He caught Argyle's dispirited countenance and shrugged. 'Not to worry for their afterlife, Sire, the asylum is part of a monastery and has its own priest who reads the rights and says masses for the souls.'

'Some small comfort for the bereaved,' Argyle remarked. He turned away from the island and was surprised by a brilliant display. 'What is that, my Lord?'

This time, Nicolò followed his gaze and smiled. 'Glass, though not such as you are used to I presume. You will find no finer craftsmanship anywhere in the world. Venice makes the finest glass. It hails from the island of Murano.'

He pointed in the opposite direction of the black smoke and when Argyle squinted he could just about make out another island.

'I confess the idea of a city made up of islands is strange to me,' Argyle said and one of the attending guards suppressed a laugh. 'Even now that I am here I still struggle to make sense of it.'

'If you were to stay longer you would become used to it.' Nicolò gave a sharp order in his native tongue and two servants turned down a narrow street. 'After all, it is as much dry land as your own country.'

Argyle's horse followed Nicolò's across one of the many beautiful stone bridges holding the city of Venice together. Beneath it, long, narrow and strange-looking boats bobbed on the soft tide. Rather than being moved by oars, only one man stood at the stern and rocked a tapered plank from side to side. Argyle did not think the boats looked very safe.

'We must leave the horses at the docks and sail to the cemetery. It is on Isola di San Michele.' Nicolò indicated. 'There, halfway to Murano.'

'You are kind to take the time, my Lord.' Argyle handed the reins to a guard sporting the Doge's distinctive gold and red colours.

'Your request is a modest one, Sire. I can spare the morning for you.' Nicolò stepped onto the deck of a boat and turned, his cloak fluttering. Unlike Argyle, he seemed unfazed by the warmth, his garb impeccable. 'Please.'

Argyle sat down beside him and the boat rapidly made its way across the shallow strait. Only two servants escorted them and they had taken their seat at the bow. Alone at the stern, he decided to prompt Nicolò about the sickness that was said to have killed Thomas.

'Did many die from the pestilence last fall, my Lord?'

Nicolò made a face. 'We do try to keep it at bay, Sire.'

'As well I can imagine. You have taken the brunt of many of the bouts, I know, my Lord.' Argyle was pleased they were on a real boat rather than the narrow canal vessels. 'Forgive my curiosity.'

'No need to apologise.' The Doge's son tugged at his cloak when the wind picked up its hem. 'It is I who must ask forgiveness, I was rash when I had no cause. It is only that every time a foreigner arrives there is a hint of fear and blame in such a question as yours. I know that you merely seek solace about your brother.'

Solace, lies. Whatever you may serve up I shall pretend to eat with pleasure, Argyle thought. 'It was a great shock.'

'The illness last year was mild and quickly passed.' Nicolò raised a hand in greeting when they passed a barge going the opposite direction. 'It took only a few souls. If your brother was among the unfortunate then he would have had a satisfactory burial.'

'I see.'

'Still, we found it best to contain the dead on the island.' Did Nicolò's cheeks colour? On the water, the sun beat down on them and even he seemed affected. Perhaps it was no more than that.

'No one has been able to find out how it transmits, I gather?' Argyle was not at all interested in disease, he just had to keep Nicolò talking.

'No, though the finest physicians in the entire world live here in Venice,' he said and pushed his dark hair from his forehead. 'That is why we must place our trust in God's hands where the pestilence is concerned. Who are we mere mortals to question His divine plans?'

'Well spoken, my Lord.' Shielding his eyes, Argyle watched the island grow with every stroke of the oars. 'We must trust in God.'

The rest of the short trip was made in silence, Argyle careful to keep his eyes on the horizon and Nicolò seemingly lost in thought. When the boat bumped into the wooden moorings, they both stood and he led the way along a low stone wall that circled an enormous cemetery. Pushing through the wrought iron gates, it seemed sound faded as they stepped foot on consecrated ground.

Marble effigies and granite headstones struggled for space on the neatly trimmed grass, pale gravel paths intersecting it. Though it was the height of summer the graves were tumbling with flowers, predominantly red and white, dots of yellow and heady lilac drawing in the eye. Some of the effigies were weather worn and so smooth that no features remained from the men and women whose bones rested beneath.

At the far side, the soil looked freshly turned, brown and barren in the sea of colour. To the right was a poorly maintained area, weeds pushing through the dry dirt where they could. 'What is that?'

'Your brother's final resting place I am afraid.' Nicolò's voice was without a trace of pity. 'We had to bury them in a hurry, before the sickness took hold. You will understand our urgency. That is why it looks, well, bleak.'

From the uneven ground, Argyle could tell that this was a mass grave. Although he knew full well that his brother was not buried here he felt sickened. 'Cannot the city do something?'

'The city's coffers are not as full as they once were. It is my father's greatest shame and he works tirelessly to remedy the situation.' Nicolò led Argyle around the far side of the gravesite. 'I shall leave you to contemplate your brother for a while if you wish? We must get back before the tide turns or we may have to stay here longer than we anticipated and I have matters awaiting my attention upon my return.'

Argyle crouched by the rugged edge. 'I shall not be long.'

Even as he looked intently at the ground, Argyle could feel Nicolò's eyes on his back. He would not have much time to himself. Argyle put a hand on the ground.

'Sad business.'

Jerking his head up, Argyle squinted against the sun. A dark figure stood a little further afield, looking at the gravesite.

'Very sad.' The priest came closer. 'I come here sometimes to say a prayer for their souls. Masses are said too, naturally, but to come here grants me a strange sense of purpose. Poor unfortunates.'

'You are kind.' Argyle half-expected Nicolò to swoop in, but no footsteps sounded on the gravel.

'I am God's servant.' The priest pushed his hands into his wide sleeves. How he managed to stand in the sun in his black garb without sweat running down his cheeks, Argyle had no idea. The priest inclined his head. You have journeyed far.'

'Yes.'

'English, I believe?'

'Yes, father.'

'You must be very devout.'

'I seek the truth.'

'Do we not all, my son?' He put a soft hand on Argyle's shoulder and he nodded. Encouraged, the priest continued. 'Your search has led you here?'

'I am told my brother lies in this grave. I wanted to pay my last respects, to see where he finally found some rest from a life of industry and… I needed to see his grave.'

Scouring Argyle's face, the priest shook his head. 'You seem to be from a family of means?'

'I doubt there is enough gold to lure anyone to undertake the task of bringing a victim of the mortality from here to England.'

'Ah.' The priest gave an almost imperceptible nod and lowered his voice. 'This is a grave for the poor. Not for victims of the dreadful scourge.' At Argyle's expression, he flickered a smile. 'They are burned – as the poor souls plagued by leprosy. We have not the lime that others possess to layer over the bodies of the diseased.'

Argyle tried hard to maintain a blank countenance and the priest gathered his garb revealing bare feet in sandals. 'Besides, these past four or five years, by the grace of God, there has been no outbreaks. No painful deaths, no families torn apart by black boils. For myself, I believe it is because the priesthood of Venice has finally decided to live up to God's rules.' He smiled in earnest. Though missing a few teeth, he had a comely appearance. 'Your search is not at an end, I fear, for what you seek you will not find here. And from your expression I think you did not expect to?

Wherever you go next I advise you be wary of the company you keep. Not all take God's truth to heart as they ought.'

Behind them, the gravel crunched announcing the arrival of Nicolò. 'Father?'

'I am saying a prayer, my Lord Venier.' The priest turned and a kick of wind made his gown flutter. 'Your guest is mourning for his brother's soul and I am trying to ease his sorrow. Fear not, child,' the priest said to Argyle. 'Your brother is with God and prayers shall be said to preserve his immortal soul.'

Not much of a comfort even if kindness is found in the most unlikely of places, Argyle thought. I know full well that Thomas must pay for his sins and that, if there is a God, he is not awaiting my brother's imminent arrival. Someone else may well be caught in eager anticipation for Thomas shall be long in purgatory.

'You are kind, father, I thank you for your words of comfort.' Argyle bowed his head for a blessing before the priest went on his way. It was clear that he had unsettled Nicolò and he struggled to conceal it.

'We must go. The tide is turning.'

'I am grateful, my Lord,' Argyle said as he followed Nicolò towards the wooden dock. 'That you were able to grant me a few moments of contemplation. If it is possible I should like to make a donation on behalf of my family that the site might be better tended?'

'I shall ensure your donation is put to good use,' Nicolò said with a tight smile and stepped aboard. 'If you will forgive me I must speak to one of my servants.'

Argyle sat at the bow as instructed. 'I shall mourn my brother in silence a little longer. Raw grief was soothed today.'

Somewhat mollified, Nicolò sat at the stern and began a whispered conversation. It continued until the boat docked on the principal island. Argyle was certain they were discussing what might be done to make the tiresome priest from the island tell them what had transpired. He was equally certain that the priest would merely repeat his parting words. To have a man of the cloth dissatisfied by the Doge's own son left Argyle wondering what had driven a wedge between the powerful church and the official head of Venice. Was there more to the Vernier family's desire for power than met the eye?

After the morning's excursion his notion had been proven correct. No one had thought he would come poking his nose in where it clearly did not belong. Everyone – whoever that might then be – had been satisfied that, upon the news of Thomas' death, the family would have mourned his passing and left it in the hands of God.

Argyle knew that God could never be trusted. And neither could anyone in Venice.

CHAPTER 63

12 July 1400 – Venice

'I am sorry we could not offer you more comfort, Sir Argyle,' Nicolò said with much loftiness.

The sea chafed against the pier and from below the waves moaned. After several days of burning sun and an almost unbearably moist heat, this morning was shrouded in a thick mist visiting cool kisses on Argyle's cheek. Windham had lamented their imminent departure for most of the evening before and had been relieved to wake to the rich morning fog that merged air and sea. Not that Argyle doubted Windham would be sick before the barge left the dock. One glance at his companion confirmed the suspicion.

'I should have liked to meet with your father and thank him personally for your hospitality, my Lord.' Argyle briefly grabbed Nicolò's arm and looked him in the eye. 'It was a solace to see my brother's final resting place. Given the option, my family would have preferred to have his bones returned, but I understand now that it is quite impossible. I pray that my humble donation might see it tended and that it will, in time, bloom to be a place of pilgrimage to those who my family's misfortune.'

'It is a pity that father is delayed in his return.' Nicolo skirted Argyle's last effort of prying open his chest of secrets. 'As I told you, all victims of the mortality are buried immediately. Had we only known that he had a family…'

'I confess that his secrecy surprises me,' Argyle said and watched Windham hesitate at the far end of the pier, giving the barge a suspicious glare when it dove beneath his testing foot. 'Perhaps he wished to protect his family. Shield them from his disgrace.'

'He has children?' Although they stood shoulder to shoulder, Nicolò's silhouette was blurred by the mist.

'Indeed, my Lord.' Argyle gestured at Windham. 'Enough dawdling. Get on board and take the horses.'

Windham scowled but went about the task all the same.

'You are set to return to England now, Sire?' There was something approaching hope in Nicolò's eyes. 'Now that you know what happened to your brother?'

'Yes, I shall.' Argyle pulled at his short jacket, the fit was snug and unfamiliar though he had worn the style for a week now. 'I suspect it may well be a difficult return journey.'

'No doubt you speak of the animosity between England and France. By no means aided by your new King.'

'How so, my Lord?' Argyle stepped onto the barge.

'Word travels fast,' Nicolò said with a secretive half-smile. 'We have heard that King Henry holds on to something that belongs to France. A certain girl '

'Perhaps all will soon be resolved.'

'She should be returned, Sire.' His voice floated over the pier to the barge, the swirling fog swallowing him up. 'For the good of both countries.'

Windham was grabbing the low railing hard, his big hands as white as his face. 'What was that about?'

'A warning from Venice to King Henry.'

'Conveyed by a liar?' Windham glared towards the hidden city, his fear of the sea momentarily forgotten. 'Now there's a turn.'

Argyle took Argent's reins and sat down on an upturned barrel. 'Yes, there is a turn…'

'Mind you, I had a very pleasant visitor yesterday while you were out seeing the sights.' Windham tried to steady his stance by grabbing his horse's mane. 'Very pleasant.'

'Is that so?'

It was a good thing that he had not divulged too much during their last night at the tavern. Some walls had ears. Especially those looking to profit from spying on troublesome strangers. Ever since the feast at the palazzo, Argyle was convinced that their every move had been watched and reported back to the Verniers.

'Thought it best not to say anything before we were out of there.' Windham echoed Argyle's musings. 'It was one of the Donna's maids, she and I'd had a bit of… Anyway, she'd been looking for me and found me in the garden behind the tavern.'

'Pleasant, you said?'

Windham covered his mouth with his hand. He had gone white although Argyle could not feel even the slightest swell. 'Go on. It might just take your mind off our crossing.'

'I doubt it.' Windham swallowed and willed himself to continue. 'She'd been in with the ladies when the Dogaressa had word of her husband's returning. Rumour is…'

'I do not care for rumours,' Argyle snapped.

'You'll care for this one. The Doge's an active fellow.' Windham's eyes shone, his discomfort forgotten. 'It's as well-kept a secret as the fact that the real politician in that family is his wife. Without her, he's nothing. Last night, he was supposed to show up, but he didn't and it seems it's got the palace in a state.'

'And O… the Donna sent word to us?' Even though they would be leagues from Venice before anyone could follow them it was foolish to believe that the bargeman would not carry back word to the most powerful family that two Englishmen had spoken about them.

Argyle had been careful to engage someone who did not speak their language, but he was far from certain he could trust the interpreter he had engaged for the task. He considered telling Windham to keep quiet until they reached the mainland but what would be the point. They had already named the Verniers and Nicolò had been at the docks when they got there. No doubt, he had issued orders of his own.

'She'd been worried that something might've happened since she'd been banned from escorting her brother that morning. So she sent her maid to see if anything could be learned.' Windham lowered his voice, 'At the docks.'

'She returned with nothing?'

'All she could discover is that the Doge's still on land. Somewhere north of here.'

Argyle stared into the mist trying to make out the shoreline. 'Did she think he was waiting for something – or someone?'

'She didn't know. The Donna'd said her father hadn't sent word, but…'

This was dire news indeed. It was ludicrous to believe that the Dogaressa had not informed her husband that an Englishman had come asking unwelcome questions. Rumours travelled far and fast and she had herself told him to wait for the Doge to return, which had made Nicolò's suggestion that they leave today surprising. He had told Argyle that the Doge was detained, adding another lie to the pile.

'What do we do?' The barge clipped and Windham gulped.

'With luck the Doge shall think us too clever to board a barge in this weather. Unless that is his plan and his son merely followed his father's orders.' Trying to ease the drab mood, Argyle said, 'It is a good thing that I carry a letter from the Donna – and the Countess.'

'Relying on women, Sire?'

'There are far worse choices, Windham.'

The mop of grey hair shifted and he grabbed the mane so tight that his horse neighed. 'That's the truth, Sire. I told her that you'd know nothing of consequence. I assumed it'd be better that way.'

'Good. I must tell you that they lied to both of us.'

Tight-lipped, Windham asked, 'How so?'

'How did this woman know where to find you?' The concern had irked him since Windham began his tale. It was too late to change what had happened, all that was left for them was to stay alert. 'The only one who knew where we lived was Nicolò. I doubt very much that he passed on that information to his sister – or even his mother. To him they are just women. Ornaments. He has his own agenda. Perhaps he followed orders, though I do not believe that to be the case. So, unless your tongue ran away from you at the feast…'

Windham shook his head vehemently and Argyle was inclined to agree. They all looked surprised at our arrival, he thought, and though they are good actors, they are not that good.

If the Doge knew of the visit he would have taken other measures had he believed Argyle to pose any real threat. Most certainly he would not have left his women to deal with their unwanted visitor.

'My tongue knows when to wag and when to stay still.' Windham wiped his brow. 'I said nothing to her…'

'We both know my brother's true fate. God's bones, you even saw it. From what I can gather all this secrecy has to do with something Thomas took with him.' He paused. 'What it might be I cannot say.'

'Time'll tell.' Windham's words came out in faint, flat punches.

'That is what I fear.'

Argyle stared into the mist, willing the shoreline to appear. He struggled to understand what part the Doge might play. This was, most likely, a matter to be settled between England and France. What business was it of the Duke of Venice to join the quarrel?

He doubted that Thomas had ever even corresponded with Venice. Then again, his brother had been full of surprises and nothing ought to baffle Argyle anymore. What worried him was what the Doge or someone in his household stood to gain from being part of the elaborate lie of Thomas' death? What secrets lay buried between here and England?

Under different circumstances, the bargeman's steady strokes would prove soothing. Instead, every stroke increased his sense of dread. Where could he go to ease his concerns and find the answers he so desperately sought? Learning the truth of La Fontaine's death had only served to sever the bond he had with one King and put another on the throne and turn Argyle into a pariah at court.

Not for the first time he wondered if he would live to step foot on English soil. And if he did decide to pass through King Charles's lands would it prove enough that his daughter had depended upon Argyle? Or would it merely serve to expedite his own demise?

Part IV

Pitfalls and Snares

CHAPTER 64

2 August 1400 – Near Vichy, France

'We're being followed.'

Windham spoke with no trace of emotion.

Argyle knew it, too. The past days had proven to him that snapping at their heels were men eager to serve a vengeful master. Only he could not quite believe it was the Doge sending his men to fetch back two tiresome Englishmen.

Nicolò would have sent word to his father that they were leaving if not confirming that he had done as bid and sent them packing. If the Doge wanted them caught all he had to do was wait by the docks on the mainland. They had come ashore with no sighting of the Doge or his men. In the back of Argyle's mind lurked Windham's comment that the true political power in Venice was the Dogaressa. Was it the demure, distanced woman who dictated their fate? If so, she had plenty of opportunity to imprison them while they were in the city and she had refrained. Perhaps she simply did not want the stain of such an act on her pristine garb. What was better than to send them on their way and there, they could be set upon by lawless men and no one would ever know the truth – whatever that was.

On the second day of their ride, Windham had taken advantage of a moonless evening and had broken into a stone shed outside a large house where they were fortunate to find a neglected sword and a couple of daggers. The next night, they had honed their blades and Argyle enjoyed once again the feel of a sword at his side. Hopefully, the old wooden handle with its worn leather binding was as strong as the steel.

'Yes.'

Windham bunched up his cloak and tied it behind the cantle. 'You want to get caught?'

'We cannot keep playing this game of cat and mouse.' Argyle wiped sweat from his brow. The afternoon heat was relentless and the skies above loomed with rain. 'Although…'

'Worried it'll be Calais all over again?' Windham sighed as the first droplets of tepid rain hit his head and hands. 'Cause I am.'

The rain increased and soaked Argyle's short jacket. Silk was fine for indoor activities, but it drank up water quicker than a man caught wandering the desert. As if on command, the skies opened and unleashed thunder and lightning accompanied by sheeting rain.

'It seems nature is offering an escape for us.' Argyle leaned towards Windham to be heard. It would not do to raise his voice and let anyone know where they were. The downpour made it difficult to see more than a couple of paces ahead, a circumstance that levelled the field against any followers.

'No reason to delay.' Windham pressed his horse's flanks. 'Mayhap we'll even find shelter before we drown.'

Careering down the narrow path, low-hanging branches whipping their arms and cheeks, mud flecking their clothes, Argyle said a silent prayer that they might just shake their unwanted companions once and for all.

Focused only on staying in the saddle and on the road, he veered at the last moment to avoid Windham who reined in his horse so hard it sat down. Close to the muddy ditch, Argyle's horse slowed to a clumsy trot.

'What the Hell?'

'Shelter.' Windham pointed straight ahead to some derelict buildings leaning against one another at the other side of the road only just visible through the downpour. 'It's no use going on, Sire, we need shelter.'

'We need to keep going.' Argyle struggled to get his horse back on the road, which had deteriorated into a small, angry river. 'If we stop here…'

'Maybe it'll trick them. They'll think we've gone on. We'd get behind them. We'd be better equipped to see what might be done.' He was already making for the buildings, a dark shadow against the grey curtain of water.

'And if they do not?' Argyle shouted after him.

'Then we'll die dry!'

It turned out that Windham was only half right. There was shelter to be found even if the stamped clay floor was a sticky mess, tiny streams of water running crisscross through dirt, grime and age-old dung. Argyle shook out his cloak, which was almost dry, having been stored inside the saddlebag closest to Argent's belly.

'Will we be able to hear if anyone comes this way?'

'No.' Windham pushed aside a rotting board. 'But we'll be able to see anyone approaching.'

Argyle did a quick tour of the dilapidated structure. 'If all else fails I think the horses can run straight through the back here.'

Nodding agreement, Windham pulled off his shirt and wrung it adding to the streams on the floor. 'We'll stay put and see if anyone comes. If they're smart they'll be in that cosy inn we passed this morning. Nice and dry while we huddle here like paupers.'

It was no secret that Windham was a creature of comfort. Although used to sleeping rough from his years in the English army, he grumbled and whined every time they passed an inn or tavern and Argyle decided against stopping. Leave it to the former warden to remember an inn, he had already forgotten.

'Better to stay safe.'

'Better to stay wet,' Windham said and gave a gruff laugh. 'I'm no fool. We're better off not stopping, but even you can't deny you'd swap these drab surroundings for a feather bed and some warm food if you had the choice.'

'If I knew we were safe then yes, in an instant.' He went to the wall and peered out of a hole in the rotted wood. 'But we are not safe.'

'Haven't been since you met me or is it the other way 'round?' Windham slung his cloak and shirt over a low-hanging beam. 'There's some damp hay. I'll feed it to the horses.'

'Rub them down first,' Argyle said out of habit and earned a displeased look. 'If they catch a cold no amount of damp hay will save them or us.'

Knotting together two wads of hay, Windham threw one at Argyle. 'I was fine playing your servant in Venice, but I'm not your stable boy. If you want a dry horse you'll have to rub him yourself.'

Working on the horse, Argyle was momentarily soothed and pushed back into the arms of childhood memories of working in the stables with his brother John. The faceless shadow.

'There's someone sniffing about.' Windham's words were barely a whisper.

'How did they find us?'

'Mayhap they want out of the rain same as we did.' He crept closer to to the wall, peering into the storm. 'They can't've seen us.'

Argyle for Windham to be silent. He twined the reins of both horses around his arm and, with a quiet tug, they followed him to the far side of the barn. Windham stayed by the spy-hole, his body tense.

He held out a hand, signalling four riders. Argyle drew breath. If it came to it he had kept the old, stolen sword well-honed. Windham was left with a dagger with a loose handle and the short blade he used for shaving. Neither was worth much if the men tracking them came barging through the doors steel drawn.

One of the horses tugged at the rein and Argyle put an absentminded hand on its neck. Argent nuzzled his shoulder.

Windham crouched, poised to pounce.

The door blew inwards and knocked him from his low stance, the rusty iron handle hitting him square in the temple. Argyle saw him go down, beads of dark red staining his brow. Time slowed.

Four horses burst through the narrow opening, the doors creaked off their hinges and the wall splintered into nothingness. When rain suddenly tore through the roof, Argyle got a minute advantage and he threw himself into Argent's saddle, a piercing pain shooting through his knee as it caught on the wooden pommel.

Windham stumbled to his feet, the left side of his face a bloodied mess. Argyle could see both his eyes shine when lightning lit up the slate sky. Without a second thought, he threw his own dagger across the room and turned Argent before he knew if the knife was caught. If not, Windham would have a short, sweet death for it would pierce his heart.

'God's blood!' Windham roared.

Wielding his sword, Argyle let Argent do the brunt of the work, pressing against two of the horses that were now caught between the thick beam at the far end of the stable and his flashing sword. Their nostrils flared and their riders flailed their blades clearly surprised by his frantic attack.

One rider screamed as his horse pushed against the beam with enough force to crush his leg. In a flash, a sword sliced the horse's throat and it fell, kicking and screaming to the muddy floor, the desperate rider caught beneath it.

A short spear sliced the air near Argyle's ear. Although most sound was drowned out by the blood beating in his ears he heard Windham curse, the sound dull. Swinging his sword once more to block the spear he sensed rather than saw a possible escape.

Windham's horse was dancing around Argent, the rein still tied to Argyle's arm. He slapped it across the rump. The horse screamed in pain and fury. The tug on the rein nearly took off his arm and he bit down on a roar as the beast flew past the two men Windham was circling. Slipping the sword into the scabbard at the side of Argent's saddle, Argyle threw his arm out just in time to grab Windham's and both men groaned as Argent leapt to join his companion in the thundering rain.

The torrent drowned out Windham's curses and numbed Argyle's pain from where his leg was pierced by a piece of wood. He tugged hard at Windham to get him onto the horse. Windham almost winded Argyle as he threw an arm around his waist and somehow managed to heave himself up behind the saddle.

The increasing darkness lent no succour. Argyle knew that Argent would not be able to carry two men for long. They would have to slow down soon. A yank at his arm told him that Windham's horse was still right in front of them, pounding through thicket and forest. It also told him that his shoulder was dislocated.

Behind him, Windham shouted something, but Argyle could not make out the words. Finally, they roared past his ear like a clap of thunder.

'They're coming!'

CHAPTER 65

2 August 1400, Midnight – Near Vichy, France

In fetters once more.

With his arms twisted behind his back, he sat awkward on the horse, his thighs aching from pressing tight to stay in the saddle. He could not make out Windham. Argyle's leg dripped blood, but he could still feel his foot and he thanked the heavens for small favours. He turned a little in the saddle and almost slid off. One of his captors gave him a rough push and growled an order.

There was no coat-of-arms on their attackers' clothes, but they must be local for even in the dense, dredged woods they made easy speed. It rained as much as before a thick curtain of water that obliterated the world around them. He had no idea where they were.

'Alors, Vichy.'

Blinking away water, Argyle tried to make out his surroundings. It was the same deep, wet darkness all around. He tried to move and the rope bit into his wound. Somewhere to his left, a voice barked an order in French and a noise died down as someone rode on ahead.

An explosion of light engulfed the world when he knocked his head into a thick branch. Next to him, a man laughed and a gloved hand groped for the horse's rein. 'Careful.'

Behind him someone cursed. 'He won't stay in the saddle.'

'Toss him across the horse and tie him on with a rope. If he doesn't make it, it's fine.' The supportive, gloved hand vanished. 'We have our prize.'

Argyle wondered if they knew who he was or if they judged their success by his appearance. He had tucked the expensive silk clothing into his pack and had lost his short silk jacket in the barn. All that was left was the gold pin from Venice which he had used to secure the cloak to his shoulder. They must have found it after they had caught Argyle and Windham in the woods.

To his left a groan eased his concern. Windham was still alive. He had once saved Argyle's life. If he could get them through this did it settle his debt? Of course, if he had stayed in England, Windham would have worked out his tenure and then returned to his family and none of this would ever have come to pass.

The thought of England turned his mind to his time in the Tower. He wondered if it had put a curse on him, had made him prone to captivity. He had not revealed that he understood even a single word spoken around him. Better to pretend ignorance for as long as he could. It had worked in Boulogne. What was to say it would not work here?

Vichy. Something about the name teased a stale memory buried deep in his brain that an uncle to the French King Charles, the Duke of Bourbon, held the city and area of Vichy.

Had the Countess gone back on her word and sent a message to her royal nephew? Argyle might never know. He had no idea what kind of a man the Duke was, but to have Englishmen on his lands in these troubled times would no doubt ensure they would stay behind bars for a long time.

He almost hoped the men taking them to Vichy were poor and had simply gleaned a chance to make a tidy sum handing over trespassers. It would make trading with the Duke easier. It would also mean that Argyle had to write to Elizabeth. It would prove no mean feat to find someone who was willing to smuggle out a message, and yet, it had to be done.

A soft sound of squelching hooves approached. 'Le Duc est la.'

Flickering light penetrated the woods, their pace increased and then they lost what little shelter the foliage awarded. The rain beat down on him as his horse was forced into a canter. The ground tilted and he leaned back just in time to not fall from his saddle.

Something heavy thumped to the ground behind him. 'Merde!'

Argyle imagined Windham's limp body rolling in the mud and willed him to live, just a little longer, just long enough for Argyle to make good his promise and return his companion to England.

The surface changed, he could feel the horse struggle to gain footing before the pace dwindled and he could make out walls, turrets and little specks of light in the distance. Again, he tried to glance over his injured shoulder. This time, the man holding the reins used them to whip Argyle's bloodied leg and he groaned in submission, pressing his dislocated arm to his chest.

Once inside the curtain wall, a torch was thrust in his face and his world turned white for a moment. He had been staring intently into the dark for so long that the flickering, sputtering light seared as fire. Blinking against the flare, he noticed blurred figures that appeared to be running here and there. Argyle was pulled off the horse and left on his knees in the sludge, the point of a sword prickling his neck. Out of the corner of his eye, he spied Windham still tied to a horse, his arm turning the puddle of water under the horse's belly a weak pink.

'In there.'

Argyle was yanked to his feet and forced across the yard into temporary shelter. Here, the torches burned bright and he tried to get a sense of the place without drawing attention to himself. He was rewarded with a rough blow to the small of his back and lost his breath.

'Not him.' What looked to be a captain pointed to an old, battered door. 'In there until we hear from the Duke.'

'Can we take him in?' Argyle's guard asked from behind.

The captain just stared until the man cleared his throat. 'We found them.'

'You attacked them.' The captain dismissed the man with a gesture. 'You were asked to watch.'

Argyle's guard stepped into the light. He was tall and slender, his hands as rough as his voice. A warped scar ran across his cheek. 'They tried to escape.'

Tilting his head, the captain looked at Argyle. 'Most likely they tried to get to shelter. In this hellish weather I'd have done the same. The Duke will see this one in the morning. Make sure they're not put in the same cell.'

The tall man's grumblings stopped when the captain glowered at him. 'You have come fishing for a reward. I doubt the Duke'll be in a generous mood. They were to pass through his lands unhindered not wind up here. Get out.'

A soldier grabbed Argyle by the shoulder and the captain turned his back. 'Water and bread,' he paused. 'And a priest for the other.'

'A physician.' Argyle could not help himself. Windham did not need prayer he needed a man with a needle. 'I beg you. He is innocent, he must be saved.'

The captain turned back and smirked. 'The Duke'll be pleased you understand us. Just don't expect that to save your companion. If he survives the night, you can ask the Duke for this favour yourself. Perhaps he'll be in an obliging mood. Perhaps not.'

CHAPTER 66

3 August 1400 – Château de Billy, Vichy

'Bow in the presence of his Grace Louis, Duke of Bourbon.'

The guard at Argyle's side kicked his good leg and he fell to the floor. He was tired and cold and his arms ached from being pinioned all night. It was well past noon and a fierce sun had burnt the rain away. The fields and forest beyond Argyle's cell had steamed for hours. But the sun had not warmed his bones.

'What is this?' a crisp voice enquired.

'A sad mistake, your Grace,' the captain replied somewhere at the back of the grand hall.

The pause that followed suggested that to call the capture a mistake was a grave understatement. The guard moved his foot a little, his toes cracking inside the old, worn leather. When Argyle shifted, his manacles clattered.

'Take them off.'

The dismissive order was carried out without delay and Argyle slumped. He tried to move his fingers, they were reluctant to obey. His leg throbbed and when he leaned on his hands fresh pain ran up his arms and down his spine. Despite the agony in his shoulder it no longer felt out of joint. The physician had done his job.

'The other?'

'Not awake, your Grace.' There was something guarded about the captain's answers. As if he was speaking to a child. 'But still breathing.'

'Come.'

The captain skirted Argyle, who dared to look up, only to stare at the captain's broad back. In the light of day, he could see that a red band adorned with yellow fleur-de-lis ran down the middle of the captain's bright blue cloak. He turned his head a little and stared into a big shaggy mop. The old grey dog beat its tail a couple of times.

The urgent whispering stopped.

'Leave us.'

As he walked past, the captain glowered at Argyle who tried to sit back on his heels but his wound burst and he fell forward once more.

'Can you stand?' The crisp voice carried a hint of concern.

'Yes, your Grace.' Argyle bit down hard and got up, blinking away dancing, black spots. 'Just about.'

The Duke rose with much dignity, great wisps of grey hair sprouting either side of his jewelled cap. His eyes skipped around the room as if unable to pause and linger on anything. Even when he looked at Argyle it was in fleeting glances.

'This is most unfortunate...' He rubbed his hands together and his thick, gold rings rattled. 'Most grievous... You were supposed to leave... to pass... I do not know how...'

'Your Grace, my companion...' Argyle stopped when the Duke finally locked eyes with him. He had seen that gleam before. Madness dwelled within. 'He is badly injured. If he might be seen by a physician? I shall pay...'

The rubbing stopped and the Duke's expression turned blank. 'Do you think me poor?'

'No, your Grace. I understand that our being here...' A gesture silenced Argyle.

'Yes... No...' The Duke sat down again, letting his eyes dance about the room looking at nothing in particular. 'He will be seen once my physician has tended your wounds. He did what he could in the dead of night, but insists you must be seen again in daylight. They say you put up quite a fight. Smashed a barn and killed a couple of men?'

Argyle nodded, his neck was stiff but at least his arms were beginning to tingle, blood running down to revive his hands. 'If they were your men, your Grace, I... We did not know.'

For the first time, the Duke smiled, a strange childish expression smoothing away the years on his face. 'I do not keep fools in my pay. If they were no match to you they were not my men. I believe my captain was callous enough to employ some local boys to keep an eye on you. He will be punished for his mistake.'

He snapped his fingers and a servant stepped forward carrying two plain cups on a tray. The boy offered one cup to Argyle before serving his master. Argyle tested the content and relished the cold, clean water.

'You are a knight I am told?' The Duke put down his cup untouched and folded his hands into his lap.

Wincing when he tried to put weight on his wounded leg, Argyle nodded. He shifted his stance and his calf screamed in protest. 'Yes, your Grace. I have been visiting my brother's grave in Venice. I was returning home when your… the men came upon me and my servant.'

'Is that so?' Once more, the Duke's eyes flitted about the room before settling on something behind Argyle. 'Well, now that you are here I hope you will be my guest of honour for a little while. Until that… Until you are well enough to leave.'

'Thank you, your Grace, for your…'

'Yes well, I think you should go now.' The Duke stared out the window.

Argyle turned, careful to keep the weight off his leg and limped towards the polished doors at the end of the hall. When he reached out it swung open the bright silver inlay glittering with movement.

'You shall dine with me tonight.'

Before Argyle could make any reply, the door closed again and a guard of eight surrounded him with the captain at their head. 'Your possessions have been moved to more suitable rooms. As has your man. The physician's seeing him now.'

'Thank you.' Argyle struggled to remain dignified. Tears pressed on as fear pulled back its talons and took flight. 'I…'

'You're not a guest,' the captain continued and nodded to the guard. 'You're here at the Duke's discretion. Until we find a way to rid ourselves of you. Take him away.'

ꕥ ꕥ

CHAPTER 67

7 August 1400 – Château de Billy

Windham sat in front of the brazier's glowing embers. He rose with an effort, clutching his bandaged arm with his free hand and offered his seat to Argyle.

The night was drawing to a close and Argyle had been caught in another strange dinner with the Duke. One moment, the old man would regale with tales from his frivolous youth, the next, he would stare vacantly into the air, lost to the world.

'It's quite an upgrade from sleeping rough these past months.' His arm was tied to his body to make the wound heal faster.

'Yes, and yet I find myself wishing for simpler accommodation.'

'We're free to leave, aren't we?' He nodded at the pitcher and Argyle shook his head. It would not do to clutter his brain with any more wine than he had already had.

'We are free to roam the castle. We may have to stay for a while.'

'How long?' Windham's question was laced with concern.

'I know you long to be back in England. I shall endeavour to ensure you are given papers of safe passage and a fresh horse.' A glance at Windham gave him pause. 'You are not bound to me by either contract or fealty – rather I feel it ought to be the other way around. You saved my life.'

'And you saved mine,' Windham said. 'I might've taken a beating for you, but I didn't have to go to Venice and I did. A man died on my watch. Someone I should've been able to protect. I'll see this through.'

'If that is your decision, there are things I must tell you.' Argyle buried his head in his hands. 'Things you cannot tell another living soul. What is said here tonight must go with you to your grave. I offer you freedom one last time.'

Windham snorted. 'Freedom? Wouldn't know what to do with it.'

Live a life in peace, Argyle thought. A life such as I will never have.

He did not argue with Windham, he knew it would be fruitless. Ever since he fell into Argyle's life in Calais there had been a strange connection between them, a feeling he had only known once before when he was a young man making ready for his first real adventure. Before he knew what the world truly was.

'If we make it to Paris King Charles may well ask for my loyalty.'

'You're to be the French King's man now?' Argyle could tell by Windham's question that he was thrown. Here was a man who had never been exposed to courtly life. How

Argyle envied him.

'I shall tell him that I pledged myself to the Dowager Queen before I left England.' Argyle considered how to proceed.

'His daughter?' Windham made a face. 'Is it true?'

'I found I had little enough loyalty left, but how could I refuse a child? The Dowager Queen has always sought my friendship. She arrived a stranger in a strange land and needed a friend. When I… I had to turn my back on her husband while he was still King. After he died, I could offer no solace. If I can now make amends, I must.'

Weak flames illuminated the chamber, casting the corners in gloom. The walls were decorated in muted colours, an old tapestry adorning one side while a row of chests lined the far side. They contained old, linen shirts, some embroidered and others plain.

Windham bit into an apple and nodded. 'Makes sense I suppose.'

'In any event, when I came to you I was locking for my brother – that much is true. I was told he had died in Venice in October. A feat utter impossible.' Argyle tried to decide how much to tell Windham. Every word from now on would only add to the danger he was already in. 'He was exiled by King Richard and I put him on a ship two years ago myself. Only he came back.'

Windham gnawed at the apple core, no trace of concern in his manner. 'He didn't really understand the premise of exile?'

'He was called back *by* the King,' Argyle said. 'Perhaps he was never to have left at all. The exile was a public declaration and the King could not go back on his word. So off Thomas went and back he came the same day I put him on the bloody ship.' Argyle felt the old, familiar twang of betrayal. 'I learned of his return many months later when he saved me from bleeding to death in the Tower.'

'It seems to me you enjoy prisons a little too much.' Windham's dry statement made Argyle laugh and released some of the tension in the room.

'Where Thomas went next, I do not know. What I do know is that he did not leave England until late September last year. Which means he was still in the country when Lord Bordeaux gave up his crown. By then, Thomas' life was in danger and he was warned to leave.' Argyle decided to be honest. 'His wife is the reason I left England. King Henry did not know though by now, I must assume he is informed of my transgression and, most likely, he hopes I have perished like my brother. You must understand that I cannot vouch for your safety.'

'No, and you've been doing so well on that score till now…' Windham grinned and clutched his arm. 'I'd rather chance it with you than attempt to return to England on my own. You heard the same talk as I did on our journey. The streets are teeming with people who hate the English.' He threw the apple core into the dying embers.

'Sometimes I wonder if an angry France is better than an insecure England?' Argyle rubbed his face. The Duke insisted on burning incense at the table and it stung his eyes. 'I believe King Charles will ask me for a favour I am unable to honour. I shall try to keep you out of it that you may honestly say that you knew nothing.'

'Knowing you is dangerous then?' Windham looked up when Argyle snorted a laugh. 'What?'

'I think you would get on with my Master of Arms. He has often said the same.'

'He's the last one you promised safety, isn't he? Your Master of Arms?'

Argyle's response drowned in a ruckus that brought them both to the narrow window. A large retinue piled through the gate, horses and men in bright clothes spilling into torch-lit the courtyard.

Argyle recognised the standard that was being packed away. A winged lion carrying a sword.

The Doge's men had arrived.

CHAPTER 68

20 August 1400 – Hôtel Saint-Pol, Paris

The Doge's embassy filed past Argyle on their way out of the great hall. He looked for the ambassador who usually wore the brightest colours and a feathered headdress. He had been the only one to speak to Argyle and, at that, little enough.

A few deigned to give a nod, most of them ignored him. Their mission was complete. King Charles had received them and taken some bothersome prisoners off their hands. Argyle and Windham was handed over without ceremony to the castellan who was still confused as to the two Englishmen. Were they hostages or guests? Argyle did not know himself.

Once in the hands of the French, Windham was taken to the cells, whereas Argyle was given a fine room and a servant to provide what he required. He had been seen by a physician and his wounds were almost mended, but he was by no means free.

The French courtiers resumed their usual distractions, gambling, talking in groups and glancing at Argyle. They took turns to seem less conspicuous, but it had the opposite effect. He felt as if he was a mythical creature that had suddenly appeared in the realm of men. A Kraken on land. He still wore the clothes he had on when he was captured near Vichy. Though they had been washed and mended they were worn and the vibrant colours faded in splotches. A few of the bloodstains had turned into brown blemishes. All in all, he cut a miserable figure.

His royal guard, a young man who puffed out his chest at the slightest glance, nudged him to one side where the wooden cladding on the wall hid a door that took them into the royal inner chambers. King Charles was washing his hands, a servant poised to dab the scented oil from his fingers and another holding a tray of rings.

'You are either very stupid or very brave to come here.' King Charles held out his hand for his groom to push the rings in place. The chamber was warm and comfortable. All the faces were hostile.

'Or I am very loyal, your Majesty,' Argyle said.

King Charles laughed. 'I am told that my daughter trusts you with her life and that she counts you among a rare, few Englishmen who offers sound advice. You appearing at my court raises a pertinent question. What has stolen you from her side?'

Argyle weighed his options. Either trust the French King with the truth that he had left England without royal approval to seek the truth of Thomas' death. Or conjure up a tale just creative enough to be believed without him being tripped up by it. Neither was very appealing.

'Well? Why did you leave my daughter alone in a shattered land?'

'The Dowager Queen is well capable of handling her situation, Majesty,' Argyle said and earned a nod. Best to stay close to the truth. 'I am here to find a servant once employed by my brother. A man who was last seen in Calais.'

'Calais you say? Then why do you hold letters of safe passage from the Countess of Boulogne and Lucia Visconti of Milan?' Pierre Salmon asked. The King's secretary had a slippery appearance. 'Majesty, I strongly advise against listening to this culprit. How can we be sure the letters are authentic, let alone that he is who he claims to be?'

'I hold my aunt in high esteem.' King Charles gave Salmon a warning glance. 'If she has accepted Sir Argyle's claims so should we. I hardly think I have to remind you just how much I owe her. How much France owes her.'

Chastened Salmon bowed his head. 'Naturally, Majesty.'

As soon as King Charles turned to Argyle, Salmon glared his way, adjusting the golden chain of office settled around his neck. The pendant that drooped towards the floor appeared to be a rough green gemstone set in silver the workmanship intricate.

'Why would one of your brother's servants make his way to my court?' The King settled on his throne, which sat just one step above the tiled floor. It was plain and all the more imposing for its lack of decoration. Behind him delicate fleurs-de-lis was carved into the wall, the edges picked out in gold and brilliant blue.

'Majesty, I have good reason to suppose this to be his destination.' Argyle summoned his courage. 'If I might be allowed to speak with you in private?'

'Most certainly not,' Salmon squealed. He wrung his pink hands, his cheeks flushed in alarm. 'Majesty, our relationship with the English is at a precarious junction, your precious daughter is in the grips of the pretender King. We ought not listen to anything from their poisonous court.'

'What I have to say is not from court.' Argyle noticed King Charles shift, the rings on his fingers gleaming. He continued, 'I am not sent here by the King of England, nor by the Dowager Queen. I am here on a personal errand.' He focused on the only man who might change his fate. 'Majesty, I beseech you.'

'Very well.' The room fell silent as King Charles rose. 'Do not concern yourself, Salmon, for I am in my house and Sir Argyle has long since been stripped of his weapons such as they were. He is limp and his one-armed man is under lock and key. I am quite safe.'

As the last, Salmon left through the secret door glancing over his shoulder. It would not be long before he had concocted some elaborate lie that would have the courtiers clawing for his attention. Argyle would know his kind in any place. Salmon was as ambitious as he was ingratiating. Thomas would have liked him.

The King dismissed his guard. 'Leave us.'

He ignored their baffled looks, but when his servant made to leave too, he stayed the boy with a gesture. This must be a favourite squire.

Merriment played in King Charles' eyes when he examined Argyle. 'I remember you, Sire, from when my late son-in-law came to fetch my daughter. You were just as severe then, so guarded and watchful. Am I wrong to assume that you have been a loyal servant to my Isabella? I cannot imagine her so deceived. She understands the games at court much better than anyone. After all, she is my daughter. It is a pity that your King Henry believes her now to be the possession of the English Crown.'

'I am sworn to her. Though she is not free to leave England, I believe she lives befitting her state.' He hoped she had been afforded more firewood and visits to court, although he doubted it. Still, a harmless lie to smooth his own path must surely be forgiven.

'I have scant news from her. I know only that her life is comfortable. However, you come to the crux of the matter. She is not free. She is not returned to her home and her family.' King Charles twisted his signet ring. 'Isabella is held captive and I want her back.'

'The Dowager Queen is partly the reason I left England.' Argyle tried to read the King's expression. 'She is as determined to return to your court as you are to receive her. Last I saw her she expressed concern that King Henry would not be easily swayed to release her and feared that perhaps you would give up…'

King Charles' beat his hand on the polished armrest, his gold rings denting the wood. 'Reckless child. How can she think so about me, her doting father…' He looked at Argyle. 'I would have the true reason you left England, Sire, for I hear rumours that your King is not best pleased. I hear he has guards searching for you in Calais and beyond, encroaching on my lands.'

It was one thing to wonder if King Henry had taken measures, it was another to be confirmed in his suspicions. Argyle knew that he could never return without paying a heavy price for his decision. Affirmation of his fears brought with it stealth.

'You shall repay my boon of having this conversation in private. The truth, Sire.'

'I have been searching for my brother, Majesty.' He fought to keep what courage he had intact under the watchful eye of King Charles.

'What has that to do with my daughter?' His rich brown and luxurious pointed beard glittered as he stroked it.

'Her Grace told me that my brother had carried with him some valuable documents when he left England.' In truth, Isabella had known very little when he had asked her for confirmation of Elizabeth's claim.

'Ah… You speak of Thomas de Mowbray.' King Charles grabbed a gold cup and drank deep. Behind him, the boy hovered, his expression blank, the tray in his hands steady. 'A mischievous man by all accounts. Why did my daughter have dealings with him?'

Argyle clutched at straws. 'Before King Richard decided Thomas was a traitor, he was high in favour. She often came across him at court.'

'Come now, Sire, you disappoint. Surely you cannot think that she would house him as a prisoner at Windsor and not tell her own father? She said that he blustered louder than those wretched peacocks Richard gave her for her birthday.' King Charles smiled a little. 'I remember your brother visiting for a jousting tournament many years ago as a youth.'

'He was here with King Henry when they were both young Lords, eager to impress on the jousting field.' When Thomas had left, Argyle had been jealous for the first time in his life. How he had envied his brother's good fortune.

'They most certainly achieved their goal for we were truly impressed. Henry was the best but as I recall, your brother held his own.'

'I believe he did.' He tried to assess how far he could go. 'He sat a horse as few others and knew how to wield a lance.

I sometimes wonder how he would have fared in battle, but it is too late…'

Leaning back, King Charles took in Argyle's appearance anew. 'He is dead?'

'In Venice. Or so we were led to believe.'

'You doubted the information?' He gestured at the boy.

Grateful, Argyle accepted a cup of wine. 'Only its origins. His death I did not doubt.'

'Refresh my memory, Sire. Richard exiled your brother is that not so?'

Nodding, Argyle washed down the rest of the wine and returned the cup to the tray. He watched the boy disappear behind a thick curtain no doubt covering up an unsightly door and drinking up any draft from the hallway behind it. Every castle had them.

'At the same time as Henry of Bolingbroke.' The deliberate slight in calling the King by his former name told Argyle what the French thought of his ascension.

He will not goad me, Argyle thought.

If he was to succeed, he had to be as shrewd as Thomas. These past months had taught him much about politics and now, that knowledge must stand its test. In order to return home, he could not afford to speak out against King Henry. However, if he wanted to resolve the mystery of Thomas' death and the lie spun around it, he had to befriend King Charles.

By now, Argyle was certain that though the King wanted his daughter back, he also sought a cause to start a with England. King Henry's reluctance to let go of Isabella was more than ample reason to raise an army.

'It fell to me to send both from the English shores. I was to bear witness to their departure on orders from King Richard.'

'The word of his uncle would not suffice?' He cleaned his nails with a small knife with a jewel encrusted gold hilt. In his inner sanctum, he appeared at ease. 'I often wondered at Richard's reluctance to accept that Lord Gaunt was ever his loyal subject and advisor. I told him that on more than one occasion. He chose not to listen.'

'He had his reasons, I am sure.' Refusing to cower before King Charles' intimidating gaze. 'Thomas was a fickle friend to the Crown and often only out to pursue his personal interests. I can hardly fault the late King his suspicions. Unfounded though they were.'

'Richard wanted rid of Henry for a long time,' King Charles conceded. 'If I had a cousin such as Henry perhaps I too would have gone to extremes to rid my court of him. What was the spat between Bolingbroke and your brother?'

'It was to do with the Crown's money. I am sure there was fault to be found on both sides, Majesty.' Argyle did not wish to stir up old memories. 'In any event, the King sent them both away in disgrace.'

'Henry came here, sharing his tale of woe.' He shook his head as if he had not quite believed all of it. 'Where did your brother go?'

Argyle drew breath. 'Home, your Majesty.'

King Charles stopped drumming his fingers. 'Home?'

'I put him on a ship bound for your shores. He returned to England as soon as my back was turned.'

Crushing silence followed his admission. In the end, the King broke the tension. 'Why?'

'It was a secret to which I was never privy. I saw him just once after his exile and, at the time, I was teetering.' Argyle noticed King Charles' demeanour change and plunged on, eager not to tear open another old and aching wound. 'In my distress, I was certain Thomas' ghost visited me. Until he pushed his hand into my wound. When I asked him why he had returned he became evasive speaking of orders to carry out and masters to serve.'

'Masters?' King Charles clapped his hands once and the boy reappeared from behind the curtain. Argyle wondered how much he had heard and if the King was right to trust him so entirely. Most likely, the boy served more than one master himself. Even as a royal favourite, he would not receive any wages of consequence. This close to the King, he was a prime target for ambitious courtiers who had money to spend and a desire for information. Men such as Salmon.

The King gestured. 'Fetch me Madame.'

Scurrying across the painted floor, the servant slipped through the doors at the far end. As the latch clinked back into place, King Charles rose, his rich garb pooling around his feet. He cut an impressive figure. It was hard to imagine that this man could wake tomorrow and be in the grips of madness. Argyle was not ignorant of this affliction and counted his blessings that, for now, King Charles was lucid and in control.

'You are telling me that your brother was at court until…'

'Until lord Bolingbroke ascended the throne.'

'Thomas was in England until after Richard died?'

'No, Majesty. Thomas' wife told me that he was roused in the middle of the night and fled within the hour. He left no word of his plan.' If only he had decided to trust Argyle. All he had ever wanted was to be close to his brother, to share his concerns and aid where he could. 'We received word of his death in October.'

'How do you know that he did not linger in England?' King Charles reached up to stroke his beard and then froze. 'This is troubling news.'

'We were informed that he died from the mortality in Venice.'

The Venetian embassy had enjoyed days of direct access to the King and his council. If they had orders to taint Argyle's already fragile reputation they would have had ample time. What was to have stopped them feeding the French King lies? And then there was an even worse option. That he colluded with whoever had killed Thomas.

'The sickness does not care if you are rich or poor.' With the flick of a wrist, King Charles dismissed months of concern. 'You know this as well as I.'

'Except Thomas never travelled beyond Calais.'

Before the King could speak the doors opened. An annoyed glance was all that was needed to scare off the boy who scrambled backwards as the doors slammed shut. After a beat, he said, 'You are certain?'

'How is Thomas supposed to cross the Channel and make his way to Venice, fall prey to the pestilence and die within a month – if that? Allegedly he died last summer.' Argyle hated that he would never see his brother again. They rarely saw eye-to-eye and yet, he still struggled to accept that he was gone.

At the King's annoyed snort, he continued, 'Tell me, Majesty, how can a man die three months *before* he left his home? Three months before his wife said her goodbyes?'

A hand crept to the pointed beard and began stroking it again, contemplation played on King Charles' face. 'Distress can warp a mind.'

'Master Windham, my unfortunate companion, was warden of the Calais prison. His ledger will attest the date of Thomas' arrival. It was this entry that set us upon the path of an ugly truth. I shall not bore your Majesty with the details. Suffice to say that my brother met his untimely death in Calais at the hands of villains.' Instinctively, Argyle rubbed his thigh. When it rained, it ached as if it had only healed on the outside. The sensation of the ground shifting beneath his feet was gone, but the memory of it persisted. Villains altered lives and he wanted to know who had altered his.

'I too could have died at their hands if not for Windham.' He pushed out the admission. 'We were left in the sea for dead.'

'And you washed up in my aunt's dominion.' King Charles flashed a humourless smile. 'She sent word.'

'She said she would.' Argyle hoped she had honoured their arrangement. 'It was she who encouraged me to continue my journey to Venice that I might unearth any truth buried in my brother's empty grave.'

Glancing at the tall, ornate doors at the opposite side of the long room, King Charles rubbed his forehead. 'You saw it?'

'I saw what they wanted me to see.' Argyle hoped that Nicoló's men had not returned to visit harsh justice upon the priest from the cemetery. He was an innocent bystander put in Argyle's path by pure happenstance. 'There was no bout of mortality in Venice last year. Not at any time.'

'Is that so?'

'Yes, Majesty.' Argyle leaned heavily on his good leg. He yearned to sit on one of the low stools by the empty hearth. On the wall, the King's crest gleamed as sunlight danced across its surface. 'A priest told me. It raised more questions than it answered.'

'I see.' King Charles clasped his hands behind his back, straining his gown to expose a budding potbelly. 'I am not so reckless as to challenge the word of a holy man. What do you plan to do now?'

If I were free? How tantalizing the prospect.

'Rather than find closure, I have unearthed a web of lies. I should like to discover the truth, though I fear it is buried deep. I may spend the rest of my life seeking justice. I wish to return to England and live my life in peace, but I doubt it will be so. I desire peace of mind. I want to be able to tell my nephews that their father's death was not in vain. That he was noble. In the end?' Argyle paused, searched his soul. 'I want the Mowbray name cleared. Thomas had an riotous streak, but he was never reckless. He had his reasons. I want to know them.'

'I wonder if you are ready to do what it takes?' King Charles said with something akin to compassion. 'Names carry with them great responsibility. That we both know.'

'Would that they did not.'

For the first time, King Charles laughed, a deep and hearty sound that bounded off the walls. 'You are not the first to make such a wish, nor shall you be the last. Perhaps I might aid in your quest.'

Not daring to contemplate the cost of such aid, Argyle let hope soar. 'How so, Majesty?'

This time when the door swung open the King smiled. 'Madame, I have an assignment for you.'

CHAPTER 69

23 August 1400 – Hôtel Saint-Pol

'What luck you had that the Venetian embassy chose to escort you to our court.'

So that is the tale they have agreed on telling, Argyle thought, I suppose it requires fewer explanations than the truth.

'For an Englishman, safe passage is hard to contrive these days. I was honoured when offered their protection.'

It was hard to imagine that King Henry had nothing to do with his captivity and equally hard to imagine that King Charles would ever concede to manage any requests from a man he clearly believed a usurper. The longer Argyle spent at the French royal court, the more eager he became to please whatever ruler might provide an escape.

'You are very quiet tonight, Sir Argyle.'

'I am sorry if I am poor company, Madame, I find that I miss my family.'

'All of it?' Madame looked into the sea of colour washing around them. Courtiers wore silk, brocade, lace and gemstones the like of which was only found at the English court.

Tonight, they were in the Queen's dwelling, one of three buildings that made up the royal castle. Queen Isabeau's Bavarian heritage dominated part of the décor. One wall was hung with heavy tapestries while two others were adorned by panels of dark blue fabric embroidered with the fleur-de-lis. Large oil vats hung from thick chains to bathe her guests in a buttery, fluttering light.

'Yes.' What was another half-truth?

'Then I shall endeavour to expedite matters.' She smiled at him, comfort hidden in her green gaze. 'To miss one's family can be a terrible thing.'

'You suffer the same, Madame?'

'Oh no, I have my brother here most of the time and my sister visits regularly.' Behind her impeccable manners lingered a darker nature.

'I meant your husband and children.' Argyle noticed the minute change in her demeanour. He had struck home.

'When the King permits, I see them.' Madame tried to brush aside her pain. 'He has much need of me.'

'And the Queen?'

Madame tilted her head towards Argyle. 'Isabeau has *no* claim on me.'

The disdain in her whisper was so ad odds with her contended joy at the sight of all the young men and women parading each other around Queen Isabeau's great hall.

'I stand corrected, Madame, forgive me.'

'You were not to know.' Something in Madame's tone

told Argyle that he had finally found a chink in her armour. A tiny flaw to pick at until it grew big enough to exploit.

When the musicians began to play, she held out her hand and he took her to the floor.

'How did you come to be in the King's service, Madame?' Argyle's feet followed the flow of the dance surprisingly well considering he still felt twinges of pain in his leg. At least she was light and his arm had mended well under the court physician's zealous attention.

She smiled up at him, white teeth against cherry lips. 'It is a long tale, Sire, and I shall not tire you with the particulars. Rest assured that our arrangement is of mutual benefit.'

Argyle lifted her from the floor, burying his hand in the layers of her silk skirt. King Charles nodded at them and she twirled a hand in his direction, flashing another smile. To his left, Queen Isabeau's gaze was fixed on Argyle who offered a polite smile in return.

'She favours you.'

'I am sure the Queen is just being polite.'

Madame turned in his arms and pinched his palm. 'Isabeau is everything but.'

The music stopped and all the dancers turned to applaud before dispersing. The musicians struck a few chords and the Queen's ladies took the floor, their bright dresses attacking the senses, their jewellery glittering.

'Refreshments?' Madame drew him to the far side of the room. 'And perhaps a quiet word.'

She snapped her fingers and a servant immediately weaved towards them, a tray of food and drink held high above his head. There was something well-known about him, although Argyle could not place him and dismissed it as a fancy. Perhaps he was simply homesick for a familiar face.

'The King is arranging an embassy to visit King Henry.' Madame shook her flaming hair from her face and drank with greed. Unlike the other women in the room, she wore just a simple golden chain around her neck, a drooping pearl pendant caressing her cream skin. 'It is as good as arranged.'

'So I gather.'

Ever since King Charles had introduced Argyle to Madame, he had been curious to know her better. She appeared to have unhindered access. Why did the King of France trust this woman above all others?

'The King believes that Jean de Hangest, Lord of Hugueville, is the man to return the Princess to us.' She let her gaze wander. 'I told Charles that he was mistaken that his diplomats were unlikely to succeed, but he would not listen. So, he sends men to a woman's work.'

Once more, he was thrown by the level of intimacy between these two most unlikely allies. Not even the Queen called her husband by name. 'How so, Madame?'

'You are not the least bit curious about my name, Sire?'

'If it was for me to know, you would have told me.' Time had taught Argyle that sometimes it was best to live in ignorance. At least it might resemble some form of blessing.

She lifted her hair, revealing her long neck. 'It is stifling in here. Escort me for a breath of fresh air. I insist.'

Argyle made for the door, her touch light and warm on his sleeve. He was well aware that everyone in the room watched them go and briefly wondered what they thought of him and more importantly what they thought of her.

Once outside in the small, enclosed garden, the caress of air made his skin prickle. Next to him, Madame raised her arms to the skies and twirled on the tiled courtyard. 'Is not this marvellous?'

'Just what I needed.'

'How are you at keeping secrets, Sir Argyle?' His name rolled off her tongue with a strange ease. 'For I have one to confide and none to confide in.'

'It depends on whom you ask,' he said and earned a curious glance. 'Most of my family would say I am too honest for my own good. It only goes to show they do not know how many secrets I carry. My brother would say I am better than most. But then…'

'He is dead.' She turned her face to the skies. 'Most of the court would say I am the worst kept secret in the world.'

'What would you say?'

'Jealousy makes people see what they want to see.' Madame tugged at a stray strand of hair. 'They believe that I am Charles' lover.'

'Are they wrong?'

A green flash told him that he was teetering on the edge of patience. 'Yes. I leave such frivolities to my sister.'

'Then why…'

'They see me at court, not her, so they assume she is unimportant and that it is I who have stolen the King's affections from his wife. But truly, Sire,' Madame looked up at him. 'Would you blame him?'

'The Queen has many qualities.' Best not to commit to too much. Compared to her ladies, Queen Isabeau appeared bland.

'Charles relies on her like none other even more than he relies on me. No one could tear him from Isabeau though many have tried.' She led the way to a bench snuggled in between two large shrubs. Although autumn was a long time away, the leaves seemed ablaze in the golden light from the windows behind them.

'His bouts of illness are truly the worst kept secret in the world. When he is ailing she rules in his place. At such times, he does not allow her to visit. For years, she suspected that he had a lover, though for all my sister's merits, she is little more than a nurse.'

Argyle had heard of the King's frail mind, but the time he had spent in the presence of King Charles, both now and when he first visited Paris, he would never have believed anything ailed him. He sat down next to her and waited for her to continue.

'You would do well to keep our Queen happy,' Madame said, her voice shattering the delicate silence. 'She is the most powerful person at court. It is to her tune we all dance. Should she ever request your attendance give it without delay. Afterwards, come to me.'

CHAPTER 70

25 August 1400 – Hôtel Saint-Pol

Madame detached herself from a large group of newcomers and came to Argyle, a smile playing on her lips. 'You are spying on my husband?'

'He came with quite a retinue.'

'Yes.' She straightened her necklace, the single pearl replaced by large emeralds that set off her eyes. 'He likes to look important so that I do not outshine him. The Prince has invited him for a hunt and he is eager to show off his new hounds. I hear they are ferocious.'

The roll of her eyes made Argyle laugh out loud. She had an effortless way about her that was hard to resist and the notion of her enduring endless chatter about dogs was absurd. She was a politician.

Her husband sidled up, distaste plain on his face. 'You

should not lurk in the shadows, my dear. I bring you here to sparkle and shine, not by stand idly. You might be happier with the Queen's ladies.'

'I am quite content here, Pierre. Sir Argyle is an honoured guest of his Majesty.' Madame flashed a bright smile and he seemed to soften to her. 'I shall be of no bother to anyone and always be of good use. If the King is happy to be in Sir Argyle's company then so am I.'

Her husband nodded at Argyle. 'Good. I do confess that when the Countess sent word that I should travel to court to attend the King, I was surprised. Now I see that she is our true and constant friend. You should invite her to come and stay some time. It would add greatly to our circle.'

'I shall, my dear.' Madame squeezed her husband's arm before he left to join a large group of courtiers.

'The Countess?'

'Joan of Boulogne and Auvergne,' she said tasting every word. 'She saved Charles' life at an ill-fated ball when she was just fifteen, ten years his junior. I suppose that makes her a force to be reckoned with. Which is why I was surprised to learn that she had taken herself *from* court.'

'As the King's aunt surely she can do as she pleases?' Argyle put aside his glass.

If the Countess appeared here how long before someone realised that she was instrumental in his own arrival? It was a surprise to learn that the King had not confided in Madame that Argyle had wound up on her shores bludgeoned and desperate.

'My husband is infatuated with her,' Madame said with a hint of contempt. 'I suppose I must take whatever kindness she might bestow. We all want Princess Isabella returned not least the Countess. It will please Charles above all else.'

'But how, Madame?'

'Much can be achieved in the shadows, Sir Argyle.' She nodded at a throng of splendidly dressed men and women who were separating from the crowd, ordering themselves into a line. The doors to the great hall opened.

'Cue the foreign dignitaries and important guests,' she said with a sigh. 'We shall speak again.'

Before he could say more, she had turned away and made her way to the very front of the line. He watched her straighten her back and flash a brilliant smile at her husband. He bowed to her and made a comment that seemed to amuse her. When the herald announced the guests Madame turned her head a little and shot Argyle a sly smile.

This is a woman who plays the game extremely well, Argyle thought. Woe the man who ever underestimates her.

As more people filed into the great hall, he slipped away, making his way towards his own rooms at the far end of the King's dwelling. He lived as an honoured guest although his chambers were under guard and his door locked at night.

Lying back on his bed, Argyle hoped he would soon be allowed to visit Windham whose whereabouts were still unknown. The court physician had mentioned him only once and had appeared to regret his slip of the tongue.

Since then, he had no news of Windham and as sleep approached, worry wormed in his stomach.

CHAPTER 71

27 August 1400 – Château de Vincennes

Madame cantered out of the courtyard on a massive bay horse, comfortable in her side saddle. Argyle did not doubt she would be equally contented in a soldier's saddle.

Yesterday, the entire court had moved from the heart of Paris to another of King Charles' favourite castles to entertain his guests. While Hôtel Saint-Pol offered safety with its location near the imposing Castille prison, Vincennes afforded leisurely activities and housed the royal stables. This became especially desirable when one of the guests had brought most of his kennel.

'What are they all doing?'

'What they have always been doing. Making sport of killing.' A young man stood next to Argyle. His face worked constantly, an unsettling sight. He turned. 'Madame wishes to see you later.'

'Where?'

The man smiled, his expression momentarily still. 'In the shadows.'

He watched the last stragglers canter through the gate, allowing himself to be a little disappointed that he was not invited. Although Argyle believed he had won King Charles' trust, even he knew that many a hunting accident was no accident at all. Put a bow and arrow or even a spear in Argyle's hands and send him hunting with a King – no, he would not have allowed it either.

Crossing courtyard he passed the stables where a few of the guards nodding at him. By now, most of the King's men had spent an night squatting outside his door and they seemed to have decided he posed no immediate threat. A few had even exchanged words with him for which he was grateful.

In a penned off area of a large field, Argent was grazing. When called, the beast's ears pricked and he cantered closer. It was not the sight of the horse that eased the burden he carried.

Windham was there too, looking no worse for wear. Was this the work of Madame? Some nights ago, Argyle had asked for news of his companion, if nothing else then to know he was well. She had given him an odd glance and skirted the topic, diverting his attention by asking him to dance with her. Perhaps this was another matter that had been kept from her. If so, she could not have been best pleased.

By now, he did not care who had acted. It was enough to see Windham free to roam, his arm no longer in a sling, no sheen of fever on his brow.

Before he could utter his relief, Windham nodded at the

flock grazing farther afield. 'Whatever you may feel about the French, they do breed wonderful animals. Yours is growing fat in his pen.'

'Argent is a great addition to the royal stables.' He clasped a hand around Windham's arm for a moment and decided to avoid a awkward conversation. Instead he leaned on the rail. 'He would not be so round of belly if only I would be allowed to ride him.'

'The sun'll shine at night before that happens.' Windham turned from the fold. He seemed determined not to speak of whatever experiences he had this past week. 'What'll you do while most of the court are gone for the hunt?'

'I thought I might visit the kitchens,' Argyle said.

'The best place for gossip and information's in the kitchens. Mayhap I should go, spare you the bother.'

Argyle smiled a little. 'And what does that leave me?'

'Free to pursue other interests.' Glancing towards the forest, Windham smiled. 'Perhaps pick up a spear and join the hunt, who's to say what might happen…'

'We would be stuck here forever.' A probable scenario even if he did nothing. 'Perhaps one of the guards can be persuaded to ride out with me. We would be back long before the court returns.'

'You'd have more luck staying put,' Windham said looking past Argyle's shoulder. 'I think you're about to get a bit of company.'

Turning, Argyle saw Madame walking her horse into the yard a stable boy rushing to her side. She gestured and pointed and the blacksmith came out of the forge, wiping his blackened brow. He bent to look at the horse and Madame handed over the reins.

'I'll get on then. See what the cooks're preparing for tonight.' Windham rubbed his arm, which was marred by an unsightly scar that the physician insisted was healing as it should. Would that the Countess brought with her Grand-Maman de Reines if she should decide to make an appearance.

'Best keep that arm still.'

'I'll get someone to help me. They're nice in the kitchen.' Squinting against the sun, Windham skirted Madame as he aimed for the main keep. 'Very serviceable.'

'Serviceable?' She pulled her gloves off one finger at a time. 'I hear your man is very popular in certain quarters.'

Rather than probe as to why she had failed to mention that Windham was well, let alone discuss his merits, Argyle turned to Argent and stroked his shimmering hide. 'What happened to your horse?'

'It threw a shoe. I found it better to return at once than risk it going lame.' She leaned over the rail to nuzzle Argent. 'You should have been allowed to come today. Such a magnificent creature must be exercised.'

'He seems to like you.' He sighed. 'Perhaps you want him saddled? You will be by your husband's side before he knows you are gone.'

She laughed when Argent nibbled at the lace trim of her sleeves. 'And ruin a hard night's work?' When Argyle looked at her, she smiled. 'Sometimes you have to force the hand of fate a little. Though your horse could use a good chase.'

They watched Argent trot away. 'We must speak. I hear you are looking for proof that your brother was killed?'

There were no secrets at court, La Fontaine had once warned Argyle. That was true of all courts – and camps for that matter. Argyle had spoken of Thomas to no one except Windham and King Charles. It was obvious from where Madame had her information.

'I know he was killed. I do not know why, not yet.'

'I heard tell your brother sent some documents here.' Madame turned led the way towards one of the gravel paths that cut from the stables to the main keep. The beds were full of late summer flowers and Argyle was reminded of his aunt. 'Have you seen them?'

'Have you?' Part of him wanted desperately to trust her. Another part screamed that she was danger in a dress.

'Men have sacrificed their lives for what those missives contain. I worry that you may have to do the same.' She paused and looked down a path, a range of emotions flickering across her pretty face. Argyle followed her gaze and noticed her servant waiting for her. She let out an affectionate sigh. 'Jacques.'

'Who is he?'

'My brother.'

CHAPTER 72

1 October 1400 – Hôtel Saint-Pol, Paris

'Sir Argyle, you are most welcome.' A heavy accent laced Queen Isabeau's words and Argyle bowed deep before her. 'Come closer.'

Crossing the room, the Queen's ladies pretended not to notice her visitor, but they made a poor show of it. She waved a dismissive hand and they left shooting quizzical looks in Argyle's direction. All save a solitary young girl who appeared completely ignorant of his presence.

'They are too curious for their own good and you are the kind of novelty all young women enjoy discussing behind closed doors. I suppose it cannot be helped.' Queen Isabeau smiled and the room brightened. While plain at first sight, the Queen could turn on a charm that was hard to rival. 'My husband has told me of your… conundrum.'

'I believe the King desires that I go to England on his behalf, Majesty.' Argyle tried to suppress the urge to retain her attention. How strange that such a nondescript woman was endowed with so much charisma.

'To fetch back our beloved Isabella, yes. But not until he has tried by means of a French embassy.' The Queen sighed and gestured for him to sit at her feet. The young girl quickly arranged a bed of pillows before scurrying back to the Queen's side. 'Odele here is quite deaf. She has never learned to write. It does not seem to catch her interest. Which makes her the perfect companion. I suspect she can read lips or minds, though she cannot convey anything to anyone.'

Her meaning was not lost on him. 'A comfort, no doubt, Majesty.'

'To me if not to her.' She gave Odele a doting smile and turned back to Argyle.

Surely being so close to the Queen as to be allowed to stay when all others were sent from the room must be some comfort to the girl as well, despite her shortages.

At her touch the girl went to a silver tray, arranging the cups with care. Queen Isabeau watched her work. 'I do not know what my husband thinks will come of his venture. King Henry is no fool, as well you know. I found him pleasant enough company when he came here during his exile – and, to own the truth, I am not sad that he replaced our son-in-law. It is unfortunate that Richard's untimely death should cast such a shadow on the transition.'

She took a glass from Odele's neat tray. 'Do not look surprised, Sire, you know as well as I that volatile Kings must be held in check. While Isabella wilful she is also still a child. She was not fit to rein in the King of England as my husband had hoped she might. It was clear to me from the first meeting with Richard that he was… troubled.'

Argyle wondered if perhaps Queen Isabeau had played some part in Bolingbroke's return to England but dismissed the idea. She would have little interest in replacing her daughter's husband with a man who would in all likelihood dispose of King and Queen alike.

'You know King Henry well, I believe?'

'I once partook in his pilgrimage to the Holy Land.'

'You are a pious man?'

Her expectant smile withered as he admitted, 'No Majesty, not particularly. I have often struggled to understand God's actions, to make sense of that which appears senseless.'

'What senselessness had invaded your life?' Her disinterested tone and scrutiny gave way to a pause.

He sipped the wine before answering. 'My master was killed in a joust and I desired revenge. Jerusalem offered another path.'

'God's ways are often shrouded in mystery.' Queen Isabeau picked a strange-looking fruit from the plate and sucked on it. 'I am pleased you were saved although I see you still grieve the loss as well as a much more recent one. My husband's aunt wrote to tell us of your misfortunes, Sire. Did you find the answers you were looking for?'

'No, Majesty.'

Last night, Madame had sought out Argyle. The court had returned to the royal palace within Paris the day before, many invigorated by days spent hunting, hawking and enjoying the abundance of early autumn in the countryside. She had spent the entire time by her husband's side, Pierre scowling every time his gaze snagged on Argyle. Now, he was gone back to his estates, satisfied that she had kept faith with him. At least that was what she claimed. That and that King Charles had told his wife of Argyle's true purpose. It should come as no surprise that he was summoned this afternoon. Rather, he had wondered at her restraint.

'Unfortunately, I found more questions and no answers that would serve to bring me peace of mind.' There was no point in denying his failure nor that he refused to give up his quest.

'Save one.' Queen Isabeau sucked on another of those strange fruits, small and orange and smooth as a cherry. 'Your man, Windham, he told one of my ladies that you met in Calais? I believe he is eager to return home.'

'Very eager, Majesty, as am I.' The longer he stayed in this hostile court, the more his morals frayed. How long before he would agree to anything to be let loose? 'I had not presumed to linger in France. Once I had visited Venice, I imagined all would be resolved.'

'Since that is not the case, Sire, I wonder if you are willing to travel under the banner of France? Is your man?'

Windham is not my man, and he would most certainly object if he heard that we were speaking thus of him, Argyle thought as he tried to decide what to say next.

She spoke before he could. 'Can you ensure that my daughter is returned to me, Sire? In the event that my husband's embassy fails. I should not like to be fooled into false hope if there is none.'

'There is hope, Majesty,' Argyle said and meant it. 'I believe some deal might be struck.'

'It must be one that sets her free,' the Queen retorted, her bright smile gone. 'She was married too young and now she must be returned that we might make a more suitable match for her. It will not do to make arrangements that she is to marry this English prince. She must be free. Can you make such a promise to me and honour it?'

'If I made such a promise, I would be a fool.' Argyle earned a nod for his honesty. 'All I can offer is to do what is within my power, and I shall do so without any hidden agenda. I am very fond of her and wish for her to be happy.'

'Your King Henry is a shrewd man.' The Queen's gaze skittered across the tapestries to her right, rich and opulent in colour they told the tale of Adam and Eve in the Garden of Eden. 'What will it take to strike an accord?'

'Leverage.'

'What kind?'

'What you offer must more than cover the loss of your daughter. As you say, King Henry is shrewd. He is not about to part with the one person who might ensure what he desires.'

'Charles has sent money. But you speak of something else.' She tapped the tray and Odele poured more wine. It was weak and sweet at the same time. 'Perpetual peace?'

'King Henry takes after his grandfather. It may be that he is not interested in peace.' If it were as easy as promising not to take up arms against England, Isabella would be in France by now.

'I hear that he has enough war on his plate to the north and the west.' This time the Queen's smile turned her features wolfish. 'The Scots and Welsh are lusting to topple him and seize power for themselves. Or better yet, for us. A word from the King could remove much concern. Is Henry so blinded by power that he cannot see the facts in front of him?'

'You know far more of current affairs than I, your Majesty.' Argyle tried to hide his surprise. 'I have been long from England and had no news.'

'And why is that, Sire?'

She was even more astute than her husband. Madame was correct the royal pair was well matched. He refrained from replenishing his own cup. 'No one knows where I have gone.'

'Including your King?' The Queen mulled over this fact. 'If I were to deliver you in chains would such an act free my child?'

'Though I am certain King Henry would be most grateful for your gesture, I believe it would only afford that I be a head shorter not you a daughter richer.' He accepted her laugh with what he hoped was a measure of grace. 'I am not that important.'

'You underestimate yourself, Sire,' the Queen said and stroked Odele's white hair. 'As so many great men do. Take Odele here: her father was a great man who thought little of himself. When he and his wife died in a fire, Odele's hair turned white and brittle from shock. I sometimes wonder what he might make of her now being my closest companion when in life he never dared ask for favours that were owed him a thousand times.'

Closing her eyes, Odele appeared appeased by the caress, a white-haired angel resting against the throne of a Queen. An unlikely sight if ever there were. Queen Isabeau continued, 'As I say, perhaps you are more dear to King Henry than you might imagine.'

She touched Odele's cheek and the child opened her startling, pale blue eyes. 'Fetch me the letter.'

Odele scurried off through a door ornamented with elaborate iron-works and Argyle heard her rummage, opening boxes and slamming them shut making a great ruckus. The Queen seemed undisturbed. 'She cannot hear and thus, she is very loud whenever she is set to a task.'

'She understood your words just now, your Majesty?'

'She has been with me for a long time and so, I have had plenty of time to observe her. I assume that she knows all that goes on even if she is cursed to keep all that knowledge to herself. I find pleasure in teaching her little things such as to distinguish seals and the like.'

Odele reappeared with a triumphant smile, her small hand held high, clutching a thick scroll. She pushed it towards the Queen who inclined her head as she took it. 'Well done, child. Now, off with you. Find something to eat.'

Argyle watched her skip across the floor the rush matting squeaking beneath her fine silk slippers. When she was out the door he looked up at the Queen who offered him the paperwork.

'Read it.'

After the first sentence, his heart sank. 'Thomas knew this?'

'A man came here shortly after your brother left England. He was ragged and scruffy and so my husband's guards would not admit him, but I heard of it and sent for him. After our conversation, I offered what comfort I could without it seeming peculiar. It was not long before he disappeared.' The tiny pearls on her long necklace rippled in tune with her breath. 'What he had to tell was alarming.'

'He was my brother's servant?' Argyle had come to doubt Elizabeth's word that Thomas had brought a servant. It would make more sense to travel alone and attract less attention. Here perhaps was proof that she had told the truth. If so, there was no reason that the message he had just read was not equally true. The mere thought of it curdled his blood.

'You know that Henry came to us when he was exiled. My husband insisted that we house him. Initially, I wanted him turned away. It was a bad decision to house an English prince when our daughter was sent to England to broker peace. Still, Charles could not be dissuaded.' Something in Queen Isabeau's words checked Argyle's objections. 'I would like to say that my husband played no part in Henry's return, but I know not what to think these days. However, if this is true, even just a small portion of it then you *are* of value to King Henry, and he will – he must – listen to you.'

Argyle bowed his head to the urgency of the Queen's demands. 'If I can be of assistance, your Majesty, I am yours to command.' A moment ago, he desired nothing more than to return home. Now, he wished he could steal away as his brother's servant had.

'Madame thinks as I do on the matter of my husband's embassy. He has chosen poorly when it comes to negotiators and yet, we are left one option. To wait.' There was no emotion in neither the Queen's voice nor her words and expression. Shortly after, she called her ladies back in attendance and they fluttered about, creating enough of a distraction that he could leave without being dismissed.

If Queen Isabeau understood the full implications of the scroll, how could she stay so calm? How could she dare send Argyle back to England, knowing what he now knew?

This at least had a simple answer. She was desperate.

CHAPTER 73

16 November 1400 – Hôtel Saint-Pol

'I struggle with your King these days,' King Charles confided in hushed tones. He had sought out Argyle once the meal was over. Now, he clung to a silver cup, his eyes watery. 'It seems he is willing to risk open war to keep Isabella in England.'

'Perhaps, Majesty, he hopes to make the same alliance with you as her first husband did.' The longer he stayed at the French court, the more he was convinced that English spies hid in plain sight. Better to be bland in his remarks.

'Then he is very clumsy,' King Charles slurred. 'If he is as clever as he says, as I witnessed when he came here during his exile, he would have sent her home the moment Richard died. England is no place for her anymore.'

Argyle longed to be in the great hall, to vanish into the

crowd of courtiers and social climbers. Here, in King Charles' inner rooms, there were no dark corners to retreat to no hidden doorways to slink out of. Here there were just bright colours, thick carpets and far too many trinkets and ornaments for your eyes to find somewhere to rest.

'Hangest should have had more sense in his negotiations. I freely admit as much. A *handshake* is hardly the way to ensure the return of a most beloved daughter.' Snapping his fingers for a servant to replenish his cup, King Charles leaned on Argyle's shoulder, his breath sour. 'He should have had something in writing. He should have brought home Isabella. How can I know that *your* King will honour his promises?'

Because you offered King Henry two hundred thousand francs in exchange for her, Argyle thought, and he needs the money more than he needs the presence of an underage Dowager Queen at his court.

Madame had given a whispered recount of Jean de Hangest's endeavours in England. It seemed the man was almost certain that no further action was necessary. Argyle was of a different opinion. If France was willing to part with such an amount for the hint of a promise what might King Henry get if he prolonged the return?

'Perhaps the Princess will take to Prince Harry. After all they are of an age.' The moment his remark left his lips he knew he had made a mistake.

'I want her back.' King Charles beat a ringed hand against the tabletop. 'She shall never be happy in England now that his own kin put her husband in an early grave. How can King Henry believe she will ever wish to be part of his family?'

King Charles' words made the wine thicken in Argyle's mouth and yet he was done coddling for the night. 'Politics,

Majesty.'

'What I did for Richard was politics. Henry's demand is tantamount to treason.' King Charles barked a laugh and sloshed wine down his pearl-studded shirt. 'That fool put himself on the throne of England without any concern for the repercussions. No monarch in Europe will think anything of it if he is removed. He has no friends, Sire, no allies to which he can turn. He should honour his promise.'

'It is my understanding that Monsieur Hangest agreed with King Henry a return of the Princess in the coming year?'

'Is it, Sire? Is that your understanding?' When the King caught Argyle in the ribs with his elbows, he swallowed a groan. 'How did you come by such information?'

Argyle how easy it would be to convince him that he had offered the details himself. But he was no common drunk. No matter how far into the wine he got, he was cunning and it would not do to underestimate the French King no matter his state. As long as he was lucid, he was dangerous.

Rubbing his side, he said, 'Madame gave me a short report. I was under the impression she had spoken with you.'

'The fair Madame…' King Charles swayed as he stood. 'Where is she this fine evening? Have you seen her? Or that vile creature that is her brother? He is a nasty piece of work, Sire, the tales I could tell you about him would make your skin crawl. Perhaps I should have sent him with Hangest. The result might be very different. A handshake? Jacques would have brought home the hand.'

Grunting he wiped his chin. 'If your King hopes to secure the Crown for his heirs he had better listen to reason and take what advice I offer. If he refuses to do what he pledged on that famous handshake I shall sack every last town until there is nothing left of England. Until it is a charred island, barren and forgotten.'

His words made Argyle's skin crawl. The idea of returning to England inspired equal amounts of hope and fear. Even with what he now knew courtesy of Queen Isabeau, he knew that he would be punished the moment he set foot on English soil. Not even King Charles could prevent it nor would he care. Hedging the return of his daughter on an Englishman was a last resort. No one would expect him to succeed.

Argyle was reduced to being a pawn, not at liberty to ask favours or expect anything. Although, perhaps unwittingly, Queen Isabeau had afforded him with some leverage of his own.

'What would you have me do, Majesty?'

'I propose a trade,' King Charles said, his eyes swimming. 'You come in search of your brother's servant. I cannot give you him, but I can give you what he brought.' He tottered closer and caught himself on Argyle's shoulder before he went over. 'In return, you will ensure that Isabella is returned to me. Without delay.'

'And if I fail?' Argyle wondered what King Charles had that Queen Isabeau had not already given him, and yet, he already knew he would agree to anything to return to England. Accept any deal no matter how unpalatable.

'You will not fail, Sire.' The King tried to drink without spilling the precious drops. Argyle's sleeve was sprinkled with wine from the futile attempt. 'You shall have horses and men at your disposal. Once you succeed you shall receive the secret your brother wished me to keep and more gold than you can carry. Think what legacy you could build.'

'You think I can be bought, Majesty?' Argyle knew he was being insolent, but King Charles only spared him a knowing glance.

'It is in your blood.'

CHAPTER 74

2 December 1400 – Hôtel Saint-Pol

'She acts as if the entire court should bow to her,' the Countess of Boulogne said with antipathy. 'I do not understand why my nephew insists on bringing her here.'

The King's illustrious aunt had arrived a few days before and made quite a spectacle of her own appearance. Tonight, she shimmered in a blush rose gown, the top heavy with beading and intricate needlework, chains dangling gemstones looped around her slender neck. She should have attracted all eyes and so, it was perhaps not strange that she was annoyed at being overshadowed.

'See there? Insufferable.'

Argyle followed her gaze and found her mark. A large group of courtiers were flocking around a striking woman with copper hair wearing an equally striking dress. It looked to be made entirely of silver, sparkling and glittering whenever she turned. 'Who is she, your Grace?'

'I had hoped that you and I might exchange news tonight, Sir Argyle. I see now that I shall have to wait.' She schooled her features into a neutral glare. 'You on the other hand are about to find out who my nephew's mystery guest is.' She turned on her heel. 'Beware. This one is nothing like her sister.'

'Sir Argyle.' A full voice with the hint of a husky whisper caressed his ears. 'Finally, we meet.'

He bowed low, not sure what position the silver woman might have at court. If the Countess' slight was any indication, she was not high in the hierarchy, but being here at the King's express invitation indicated that she was by no means a nobody either. When he straightened, she was smiling at him, a faint glimmer of curiosity in her bright green eyes. *That* sister.

'Alors, leave us.' She waved her hand, and the crowd around dispersed, the men sending sour glances back over their shoulders, while the women seemed relieved. They were quick to pick out arms to cling to.

'Do you know, I met your brother, Lord Mowbray once – just once – long ago. As did my sister. I am surprised that she has not confided in you.' She smiled and Argyle lost himself in the silky green gaze. 'We were little more than children, yet old enough to be at court. He old enough to joust.' Her voice was soft with nostalgia. 'Once the tourney was done I sought him out and tried to strike up a conversation.'

'Your sister mentioned the occasion in passing. Why did you seek him out?' What he truly wanted to ask was her name, but since she had not bothered to divulge it, he decided to play along for a while. He was intrigued why this creature would prefer Thomas to a young Bolingbroke who had a way of turning heads.

'He was interesting, distant – aloof, I think is the word?' She switched from French to English with ease, displaying only a hint of an accent. 'I had to pour much wine into him before he could be persuaded to speak to a girl of my age and standing. He was much more interested in the young men, most of whom he had tipped from their saddles with ease. But then that is the way of young men in their prime, is it not?'

As the rest of the guests formed little groups, one man lingered alone near the door. She followed Argyle's gaze and sighed. 'My brother Jacques. He serves my sister but believes himself destined to be my protector although I do not need one.'

At her mention, Jacques came closer. His brown eyes shone with a strange possessive glitter, his mouth set hard against the constant movement of his face. If it had been still, he might have be handsome, instead, the twitching marred his features. 'Why do you speak to this vermin?'

'Sir Argyle is Lord Mowbray's brother.' The silver woman let out a peal of laughter at her brother's pinched expression. 'Him you never met, though he was formidable in his own way. Though if I am to be honest you are much more to my liking than your dark, distanced brother.' She turned her attention back to Argyle and everything faded but her presence. 'I hear that you have been entertaining my sister, much to Jacques' dislike. I see why she favours you to a hunt with the King.'

She flicked her wrist. 'Some wine.'

Jacques went about fulfilling his sister's command and she linked her arm with Argyle's. 'He is my half-brother – of sorts.' A grudge clung to her admission 'Ah, what strange things the pleasures of the flesh will lead some men to do. While others are driven by loyalty or personal debt. And some again by unearthing secrets.'

'You were telling me about your meeting with Thomas?' He was confused by her flittering comments, the strange undercurrent of her voice.

'He was strangely alluring to a girl who was not yet a woman.' Her words flowed as honey. 'So are you, though I cannot believe how different you are to him. Is it true that you are here to secure some documents?'

'Yes.' As her sister, she had the gift of getting Argyle to drop his guard. 'How do you know, my Lady?'

She accepted a glass of wine from her brother then sent him off with a curt nod. He slinked back into his dark corner. 'Someone has been telling you that my sister and I are at odds, I can tell. Do not believe every whisper that reaches your ear. We stay in touch. It is she who told me that a man bearing your brother's coat of arms came to court and was turned away by the King's secretary. Such a tiresome little man.'

King Charles' secretary, Salmon, was cautious to a fault as no doubt he had to be as the servant of an erratic ruler. The longer Argyle spent at court, the more he noticed how everyone tiptoed around their King careful not to tip his delicate balance. Once or twice, he had heard servants whisper about his nightly terrors, but in the light of day, he showed no sign of the malady he was rumoured to suffer.

'Have you seen the documents?'

'Did your sister ask you to ask me?' Argyle probed.

'Non.' She flashed a set of perfect, white teeth. 'I never take orders. Not from her. If Charles has the documents now then someone else must have seen your brother's servant. It has the Queen's mark all over it. My sister agrees.

We must recover the documents before Charles decides to use them. Whatever they contain, which I have not been able to discover. I cannot even get him to admit that he has read them.'

Although he knew in what capacity Madame's sister served it was jarring to witness her intimate mention of the King. Best to be careful in her company. 'If Thomas did send a servant here, surely he was meaning for his Majesty to have whatever the man brought. It is out of our hands, my Lady.'

'If you insist.' She swept a shallow curtsey. 'I am Eloise la Furniér. Younger sister to the fabled Madame, which you have already gathered. If she has not yet told you, her name is Maud. I am at your service.'

Argyle felt her eyes caress his face. 'Are you?'

Eloise tipped her head. 'Though my sister enjoys keeping her secrets, she is, in part, responsible for my close affiliation to Charles. She must have told you that I tend to his needs, such as they may be.'

'She did, my Lady.' Argyle clutched his cup. Since learning Isobel's secret, he had forsaken temptation, now it reared its head.

'Dis she detail the *nature* of my services?' Her eyes narrowed. 'While she is handed delicate diplomatic assignments meant to keep the peace in court and country, I am handed delicious titbits on silken cushions.'

Politics take many forms, as my brother would attest to, Argyle thought. Perhaps that was why she had been attracted to Thomas, it was too far a stretch to imagine his brother making a connection that would not work in his favour.

Jacques prowled closer, his face contorting.

'I look forward to seeing you again, Sire.' Eloise held out

her hand, and Jacques grabbed it clearly eager to drag her away, but she was not to be forced. 'After all, it is so rare we are treated to novelty. Perhaps we might share tales about family-life when next we meet.'

'Family-life, my Lady?'

'You are married, I believe?' She ignored Jacques' twitching features. 'Yet at the mere mention of marriage, you seem in pain I have always found life to be too short for misery and regrets.'

'I should rather discuss the matter of my brother's documents.'

'It would not do to hand over secrets of such magnitude to an Englishman.' Jacques gave a wolfish smile and Eloise put her hand on his. 'Imagine what he might do with them.'

'That is why Charles has left you with Maud,' Eloise sneered her sister's name. 'To ensure no more is divulged than is required.'

Argyle offered a half-smile, clearly the Furniér family knew about the content of Thomas' documents. Now, to discover a way for them to divulge their information. 'You have roused my interest.'

'As well I might. More things tie your brother to you than blood. Secrets lurk below the surface that might alter history.' She nodded to Jacques. 'We must go – I am expected.'

They made their way through the crowd and Argyle noticed Madame – Maud – hover near the door that led to the King's chambers. In the candlelight, it was impossible to make out her expression.

Secrets and shadows, Argyle thought, I have had enough of both.

Windham sidled up next to him. 'She's a treat.'

'How did you come to be here?'

'There're two hundred people here every night, d'you think one more makes a difference?' He let his gaze wander. 'I've never been to the English court, but if it's anything like this I think you're a fool for ever leaving.'

Argyle sighed. 'It is very much as this. Tapestries, candles, gemstones, luxurious fabrics and plenty of whispers.'

'You don't care for whispers, I know.' Windham flashed a smile. 'And yet, I've got a whisper you'll want to hear.'

'Not now and certainly not here. I think we can make ourselves…'

The Queen cut through the crowd and Argyle bowed low before her. 'Sire. Come see me on the morrow.'

She did not wait for an answer. He watched her go and drew Windham into the shadows where it was easy to escape prying eyes. They soon found a door leading into a walled garden and searched it.

'We're the only ones mad enough to be out in this weather.' Windham's words came out in white puffs. 'But you're right, better here than in there.'

'How did you come to attend tonight?'

'Made me some friends.' He shivered. 'I've got naught to do except wait so I've been a *good dog* and sniffed around where you don't go. This time, you didn't even need to ask.'

'You have been flirting in the kitchens.'

'And the dairy, the stables…' Windham's soft laugh rolled over the barren walls. 'It's something to do when it's dark and cold outside.'

'And there you are privy to whispers?'

Rubbing his hands, he looked about before he spoke. 'It's as if servants are invisible. That's how secrets get told far and wide. Not because of some nobleman's indiscretions in a drunken stupor, but because he can't keep his gob shut around his servants.'

'Everyone is for sale?'

'Those not born to riches are.' There was no apology. 'Your brother dealt in secrets and had spies everywhere. You told me that yourself. If you want information you don't go to the courtiers you go to their servants. There'll always be someone who's an axe to grind.'

Argyle nodded. 'Whose axe did you grind?'

'The Queen's got nice girls in her service,' Windham said with a satisfied smile. 'Though she's not nice to all of them. As I've heard, she only has love for a little white-haired freak.'

Odele. The nip of frost stole into Argyle's bones. 'It is cold out here. Can we get to the point?'

'Some say it's because she's the Queen's little bastard by some nobleman or other. That she keeps the girl around all the time to taunt the King. He's got his own bastards, of course, although that's no excuse.'

'The Queen tells another story.'

In an effort to keep warm, Windham paced the garden, frozen gravel crunching under his heels. 'Wouldn't you?'

'This is the secret you have for me?' Argyle hid his hands in his silk sleeves. 'I will not freeze to death for frivolous gossip.'

'You've been too reliant on women,' Windham said with a shrug. 'Maybe you should look for truth somewhere else.'

'The secret?'

'That knight who raised you.'

'La Fontaine.'

Windham nodded. 'Him. He's got family right here at court.'

Argyle shook his head. 'He had no family, he was the last of his line. He made me his heir for the same reason. There was no one to inherit.'

'It's a couple of girls. About your age.' Windham gave the golden windows a longing glance. 'You've been talking to one of them tonight.'

'Eloise?'

'Don't know her name only that she's got fiery red hair.' Windham's piercing look was as cold as the night. 'The girl I've been talking to don't know how they're related, but when news of his death reached them it's said they were devastated. Left court and even the King had to part with more gifts than he wanted to get them back. Now, one of them wants revenge.'

'Only one of them?' Argyle was still processing the idea that La Fontaine was a father. What of the woman he had the children with? He was an honourable man why had he not married her? No, Windham must have been mistaken, fed a lie.

'Can't tell you which one. It seems they're so alike that some of the servants don't know them apart. Except that one shares the King's sheets and the other doesn't.' Windham resumed his pacing. 'It's just… if they're planning revenge maybe they know something about your brother. About what you're looking for.'

'Lady Eloise did mention meeting my brother many years ago.'

'Then she'd be the one to ask don't you think?'

Argyle could not feel his fingers anymore. 'I am not sure. There is something about her…'

'You don't trust her?'

'I do not know her.' He tried to hide his concern. 'She promised to tell me more when next we meet.'

'Best you make that soon.' Windham stomped his feet. 'God's blood, it's cold.'

'Next time, tell me your secrets under the hot summer sun and I will happily discuss them with you until the early hours of the day.'

Windham harked a laugh. 'We'd better be home by then. And I'll have no need for secrets and friends in kitchens.'

'I hope not.'

'I'll be well and truly surprised if my family's suddenly got kitchen maids and cooks.' Windham jerked his head towards a door at the far side of the walled yard. 'Coming?'

Argyle looked at the great hall's golden windows. 'Why not? No one will miss me.'

'So long's you remember to visit the Queen tomorrow. I hear she's taken with you,' Windham said and pulled the door open. 'You've got things to brood over. I've got a maid to thank.'

Argyle squeezed his shoulder. 'Leave a girl or two for someone else.'

'I'll try. It's not my fault if they like my accent…'

Watching Windham disappear into the darkness of a narrow hallway, Argyle warmed his hands in his armpits. The cold had seeped into the pit of his stomach where it nestled, brewing concern.

If Eloise was somehow related to La Fontaine perhaps that was the secret she hinted at, but then she too had known Thomas. She was the second person to link two sworn enemies together.

Argyle did not like it.

CHAPTER 75

3 December 1400 – Hôtel Saint-Pol

The crowd parted before the Queen walking slowly as was her fashion. In the privacy of her own chambers Odele never left her side, but when the Queen moved about the castle she was surrounded by her young, beautiful ladies, no white-haired child in sight.

Today, a couple of young girls bobbed in her wake dressed in deep blue and with little coronets adorning their dark brown hair they looked the spitting image of their mother. Isabella's younger sisters. They looked as she did when he had first met her. It felt a lifetime ago.

'Sir Argyle.'

He swept a bow and the girls mimicked their mother's courteous nod. '*Mes filles, Jeanne et Marie.*'

The girls held out tiny, dainty hands and Argyle took one

at a time and bowed his head. 'I am honoured to meet you, Princesses.'

When he straightened, merriment played in the eyes of the Queen's ladies spaced out around the room.

'You may be excused. Go and see your father and then your tutors await.' She watched them go, three ladies to each little girl. 'They grow up so fast.'

'I sometimes wonder if my boys will know me when I return, Majesty,' Argyle said. 'Perhaps my first-born will, but my second son was in swaddling when I left. I am a stranger to him.'

'Children forget their parents, Sire, even if they did know you when they were young.' Satisfied sadness rode on her words. 'It is the way of life. I hardly remember my mother and my father is but a portrait on my wall. The future is for our children, they should not dwell in the past.'

She held out her hand and he offered his arm to her. Together, they resumed her slow procession. 'We are expecting the Dauphin to come to court for Christmas. And the Lady Margaret of Burgundy, whom he is to marry when they are of an appropriate age.'

'A blessing to be surrounded by your children, Majesty.' Argyle tried to conjure up images of his sons, although only Ned's golden curls lingered in his mind's eye.

'I am afraid you will still be here by then, Sire. So you can see for yourself all of my children. If I had my way they would never leave me.' The doors at the end of the great hall opened for the Queen and she glided through into a wide gallery. 'You may have heard of my husband's failed dealings with King Henry?'

Her voice was pleasant and low, even if her tone dripped disdain. 'A member of our embassy died. Died. And Jean de Hangest was of no use at all. How could he leave our money for a handshake. He has no proof that our Isabella will ever be returned.'

In front of them, the doors to the Queen's apartments opened, a warm embrace awaiting the return of its mistress. 'We shall proceed alone.'

She did not look back, but Argyle could hear rustling stop and a few murmurs. He had been long enough at court to forget how many courtiers and ladies trailed behind the only people who mattered. The richest men and women in the country, and the royal couple.

'King Henry will honour his commitment, Majesty.' He felt strange to champion his King. 'I have no doubt.'

'I know him too, Sire,' she said as the doors closed behind them. She let Argyle lead her to a chair before a great, roaring fire. 'You are relying on his nature, his inherent integrity.'

'And his political understanding.' He watched the Queen tuck an extra blanket around her legs. Although the palace was new, its vast rooms were difficult to keep warm. 'He knows that to keep the Princess much longer will be seen as a provocation, an act of war. I have no doubt that Monsieur Hangest conveyed his Majesty's intentions…'

She held up a hand. 'I doubt it. Hangest tells a good tale, Sire, but he was taken with Henry when he was here in exile. The two often spoke in private. Place a crown on Henry's brow and Hangest was bound to fawn over his friend. I told my husband that we should have chosen someone else, but he believed their intimacy would play in our favour. Now, we know he was wrong.'

Although she was displeased with King Charles' diplomatic choices it seemed she did not blame him. 'I have convinced his Majesty that other measures should be taken. We have written to reaffirm our agreement with King

Henry. This is his final opportunity to please us.'

Argyle moved a little closer to the fire. 'Then what happens, Majesty?'

The Queen's smile engulfed the room. 'Then we send Madame – and you.'

'With a threat that France will take up arms against England if the Dowager Queen is not returned?'

'That too.' She turned her smile to the creak of a door. 'There you are my darling. What have you been up to? Nothing mischievous, I hope?'

Odele ran towards the Queen and then stopped, turning her big pale eyes at Argyle. He gave a trying smile but the child was pinned to the floor.

'She struggles to remember people that are not here every day. My husband terrifies her although she has lived with me since she was a little girl.' The Queen held out her hand and Odele took a trying step towards it. 'Come child, it is Sir Argyle. You have met him before.'

He bowed to the girl, the white-haired freak they called her in the kitchens. Argyle wondered if they knew how silent she moved or how much she understood. In her eyes, he saw keen cunning and intelligence. Never underestimate a servant, Windham had said and, in this case, those were wise words to heed. Odele was much more clever than anyone knew, save perhaps the Queen.

The girl finally relented and ran into the awaiting embrace. She looked up, her pale eyes whisking over the Queen's face, her lips forming mute words. Queen Isabeau smiled.

'No, no, my dear, you are quite safe. It was just a piece of ribbon.' She cradled Odele's face in her hands. 'I shall explain to Madame.'

The girl struck her little fist into her palm. Then she drew lines in the air, her face alight with contempt. The Queen glanced at Argyle and gave a single, minute shake of her head. Odele's arms fell to her side, tears in her eyes.

'Later. Run along now and make something pretty with your ribbon.'

The smile on the Queen's face as Odele danced from the room almost made Argyle believe the rumours Windham had mentioned last night. Perhaps this was a child born from illicit love.

'When the time comes I shall put into Madame's hands something that I am most unhappy to surrender,' she said to the flames in the hearth. 'But it must be done.'

Argyle felt the weight of her words and knew better than to ask what she was implying. Instead, he pursued another avenue. 'Have you decided how long to give King Henry to reply, Majesty?'

'Until February. Then we will unleash upon his head such torment as will break his determination and curse his life.' The Queen looked up with eyes that had consumed the fire before her. 'At your hand, he will be undone.'

CHAPTER 76

23 January 1401 – Hôtel Barbette, Paris

'Did you enjoy Christmas at court, Sire?'

'Much to my surprise, I did.' Argyle tipped his cup to his copper-haired companion. He had missed her immensely, and yet, now that she was here he wanted her gone. 'I met the Dauphin, a strapping boy.'

'He carries a heavy burden upon his little shoulders.' Eloise looked out over the crowd. 'I am certain the Queen would want him to stay longer, but Charles has little appetite for his offspring. I cannot blame him, children can be tiresome.'

'Is that so, my Lady?' The feast had been long and speaking French these many months had begun to set his teeth on edge. Even Eloise's easy company was unwelcome tonight. It showed and he did not care.

Jacques growled low and she threw him a sharp glare that made him cower. 'Go.'

They watched Jacques retreat to a corner, his face alive with spasms. Tonight, the Queen was hosting a grand feast at her own residence set aside from the main palace. The whole court had retired to her great hall where they jostled for space by the trestle tables. On the dais, the thrones stood empty.

'He is named after some tedious uncle on his mother's side, though he believes he should have been named for our father's nephew – Edmund.' She looked up at him with an amused smile apparently immune to his grim mood. 'Edmund la Fontaine.'

Argyle saw the reflection of his frozen expression in her deep green eyes. 'La Fontaine?'

'You are just like him.' She licked the rim of her glass. 'A great knight.'

'That he was.' Argyle forced his eyes from her face. 'Though I know little about his life beside that which I was part of.'

Eloise awarded him another glittering smile. 'Perhaps it is for the best. Should you be curious and must be satisfied I am certain we can come to some arrangement.' The musicians struck the first cord and Eloise nodded to someone across the room. 'Later.'

Argyle heard a shallow breathing to his right. Jacques looked after his sister. 'Busy, so busy.'

'Where is Madame?'

'With her family.' Jacques watched the dancers form a ring around Eloise's flaming presence. 'They are rarely here at the same time. Too much for the Queen, I am told. Though if she was as clever as they say she might favour Maud to Eloise.'

'Cut from the same cloth.' Argyle tried his best to be civil.

'Not even from the same roll, I should say. They may look alike, but all similarities end there.' Jacques sneered. 'Maud left it for me to advise you to stay well away from Eloise lest you forget that French hospitality comes at a heavy price. Our sister is watched wherever she goes it is best not to get caught in her wake.'

Watching the dance, Argyle wondered if Eloise's arrival was why the Queen had retired. A few days ago, Windham had come bearing a tray of leftovers from last night's feast and a serving of gossip. Queen Isabeau was said to be with child. The smile on Windham's face told Argyle that perhaps King Charles was displeased. He had been unwell for most of January, his groom sending away all visitors even the secretary Monsieur Salmon.

Instead, the Queen had presided over meals, feasts and parties. Perhaps that was why she had decided to take up residence at the Barbette palace. It would reward the King some peace and the Queen the opportunity of leaving when she wished. She was not a young woman anymore and if rumours were true, carrying a child might be proving added fatigue.

The music stopped and he applauded out of courtesy. He had not heard a single note. One of the doors to the great hall was open and he sighed a breath of relief. It was a short ride through Paris to return to his quarters in the royal palace. He would be there before midnight.

'Leaving so soon?' Eloise touched his arm. 'I had hoped you would lead me in a dance as you have led my sister. I hear you are a great dancer and I am tired of going to bed with aching toes because some old fool cannot keep up.'

Argyle had no desire for rivalry and shook his head. 'I

was hoping to slip away. The company…'

She gave a serious nod. 'Then I shall come with you. I find I grow weary of the company as well. Too many women.'

'Staring at you?' Argyle could not resist. 'Envying you? Cursing you?'

'They are all so terribly afraid that I will make off with their husbands,' Eloise said and looked at him. 'They do not understand that they can keep their little, tiresome, clammy-handed men to themselves. If you can call them men. Most of them wear more perfume than their ladies and take longer to dress. They are of no interest to me. They are not what I want.'

He let her take his arm. 'Is that so?'

She gave him a grave look. 'No more games. I am done with games.'

They brushed past Jacques, who was lurking in the shadows, spasms of anger and madness running across his face. It was haunting.

CHAPTER 77

23 January 1401 – Hôtel Saint Pol, Paris

The door to her apartment closed softly behind them, Eloise's hand still on his arm. Her fingers brushed his hand as she passed him and went to the window where a silver tray with glasses and a carafe stood, glinting in the warm light from the hearth.

At her invitation, he had left his horse in the Queen's small stable and joined Eloise in her carriage. They had trundled through Paris in silence, her head turned from him, her gaze fixed on the carved wooden panel of the door. Without uttering a word, she had led him down a narrow, outside gallery that stretched the length of the palace.

Now that they were inside, he took in her spacious chambers. The walls were lined with thick dark green fabric and otherwise unadorned and the furnishings were sparse.

A half-open door to the side revealed Eloise's innermost sanctum, her bedroom, and Argyle glimpsed an ornate bedpost and a carpet on the floor, a tell-tale sign of importance and wealth.

'I meant what I said.' Eloise gestured to a chair and turned to the silver tray. 'I want no more games. I am done playing. I want to be liberated. I want to be rid of secrets.'

'You think it wise to tell *me* your secrets?' Watching her pour wine, Argyle took off his jacket before he sat down by the fire. 'How do you know that you can trust me?'

'We go through life blind. We cannot trust our eyes. We can only trust our instincts.' She turned with a glass in each hand. 'We are the same, you and I. You wear your scars on your skin I wear mine on my soul.' Eloise gave him an appraising look. 'Though you wear some on your soul too, I should warrant.'

'Life leaves marks.' Argyle did not want to commit to anything. Her scars might be hidden, but warning signals shone bright in her eyes.

'Let me guess,' she said and handed him a glass. 'If I am right you will do something to please me. If I am wrong…'

Leaning back, he considered whether he might be able to divert her attention should she come too close to the mark. 'You said no more games.'

'All I ask is permission to pose a question.' Eloise's green gaze weighed him down. 'Not a cunning ploy to probe into your darkest secrets just a guess aimed at something much more benign. How can you refuse me?'

He turned the glass in his hand. If she were to ask questions best not to let her read his expression. 'Very well. The reward I cannot contest.'

When she did not pursue the matter, he glanced over and saw her let down her hair, coiled copper spilling down her back. Then she turned and stared into the darkness outside the window.

'I want to ask about your brother.'

'He is dead.' Argyle drank some of the wine and found it bitter. 'Thomas is not my favourite subject. Best leave it be.'

'You promised me a question and you do not know what I will ask.' She twisted her hair absentmindedly and kept looking out of the window. 'Therefore, I shall continue for you cannot change the premise of my request now. You have agreed.'

Argyle watched her hands twirl locks around and around the sight mesmerising. Rather than ask right away, Eloise took her time as if she was trying to decide how to proceed.

To win her prize, she means to ask in a way that will force me to lose, he mused. Gliding his eyes over her bodice, he wondered just what she meant by pleasure.

'Did you love him? Was he the kind of brother who inspired love?'

Thrown by her question, he leaned back in the chair. How often had he not asked himself that? Every time Thomas brought mischief and malice to Argyle's life, and even before then. His brother had been a constant force in his life, working to provoke, stir up trouble and complicate that which should have been uncomplicated.

She put a hand on his shoulder, her fingers resting on the scar beneath the cloth. His skin tingled, the sensation mingling with blooming, deep-rooted dread.

'Even in death, Thomas comes to haunt me.' Argyle did not know how to proceed. How had he felt when he learned about Thomas' death? When Margaret had asked the ultimate sacrifice Argyle had counted it the last wish of a concerned sister. He wanted Thomas laid to rest. He wanted to outlive the memory. Which seemed impossible.

'You win.' His hoarse whisper removed her hand. 'You win.'

'That is no answer.' Eloise turned watchful. 'It is a simple question.'

'And if I were to ask you the same? Do you love your sister? What would you say?'

Shaking her head, Eloise curled up in the chair opposite his and hugged herself, her glass of wine abandoned on a table beside her. 'I ask the questions.'

There you see love is never easy. It is messy, complicated and it leaves scars on the soul, he thought as he studied her. Whatever your secrets with your sister, I do not want to know them. If you know how I feel, the only reason you are asking is because you were tasked to. Someone else wants to know how far I would go for Thomas.

Sighing, he wished she had asked how far he would go for Margaret, for Princess Isabella – for his boys.

'Yes, you do ask the questions. And since I cannot provide a suitable answer, I have lost. Is that not so?' Irritation pushed aside anxiety. 'Now claim your prize. What will you have me do?'

Eloise held her breath for a moment and then picked up her glass. 'I will claim my reward some other time. You are right, even asking questions is a game. I find I grow weary of it now.'

Argyle got up and went to the table by the window where the silver tray now plunged in shadow looked dull and dead. He poured wine into his glass and turned around. 'I saw where they make these. In Venice.'

She stayed by the fire, a pale shadow against the orange glow. 'What was it like?'

'Murky.' He emptied the glass. 'I have been awarded

much time to wonder how such a place can produce something as clear as this. So simple and beautiful – and transparent.'

Through the glass, he watched Eloise raise her own glass and look at it in wonder. 'It was a gift. I never truly appreciated it until just now.'

He rested on the windowsill and looked out into the night, specks of light illuminated the walls of the enclosed garden below, barren branches reaching towards the night sky.

Eloise slipped past the table and sat down next to him. In different circumstances her proximity could have been enticing. 'Do you ever wonder what life wants from us? What sacrifice are we sent here to make? I have asked God, but he is silent on the subject.'

A strange desire to renounce God surged and he forced it down. 'I have gone through Hell to get here, to find out what really happened to Thomas. I have to know. If that is what life wants from me, so be it. Though for my part it is down to my own cursed curiosity.'

'I suppose you have earned the truth.' She traced a finger along one of the windowpanes. 'God knows I do not want to bear the burden anymore. You have no idea what…'

A pummelling on the door interrupted her. 'Yes?'

Jacques stuck his head through the opening, spasms contorting his face. 'He is coming.'

'You have to leave. Jacques, take him by the back passage.' A hint of regret and apology rode on her clipped commands. 'Trust him.'

Although he had no intention of ever trusting Eloise's half-brother, hurried footsteps outside her door left no time to argue. She dropped one glass into a wicker basket next to her bed and threw a sheet on top of it. Argyle tensed in

Jacques' violent grip and was pulled through a narrow door into a pitch-black passageway.

'Quiet,' Jacques hissed.

Argyle felt around in the dark and touched a raw wall. Leaning against it, he felt the cold seep through his shirt. Jacques thrust something in his direction.

'You forgot this.' In the dark, Jacques' hoarse voice mirrored his always-moving features. 'She is a fool.'

Gripping his jacket tight, Argyle cursed himself. 'Why?'

Jacques' hand shot through the dark and grasped Argyle by the neck. 'If only she did not bring mongrels to her rooms perhaps I would not always have to duck out of sight. Perhaps we would avoid trouble.'

'Who was coming to see her?' He croaked and Jacques released some of his pressure.

'Who do you think?' He moved as a cat in the gloom, dragging Argyle along. Clearly, he had taken this hidden path many times before.

When his knee hit what sounded like a barrel, he swallowed a groan and asked, 'Where are we?'

'In a place no one knows about – and you will keep it that way if you value your life.' Jacques had an eerily commanding presence in the dark. 'She told you?'

'About what?' Having a longwinded conversation with a madman had to be avoided. Unlike Argyle, Jacques was no doubt armed.

'About what we all have in common?' In the dark, Jacques' voice was almost palpable. 'You, me, her… and *him*.' His voice gave away his impatience.

Argyle could imagine the contorted face, but before he could ask what Jacques was talking about, he stopped Argyle with a hard hand on his chest.

'Wait here.' His footsteps disappeared with alarming

speed. Soon, the quiet darkness began worming its way into Argyle's mind and body. It snaked around his neck, slid into his mouth, drowning him.

Just when his panic was about to win, a flickering light bobbed its way towards him. Although the flame was weak it hurt his eyes and he turned away.

'Sire?' Windham's sleep-puffed face floated above the faint yellow globe. 'I was told to find you here?'

Cursing Jacques for leaving him, he ignored Windham's curious expression. 'You know how to get back to our rooms?'

Windham's detached head nodded above the flickering flame. 'This way.' He paused. 'Some stranger came to fetch me. I know I've seen him around court, lurking. Who's he?'

Shaking his head, Argyle stared at the floor, following Windham in a silence that was both comfortable and painful.

Eventually, he pushed open a thick oak door and they spilled into a brightly lit room that was foreign to Argyle. He blinked against the onslaught of light.

'His name is Jacques and I am fairly certain he is my gaoler. Though Madame never said as much I suppose she deemed it unnecessary'.

And no matter how hard I press the matter, Eloise will never admit it, Argyle thought. But if I play my hand right, she might just tell me the secret for which I came.

ꙮ ꙮ ꙮ ꙮ

CHAPTER 78

26 March 1401 – Château Gaillard, Rouen

'You say we're free and yet, we can't leave. That's not much in the way of freedom.' Windham kicked the fence. 'It's maddening.'

'I thought you were making friends.' Argyle was tired from another sleepless night. If only the reason was a pleasurable woman and not a pack of ghosts. 'At least we are moving, we are going somewhere.'

Windham looked into the enclosure where Argyle's silver gelding was making friends of his own.

What a pity he cannot sire foals, Argyle thought, I would have made a fortune these past months.

Now, Argent careered round the field chasing three mares. Argyle wondered if they knew that nothing would come from the advances.

Turning from the horses, Windham stared at the castle wall. 'We may be moving, but we're not going anywhere. I've a mind to speed up the process only that'll probably land me in new trouble.'

'You will be home soon.' Argyle heard the hollow of his words. 'Forcing the issue is certain to land you in trouble of which I believed you had had enough. I know I have said so far too many times, but I do believe you will be free to go before long.'

'When you go to fetch the Dowager Queen – or is she Princess once more?'

'The only reason we are still here is because of the weather.' Argyle was losing his already threadbare patience. 'You of all people know how treacherous the waters are in the winter. And since you have little love for the sea, I should have thought you would appreciate our hosts' concerns that we get a smooth passage.'

'It's winter no more. In Calais, they would've resumed the regular crossings back in February. You're right, I have no love for the sea and yet, I find I'm full well ready to step foot on a boat.' Gazing north over the vast forest, he sighed. 'I'm tired of waiting.'

So am I, Argyle thought and put a hand on Windham's shoulder. 'You had something to tell me?'

'Show you.' He fumbled for something inside his cloak. 'I'm sure someone's been in my rooms.'

'We are at court, there are spies everywhere. Hell, you spy for me in the kitchens.' Argyle reached for the leather pouch. 'When?'

'Regularly.' Leaning on the fencing, Windham lowered his voice. 'Too regularly.'

Untying the leather strap, Argyle noticed the stamp on the front of the pouch. 'How long have you had this?'

His face hardened. 'Since Venice. It's leverage, she said.'

'Who gave it to you?'

'A servant girl.'

'Who?'

Rather than rise to the challenge, Windham turned and pointed to nothing in particular. 'We're being watched. That wretched Madame of yours.'

'She is hardly mine.'

'Not how it sounds in the kitchens, where, as you say, I spend much of my time,' Windham said and then laughed loudly, nudging Argyle to join in. 'Don't read it here. Wait 'til you're in your rooms. It'll keep. And don't worry, I didn't peek.'

Tucking the pouch inside his cloak he smiled for show. Irritation mingled with worry that Windham was not as trustworthy as he had hoped. 'Why have you not given it to me sooner?'

'I've not had the chance. You're always in the company of someone, they keep you busy, they feed you whatever information they see fit…' Windham winced as Argyle squeezed his weakened arm, a smile fixed in place. 'I'm just saying you'd best be on guard. They'll be asking something that you don't want to give – they always do.'

'Suddenly you are an expert in courtly business.'

'They think I'm your servant. Your man. Isn't that what you tell them?' Windham dislodged. 'You're brought up in this mess, but I'm the one swimming in the sewer.'

'I have never called you my man, though I admit I have never denied it either. If it keeps you safe, I would vow you are the Pope in disguise. And what does it matter? I would rather know what gets said in your sewer.'

With a genuine smile, Windham relented. 'They're planning to squeeze King Henry until he surrenders the

Princess. Before you ask, I don't know how. That's a part no one seems to know, at least in my world, which is strange, because if there's anything rich people like to dwell on in front of their servants it's how they can make others dance to their tune.' He began walking along the fence, one hand on the wood worn smooth by hundreds of hands before his. 'From what I've heard, you'll be part of the exchange if need be. What do you know that King Henry'll pay for with a French Princess?'

'Nothing that I know of, but who can tell when it comes to Kings?' As long as Argyle could ensure that Windham was released once they reached England he would be satisfied. It was time to part ways before another was caught in the net. Stephen had survived many years ago, but only just. Windham was tough, but every man could break. 'Have you been able to send word to your family?'

'Chose not to.' Windham sniffed at Argyle's look. 'It's better they don't know, just in case. And then they can scold me in person when I pop up one day. I like to keep it light, as you know.'

Despite their dire situation, he laughed for the first time that week. 'Yes, you do. And fear not, your wait is almost up. We ride tomorrow for the port of Barfleur.'

'What waits on the other side? What'll happen once we're back in England?'

'Your guess is as good as mine.' He ran a hand through his hair. While in Paris, he had gone to get it cut and now, it was growing unruly, curling around his ears. 'All I know is that you will get to go home. Take comfort in that.'

They made their way back towards the castle in silence, Argyle wondering what he might find inside the leather pouch. It weighed in his pocket and on his mind. Windham seemed satisfied to be exempt from speaking and paused only long enough to nod his head before turning to the stables.

Argyle watched Argent career towards the gate in pursuit of Windham. The short time in the saddle from Paris had been such solace, and his heart ached for a brisk ride. But the French guard would never let him out of their sight.

'Sir Argyle.' Maud emerged from the stable, her skirts dotted with mud and her short cape moist. 'You should have come out with me.'

'Extend an invitation and I shall.'

She laughed, the sound as soft as silk. 'Then I invite you to ride with me tomorrow on a long journey. What say you?'

'I accept, Madame.' Argyle looked for Jacques who was strangely absent. 'How many are going?'

'We shall be a small party. Twenty-five I believe.' She pulled off her gloves and handed them to a servant. 'Off with you. There is much to pack and I need you to survey the process.'

She watched her servant dash off without a backwards glance. Unlike most other noblewomen, she enjoyed many freedoms such as being quite alone with a man. 'We have precious little time to ourselves, do we not, Sire, we who are somehow of interest to the Crown.'

'We do,' Argyle said and let himself enjoy her light touch.

It had taken some time for him to riddle out who was the eldest, but in the end Eloise had told him and now, it was so very obvious. Maud shared traits with Margaret that were undeniable. Such as having affable manners when she chose.

'Do you know how long it will be before we reach England?'

'Though we sail from Barfleur I do not believe we shall land at Lyme.' She shook her head at Argyle's questioning glance. 'Charles has his own ideas.'

'Does Queen Isabeau know?'

'You tell me. She has grown quite fond of your company, I hear.'

He did not like the teasing edge to her words. 'We have spoken a few times.'

'Which is more than any other these past months.'

'Save King Charles.'

'Save the King, yes.' Maud paused to scrape mud off her boots with a stick. 'They are thick as thieves these days. It has been years since the Queen has travelled in the royal train, and now, here she is. I should like to believe they are reconciled, but I believe she is here for a different reason – one to which I am not privy.'

'Perhaps she too grew restless. The winter has been long at court.'

'Charles leaves us little to do.' She rested her hands on the fence where, not long ago, Argyle stood with Windham. 'He likes to have everyone close at all times and he is not happy that he has to part with anyone to go fetch Isabella, though she is dear to him.'

'To her mother too.'

'If you say so.' It was no secret that the la Furniér sisters considered Queen Isabeau a lacking parent at best. 'I have not come here to argue about those well above us. I have come to present a gift.'

'Will I like it?'

At her harsh glance, Argyle smiled and she seemed mollified. 'Perhaps. For what it is worth at least you shall find comfort in it. Of that much I am certain.'

'Then by all means do not keep me in suspense a moment longer, Madame.'

'Once we have dealt with King Henry – and secured the return of Isabella – you are free to return to your family.' For the first time since Argyle had arrived at the French court, someone voiced what had never been openly stipulated. That he was a prisoner.

She smoothed her skirt. 'No one expects you to return with us and nor that you keep faith with Charles once the deed is done. Your future lies in England. Surely on that we can agree?'

'That is good news, thank you.' Argyle was numb. He longed for England, for his boys if not his home. He had no place in his household, it was ruled by a stranger, an enemy. The future Isobel offered was just another kind of prison.

'I thought you would like to hear it now, so that you might exert yourself once we come face to face with King Henry.' Madame smiled, her green eyes twinkling. 'Sometimes it is better to offer great gifts than great threats if you want to succeed.'

'Allow me to walk you back to the castle, Madame,' Argyle said skirting her final comment. It felt as if he knew a secret about her that might corrupt their relationship, which made him hesitate to call her by her name.

'At least twelve days on the road lie ahead of us, Sire. It will be a while before you are truly free, but the prospect might make the ride more comfortable.' She accepted his arm and squeezed it for just a flash. 'I managed to persuade Charles that I do not need a carriage or we would have added weeks to our journey.'

'I have seen you in the saddle,' Argyle said with true admiration. 'Why would the King suggest you ride in a carriage?'

'He does not believe women should ride horses for such a distance.' She shook her red hair. 'We all know that it is he who cannot ride for long. When we move on, the court will return to Paris – to a place he knows well.'

Argyle watched as Jacques hovered near the main gate. 'Your brother is coming with us?'

'Of course.' Maud glanced at him. 'Jacques is desperate for an adventure. No one would be able to persuade him to stay put once we get to Barfleur and I see no reason why he should not join us. He has his uses, despite what others might think.'

'I hope he is not disappointed. Politics and negotiations are hardly grounds for a great adventure.'

The smile she wore held a hint of sadness. 'He is about to rescue a princess from an evil king. He believes he shall return a legend.'

'You have not told him that even if King Henry agrees we cannot expect Princess Isabella to come directly?'

'You try. Jacques has long since stopped listening to me.'

No, Argyle thought as she dislodged and went to her brother, her hands outstretched, for he is as mad as he appears sane.

The constant spasms of Jacques' face revealed the beast within. Why would King Charles send a madman to negotiate with a King? Unless he was there for another purpose, much as she had implied.

As soon as they vanished into the castle, Argyle turned right and found his own, modest rooms. The interior was comfortable and the view spectacular, but he would be glad to leave. Madame's promise of freedom left a jumble of overwhelming emotions. Unless they were successful, freedom was a dreamscape if not a pleasant one.

Windham's parcel tumbled onto the floor when Argyle threw his cloak on the chest, the lid standing upright at the end of his bed. He had little enough possessions and most of them were already packed, though not quite in the order he left it. It reminded him of Windham's concern that his rooms were regularly checked when he was out. Argyle picked up the pouch.

Might as well look inside, to pass time, he decided and brought the small bag to the window. The light was fading fast as the sun crept around the castle before it nestled in the forest for the night. He lit a tallow candle, the smell rancid and the smoke black against the golden windowpanes.

The first letter he pulled out was a brief note sent by messenger from Thomas to the Doge of Venice. Proof that they were better acquainted than the Dogaressa and Nicoló would admit. Argyle had suspected as much. The broken seal sported the Mowbray crest, but it was not Thomas' writing, he would recognise that spidery scrawl anywhere. Then again, his brother had scribes as all noblemen did.

Tedious content until the last sentence, which conveyed that Thomas would soon leave England and that he was eager to find welcome in Venice. Below it, in writing that had faded to a light grey was a note: *Not the Lord.*

Argyle pulled out the next piece of parchment.

We shall come for you.

He put down the note and tapped the window to lure in an early swallow, which swooped at the last moment and soared into the dwindling light.

Was this why the Doge had stalled his return while Argyle had visited? Or was the reason quite another and completely unrelated to Thomas? If that was the case why send an embassy that just happened to pass Vichy when Argyle and Windham was in the area? It seemed too much of a coincidence.

He scratched his neck looking at the message. Thomas and the Doge seemed to know each other well enough for him to offer safe passage by way of an escort. If they were on intimate terms, would not the Doge be discerning enough to know that Thomas did not write the message – as well the note indicated.

– *Not the Lord* –

Biting the inside of his cheek, Argyle stuck his hand into the pouch and cursed. Something sharp lurked in the dark leather bowels. He upended the pouch and a handful of paper scraps and longer missives tumbled out along with a pin, one end studded with small garnets the other as sharp as a needle. He picked it up and turned it. Most of the garnets were dull, but one shone brightly in the fading daylight.

Gold and red. The Doge's colours. A gift perhaps? Or a bribe?

Pinning the trinket to his collar he picked a random scrap of paper. He re-read it several times, the rush of blood rising to a throb in his ears. It was short and to the point.

– *The Lord is captured. Turn back* –

The longer letters contained a lengthy exchange about various political debates including something that gave Argyle as much pause as the short message had. They continuously referred to "the bastard" which Argyle initially dismissed, however, the more he read the more he realised that Thomas was referring to a someone at court who outranked even himself.

There were only a few men in England more powerful than Thomas had been. Barring de Vere, who had been exiled for years by the time these were dated, the only other men who fit the bill were of royal stock. And a man it most certainly was.

As the exchange was fragmented and several letters seemed to be missing, he struggled to make sense of it all. Lining them up did little to aid his progress. He pulled the candle closer, holding each missive to the flame lest he had overlooked something.

Suddenly, the pieces fell into place, interlocked and showed him the full, terrifying picture. Thomas' secrets sent to Paris, his communication with the Doge. It all fit. It all pointed to one man.

He now ruled England.

CHAPTER 79

22 April 1401 – Port of Barfleur, France

Argyle watched the sailors load their belongings onto the ship. It lay gently chopping on the crosswinds, the current dragging at the anchor chain. He remembered his very first sea voyage travelling into the unknown with a weight on his shoulders and enemies all around. It seemed to him that no matter when he boarded a ship it never boded well.

Windham sidled up beside him. They had spoken little since Rouen for the journey had been arduous and there had been few breaks. Now that their time together was almost at an end, Argyle admitted to himself that he would miss Windham's brazen manner. More than once, they had faced enemies together and had taken turns saving each other's lives. They both had the scars to prove it. Argyle hoped that Windham would return to his family and find that a quiet life was just as welcome as he had dreamed.

'Looks unsteady. It's hardly a vessel fit to convey such fine folk as them we're travelling with.' Windham's dislike of the sea seeped through his sullen comment.

'As soon as we clear the harbour it will change.'

'For the better?'

'We need the wind or we will be stuck on sea for a lot longer than any of us desire.' Argyle looked towards the docks where Jacques was instructing two ship boys who stared at his face with open fear. 'There is a man I would rather leave behind.'

Windham followed his gaze. 'He's necessary, isn't he? He'll be leverage to Madame's soft touch.'

'Madame insists – as does King Charles. Though if you were to ask me I would call him more trouble than help. And you are correct, he is most certainly equal to the task of levelling out Madame's political savvy.'

Argyle was certain that, to the English, Jacques would be about as welcome as a rabid dog in a kennel, but since King Charles would not listen, he had settled for keeping his distance. Maud would rein in Jacques if the need arose of that Argyle was certain.

Now, Jacques offered his arm to his sister and together they walked up the plank. Watching them go, Argyle wondered what they knew that he did not. Thomas' letter had spoken of leverage, but what did that mean? Was it as Argyle imagined? Or had he made a connection because he wanted to and would find himself woefully mistaken?

'You think him mad, don't you?'

'What?' Argyle looked at Windham.

'Jacques la Furniér. In the kitchens at court, they said only a lucky few'd ever seen his face still. It's supposed to be quite a spectacular. More like an angel with its wings clipped than his usual, mad whirlpool.' Windham turned his back to the docks. 'It seems he enjoys some things as much as you and I if not more. When he's with a woman, any woman, he lets them see his true self.'

The idea of Jacques with a woman made Argyle's stomach churn. 'And what is that?'

'Don't know, none of the women I got with had ever dared approach him. It's something to do with his childhood, the twitching.' Scratching his cheek, Windham gave the ship another repulsed look. 'It's something to do with one of the sisters, though no one knows what.'

'Curious is it not.' Argyle watched as Argent was brought aboard. 'That no one knows anything about the Furniérs? Considering that the servants' quarters are riddled with gossip and rumours.'

'And truths.' Windham sighed as his brown mare walked up the plank, placid as ever. 'Maybe someone knows something but they won't say. It's as if there's some arrangement made, some deal struck with all the servants at the castle not to speak about the red women. Good or bad, nothing filters through. It's a mystery to me. Somehow, they've managed to be spared, protected…'

The last of the crates, barrels and animals were loaded, and Argyle readied himself. 'I would say it is because they are not interesting…'

'If that be the case, no one'd ever gossip about you.' Windham gave a weak laugh. 'And that's all they do.'

'When we were at court?'

'No. And that's when it was fun to speak of you.' His words carried odd concern. 'From the moment you met Madame no one breathed a word about you. It's like you simply ceased to exist. I'm still the only one who knows about…' Windham gestured. 'The sister.'

A call went up and Argyle led the way towards the ship. 'Perhaps, some day, I might learn the truth. Discover why the court never mentions the sisters. It seems odd to me, especially as any court loves to gossip about royal favourites – for better or for worse. Now is not the time.'

'You're free when we return, aren't you? They can't expect you to stay faithful once we're home. Why would you?'

'If I succeed, I am free. Whether or not I am faithful is beside the point. No doubt that is the true reason Jacques is coming with us, to keep me in line.' Argyle paused by a stack of barrels that afforded some shelter from prying eyes. 'When we land in England you and I go our separate ways. You are free to return home providing you honour your promise and keep to the story upon which we agreed.'

'That my contract was extended.' Windham nodded. 'I'd say I'm sorry for parting ways, but I'm not. It's been an adventure I wouldn't wish on anyone. Best forgotten for the most part, so I'm happy to keep my trap shut on the subject. Do you know where we'll land?'

'They will not tell me.'

At some point since leaving Paris, the French had decided it was too great a risk to tell him. Not even Madame had alluded to a destination. The lack of information had forced Argyle to make his own assumption.

He adjusted his heavy, travel-stained cloak. Although spring was in full bloom the sea cooled the air. 'The most common port to reach is Lyme Regis. If it were left up to me, I would dock in Portsmouth.'

'Why?'

'The English know we are coming.' Argyle pointed to the horizon. 'Would you welcome an enemy to an open road? Or a fortified castle?'

When the ship's keel tilted, Windham turned his gaze to the wooden dock. 'You think King Henry doesn't know you travel with the French?'

'Our King is no fool.' Argyle walked up the plank. Somewhere behind him, Windham groaned when the gangway shifted. It drowned out Argyle's comment.

'He knows I am coming.'

CHAPTER 80

2 May 1401 – Portchester Castle, Portsmouth, England

'A ghost returned from the dead.'

King Henry sat on his throne the room empty save from two guards at the door. 'I never believed I would clap eyes on your sorry face again, Sire, and I freely admit that I would have been better pleased if the rumours of your death were true. But then, I was bound to be disappointed. After all, you often enough proved to my cousin that it is impossible to be rid of you.'

The floor creaked when Argyle shifted. 'Yes, your Majesty.'

'And now that you are here you presume that I will simply give up Isabella because you ask it of me?'

'It is not I who ask, Majesty,' Argyle said still on bended

knee. It made his leg ache. 'It is King Charles of France.'

'It is his despicable witch of an envoy.' King Henry's temper was on the rise and Argyle once more wondered what Madame had said behind closed doors last night.

Their meeting had ended abruptly and she had swept past him with a triumphant smile on her face, Jacques prowling in her wake, face contorting. He had not seen them since as they were housed in the upper part of Portchester Castle's impressive sea tower while Argyle was taken to the old inner ward building where the floors creaked and the shutters did little to keep out the fresh breeze. The walls were stained from rain seeping in and the windowsill wore a thin coating of crystallised salt. Still, it had a bed with fresh linen and a roaring fire and for that he had been grateful.

The crossing had been uneventful if a little prolonged by a few days of quiet weather, but he and Windham had been crammed into a tiny cabin and the stench of sick had made it an arduous journey.

On the throne, King Henry tapped his fingers on the armrests. 'She comes spreading vicious lies. A French disease sent to cripple England and all who live here. Why do you insist on consorting with untrustworthy women, Sire? Are you truly that simple or do you stand to gain something from this alliance? My cousin always praised your honesty. I am prone to believe we were all deceived by you – that you have bested even your own brother in your scheming. Tell me, Sir Argyle, what do you think her poison words will achieve?'

'I am not privy to what she has told you. I can neither defend nor atone for her comments.' Despite the severity of his situation, Argyle could not suppress his own rising temper. 'As to my choice of women, you must rejoice in knowing that at least one, my own wife, serves only you.'

'Wine!'

One of the guards opened the door and barked an order. In the ensuing silence, Argyle dared to rise, rubbing his pained leg and easing the ties of his collar, which cut into his old wounds. King Henry did not move.

Finally, a servant slid into the room with a tray of wine and one cup. He quickly poured and handed the drink to the King before leaving. Argyle watched him drink deep and then turn the cup in his hand.

'You have me to thank for the warning,' Argyle said. 'I risked my life.'

'If you had never left …'

He pushed a hand through his hair. It still smelled of saltwater. 'If you had never detained the Dowager Queen, your Majesty.'

Above the rim of his cup, King Henry looked at Argyle, appraising him, considering his words. 'I shook hands with Monsieur Hangest. I would have returned to the matter sooner, except I have been preoccupied, as you must know.'

'The French did not see fit to provide news from home.' Though Argyle had thirsted for it, the only time he had any news was when Queen Isabeau had told him of King Henry's troubles from the north and the west. 'Part of my punishment no doubt.'

'Or to sway your loyalty to Charles' side.'

'They would have been better off telling me what was going on,' Argyle said and King Henry inclined his head. 'In telling me nothing, they starved me and I grew hungry for information.'

The King put aside his cup. 'How hungry?'

'Enough to read old documents. My brother's.' He watched for a sign that the King was somehow privy to the content. 'The papers contain something quite interesting.'

When King Henry pounded a fist onto the armrest, one of the guards at the door took a step forward and was checked by a glare. Instead, he rose and turned his back to the room. 'How did you come by such documents?'

'They fell into my hands, after a fashion.' That part still irked Argyle although he would not admit as much.

The King went to a window, leaning on the sill. The views beyond were of the sea, the French ships and, most likely, of his men standing guard only a few paces from the docks.

Yesterday, a contingent of soldiers had come out in force before anyone had stepped foot on English soil. Silently, they had watched as the French delegation disembarked and when Argyle had swung into the saddle, Jacques had sent the soldiers insolent glances, his face working. With Madame at their head, the procession had proceeded to the castle, English soldiers flanking the road all the way. When called upon, Madame had shown King Charles' seal and been admitted.

While Jacques, Argyle and the rest of the party had spent some hours in the sun waiting for the gates to open, Windham had trotted away his face still ashen from the sail. As he crested the first ridge, he had turned in the saddle and held a hand in the air before he disappeared into freedom.

Windham who had provided the papers. Since first reading them, Argyle had pressed the subject of how they had come into his possession, but he had been tight-lipped and dismissive. They had been delivered by a girl in Venice. After the struggle near Vichy and his injury, he had forgotten about them and only when they had packed for Rouen had he come across the pouch again.

A truthful story? Argyle could not tell, only that it had

never changed. Windham kept to the same tale and after a few more tries, Argyle yielded. He was satisfied that Windham had never read the contents, although last night he had wondered why Windham had never asked about anything. Now that he was gone, Argyle would never know.

'Well?'

Argyle blinked and King Henry gave him a piercing glance. 'I ask again, Sire, who is she?'

'Madame?' Argyle was at a loss. They had spoken for hours last night; how could he not know? 'She is Lady Maud de Furniér, a nobleman's daughter and the French King's close confidant and now his chosen emissary. I believe she is sent to handle the most delicate matters when others before her fail.'

'And you?'

'I am a prisoner. In these times, King Charles is unlikely to trust an Englishman. You cannot blame him for taking the opportunity to use my presence in Paris to send you a clear message. I may not have come in shackles, but make no mistake, I am by no means free.' Behind him, one of the guards cleared his throat and Argyle added. 'Your Majesty.'

'I would know the content of your documents.' King Henry turned to the view once more. 'We shall revisit the topic when the French harlot and her mad dog is gone.'

Argyle looked at the floor, swept clean and washed, the walls adorned with tapestries. If needs be, King Henry could dwell here watching for a French fleet to descend upon his shores. No doubt the soldiers they had seen yesterday were just a small part of a greater force camping out of view.

'The lady is not under my command.'

'You will know how to please her.' His comment was thick with disdain. 'You always know. I believe your brother considered it one of your greatest gifts. "My brother knows how to bend any woman to his will" Thomas would say, and we would all believe him. Was he mistaken?'

King Henry's imitation of Thomas was eerie and his comment made Argyle's neck burn. 'In this instance, yes, and he would be the first one to admit it if he were here to see me.'

The heartless laugh congested in the air. 'That is a turn. If you knew how many women have pleaded your case since you left you would understand why I am quick to believe what your brother boasted. Not just your wife, although as you may imagine, she was – and still is – livid. You left her alone and pregnant without a single word. Since then, I have on occasion written to ask if she had any news and have been met only with silence from Beauworth.'

Against the blue backdrop of the window, King Henry was a black shape. Only his rings glistened when he moved his hands. 'Your callous behaviour was a surprise. Even though she has disappointed you, I thought you would have more honour, more benevolence. The years have left you cruel and cold.'

As they have left you, Argyle thought and shook his head. 'I did it to keep my children safe.'

'If you believe I feel obliged to take care of my so-called cousin, you are mistaken. She might have swayed my father, after all he was feeble towards the end, but I am not so easily convinced. It is her word and the word of a castrate that puts her in my family. Unless I get evidence beyond doubt that she is who she claims to be, I shall continue to presume what I have always presumed. That she is ambitious and calculated. As are all your women.'

'Believe what you will, Majesty,' Argyle said and earned a cold glance. 'I heard her tale and have no reason to doubt her.'

King Henry stroked his pointed beard, it looked thin and straggled compared to King Charles' rich growth. 'Even though you know what it means if it is true?'

'Yes.'

'It is just as well that she only claims to be a bastard. If she had dared to reach higher I would have cut her down myself.' He left the window. 'As it stands, her blood is diluted and your children's claim is weak.'

Argyle watched King Henry pace the room. 'We make no claim. I want for them to live a quiet life away from court, your Majesty.'

'You always were a most unnatural Mowbray.' He paused and rubbed his arm. When a stray ray of light hit his face, it was patched in red scabs. 'Most unnatural. And what of your sister-in-law? Thomas' widow. She has been constant in her attentions.'

'She looks to further her children, for which you can hardly blame her.'

'She shares your brother's ambition. For a year, I have had monthly reports from her. Where you were, what you did – how you fared.' He stopped. The Lancaster crest set into the wall above crowned his bare head. 'When she was called to court, she was slow to produce evidence. From her I know only that you were in Boulogne and Paris, though other friends have reported seeing you in Calais and as far afield as Milan?'

The Donna's nosy maid. Argyle tipped his head. 'I wanted to visit Thomas' grave. Learning of his death was a shock to the family, to me.'

'He is not buried in Milan.'

'No, Majesty, Milan was merely on the way,' Argyle said with spite. 'He died from the pestilence and was buried in

Venice. Or so we were led to believe.'

Fleeting shock revealed an unpleasant truth. He was quick to recover. 'If that is what you have been told then surely it is so?'

'If that be the case, then he was buried in a pauper's grave.' Argyle remembered the priest. 'Which is odd because in Venice, they burn victims of the mortality.'

'Barbarians,' King Henry murmured. He looked ill at ease. 'Since I know not to underestimate you, I will ask this: Did you leave to seek out your brother's final resting place or did you leave to find out what had happened to him?'

'Both.'

I went to lay to rest the greatest ghost of them all, Argyle added in thought. A man your father loathed and more than half of the English Lords feared. I needed to get away to put La Fontaine out of my mind and yet, he returned in force when I reached Paris.

To learn he was the father of two girls had been a shock, more so because La Fontaine had never once mentioned their existence. How could a great knight ignore his own kin?

King Henry turned his signet ring, slowly and deliberately. 'Is that what brought you to Paris?'

'An Italian embassy brought me to Paris.' He saw no point in revealing in what state the embassy had found him or what had transpired before they had arrived. 'King Charles was gracious to welcome me.'

For the first time, the King almost smiled. 'Charles never does anything without a hidden agenda. What has he asked of you?'

'That I ensure the return of the Princess Isabella to France. As you no doubt discussed with Madame yesterday. King Charles and his Queen are eager to have their daughter home.' Argyle shifted his feet, his leg hurt. 'As eager as she is to leave, no doubt.'

'So you say, but what if she has changed her mind?' King Henry asked the question with a disturbing listlessness. 'It has been more than a year since you last saw her. She may have changed her mind.'

'Have you released her from her prison, your Grace?'

'She is not in prison.'

'She still lives with the Bishop?' A nod from King Henry confirmed Argyle's suspicion. 'You will no doubt find that she thinks of that arrangement as a prison. If she is still in his care she will not have changed her mind. She will want to return. England was disagreeable to her long before she was placed under his roof and she is unlikely to have changed her mind. Ever since she came here she has longed for France. What might sway her now?'

King Henry sat down, cloth-of-gold enveloping his dark garb. 'My son.'

If not for the severe situation, Argyle might have laughed. 'She desires to return to France, is that not so, Majesty? And you struck an accord with Monsieur Hangest in October of last year. You have your payment. What is the delay?'

For some reason, King Henry accepted Argyle's pounding questions. Any other time, he would never have dared to be this outspoken, but now that he knew for certain that Isobel and Elizabeth had sold him out he had little left to lose.

Rather than evade the questions, King Henry sighed. 'To govern a country is no mean feat, Sire. I have much on my mind and even more on my plate. Ensuring the return of a child to her parents was not as pressing as ensuring peace to the north – and the west.'

Queen Isabeau had it right, Argyle though and smothered a smile, how easily she had read the situation. He pushed his fingers into his belt. It was light without a blade. 'The lack of attention has brought an enemy to your shores, your Grace. You could have avoided it if you had paid heed to your accord with Hangest.'

'You threaten me with a French invasion? When just last night your Madame promised me it would not come to that.' King Henry pounded a fist on the armrest, the sound crisp and stark. This time, his guards stayed in place. 'Is this your role, Sire, to provoke while she honeys her words? To be a fierce warrior while she plays the frail damsel? Know this: I shall succumb to neither ruse. I shall return King Charles' daughter this year. If you force my hand I cannot answer for the consequences.'

'I know of your consequences. I felt them in Calais.' He was unable to rein in his tongue. 'Your men beat me to within an inch of death. If not for a fellow Englishman I would have been killed. As it were, we washed ashore in Boulogne while your foul creatures vanished. You threaten with consequences though you can bring nothing down upon my head that I have not already survived.'

In the trembling silence, King Henry sat frozen in place, gripping the armrests of his gilded throne. His face was hard and flickered with fury. Had it run wild with spasms he would have resembled Jacques.

He waited for the King to call his guards and order that Argyle be thrown in a cell no doubt already fitted out for him. Nothing happened. The sharp sea breeze sang through the open, cold hearths, accompanied by the scream of gulls outside the windows.

'What about your boys?'

The whisper crashed around Argyle. Paralyzed, he stared

at the King, his mind blank, a white backdrop devoid emotion, feeling, reaction. Then invisible shackles curled round his legs and arms, biting into his lungs and heart, relentless in their embrace. The world tilted.

'If you push me, I will take them from you.' King Henry leaned forward. His hands shook, but his expression was calm. 'Beware, Sire, that sometimes we must reach for means we do not wish to employ. Keep the mad French dog on a leash and I will negotiate with your *Madame*. We shall strike an accord. Until we do, you shall be locked in your rooms awaiting my judgement.'

Argyle left the room in a daze. His children. King Henry had not even bridled at the accusations that he was responsible for the attack in Calais, he had neither denied nor confirmed Argyle's insinuations. Had he seen fear or shock on the King's face? Was it not the same? In his current state, he did not know. He could not think.

Jacques dislodged from the shadows, a silent companion with a screaming face. Argyle could not look at him, could not leash the dog. He was left to pray that Maud would broker a deal that might keep his children safe.

He knew that if it came to it, she would not care what happened to them. She had one mission and she would sacrifice anything to succeed.

CHAPTER 81

3 May 1401 – Portchester Castle

Argyle lay awake, images racing through his mind of his little boys cowering in the Tower, Isobel powerless to help them. It chased sleep from him and for that he was grateful. His dreams would be even more haunting.

When Maud slipped in to his room he scarcely noticed. Leave it to her to find a way through a door locked by a King. She sat at the edge of his bed and reached out only her courage failed and instead, she put her hands in her lap.

'It is done.'

'What?' A night and a day of speaking to no one had turned his voice dry and brittle.

'She will return. Henry has relinquished his greatest prize.'

Argyle turned his head and looked at her. Could it be

true? 'When will she be set free? When can she return home?'

'Once he has defeated the Welsh princes.' Madame's dress rustled as she shifted. 'I have promised that France shall not attack England while he fights in Wales. Until he returns to London you are to go to the Princess and provide what solace you can.'

Go to Isabella? No, he had to go home. 'My children?'

Rising, Maud looked down at him, in the dark her green eyes were reduced to dark circles in her pale face. 'He told me what had transpired – or the gist of it. It appears you are wrong in certain aspects and your King is keen to impress that what you told him about Calais was the first he had heard of it.'

Pushing himself up, Argyle shook his head. 'Why did he not say so himself? And if not him then whom? Who else might want Thomas dead?'

'I believe your brother had many enemies.' She did not move. 'Perhaps you are looking in the wrong direction. Perhaps his true enemy dwells elsewhere, but Argyle…' This time she did put a hand on his shoulder. 'Have you not suffered enough? Has not your family? You have discovered much about your brother's demise what more can you want? Your man told you what happened to Thomas in Calais. You know where he died.'

Argyle had nothing to say to her. Thomas' death was a scab he could not help but pick at although he knew it would leave a scar that he was forced to bear forever. Did she truly expect him to relinquish? Trust a man who was utterly untrustworthy?

'You almost died yourself in the pursuit.' There were tears in her words if not her eyes. Now that she was close he could see the dark emerald abyss and wanted to drown in it. 'It is time to lay the dead to rest. They deserve it. You deserve it. Take this olive branch for that is what it is. Go to London and care for Isabella. When the time comes and she is returned to France, you are free to return home. To your children. Your wife.'

'How did you get the King to agree to such terms?'

For a long time, she looked at him, calm, composed. Only her silence revealed the inner turmoil. Argyle let her think. He was in no hurry. The idea of staying in England was a branch of thorns.

It could not be, it was too easy. The longer she paused the more his concern grew. She promised him freedom, but perhaps it was a ruse. As soon as he reached London King Henry's men would seize him and throw him in the Tower. This time to rot to death.

He shivered and she finally spoke. 'Charles did not want you to know.'

'Know what?'

Madame nudged for him to move and slid up to sit beside him, rearranging her skirt. It was an odd feeling to have the light silk weigh down his legs. She took his hand in hers, a motherly caress.

'You must swear never to repeat what I say. Not while I live, not even beyond. This is a secret to which few are privy, chief among them my sister and Queen Isabeau.' For the first time ever, Argyle heard her mention the Queen with warmth. Maud sighed. 'Not even Jacques knows. Not because he cannot be trusted, he is as loyal as any man I have ever met. If he knew then his life would be in peril. You cannot tell Princess Isabella. You cannot breathe a word of it to anyone. You must take the secret with you to the grave, a secret even your brother could not keep.'

'Has it to do with the letters?'

'What letters?' The confusion in her voice clashed with the calm of her eyes.

Argyle pointed to the stack by the window. 'Those.'

Rather than rise to fetch the missives, Madame put her head on his shoulder. 'Yes, in part.'

'Windham was right.'

'About what?'

In the dark, her whisper was strangely comforting and he rested his head on hers. How long would it be before he was afforded any comfort? 'That you spied on us the whole time. Why should I trust you now?'

'I have left Jacques further down the hall. We are free to speak – if you wish it. I cannot undo what has been done.' Madame moved her head and his shoulder grew cool. She still held his hand. 'If you would rather not, I understand. As for whether you can trust me, it is up to you. Ask and perhaps I may console you. But beware you might not like the truth.'

'Did you provide the letters? Did you slip them into Windham's possessions or into his hands?'

Her elbow prodded his arm, creating a dull, comfortable ache. Argyle could feel her breathe, her shoulder rising and falling at an even pace. she was deciding on something.

Where Eloise was quick to act and often rash, Maud had the air of an older sister about her. Perhaps Margaret would have taken to her, though Argyle doubted it. The pure cunning that had dwelled in his sister was not mirrored in Maud. Hers was a calculated mind, she weighed her options before acting.

She was right. The dead should be left to rest. With horror, Argyle realised that he had spent more than half of his life chasing ghosts. Never at ease, never able to rest, moving always from one place to the next, and for what?

Who would thank him when his life ebbed? Would anyone sit by his side? Would anyone remember him? Or would he be a ghost for his own children to chase?

She took a deep breath and Argyle cut her short. 'No. I do not need to know. If you can ensure that I am free once the Princess leaves England that is enough for me.'

Rising, she glanced at him. 'Time to make peace?'

'Yes. With all of it.'

CHAPTER 82

4 May 1401 – Portchester Castle

'I have orders to take you to London, Sire.' The captain of the guard looked uncomfortable. 'We're not to make any stops along the way, save to sleep.'

Argyle looked at the ship vanishing on the horizon. A sudden desire to be aboard and not left here to fend for himself rose in his chest and tied his tongue. The French had gone without him. Dismay seized him and he had to shake his body to resume control.

The captain glanced at him. 'Sire?'

'Has the King left? Only he said we were to have words once the French had gone.'

The captain nodded to one of his men who brought Argent to the mounting block. At least Argyle still had his horse. The sight instilled a little comfort in his bleak world.

He reached out and stroked Argent who leaned into the caress. How much they had experienced. By some miracle, Argent had survived the hardship Argyle had endured and now, they were here in England together.

He had offered the horse to King Charles as a gift of gratitude that he had been kept safe at a hostile court. The King had refused, arguing that he could afford to pay de Reines for a steed of his own should he so desire.

'King Henry rode out at sunrise, Sire.' The captain held the reins loosely in his hand as if weighting whether or not it was wise to let Argyle ride on his own.

'To Wales?'

Tying Argent's rein to the saddle of his own horse, he walked it to the mounting block. 'I wouldn't know, Sire. What his Majesty plans is none of my business. I have my orders. He left you this.'

Presenting a small, sealed letter, he called for the gates to be thrown open. Argyle pushed the paper into his sleeve careful to tie the ribbon of his cuff tight.

Surrounded by six men, Argyle rode out of the castle, looking up as they passed under the portcullis. The teeth were jagged and caked in rust. King Henry had not deemed it necessary to prepare for an invasion. Perhaps he would have to change his mind if he did not live up to his agreement with Madame.

Argyle had woken up at sunrise to find a slip of paper on the floor.

– I am sorry –

The pouch under his garments had been empty except from the gold and garnet pin. She had taken what evidence he had had, except for once, he had anticipated her move.

The letter from King Henry scratched against his skin.

He wondered what it might contain and if he even wanted to read it. Still he knew that, in the end, he would not be able to leave it alone. Curiosity was his true curse. He had indulged so often in the past and would do so again before they reached London.

Besides, if what he had read in the letter Queen Isabeau had showed him was true, there was still something to be done.

As the castle grew smaller in the distance an idea formed in his mind.

Promises could be broken, and he owed no one anything.

ഗ ര ഗ ര

CHAPTER 83

4 August 1401 – Portsmouth

Argyle looked at the ship rolling out of port. Three months ago, he had set foot on this very dock to claim back the Princess to her country, a French embassy at his back.

King Henry had agreed and Isabella was finally to return to a place Argyle missed with ever-growing intensity. He did not know how to be a knight in England, he only knew how to be a prisoner in France. What irony life offered.

For the past three months, he had been a constant companion to the greatest prize in King Henry's treasury, the Dowager Queen, once more known to all the world as Princess Isabella. She had been relieved to see him at her doorstep, so much so that she had fallen into his arms with a wail and had clung to him for the better part of a day until one of her ladies-in-waiting had managed to pry her little fingers from his arm.

Since then, they had shared many quiet moments together and she had been partly instrumental in putting back together pieces inside Argyle that he had thought shattered beyond repair.

Isabella's parting words had held little comfort though they were spoken with great sincerity. 'I make for home, Sir Argyle. I fully intend to be happy in the future. Take heart, dear friend, for we shall meet again, I am sure of it. Now, I take my leave and wish you all the luck in the world – I release you from your duty to me.'

Her lower lip had trembled just a little but she had not lost her composure. Nor had he, although a lump in his throat had forced him to stay silent and merely incline his head at her little speech.

Realising he could not speak, she had straightened, her cloak and skirt flapping in the strong western wind. Her ladies-in-waiting had boarded the grand ship already, gripping their headdresses to keep them from blowing into the sea. She had offered one last little smile and then made her way up the gangway. Isabella had disappeared from view only to reappear next to the captain, transformed back into a child. Argyle was certain she had looked straight at him even if she was so minute at the helm that he could not swear to it.

The ship made slow progress at first, oars spouting to force it out against the tide. It rolled on the swell and Argyle hoped Isabella was not fearful that the entire crossing would be this way. He remembered Windham's haggard face and thought that, today, the breaking waves were much taller than when they had made the crossing back in April.

He watched as the ship made it past the natural bay and cut into deeper waters, a strange feeling of abandonment aching in his chest. More than anything, Argyle wanted to be on that ship. Maud had advised he make amends with his family, but she did not know what waited for him when he returned.

For three months, Argyle had avoided sending any message, any warning that he had returned. Every night, he had sat at his desk in the Bishop's palace, quill poised waiting for words that would never come. Other words came though, for other eyes to read, and those he recorded with great care. When his candle burned low, he would lie on the bed, trying to avoid sleep. For sleep brought with it a deep-seated roar of anxiety.

Now, his excuse to stay silent, to avoid drawing attention to himself grew smaller on the horizon, as the ship took the wind in its sails. Soon, Isabella would be back in her mother's household, held in her doting father's arms. The idea tugged at Argyle's heart. He too would see his children soon. Look upon his third child for the first time, mirror himself in Edmund's big blue eyes and hope that Thomas' hair would in time fade to gold.

Around him life continued, sailors and merchants bustling on the docks, big batches of wool were carried from the shore to the waiting ships. He thought the product looked a little loose. It had been so long since he had cared about sheep and wool that perhaps his eye was out of practice.

He wondered what might await him at Beauworth. Stephen was a good master of arms but as a steward he was less than perfect. Isobel would have handled the household, she had a knack for coin and negotiation. Argyle remembered once seeing her haggle with a merchant who sold buttons and ribbon, driving the price down until the man almost wept. Later, when she had returned to her rooms triumphant, Argyle had caught up with the tradesman and pushed a small purse in his hands.

In the back of his mind, Argyle heard Thomas telling him that he had a kind heart. He did and it had taken him far too long to appreciate it. Perhaps the situation with Isobel could be resolved. Perhaps all was not lost.

In the jumble of people, a dark-haired man bumped into Argyle. A blade slashed his skin, biting into his flesh.

He slid sideways to escape the dull pain and warm fluid spilled down his side. His breath caught somewhere short of his lung. He tried to get up and failed.

As the cold wrapped itself around him, Argyle took comfort in a simple truth: He had left his legacy in the hands of the only person he dared trust.

Elizabeth.

She would know what to do with King Henry's last words to him, etched onto paper, sealed with the royal crest.

– I understand now that you know too much for me to be rid of you – and so I only ask that you keep my secret. I am every bit as royal as you are and we are both forced to live with the sins of our fathers. Should you fail me, cousin, *the consequences of your actions will be beyond your imagining. –*

HISTORICAL NOTE

Towards the end of his reign, Richard II Plantagenet decided to bring the Irish to heel. Whether because they had killed his Lieutenant or if he did indeed intend to make his maternal brother King of Ireland, he left his child-queen Isabella in England and turned his back on a country that was fed up with his whims and erratic behaviour.

Most historians agree that Henry of Bolingbroke came to hear about Richard's departure through either their mutual uncle Edmund, the Duke of York, or possibly his son, Edward of Norwich, in this book styled the Duke of Albemarle (also referred to as Aumale in some historical sources).

As soon as Henry of Bolingbroke returned, most of the English nobility decided to back his claim to have his lands and titles restored – all of which Richard had taken for the Crown when John of Gaunt, Henry's father, died in February 1399.

Whether Henry had planned on usurping Richard before he broke exile and returned to England is a much debated topic. Whatever his previous plans, the nobility soon convinced him that he would be a better king than Richard had ever been. And thus, Henry set out to conquer England and expel his tiresome cousin.

The words exchanged between Richard and Henry when they finally met at Flint are near as can be to what actually happened on that day. Richard was in the custody of the Percy brothers, who were sworn allies to Henry and Richard must have known that nothing would come from him making a big display. Instead, he agreed to Henry's claim that he – Richard – had been a bad king and let himself be taken to London only attempting to escape once. Which failed miserably.

When he returned to London, perhaps Richard hoped he would be able to persuade the Londoners that he should be allowed to keep his crown, but events would have it differently.

As the first king of England, Henry crowned himself to the cheers of most of the noble houses in England, sparing a few including the Earl of Salisbury who did indeed attempt to seize king Henry IV and his sons at the Epiphany Tournament which was held on 2 January 1400.

Not long after, rumours from France reached the English court that Richard had been killed by Henry IV, something he arduously denied for his entire reign. Some historians believe that Richard was starved to death on Henry's orders, others think a royal order might have been misheard and the deed carried out without Henry's knowledge.

Whatever the truth, by the middle of February 1400, Richard was dead and brought back to London for all to see. No doubt, Henry hoped this would stamp out any further attempts of rebellion from the few noble families still loyal to Richard.

Henry's reign was not to be the golden age he hoped for. He was constantly threatened from all sides by the Scots, Irish, Welsh and, of course, France. Why he chose to keep the Dowager Queen Isabella against her own express wishes as well as those of King Charles of France is anyone's guess. Most likely he wanted Isabella and Prince Harry (also called Prince Hal in historical sources) to form an alliance.

Being of a warring nature, Henry later revived the war on France his grandfather, Edward III Plantagenet, had started many years earlier. It seems that striving for a crown is simply in the blood of a true Plantagenet.

In this book, I play with the idea that Thomas Mowbray did not die in Venice as historical sources claim, but that he had broken exile on Richard's command and was killed much later in Calais. I did so to drive the story forward and because it has never been ascertained without a doubt that Thomas did indeed die in Venice.

Another interesting element is the death of two of Argyle's sisters. While the lives and deaths of the male line of the Mowbray family are consistent and well-documented, it is another matter when attention turns to the female side. As I researched for this book, I came across several different dates of death for Eleanor Mowbray (m. de Welles) and Margaret Mowbray (m. de Lucy).

Eleanor is said to have died at any time between April 1399 and late 1426, rendering her anywhere from the age of 35 to 62 years when she died.

Margaret is said to have died any time between late 1399 and the middle of 1404. For the purpose this story, I chose to have the two most troublesome sisters die within a few weeks of each other.

Only one sister all sources agree upon, Joan, who is said to have died in 1402.

The timeline of this book spans just a few years. The last year of Richard II's reign and the first two of Henry IV's reign. I take you on a journey of Europe and we visit some of the most notable cities and the people who lived there at the time.

The French king's aunt, the Countess of Boulogne is a perfect example. She was instrumental in saving her nephew from burning when a party got out of hand and candles set fire to a ring of dancers, one of which was the future king Charles. He is said to have hidden under her skirt, which – if nothing else – makes for a fun image.

Argyle returns home with an embassy that never existed, although the time of Isabella's departure from England is historically accurate. She returned to France and was later betrothed to a distant cousin.

ACKNOWLEDGMENTS

There are more than a few people without whom my books would never exist. In a performance, I like to think worthy of the Oscars, I would like to extend thanks to:

My editor and excellent friend, Steve, who never lets me off the hook for something, I could do better.

The fabulous three, I am blessed to have you as companions on my journeys into the unknown.

Thank you to Hannah, my enthusiastic and wonderfully critical proof-reader who helps me weed out all the little linguistic rascals that inevitably lurk in the dark corners of any manuscript.

Thank you to Tairelei, my amazing graphic designer. You are a true artist and an exceptionally patient human being.

My family and friends for their unfailing support. You make me keep going when things get rough.

Most of all, I thank you, my wonderful husband for supporting me at every turn and for never doubting my efforts, even if I do. I love you.

And a big thank you to you, my dear reader, for going on this epic voyage with me. You are what makes me aspire to greatness.

ABOUT THE AUTHOR

Mette Holm is a writer of historical fiction focusing on last of the Plantagenet rulers beginning with Richard II. The Mowbray family caught her eye when she was first researching the age and especially Thomas Mowbray was so fascinating, she simply had to write about him and the Mowbray family. The decision led to her first book: *At the King's Command.* In this sequel, she once more delves into the vipers' nest that was the English court.

Mette Holm has been telling stories all her life, be it in school, at university or even in her day-job as an independent business owner and copywriter. While historical fiction holds a special place in her heart, she has an alter ego that has published an eight-book dark, epic fantasy series that draws on certain historical aspects. As a quirk despite her Danish heritage, she knows more about medieval England than she does about Danish medieval history, although that is about to change.

Sign up to her newsletter (ensuring you get first dibs on all new releases) here

Go on one more adventure with
Argyle Mowbray in

Turn the page for a sneak peek…

To be placed in the hands of Sir Argyle Mowbray
In the event of his death, burn this without opening it.
By the command of Isabella of France and England, Dowager Queen.

11 July 1401
Hôtel Saint Pol, Paris

My dearest friend!

Put me out of my misery. Write to me this instance and reassure me that you are well. That the cruel rumours fluttering around my father's court as black-winged butterflies are naught but malicious lies spilled to make my life unbearable.

I cannot survive if you died to set me free!

I cannot breathe, I cannot eat. I feel so very wretched. This is all my doing. If I had not demanded you attend my return. If only I had heeded the King's command to leave you in London. But no. I had to have my way. One last time, I wanted to thwart Henry and prove to him that he will never, in my heart of hearts, be King of England. He will only ever be a demon ascended from Hell to spew fire and discord across the country I grew to love. That you taught me to love.

You are an angel to his demonic reign, you must survive, you must guard the realm I have lost forever. You cannot let his devilish ways consume a kingdom. You are all that stands between England and destruction.

Oh, my friend, I pray day and night for your life. I wish for nothing more than to hear you are well. My mother is as disturbed as I by this news. This terrible, horrible tale of your fate. She is with me in the chapel early and late, her features harried, her hair greyed by the lack of news. Two Queens pray for you. Surely, God must listen?

My father… No, I cannot begin to tell you what happens here when you might be battling death. I dream such vivid dreams, such nightmares of you brandishing your sword against Death. He seeks to swathe you in his robes, to claim you for himself. I will not have it. You are only just returned to us, to me, to your family.

I know you can defeat Death! I have seen what you can do, what you can endure. You are not allowed to die. I will not have it. I demand that you live. Breathe. Recover. And guard your family with the vigour that you once guarded me.

Defender of England, rise anew and be my eyes in a court to which I shall never again return. Do not turn your back on a country that needs you, on friends who desire nothing but to trade places with you that we might know you will survive. Do not fail your family now in their hour of need. Do not fail me.

Argyle, I beseech you. Live. For me, your greatest friend in the world.

Isabella

Keep reading here

ALSO BY METTE HOLM

THE MOWBRAY CHRONICLES – MAIN SERIES

At the King's Command

Court of Deadly Whispers

Web of Lies

Legacy of Kings

Coming in 2025: The Rogue's Son

THE MOWBRAY CHRONICLES – NOVELS

Shield of Blood – La Fontaine's Story

MOWBRAY NOVELLAS

The Golden Squire

Printed in Great Britain
by Amazon

62976374R00394